# FERN MICHAELS

*Wildflowers*

D0017872

HQN™

Recycling programs
for this product may
not exist in your area.

ISBN-13: 978-0-373-77506-4

WILDFLOWERS

Copyright © 2010 by Harlequin Books S.A.

The publisher acknowledges the copyright holder of the individual works as follows:

SEA GYPSY
Copyright © 1980 by Fern Michaels

GOLDEN LASSO
Copyright © 1980 by Fern Michaels

This edition published by arrangement with Harlequin Books S.A.

® and TM are trademarks of the publisher. Trademarks indicated with ® are registered in the United States Patent and Trademark Office, the Canadian Trade Marks Office and in other countries.

www.HQNBooks.com

**Printed in U.S.A.**

# CONTENTS

# SEA GYPSY

## CHAPTER ONE

BURGUNDY SHADOWS graciously gave way to the soft pinks and grays of early dawn, Cathy Bissette's favorite time of day. She loved the morning and its peaceful quiet with a comforting knowledge that the new day would bring, if not happiness, then contentment. That was why she had asked for a three-month leave of absence from the publishing house where she was an editor and subleased her New York apartment in the Village.

She had come home to the coastal flatlands of North Carolina, and here she could shrug off the acquired veneer of sophistication and return to the uncomplicated life she had left behind. Here in Swan Quarter, surrounded by a loving father and old friends and the lush grassy banks leading down to the waters of the Pamlico Sound, she could restore her spirit and mend her soul.

The soft lap of the sound against her sun-darkened feet was soothing, a balm to her erupting emotions. It was a gentle feeling, like when Marc Hellenger touched her and held her close. Yet, she didn't like the feeling now, here in this peacefulness with only the shriek of the gulls to break the quiet and the ghostly specters of the shrimp boats testing their moorings to the long rickety piers.

She withdrew first one foot and then the other, tucking them firmly beneath her. She would not think, would not feel. But once again the familiar self-doubts began to creep in despite her resolution. Had she been wrong to run like a frightened puppy? She recalled her squeaky reply of, "If *you* loved me you would marry me." It had sounded archaic to her own ears and God only knew how it had sounded to Marc. Why couldn't she be sophisticated and clever like the other girls in the office? They would have known how to handle Marc and his insistent demands of, "If you loved me you would sleep with me." Well she wasn't like the other girls and she couldn't handle it. Right or wrong, she was stuck with her decision and would no doubt end up a dried up old maid.

Cathy shifted her position on the dock to a more comfortable one and almost knocked her carryall into the water. Her heart hammered at the near mishap and she moved the canvas bag to a more secure position. Teak Helm's galleys of his newest manuscript and a romance novel she had promised to line edit for her boss, along with a breakfast roll and a thermos of coffee rested inside waiting to be devoured. The coffee and roll for sustenance and Teak's galleys for mental nourishment.

She was comfortable here, safe from Marc. Now why did she keep using the word *safe*? *Safe* was a word children used, or mothers when they referred to their offspring's well being. She wasn't a child, she was twenty-four years old with a responsible job and an apartment of her own, not to mention a second-hand

Mustang and her day sailer. Why couldn't she accept an affair for what it was without benefit of that small piece of paper called a marriage certificate? All her friends were embroiled in affairs and happy with the arrangement. Why did she have to be different?

She squared her shoulders imperceptibly and muttered to the emptiness around her, "Because it isn't something I can take lightly." And that was that, she thought, dusting her hands together and scrambling to her feet. A quick run along the shoreline to empty her mind of Marc and she would be born again on the banks of the Pamlico Sound. This was where she belonged, where she wanted to be...wasn't it?

She ran, jerkily at first, until her muscles limbered up and she got the hang of her old style; head up, elbows bent, fists loosely clenched. Her breathing was deep and regular, the tang of salt air perfume to her senses.

A soft whoof at her heels made her swivel, never breaking her running stride. "Hey, Bismarc, good to see you. Beat you to the end of the strip." The Irish setter dug in his paws and sprinted ahead of her, his russet sleekness there one moment and gone the next. He knew if he made it back to the dock ahead of the slim girl with the blond flying pigtails, he would find a treat in the carryall resting on the end of the dock. And if he were extra lucky and the girl obliged, he could fully expect to have his belly scratched for at least ten minutes.

"Look at you, you're not even panting!" Cathy gasped as she collapsed onto the smooth planks. "I'm out of condition," she said, fondling the dog, "but it's a temporary state of affairs. By the end of summer, I'll race you to the point and win it hands down. Here, you deserve this," she said, handing him a salmon-colored biscuit.

Cathy poured herself a cup of coffee from the thermos and sat nibbling on her sweet roll. "Bet you're surprised to see me home, right? Well, you see it was like this: things got a little sticky back there in the Big Apple and I sort of cut out and ran, back to Dad and you. I'm not really different from the others. It's my values that are different. I know this sounds corny and girls my age don't think in terms of saving themselves, but I do. I don't know how to make the bar scene and I don't bed hop. Maybe I'm right and maybe I'm wrong. I just don't know anymore."

Bismarc ceased gnawing on his biscuit. His ears pricked up, not at the words she was uttering but at the tone of her voice. He slinked his way up to the girl on his belly and forced his shaggy head into the crook of her arm, willing her to laugh and hug him like she always did. Cathy laughed. "I have you. Is that what you're trying to tell me? Girl's best friend. Loyal, devoted and loving. You've got it all, Bismarc. You'll never forsake me. However," she said clasping his head in her hands, "you don't make my heart pound and my senses reel. And what good are you on a cold winter's night? Roll over," she ordered, "so I can scratch your belly." Bismarc didn't have to be told a second time. This was what life was all about.

"I brought Teak Helm's galleys for his new book with me. His last book was a million-copy bestseller and this one promises to be even better. If I were his editor,

Bismarc, I'd take him in hand and…actually—" Cathy lowered her voice to a mere whisper "—I just might get to do that when I go back to New York. Teak's editor is moving to the West Coast and my boss told me I'm in line for the job. Imagine me, Cathy Bissette, a little ol' North Carolina girl, being Teak Helm's editor. What a life he must lead, all those wonderful sea adventures, the true life stories he creates. Now there's a man I would like to meet."

Cathy turned at the sound of her name being called in time to notice two things. Her father sauntering down to the dock and a swift motor launch churning through the brackish water to her left. Bismarc, shaken from his moments of ecstasy, scrambled to his feet, barking wildly at the intruding launch.

"It looks like we've got company," Lucas Bissette said in his gravelly voice. "Powerful company, from the sound of that launch. Rich, too, from the looks of that motor yacht riding at anchor out there."

"A bit early for visitors," Cathy said, an ominous feeling settling between her shoulders. Her breath quickened at the sight of the sleek launch, bow raised, water cutting back in white pluming arcs as it sped by the hull. The now golden dawn cast everything into a yellow nimbus and she could see the occupants of the launch as the pilot cut back his engines. A tall, broad-shouldered masculine figure manned the wheel and a breathtakingly beautiful woman was at his side.

Lucas Bissette and Cathy stood waiting, a welcoming committee of two, for the arrival of the launch. The man's handling of the boat was admirable as he nosed it into the dock and expertly tossed the bow and stern lines which Cathy and Lucas secured to the pilings. No Sunday sailor, this one, Cathy thought, somehow pleased that such a beautiful craft was in the hands of a capable seaman. Too often she had seen luxurious vessels run to ruin at the hands of careless, inexperienced owners who were known to salty, able seamen by that deprecating term as "Sunday Sailors."

An indrawn breath escaped Cathy as the man leaped to the dock with athletic agility. It was impossible not to be aware of his striking good looks which were enhanced by a golden tan. Dark hair brushed casually off to the side and trimmed just a trifle shorter than was the current style offset piercing gray eyes that flicked over her cutoff jeans and washed-out T-shirt, yet seemed to survey the soft curves of her figure beneath. When he smiled in greeting, it was warm and friendly and displayed a humorous irony and dazzling white teeth.

Cathy felt her gaze narrow as she took in the sight of the woman who had accompanied him and was mournfully aware of her own hastily braided hair and bare legs that ended with bare feet. This woman was beautiful and meticulously groomed. Even at this early hour her makeup was perfect and her platinum hair had the appearance of being styled by a New York hairdresser.

Out of the corner of her eye, Cathy watched her father straighten his shoulders and hitch up his baggy blue jeans; a silent tribute to the woman standing on the dock.

"Jared Parsons," the man said, holding out a bronzed hand. "And this is Erica Marshall…my secretary."

I'll just bet she's your secretary, Cathy thought uncharitably as she noticed the proprietary look on Erica's face.

"I'm looking for Lucas Bissette. According to the marine mechanics on Ocracoke Island, he's the best damned mechanic on the coast. I started out from Maine a few weeks ago, and my chief engineer became ill and is now hospitalized in Virginia Beach. I was going to pick up another engineer in Cape Fear but developed engine trouble out at Ocracoke. We made it here by the skin of our teeth and I mean that literally. I'm on my way home to Lighthouse Point, in Florida. Now, can you tell me where I can find this Bissette fella?"

A half-smile formed around the corners of Cathy's mouth. It didn't seem like a question to her but a demand. How would her father react to this demand? She was chagrined to see a wide smile stretch Lucas's mouth as he looked at the woman as he answered.

"You're talking to him," Lucas drawled. "And you heard right. I am the best damned mechanic on the coast."

"I just knew it," Erica smiled winningly. "You have that…that look about you that…that speaks of knowledge."

Cathy grinned when Jared Parsons winced. So much for eloquent secretaries, she thought nastily, disliking the beautiful Erica on sight.

Jared extended his hand toward Lucas and gripped the other's firmly. "Glad to meet you, Mr. Bissette. Sure hope you can help me."

"I'll try. Can you tell me what's wrong?" Lucas

asked, expecting to hear a series of complaints in the most untechnical terms, such as, she's dragging, can't get any speed out of her, the head's plugged and won't flush, or she's making a sort of thumping noise. Instead, Jared Parsons seemed to have a very knowledgeable opinion of what was wrong with his motor yacht.

"Firstly, I know it's the primary marine generator. We were supposed to pick up another at Cape Fear. The replacement engineer has ordered it, picked it up and it's all ready to go. Secondly, I believe the exhaust manifold is on the fluke. Last, but not least, I think the raw water intake is giving me trouble. Again, I might add. It was taken care of, or at least I thought it was, in Kennebunkport, Maine. Now, I'm not so certain."

"Sounds like you've got a real ox in the ditch, son. I'll have a look at it for you, later today, when I have time. If it can be fixed I'll be glad to oblige. Better be prepared to stick around for a week or so."

"A week! Mr. Bissette, I don't have a week! I have to be back at Lighthouse Point at the end of *this* week. Look, I'll pay you double what you charge, triple if necessary. But I need the work done today, tomorrow at the latest."

Cathy's back stiffened at the man's arrogant tone. Why did men like him always think money could buy everything? She clenched her teeth. If Lucas buckled under, she would push him off the dock and that fancy looking Erica right along with him.

Bismarc was in tune with Cathy's emotions and began a deep growl in his throat to show his own disapproval. And then he did something that lightened

Cathy's heart. He had slowly maneuvered himself over to Erica and was slowly licking her leg.

*"Eeek!"* Erica squealed, backing away and at the same time losing her balance, toppling into the brackish water. "Filthy creature!" she shouted as she surfaced with an undignified splash.

Bismarc, unconcerned with what he had done, reared up and placed his paws on Jared's shoulders, demanding attention.

Jared wasn't in the least angry and issued a deep chuckle as he watched his secretary. Lucas seemed concerned and made a move to assist the woman when Jared stopped him. "She knows how to swim and the ladder is right there." He scratched the big dog's head and grinned at Cathy. "Affectionate dog you have here. He seems to have firm likes and dislikes."

Cathy stared into slate-gray eyes, again aware of her shabby appearance. She felt out of place and uncomfortable at the man's close scrutiny. She had to say something, make some comment. "I thought you said your secretary could swim. Looks to me like she's going down for the third time."

"She'll come up when she realizes I'm not going in after her," Jared said coolly.

Cathy shrugged as she bent down to pick up her carryall. The contents had spilled with Erica's wild plunge into the water.

"Allow me," Jared said, bending down. He handed the Teak Helm galleys to her along with the thermos.

Cathy couldn't conceive what came over her, but she snatched the galleys from his hand. "Give me that!"

The gray eyes were mocking when Jared handed them over. "I wasn't going to keep it. I was just putting it in your bag." His smile was tight, almost grim when he watched her place the rolled leaflets in her bag as though she were handling eggs.

"Darn you, Jared. You could have pulled me out," Erica said as she wiped straggles of hair from her eyes. Angrily, she lashed out with her foot, her aim directed at Bismarc.

Jared's face was hard and cold as he grasped her arm, pulling her back from the dog. "The animal was just being friendly. Get in the launch and I'll take you back to the *Gypsy* so you can get cleaned up." He looked at Lucas and said, "I'll be back as soon as I get her to the yacht and we can talk."

Bismarc advanced a step by way of apology to Erica who squealed in fright.

Cathy couldn't help but burst out laughing. "Come on, Bizzy, time to go back to the house." Without another word she turned on her heel and sprinted after Bismarc who had taken the lead. She would have been bewildered if she could have seen the look on Jared Parsons's face as he watched her running retreat, the yellow tote bouncing against her side.

Back in the house, Cathy set about making breakfast. She cracked eggs into the bowl and automatically beat them wildly. She was angry and she didn't know why. She certainly wasn't angry because Jared Parsons touched her precious Teak Helm galleys. She had just met the man and here she was beating the eggs with fury yet her blood was churning wildly in her veins.

Suddenly, Cathy realized it was Erica. No one in the whole world should be allowed to be that beautiful. Even Lucas, her very own father, fell for her good looks. Men! And, Erica belonged to Jared Parsons. She belonged to him the way Cathy, herself, could have belonged to Marc if she had given in to his demands.

Would Marc have let her go down in the water for the third time? she wondered. Then make some scathing comment as Jared had done? Yes, she admitted to herself. Men did things like that when they believed they owned women. She wondered, fleetingly, if Jared Parsons paid the beautiful and ravishing Erica a salary for her secretarial duties. But the sharp hiss of the eggs as they hit the hot butter in the pan brought her thoughts back to the task at hand.

Lucas Bissette walked though the door just as Cathy slid the eggs onto his plate. She said nothing but waited for him to make some mention of their early-morning visitors. As she busied herself with spooning food into Bismarc's dish and refilling his water bowl, her thoughts raced. Jared Parsons was good-looking, down-right handsome. He was virile and athletic and obviously very rich. He was also arrogant and demanding and sported a slightly condescending attitude. There had been a moment when she had actually expected him to pat her on the head like he had done to Bismarc. He also had a live-in woman. How old-fashioned that sounded, how jealous and spiteful. Why should she be jealous? She had only met the man, a man who looked at her the way he would a grubby child.

Cathy stood up facing the kitchen window, watching

the return of the power launch. She felt a tremor in her legs and her heart began a wild fluttering. Some instinct, some intangible force, was making her aware of this man with the gray eyes and wry smile. She envied Erica and all the women like her. Was she wrong? Were they right, to live for the moment and enjoy it for what it was? Cathy sighed, the sound loud in the quiet of the kitchen.

"Did you make enough eggs for Mr. Parsons?" Lucas asked, biting into a crisp piece of toast.

Cathy swiveled from her position at the window. "No, I didn't make enough eggs because I didn't know he was coming for breakfast. Since I'm the cook around here, it would have been nice if you had informed me," she snapped.

"I've invited people on the spur of the moment before and it's never annoyed you," Lucas said, pushing his plate toward the center of the oak table.

"Next time, please ask me," Cathy said quietly. "Open the door. He's here." She turned, busying herself at the stove. She was ill at ease, uncomfortable in the man's presence. Somehow, deep within her, she knew her life was changing, had begun to change, the minute Jared Parsons stepped from his launch.

Bismarc's loud bark of welcome made her drop the egg she was holding and the laughter in Jared's eyes made her grit her teeth. Even the dog liked him. Dogs were supposed to be astute judges of character. A pity Bismarc wasn't perfect.

Cathy cleaned up the broken egg and turned to face him. "What would you like for breakfast, Mr. Parsons?"

"Anything you'd care to make will be fine. I hope I'm not putting you out or keeping you from something."

Was it her imagination? Did his eyes go to the yellow tote or was he looking at the copper-and-wood butter churn that sat in the corner?

"Cathy's never too busy to cook. It's one of her favorite pastimes," Lucas said affably. "Why, she always wins the prize at the July Fourth picnic for her She-Crab stew. Won it four years in a row. Yes, sir, all the young bucks around here come on Sundays and Cathy whips something up for them."

Dear heaven, Cathy groaned inwardly. Here she was yearning to be glamorous and seductive like Erica and Lucas was extolling her homey virtues.

"If there's one thing I really can appreciate, it's a good cook," Jared laughed.

Cathy pursed her lips. Among other things, she thought nastily as she liberally sprinkled chives and cheddar cheese into the whipped eggs, and hoped that Jared Parsons attributed her flushed face to the heat from the stove.

# CHAPTER TWO

JARED PARSONS wolfed down the breakfast Cathy had set before him. She hoped Lucas didn't notice that their visitor's eggs had been laced with chives and cheese while his own had been served plain. She thought she noticed amusement in her father's eyes as he glanced at the cinnamon toast and fancy mug resting near Jared's plate.

Lucas managed to catch his daughter's eye by clearing his throat and winked slyly. Cathy in turn banged the frying pan into the sink and flounced out of the kitchen, then stopped in her tracks and returned. She wanted to hear what Parsons had to say with her own ears. The day any man could bully her father was a day she wanted to see. What would the stylish yachtsman do when his offer of triple money failed to hurry Lucas Bissette? A vision of the muscular man in his natty ducks and yellow pullover being frustrated by Lucas's unhurried Southern habits made her giggle. Bismarc heard her, and Lucas and Jared both looked at her. Her father with amusement, and Parsons with speculation.

"If you've finished your breakfast, let's take a look at that engine," Lucas said, getting up from his chair. Jared dabbed at his mouth with the checkered napkin and then pointedly placed it beside Lucas's paper napkin, a wicked smile playing on his lips. Cathy's eyes followed his movements and a dark flush worked its way over her cheekbones. Damn Jared Parsons.

"Anytime you're ready, Mr. Bissette. I meant what I said down at the dock. I'll pay you whatever you want, if you do the job tomorrow at the latest. It's imperative I reach Lighthouse Point before the end of the week."

His voice was cool and businesslike, making Lucas frown. You didn't issue orders to Lucas Bissette, not in his own house or anywhere else, for that matter. And it was an order, regardless of how the man worded it. Cathy knew it and Lucas knew it.

"Well now, Mr. Parsons," Lucas drawled as he sucked on his pipe, "I don't rightly see how I can accommodate you, since I haven't seen the extent of the problem. Besides, if it is that new generator you'll be needing, it will take time to order it. Even if we get it up here from Cape Fear, that's going to take a day or so."

"A day or so!" Parsons protested. "It's only about five hours from here by land!"

"Best you bear in mind that we…hayseeds down here in the boonies operate at two speeds. Slow and stop. Least that's what I've heard said."

Cathy grinned openly. Good for you, Dad, that's telling him money is just something you buy things with, not people. Jared's mouth tightened at Cathy's grin. He had been put down and by an expert, something Cathy knew rarely, if ever, happened to him. Jared nodded, his gray eyes murky as the river on a bad day.

Lucas laid a rough hand on Jared's shoulder, taking the sting out of his insult, and said softly, "Just because

we all live here in this little backwater called Swan
Quarter doesn't mean we aren't aware of the outside
world. We also have priorities, and today I gave my
word I would help Jesse Gallagher repair his shrimp
nets. Now, Mr. Parsons, even if you were to tell me you
had a multimillion-dollar business deal going in Lighthouse Point, I'd still tell you that Jesse's shrimp nets are
top priority. Just want you to understand that…son."

Never one to let things simmer when she could bring
them to a boil, Cathy spoke up. "What Dad is trying to
tell you, Mr. Parsons, is your money isn't important here
and neither are your cool-voiced arrogant demands.
You came to us, we didn't come to you."

"This may surprise you, Miss Bissette, but I understood your father perfectly down at the dock and I
understand him now. There's no need for you to inter-
pret his words for me." He was angry, probably more
angry than any man Cathy had ever seen. It was evident
in the grim set of his shoulders and the stiff bunching
of the muscles in his jaw. People liked Jared Parsons
didn't bend to anyone, they were the ones who toppled
others and stood by while someone else picked up the
remains.

"If you're ready, Mr. Bissette." Jared turned and
looked around, his next words stunning Cathy. "I like
this kitchen. It's very homey with all the copper and
greenery. I particularly like the open hearth and the
overhead beams."

For a hairbreadth of a second, Cathy would have
sworn there was a wistful look in the gray eyes and then
it was gone.

"Cathy fixed up the kitchen like this from one of those fancy magazines. She's got a good eye for what makes comfort," Lucas said, winking at his daughter.

Jared Parsons turned and faced Cathy. "I guess one could say you're a homebody at heart." He grinned, but the emotion never reached his eyes, they were cool and unreadable. Cathy flushed beneath his steady gaze.

"I guess you could say that. What you see is what I am."

"Cathy, why don't you follow us out in the runabout so you can bring me back and save Mr. Parsons an extra trip? After all, he does have a guest on board and we don't want to take up all of his time."

"I'll be out after I clean up the kitchen. You go ahead," Cathy answered, refusing to turn away from the sink and see those inscrutable gray eyes piercing through her as though they could read her mind.

Bismarc got up and stretched from his comfortable spot on the wide hearth, looking first at Lucas and then at Cathy. Lucas laughed, a great laugh, starting at his toes and erupting from his throat. "Best lock Bizzy in the house when you leave. If we don't take him with us he'll only swim out after us."

Cathy grinned inwardly at what she imagined would be the scene on Jared Parsons's varnished deck and Miss Beautiful Marshall squealing her head off.

"Don't lock him in, Mr. Bissette," Jared protested. "If he wants our company, it's okay with me," he added agreeably.

"If we're going to do business, call me Lucas."

"Fine with me, and I'm Jared."

"Let's go, Jared," Lucas said, striding out the kitchen

door and leading the way down the footpath to the dock that sat out in front of the house. Jared obediently followed along with Bismarc trailing contentedly beside him. Cathy watched as his big bronzed hand fondled the dog's head from time to time during the short walk.

Filling the sink with hot soapy water, Cathy then poured herself a cup of coffee and sat down. She stared at the cup without drinking. Instead, she picked up the cup Jared had used and ran her thumb around the handle. Her own blue-green eyes darkened at the cup. There seemed to be a faint scent of masculine cologne near her, a reminder that Jared had sat where she was sitting. Her heart thumped as she recalled his handsome good looks. He was definitely what was known as "macho." If only he weren't so arrogant and conde-scending. She wondered fleetingly who his tailor was. He hadn't bought those sport clothes off any rack, she was certain of it. And, thank heavens, he didn't jangle with clanking jewelry. He was definitely a man to turn a girl's head, and Erica what's-her-name had him all to herself.

But he had liked her kitchen. He liked her father and Bizzy and he had also liked her eggs. She could tell by the way he had wolfed them down. What did he think of her? Cathy grimaced. As if she didn't know. If she were standing beside Erica what's-her-name, even her own father wouldn't notice her. There was no contest, that was for sure.

Darn you, Jared Parsons she thought. My life was just getting back on an even keel and here you limp into our port and already my life is changing in front of my eyes. Somehow, someway, you're going to change us. I can feel it, sense it, and I'm not sure I like it.

Lucas liked Jared Parsons, Bizzy did, too. So why did she have this strange sense of forbidding when it came to her opinion of the man? There was something about him, something that didn't ring true. Not that it was any of her business, but she would have liked to know just what his pressing business was in Lighthouse Point. What did he do for a living? Suddenly, it seemed very important to know. It wasn't fair, she told herself, to make judgments without knowing the whole picture. Yet somehow the word *phony* came to mind when Jared Parsons's face came into her line of vision. But now that Lucas had straightened him out, the two men would undoubtedly become friends. Everyone liked Lucas Bissette and Jared Parsons was no exception. Her father would have the yachtsman eating out of his hand before the end of the day.

This speculation wasn't getting the chores done. The dishes had to be cleaned and she had planned on mopping up the flagstone floor before she settled herself with Teak Helm's galleys. That alone was enough to anger her. She had looked forward to sitting down and devouring Helm's latest sea adventure undisturbed. Now she had to take a run out to the yacht and bring Lucas back, and if she knew her father, he would pore over Parsons's engine for hours before he made his final diagnosis of the problem.

To Lucas Bissette, an engine was like a woman, a complete mystery that only the best of men could master. Of course, that didn't apply to women like Erica

Marshall. There was no mystery there. "I'd give seven years of my life if I could look like her," Cathy groaned as she swished the dishcloth over the breakfast plates.

Men like Jared Parsons didn't look at girls like Cathy Bissette, who had brains; girls like Erica got the looks. Cathy sniffed as she squeezed the cloth, pretending it was beautiful Erica's neck.

What's happening to me? she demanded of the empty room. Why am I feeling so spiteful and catty? She didn't even know Erica Marshall and she didn't know Jared Parsons. She would put both of them out of her mind and get back on an even course. She would pick up her father and then the rest of the day would be hers to pore over the galleys. Things could only change if she allowed it. What was it her old psych prof had said? When it comes to dealing with emotions there are no tried and true answers. One is not responsible for one's emotions. They are intangibles, without substance.

Well, the first order of the day was to stop feeling guilty about her feelings and to batten down her emotions and begin enjoying her summer. She had slaved all winter long for this time and by all that was holy, no rich playboy with a live-in girlfriend in tow, was going to spoil it for her.

Cathy brought the runabout's engine to life with a flick of the switch and carefully backed it out of the mooring. She was proud of her ability with boats and her knowledge of the water. She steered deftly, heading out into the sound, loving the salty spray from the water as it misted about her, causing the golden strands of hair to curl at her temples and giving her the look of a child of twelve. As she brought the bow about to give her a heading, which would take her to the disabled motor yacht, she was surprised at the size of the vessel. It was an Italian vessel, fifty feet on the keel, at the very least. Mentally, Cathy recalled all she had heard or read about the elegant yacht. If she wasn't mistaken, Teak Helm had also glorified their delights. Wantonly powered, he had called them in one of his books. Only a rare man could afford them, and only a rare man has the style and the women to match their stunning beauty and excess.

Cathy noticed the yacht's name painted in gold leaf on her stern, *Sea Gypsy III*. From the looks of the flying bridge and the appointments of bass and gleaming chrome, she could imagine that the interior would bring a blush to Hugh Hefner's cheeks. A veritable floating Bunny Hutch, she snickered in disdain. Yet her innate love of beauty and the pleasure she took in the sleek lines of sea craft overrode her scorn.

It was Erica Marshall who greeted her as Cathy cut her engine and secured the craft to the mooring lines of the *Gypsy*. Deftly, she maneuvered her way up the gang-plank and Erica grasped her hand to help her aboard.

"Thanks," Cathy murmured as she took in Erica's appearance. She was clad in the barest of string bikinis, two miniscule strips of cloth that showed off the most gorgeous golden tan Cathy had ever seen.

"Can I get you a drink? I just mixed a batch of Bloody Marys."

"Isn't it a bit early in the day?" Cathy asked, peering at her watch which clearly said the time was 10:45.

"Early?" Clearly, it was a question out of Erica's depth. "Oh, I see what you mean. You think there's alcohol in the drinks. Goodness, no! Perhaps I should have said they were Virgin Marys. I never drink spirits. Alcohol gives you pimples," she said, patting her flawless cheeks. "Jar…Mr. Parsons is the one who drinks the liquor. I just pretend," she stated. "That's our little secret, just between you and me. I know I can trust you not to give me away," she gurgled as she waved a long pointed fingernail under Cathy's nose.

"You can count on me," Cathy said agreeably. "Is my father in the bilges?"

"Bilges?"

"Let me put it another way. Do you happen to know where my father is at this moment?"

"Of course. He's with Jar…Mr. Parsons."

"And where is Mr. Parsons?"

"Oh, well," Erica shrugged and waved her arm. "They're somewhere aboard."

"Somehow I thought they were," Cathy said snidely, watching Erica to see what effect her tone had on the scantily clad girl. There was no reaction. Obviously, Erica had become used to having people cast her snide remarks.

"Sit down and help yourself to the sun," Erica invited as she stretched out on a brilliant orange lounge chair, her long silky legs caressing the tufted cushions.

"Thanks," Cathy muttered as she sank down onto a low deck chair. As she glanced around, Cathy knew her assessment of the luxury aboard the *Gypsy* had been underestimated. Never in her life had she seen such outspoken hedonism. It was almost scandalous. From the cockpit, where she was sitting, she could look through the glass doors leading to the salon. The floor was richly carpeted in a dark emerald-green, which accented the contemporary styling of the sofa upholstery. Long plush benches surrounded the area making the focal point of the room the glass and chrome bar at the far side. The area was sky-lighted and off to one side was a winding staircase leading to the flying bridge above. Soft music flowed through the doors and also from a speaker set in a niche in the bulkhead. She imagined the entire ship was wired for the stereo system. As she watched, a white-coated steward came into the lounge from the forward section to refill the ice bucket.

"How many men make up Mr. Parsons's crew?" she asked Erica, waiting for another of the girl's vague answers.

"Three, altogether, including me," Erica answered. "You know we had to leave the engine man at Virginia Beach. Appendicitis or something."

"You mean the chief engineer, don't you?"

"I guess so. I don't pay much attention. Not to those things, anyway."

"Don't you have to use any suntan oil or sunscreen?" Cathy asked, envying the girl's deep tan.

"Heavens no. My dermatologist says I have perfect skin and nothing in this world can ruin it. He said I was one of those rare people whose body actually demands the sun to stay alive. He's absolutely right." Erica squirmed and stared at Cathy. "Do you use something?"

If there was one thing she wasn't going to admit to

Erica, it was that she had to use baby oil and iodine to get even the faintest of color. "I'm not a sun worshipper. I prefer to while away the time under a tree with a good book."

"How boring," came the reply, as Erica turned her face a slight degree toward the sun. "I hope I don't get a tan line," she complained as she adjusted the string of her bathing suit bodice.

"Yes, I certainly hope not," Cathy agreed, noticing for the first time that Erica was completely tan, without the white marks left by any suit. It was obvious she was used to bathing in the buff.

"Tell me, Miss Marshall. What does Mr. Parsons do for a living?"

"Do?"

"Yes, do. You know. What does he do for a living? How does he support himself?"

"Oh. He sends out bills. Actually, I send them out. I'm his secretary, you know. Right now, I'm on my break."

"Amazing," Cathy cooed. "Well, I guess someone has to do it."

"I hate typing numbers. I always break my nails. Jar…Mr. Parsons is getting someone to do the numbers for me when we get back to Lighthouse Point."

Cathy was saved from further comment by the arrival of her father and Jared Parsons. Her eyes went from one to the other. Sometime during the past hour the two men had reached some sort of mutual respect for one another. Jared was wiping grease from his hands and nodding while listening to Lucas.

"You have one hell of a problem, Jared," Lucas said

quietly. "Ten days, and that's only an estimate. If you have to be back in Lighthouse Point, I suggest you fly. This little beauty won't be taking to the water for some time. I'll put in a call and see what I can do about getting you that raw water pump you need and the exhaust manifold. As for the generator, you'd better bring up that one from Cape Fear. You're free to try another mechanic if you want, but if they're worth their salt, they'll tell you the same thing I did." Jared nodded, his features said he was resigned to Lucas's statement.

Cathy grinned when she noticed Jared glance at Erica. He looked embarrassed. Lucas was openly ogling the luscious display of satiny skin, but refrained from comment.

"Look, son," Lucas said, throwing his greasy hands around Jared's shoulder, "why don't you and Miss Marshall come by for supper tonight. Cathy can whip up some of her bisque. Won't you, Cat?" he turned to his daughter, silently pleading with her by the use of her pet name. "By then I should have some news for you from the marina. Best I can do for the moment. We eat at seven, give or take an hour or two, depending on Cat's mood."

"We'd be delighted, and you must call me Erica. Everyone calls me Erica—even Jared," the girl said sleepily from her position on the chaise. Cathy smirked and Lucas grinned at the uncomfortable expression on Jared's face.

"Yes, we'd be delighted," he replied coolly. "Dress or casual?"

"White tie," Cathy snapped irritably. "And after dinner we always go skinny-dipping in the river."

"Really!" Erica squealed.

"Really," Cathy said, swinging her legs over onto the gangway, her furious eyes locking with Jared's.

"Is that a promise about the skinny-dipping?" Jared asked in a husky whisper as he leaned over Cathy's descending head.

In spite of herself, Cathy laughed, her sea-green eyes full of mischief. "Scout's honor. Boys on the left bank and girls on the right." Jared laughed, the sound boyish and full of fun. At that moment, Cathy felt the man go up three notches in her opinion.

Lucas gunned the outboard motor and Cathy shouted over the spurring of the engine. "That was a rotten thing you did, Dad. Now I have to spend all afternoon in the kitchen."

"That man's starved for good food and good decent people like us," Lucas shouted back. "Be charitable. A few hours of your time to make a man happy isn't asking a lot. For shame, Cathy Bissette, what kind of daughter am I raising?"

"You've already raised me and done your best! Mr. Parsons bothers me and that Miss Marshall does, too. I wish you hadn't invited them. They're different from us, Dad. He's rich and she's...she's..."

"His woman," Lucas shouted extra loud to be certain Cathy heard him over the roar of the runabout.

As Lucas helped Cathy out of the boat, he put his arm around her. "Cat, don't envy her. She's what she is and you're what you are. She's the icing and you're the cake. What I'm trying to say is that you're..."

"I get the message, Dad, and if one more person

jams the fact that I'm a real person and a homebody
down my throat I'm going to get physically sick. And
you don't have to patronize me, either. Stop telling me
how good I am, and stop acting like a father," she said
tartly, as she flounced up the path that led to the house.

She couldn't remember when she'd been so angry.
She banged one pot and then another. By heaven she'd
cook him a dinner he'd never recover from. If that was
all she was good for, she would at least make sure it was
a dinner he would dream about for the rest of his days.
He could have the delicious Erica, but she'd serve the
main course, and if she was lucky, he'd be too sated to
enjoy his platinum-haired dessert.

Cathy busied herself, her thoughts on the dish she
was about to prepare. The secret was in the cast-iron
kettle, and she would die before she divulged it to
anyone. Herbs and spices were great, but if you didn't
have the right pot all you had was herbs and spices and
fish. Hmm, buttermilk biscuits and a salad from the
kitchen garden out back. She'd also make a strawberry
shortcake and just see which of the sweets Jared Parsons
preferred.

If she was going homespun, she might as well go all
the way with checkered tablecloth and napkins. A bowl
of daisies from the garden and a bottle of scuppernong
wine would do the trick. It was a pity Erica was coming
to dinner, it was a perfect seduction scene. Bills! He
sends out bills! Cathy shrugged and then grinned. Oh
well, there were jobs and there were jobs.

Her domain in perfect order, Cathy retired to her
room to ready herself for the evening, the yellow tote

in her arms. Darn, she still hadn't gotten to the first paragraph of Teak Helm's galleys. Tonight for sure, the minute their company had gone, she would unroll the galleys, make herself a cup of tea, lace it with rum the way Teak Helm did, and snuggle into her nest in the high four-poster and read all night long. She knew she would live every minute of Teak's adventure right down to the last punctuation mark.

Cathy finished her leisurely bath and stepped from the tub. Wrapping a cherry-colored towel around herself, she padded her way to the closet. What to wear. Her eye went to an aquamarine silk shift and then to her blue jeans, neatly folded on hangers. "What you see is what I am." Those had been her words. If she dressed up now she would definitely be suspect in Jared Parson's eyes. And that slinky dress was the one she had worn the last time she had seen Marc Hellenger. If she got dressed up her father would tease her unmercifully, and probably in front of Jared. Jared. She liked the name, it rolled off her tongue easily. It was a strong name. She finally selected a pair of designer jeans that hugged where the ads said they hugged and a daffodil-colored silk shirt with a V-neck. Definitely casual, her father wouldn't be the wiser. Jared would be so busy eating he wouldn't pay her the least bit of attention, so why was she fussing? She couldn't wait to see what delectable outfit Erica would wear to the *homey* little dinner party. No doubt *Vogue* had some tricky little number that cost a fortune, which Erica just *happened* to own.

A few quick swirls with the blow-dryer and a quick

one-two at the temples with the curling iron and she was ready. She slipped her feet into rope sandals and left the room without a second glance in the mirror. She was Cathy Bissette. She wasn't beautiful by her own standards but she would only do the best she could. I am what I am, she repeated to herself.

Bismarc was up and sniffing at the door waiting to be let out when Cathy heard the sound of the motor launch sidling up to the pier. "Oh no, Bizzy, you're staying here. We don't need another incident like this morning. Lie down now and be polite." The dog whined and made his way back to the hearth where he managed to squeeze himself between tubs of ferns and the andirons. He lay with his head on his paws, his ears cocked for the sound of a knock on the oak door. When it came, he whined again, but remained where he was.

Cathy whistled lightly when her father came in from the living room in what he called his classic golf shirt. Cathy grinned at him, then giggled. "It's wasted on me since I know you don't play golf, but Erica will never know the difference. Five dollars says she thinks it's a tennis outfit."

Lucas gave her a sheepish grin and opened the door. Her gaze went to the fourth place setting on the table and then back to Jared Parsons who stood in the doorway. Her pulse quickened as she took in his appearance.

Hmm! Cathy murmured to herself. This must be what they call separating the men from the boys. Again, she knew the casual sports outfit didn't come off a rack. Jared wore sleek white slacks and a multicolored silk shirt. He looked loose, comfortable, poised, ready for anything. He smiled and held out a spray of greens and blossoms.

"Usually I manage something a little better than this, but it was all I could find on such short notice."

"It's a good thing none of us is allergic," Lucas drawled. "That's ragweed."

Jared shrugged. "Miss Marshall wasn't able to come and wants me to extend her apologies," he said smoothly, watching Cathy to see her reaction.

Cathy lowered her eyes, not wanting him to see the relief there, and tossed his bouquet into the trash.

"Sit down, Jared," Lucas offered. "Can I get you a drink? Brought back some of Jesse Gallagher's home-made moonshine for the occasion."

"Dad, you aren't going to give him that, are you?"

"Certainly I am. I want to see what he's made of, and what better way than to have him sample some of Jesse's finest. It's the mark of a man in these parts if you can put away half a jug."

Bismarc whined again and pawed the bricks at his feet. If there was one thing he loved it was the sight of a Jesse Gallagher jug and a few drops in his saucer.

"You take this dog here," Lucas said, pointing to Bismarc. "Why, he can drink both of us under the table in sight of an hour and still get up on his feet."

"That's because he has two more feet than you do," Cathy said, enjoying Jared's close scrutiny.

"Is this serious drinking we're talking about or just a friendly toot?" Jared asked.

"Hell, man, it's whatever you want it to be. We've got the whole dang night ahead of us. The only thing we have to do is eat this dinner Cat cooked for us and from then on we're on our own."

Bismarc settled himself at Jared's feet and watched him with adoring eyes. Why he could walk right out of here and take my dog with him and Bismarc would never give me a second thought, Cathy thought dismally. He was fitting in just a shade too perfectly. Here he was, sitting in her kitchen like he belonged. Drinking Jesse Gallagher's moonshine like he was born to it and carrying on an easy conversation with her father on a subject very few people knew anything about: meaning one writer named Lefty Rudder.

"You're not going to believe this, Jared, but I have every work Lefty Rudder ever wrote. That man knew everything there was to know about the sea and every manner of boat you can think of. He had a way with words that the young writers today know nothing about, with the possible exception of Teak Helm. He's about the closest to Lefty I've ever come across."

"I'm afraid I'll have to take exception to that, Lucas. I've read Rudder and Helm both and I think Teak Helm is better than Rudder. Lefty Rudder was too heavy on the narrative. You take *Sea Gray Mist* for instance. I couldn't get into that book until the fourth chapter. An author has to get your attention on the first page, the first paragraph, and that's what Helm does. He grabs you in a vice and you don't shake loose till the last paragraph. Of course, that's only my opinion."

"I couldn't agree more, Mr. Parsons," Cathy said staring at her father. Now what was he up to? He adored Teak Helm's books as much as she did.

"Can't you call me Jared like your father does? And, if it's all right with you, I'll call you Cathy." Cathy shrugged. But inside she knew anything was all right with her.

"Are you a Teak Helm fan?" she asked curiously.

"I think it's safe to say so. I've read and admired all his books. I don't have much time to read, but when I do, I'd rather read one of Helm's sea adventures than anything else. Actually, I consider it a luxury to be able to sit and read for the sheer joy of it."

"Dinner's ready," Cathy said, sitting down on the chair Jared held for her. She ignored her father's smirk and waited for the serving bowl to be passed to her. Everything was perfect; the table, the food and the wine. Not that either of the men would appreciate the wine after Jesse's homemade concoction.

"Tell me, Cathy, what do you do? Are you home on vacation or do you live here all year long?"

"Me?" Cathy asked, shifting her eyes toward her father. "Why I just shrimp with my father." Lucas reached for his wineglass as he started to choke. "Are you all right, Daddy?"

"Fine, fine. It just went down the wrong way." He cast a watery glance at his daughter and shrugged. If she wanted to pretend she was a shrimp girl, let her. Cat always had a reason for everything she did. She was like a dog with a bone, once it got a taste of the marrow. He stared at Jared Parsons and said bluntly, "It's my personal opinion that Teak Helm has been using Lefty Rudder's work. I told you I read all of Rudder's books and Helm just takes the same plots and adds a new twist here and there, and because he writes in the first person, they're his adventures. Course I can't prove it, and I've no mind to, but it's my opinion."

"Dad! Do you know what you're saying?" Cathy cried in outrage.

"Of course I know, and I said it was just my opinion."

Jared Parsons had stopped eating, his face was a mask of controlled fury. His voice, when he spoke, was deadly. "The opinion you just stated should never be uttered before witnesses. If I were to repeat it, it could mushroom and a man's reputation could be ruined."

"He's right, Dad. How could you say such a thing?" Cathy cried, annoyed at her father and puzzled by the vehemence in Jared's voice when he defended Teak Helm.

"Anytime you've a mind to put my opinion to the test, I'll be glad to point out the similarities. I told you, I have every word Lefty Rudder ever wrote and Cat here has every book Helm ever wrote. Since no one agrees with me, it's of no matter," Lucas said, getting up from his chair. "I'll be going over to Jesse's for a while. They hooked up his cable TV and there's a movie he invited me to see. And, Parsons, I was right about your engine. The parts for the raw water pump and exhaust manifold will be here in four days, possibly five. Best I could do. And if you want to send your crewmen down to Cape Fear to pick up that generator you ordered, be glad to lend you my pickup truck. You two enjoy yourselves and save me some of that shortcake, Cat."

Cathy blinked, stared at Jared, her mouth open at her father's apparent rudeness. Jared controlled his fury and forced a grimace that Cathy supposed was to pass for a smile. She should say something, defend her father, but the words wouldn't come. Instead, she got up and removed the dinner plates. "Would you like a big piece or a little piece?" she asked inanely.

"What?"

"Cake. Do you want a big piece or a little piece?"

"Actually, I'd much prefer to have only the strawberries," Jared replied in a tight voice.

While Cathy spooned the strawberries into a dessert dish, she watched Jared out of the corner of her eye. Her throat was dry and her heart was fluttering like a trapped bird. "Tell me, Jared, what do you do?" she asked, striving to wipe the angry look from his face.

"I'm in sales. Supply and demand, that type of thing," he answered shortly.

"And then you send out bills," Cathy muttered as she turned to the counter for the cream.

"I'm sorry, what did you say?" he asked a frown settling on his handsome features.

"Nothing," she answered nonchalantly. "I was wondering aloud what movie Dad was going to see. How are the strawberries?"

"Delicious. And your dinner was extraordinary. I've eaten in some of the finest restaurants around the world and I can truthfully say yours was one of the best dinners I've ever eaten. Now I know why you won first prize for your recipe."

Cathy laughed. "It's the pot." Now why had she admitted that to this man? It was her closely guarded secret, the success of her She-Crab stew, and here she was babbling like a schoolgirl. Was she looking for that pat on the head from this strange man sitting beside her?

Bismarc made his way to Jared and nuzzled his leg. He backed up and stared at the man.

"I usually take him for a run along the shore about this time of day. I guess he thinks you're going to take him. He's certainly taken a liking to you." Now why was her voice so defensive?

"Then let's take him for his run," Jared said, rising from his chair. "I like to walk after dinner, something I rarely get a chance to do when I'm living aboard ship. You can clean this mess later."

"Oh, I can, can I?" Cathy sputtered. "You ate here, the least you can do is offer to help me clean up."

"That's woman's work," Jared defended coolly. "Come on, before this dog takes a fit here at my feet." He took her arm and pulled her to him. Cathy's breathing quickened at his touch and she drew in her breath. Bismarc, hearing the sound, nudged his way between Jared and Cathy, separating them, showing Jared that while he, Bismarc, might like him, Cathy was his mistress.

Dumb dog, Cathy groaned silently. When I want you to protect me I'll let you know. Jared was amused and fondled Bismarc's ear. "Clever dog you have here."

"Among other things," she said tartly, opening the door for Bismarc's wild charge. The dog waited, his eyes on Cathy. "Go ahead, Bizzy." The dog wouldn't move, he emitted a whining from deep in his throat. "Fetch me a catfish and I'll cook it for your breakfast," Cathy said, shooing the dog out the door. Bismarc needed no second urging, he was out the door like a streak.

Jared stared at Cathy. "Can he find a catfish at night in the dark water?"

"No, but he doesn't know that and it did get him out of the way."

Jared laughed, the boyish sound rippled through her. Suddenly, he took her hand in his. "I'll race you to the dock!"

"You're on!" Cathy cried, breaking loose from his hand and racing off in her long-legged stride. Midway to the dock, Jared passed her, his athletic grace evident in the way he ran with his head up and arms tucked closely at his sides.

Before she could reach the dock, he stopped and turned and she found herself running into his open arms. Laughing, she struggled for balance and it was only Jared's strong embrace that kept her from falling.

"No fair, you said to the dock."

"I changed my mind," he teased, the sound of his laughter ringing through her and tingling her toes. "Besides, I don't want to tire you out and give you an excuse for not clearing up the kitchen."

"Beast," she smiled. "You're no better than Bismarc. Eat and run," she sighed dramatically. She wished Jared would release her from his embrace. His nearness was doing odd things to her and she couldn't seem to catch her breath.

As if sensing her thoughts, he draped his arm around her shoulders and walked with her along the length of the pier. In the distance, the lights of *Sea Gypsy III* glowed through the darkness.

"It's a pity Miss Marshall couldn't come to dinner,"

she murmured, waiting to see if Jared would offer a further explanation of Erica's absence.

"I didn't want her to come with me and I told her so."

Cathy drew away from him and looked up into his eyes. "And are women used to doing as you say? She was extended a personal invitation, she would have been well within her rights to come to dinner, in spite of anything you said." The challenge in her voice was clear.

"Yes, I usually have my way where women are concerned," he replied, his gray eyes twinkling in response to her challenge.

"And why is that?" Cathy demanded, so angry she had to force the words from between stiff lips.

"Because I expect it," he smiled. "And also because I'm confident in my own ability to satisfy a woman in other—more pleasurable ways that make her forget my shortcomings, shall we say."

Cathy blushed vividly and was glad for the descending darkness that hid the revealing flush of color staining her cheeks. "Are you always so conceited?" she retorted, withdrawing from him until she stood precariously near the edge of the weathered planks.

"Conceited? I prefer to think of it as self-assured." A wry smile played about his lips and his eyes locked with hers and seemed to delve into her being.

Cathy could almost understand why he was so confident in himself and his effect on women. He had the handsomeness of a prince and the smile of a rogue. His broad shoulders seemed to stand between herself and the darkness, and he possessed the lean, stalking grace of a panther. She realized, to her own dismay, that she was vitally aware of his presence and of his emanating prowess. He was all that was masculine and manly, yet there was a playful hint of the boy in him. Jared Parsons would always remain young, regardless of the years he added to his age. His charm was infinite; his magnetism was boundless.

Aware that she was being drawn under his spell, Cathy tore her eyes away, eager only to put distance between herself and this overbearing man. In her haste, she came dangerously close to the edge of the dock, nearly losing her balance for the second time that night.

With the quick reflexes of a cat he snatched her away from the edge and pulled her up close against him, pressing her against his body, making her aware of the lean, hard strength he possessed.

"You see what I mean?" he said huskily, the tone of his voice sending shivers up her spine. "I simply sweep women off their feet and they fall into my arms." His mouth was close to her ear and a roaring sounded in her head. She had never been so sensitively aware of a man in her entire life.

Cathy clung to him, aware for the first time of the shock of desire that swept over her like a rising tide. "Not *this* woman," she protested, and her voice sounded unconvincing, even to her own ears. "It would take more than a plunge into the river for me to fall into your arms."

"Perhaps it would take this…"

Spellbound, she felt him move against her, watched him bend toward her. His mouth found hers and he kissed her, gently at first, then, as her traitorous body responded with a will of its own, the kiss became deeper, masterfully sensuous. His arms closed around her, molding her to the full length of his body. Her senses came alive, aware of the black sky surrounding them and the ebony waters beneath them. She was conscious of the soft, dark night and the glimmer of the bravest stars which dared to outshine the moon. The long needle pines seemed to whisper his name while the gentle sea breezes caressed and cooled their cheeks, bringing into sharp contrast the warmth of the contact between their lips.

His mouth trailed across her cheek in a caress as soft as a butterfly's wings and ignited a flame on the smooth skin just below her ear. Desire and passion licked through her veins like brushfire as she clung to him, a stirring response thundering through her that was astonishing in its intensity.

When he released her she was breathless, unable to fathom the emotions that swept through her. "You had no right to do that!" she protested hotly as his fingers wound around the base of her throat and tipped her face up to his.

"I don't think your body agrees with you," he said, his deep laugh sounding in her ears. A laugh that held all of the man and none of the boy.

Before he could capture her lips again, Cathy stumbled free of his grasp, running headlong for the riverbank, knowing only that she must put distance between herself and this man who could make her pulses race and her heart pound. A man who could make her forget her principles and conspire with him for her own seduction.

She heard his footsteps pounding down the dock in hot pursuit. She heard herself squeal in dismay and was aware of a red-coated streak leaping through the trees to take a stance at the end of the dock. Bismarc set up a ferocious barking, holding Jared Parsons at bay while his mistress made her escape.

Feeling secure in the small measure of safety Bismarc allowed, Cathy turned on her heel and faced her pursuer. "Stay away from me, Jared Parsons. I know all about men like you and I have no use for your kind. Stay away! I never want to see you again!"

Jared placed his hands on his hips and leaned backward. A deep, hearty laugh that teased and mocked her with its mischief rasped against her nerves. "That's quite impossible, *Miss Bissette*. Your father invited me to go shrimping in the morning with both of you. Needless to say, I accepted."

# CHAPTER THREE

ALWAYS AN EARLY RISER, Cathy thought this particular morning the same as the others. If her movements were a little less agile, her mind a little fuzzier, she chalked it up to the approaching storm that made itself evident through her bedroom window.

Bismarc whined at the foot of the bed. It was time to go out, and he tugged impatiently at the bedspread to show his irritation. Cathy hastily pulled on her shorts and knotted a tailored shirt at her waist. She might as well get a move on; she still had the remnants of last night's dinner to clear away before she could begin with breakfast.

She dreaded facing Lucas at the breakfast table, listening to him ramble on about his evening with Jesse's cable television, and then the inevitable questions about her own evening. And she knew she wouldn't be spared his sly looks when he noted the disastrous condition of the kitchen. No one in Swan Quarter left dinner dishes sitting on the table overnight. "I think I'm living under a black cloud, Bizzy. Do you get the feeling somebody is out to get me?" The Irish setter whined impatiently, eager to be let outdoors.

On the dock, Cathy sat with her long legs drawn up to her chin, the wind whipping her light blond hair about her face. The mist over the water swirled to the north, covering the water's surface and making it impossible to see Jared's yacht. Bismarc frolicked on the beach and soon came to join his mistress, nuzzling Cathy's hand for attention. "You know that black cloud I was telling you about? Well, I think I'd better get myself an umbrella, or I'm going to drown in the rain of my own emotions. And I don't mean from the oncoming storm, either. At least I'll be spared his company today. Dad won't be taking the trawler out with a storm coming."

Bismarc settled himself comfortably at her side and from time to time his paws took a swipe at the low gray mist encroaching the pier. Suddenly, he growled, a low sound in his throat, and stood up, ears erect. "He's out there, and he's watching us. That's what you're trying to tell me. He can see us, but we can't see him. He's insufferable, Bizzy. If there's one thing I know about, it's people, and there are two kinds—givers and takers. Jared Parsons is a taker. He thinks he's going to take me and add me to his collection...of women. That conceited, insufferable, arrogant, chauvinistic..." she sputtered angrily. "Maybe Erica what's-her-name wants to give her all to Jared Parsons, but Cathy Bissette doesn't." She laughed and threw her arms around the setter. "What I'm saying is, Jared Parsons can just go fish in some other stream. And do you know something else, Bizzy? When we get back to the house, I'm going to call Dermott McIntyre and ask him if he wants to go to the Fourth of July picnic with me. I'll even let him kiss me good-night," she said defensively. "Come on, it's going to pour any minute. If we're lucky, he might get washed overboard." Bismarc howled his protest at being led back to the house.

"I cleaned up the mess you left here," Lucas Bissette grumbled as he poured his daughter a cup of coffee and set a plate of toast in front of her. "You must have had a grand evening if you couldn't clean the kitchen."

Cathy casually sipped her coffee and told her father about her evening with Jared. Suddenly, his chair settled into place with a loud thud. Lucas leaned across the table, his eyes locked with Cathy's. "For a girl who makes her living in the city of New York, and who is supposed to be as smart and intelligent as you claim to be, it just eludes me why you're making this much of a fuss over a simple little invitation."

Cathy bristled, her eyes changing to the green of emerald fire. "Most fathers," she said through clenched teeth, "would react somewhat differently if their only daughter told them a rich playboy tried to seduce her on the riverbank. Or is it that you think I'm so ugly and unattractive no man would ever try something like that and you think I'm lying!"

"Women! You're just like your mother, trying to put words into my mouth." Gruffly, he touched her shoulder with his calloused hand. "No, I don't think you're ugly and unattractive, and no, I don't think you're lying. I just think you're afraid of men, Jared Parsons in particular, because he stirs something up in you and you're afraid of it. Parsons ain't the run-of-the-mill man you've been used to. I think you might have misconstrued what happened last evening. I'm not saying Parsons isn't a playboy. He sees you as a desirable, beautiful young woman, and not the kind of woman he's used to coming in contact with. He reacted like a man; is that so terrible?"

"It's evident you're on his side. So, why don't we just drop the subject? Thanks for doing the dishes," Cathy said curtly.

"My pleasure. I'm going down to the water and check out the pier. That's a wicked wind whipping out there. What are you going to do with yourself?"

"I'm going to settle down with Teak Helm's galleys and read nonstop. On second thought, I think I'll take the pickup and go into town and pick up a few things."

"Ah...Cat...you can't take the pickup. I told Parsons his crewmen could use it to go up to Nags Head to see if they could get a few parts for his engine."

Cathy seethed. She'd been right the first time. It *was* a black cloud over her head, and it was getting lower by the minute. Her back stiffened as she marched from the room, Bismarc in her wake.

Cathy's anger evaporated the minute she unrolled the galleys and lost herself in the latest Helm sea adventure. It was two o'clock in the afternoon when she noticed her muscles were cramped and the sun was shining bright and clear. It had also gotten hot and muggy and she longed for a cooling swim.

Tenderly, she straightened the long galley sheets on her bed in neat order and quickly donned her swimsuit, a modest two-piece affair of grass-green Lycra. Without the use of the pickup she would have to use her old bike and pedal to her favorite inlet. Quickly, she gathered up her beach towel and a pair of thong sandals and tossed them into a bright green beach bag that matched her swimsuit. At the last moment, she scooped up her portable radio and a tube of zinc oxide to protect her nose from overexposure to the sun. Packing in a slim sheaf of the galleys, she was ready to go.

Bismarc nudged her leg pointedly, pushing her toward the refrigerator. Cathy waved a bag of Oreo cookies for him to see, and he barked his approval. "To the inlet, Bizzy, and the first one in the water gets to eat the whole bag!"

Bismarc hit the water just as Cathy leaned her bike against a tall, whispering pine tree. "If you're not a chauvinist, you'll share," she said, waving the cookie bag in the air. Bismarc ignored her as he cavorted in the water.

Cathy looked around to be certain she had solitary domain of her secret place where the water was cool and calm and the sun dappled through the trees. A perfect place for skinny-dipping. She shed her two-piece suit and waded out into the water. One second there was a flash of skin and the next a mermaid broke water. Laughing happily, she played with her dog, splashing and whooping just as she had done when she was a young girl and Bismarc was a puppy.

It wasn't his words but the timber of his voice that shocked her to awareness. "Skinny-dipping, Miss Bissette?"

How had he found her? Was he spying on her, following her to finish what he'd started the night before? She tried to speak but the words wouldn't come. She nodded, her body weightless in the water. Her heart fluttered madly as she saw him standing on the riverbank.

"Are you going to stay in there all day, Miss Bissette?" he asked mockingly.

Cathy found her voice. "For days, if necessary. How did you find this inlet?" she demanded, knowing he was relishing every second of her embarrassment. And to make matters worse, Bismarc had deserted her and Jared was opening her bag of cookies. He handed one to the dog and then squatted down, watching her through narrowed eyes. From time to time he nibbled on a cookie, his gray eyes laughing at her. He was going to wait her out, and when she did leave the water, she would be as wrinkled as yesterday's newspaper. He would also see the smear of zinc oxide she had smeared all over her nose. She knew his secretary never used zinc oxide. People who had perfect skin didn't need sunscreens.

Bismarc daintily nosed another cookie from the bag, and in doing so the sheaf of galleys from Cathy's beach bag fell onto the washed-out beach towel. Cathy watched angrily as Jared picked up the long sheets of paper and scrutinized them. "Take your hands off those!" Cathy shouted angrily. "And stop feeding my dog!" Tears stung her eyes at her predicament. "Bismarc, chase him out of here," she cried.

Jared Parsons laughed and Cathy's head reeled with the effect of the sound. "This animal well may be a champion of champions, a staunch defender of womanly virtue, plus a great bird dog, but right now, right this minute, he's a dog who is smart enough to know who is holding the cookies." He laughed again and

Bismarc sat at attention waiting to be fed his special treat. "I'd almost be willing to place a small wager that he could be trained to attack for one of these delectable morsels."

He was right. Bismarc would do anything for a cookie. "You…you…" Words failed Cathy as she sputtered, trying to tread water.

"Insufferable, unbearable, conceited, arrogant male chauvinist," Jared completed her statement and laughed, feeding Bismarc still another cookie. He stood, his hands on his hips, and grinned. "You're beginning to look a little…puckered. You better come out. And to show you what a gentleman I am, I'll turn around."

"Never!" Cathy stormed. "Sooner or later you're going to run out of cookies and then you'd better watch out, Bizzy will tear you apart."

Cathy stared at him grimly. In spite of herself, she couldn't help admiring his slim litheness, the bronze chest that stood out starkly above his tailored white shorts. How well she remembered the feel of those muscular legs pressed against her own. She had to get out of the water, trick him somehow so she could get away from him. Deliberately, she took a mouthful of water, coughing and sputtering. Instinctively, she started to flounder and gasped, "I have a cramp! Bizzy, help me!" Another mouthful of water and more coughing and sputtering. Bizzy ignored her as he chewed on a fresh Oreo. Out of the corner of her eye, as she let herself slip beneath the water, she saw Jared tense and move toward the river's edge.

From under water she could hear his legs thrashing the water as he waded out to a depth where he could swim.

Cathy had always considered herself a strong swimmer, but she was no match for Jared's powerful strokes. He had her pinned to him within seconds. Drops of water sparkled on his long, dark lashes, making her want to reach up and brush them away.

"You're a beautiful woman," Jared said huskily as his eyes devoured her hungrily.

Cathy's trembling body was not lost on Jared as he drew her closer. "You're freezing," he said softly. He laughed. "Or are you?"

Cathy struggled, fighting for escape. Her face flamed and her temper flared. Her plans had gone askew. She had intended to lure Jared into the water, and while he was swimming out to her, make her escape by heading for the shore, and at the very least, wrapping the towel around her nakedness. Now, she realized how foolish she had been to assume that Jared wasn't an excellent swimmer, as he seemed to be at everything else.

As her struggles increased, she involuntarily rose in the water, her naked torso becoming visible. One quick glance in Bismarc's direction told her she would get no help from that quarter since he had the whole bag of Oreos to himself. Jared had fed him, and now Jared was holding her and Bismarc was making no effort to help. Bismarc was not the smartest dog in the world, she decided and reluctantly stopped trying to get away.

"Have you resigned yourself to be rescued?" Jared

grinned. "Admit it," he demanded, pulling her tightly against him, making her aware of his lean, hard strength and his hands holding her fast, aware of the sun glinting through the trees, the feel of the water caressing her skin. "You tricked me into the river because you didn't have the nerve to come out." There was a new note in his voice now. A throbbing note of masculinity, a teasing, sensual sound that feathered through her senses and made her feel weak.

"Admit it," he repeated against her ear, his lips caressing and finding the smooth softness near the base of her throat. "You were afraid to come for what you wanted, so you sang the song of the Lorelei and lured me in here after you." His arms became possessive, blocking out all sight and sound except the reality of his caress. His lips found hers, tasting of the slightly salty river water, cool and wet; yet, somehow, that kiss burned through her, assaulting her defenses and overpowering her protests. Mindlessly, she wrapped her arms around him, feeling his power and strength. She clung to him, weightless, buoyant, as though in a dream, and the fabric of her resistance frayed like tattered threads of flotsam and jetsam. His hands wound in her hair, his lips sought the hollow of her throat and began to trail lower.

Cathy stiffened. He thought…he actually thought… he believed she enticed him into the water to make love to her! *Crack!* She brought up her hand and at the same time kicked her legs, pushing him off balance. She dove, clean and deep, surfacing as far away from him as she could get. She was tired and she knew she could never reach the riverbank before him if he decided to pursue her. A backward glance told her he was doing exactly that, a murderous glint in his eyes. She still had some fight left in her, and would go down fighting if she must. "You stay away from me," she gasped, taking an unintentional mouthful of water. Jared was upon her, holding her head above water with one hand, the other was locked about her waist. Tears scalded Cathy's eyes as she realized what was to come. "Please," she begged, "let me go! I didn't...I only wanted to get away from you. I didn't mean for this. Let me go."

Jared frowned, noticing the tears in her eyes. She couldn't be...not in this day and age! A virgin!

Cathy stared into his gray eyes and knew immediately what he was thinking. She felt ashamed, prudish, like a little girl all rolled into one. Then she became angry, defending herself against his silent mockery. "Yes, I'm a virgin, and I intend to remain that way until the day I get married. If that makes me hokey or cornball in your eyes, then so be it. You see, Mr. Parsons," she said, making his name sound like a disease, "I can handle my decision. It must come as a shock to you to find there's at least *one* female who can resist your charms. And I'm her!"

She turned and struck out for the riverbank with sure, even strokes, belying the fact that her heart was pounding and her breathing was ragged.

Jared didn't follow, but she felt his eyes stinging her. She watched him from the shore as she stepped into the bottom of her swimsuit and then knotted the top securely. She gathered her belongings and stood a moment, staring at Jared as he treaded water exactly where she had escaped him. With four cookies still to go in the cellophane bag, Bismarc yelped in outrage as Cathy climbed onto her bike and pedaled away. Dejectedly, he followed the wobbling bicycle, hoping for a stray crumb along the way.

Even though Cathy knew she wasn't being followed by Jared, she pedaled furiously, skirting rocks strewn along the path. At the last moment, before turning into the road which led to her house, she decided to ride into the village and get the few things she needed from the drugstore. Just in case, she told herself, Jared Parsons took it into his head to follow her home.

Cathy kept her pace an easy one for Bismarc to follow. The ride to the center of Swan Quarter's business district was less than a mile, and Bismarc kept an easy lope beside her. Her circuit took her past the ferryboat landing, which all summer long took happy tourists out to the island of Ocracoke, where some say the infamous pirate, Blackbeard, buried his treasure. The ferry landing was quiet now, and she followed the road to the center of the tiny town.

"Wait here, Bizzy," she instructed as she leaned her bike outside the corner drugstore, "and don't chase any little old ladies. Be a good dog and I'll get some more cookies," Cathy said, trying to bribe the dog. If there was one thing he loved, it was padding after little old ladies and snouting against their shopping bags.

Her purchases secure in her beach bag, Cathy mounted her bicycle and made her way down the quiet village street. She glanced up at the sun and estimated the time. She had spent much longer than she had anticipated talking to Mr. Gruber, the druggist, and his wife, who insisted she have a root beer float and tell her all about New York City. Cathy almost missed his tall figure, but there was no way she could have missed Erica's striking good looks in her colorful shorts and T-shirt. "Hide, Bizzy," she hissed as she skirted into the nearest alleyway, almost toppling from her bike.

In the shadows of the alleyway, between the grocer's and the hardware store, Cathy could hear the click of Erica's high heeled shoes on the pavement and recognized the deep timber of Jared's voice. They were heading her way! How had Jared and Erica arrived in town so quickly, she wondered. Then she remembered his runabout and the public dock. He had left the inlet and gone back to his yacht, picked up Erica and had come into town. The public dock was only a block away from the village.

Cathy felt her heart sink. By the sound of their voices, they were heading right for her. If they should notice her hiding like a criminal in the alley, she would appear more foolish than ever. What was happening to her? Here she was, a full-grown woman, hiding!

"If you have something to say, Erica, say it!" Jared demanded. His tone was a far cry from the amused tone he always used with Cathy. Jared was angry, angrier than she knew he was capable of being.

Erica stopped just at the end of the alley where she turned on her incredibly high heels to face Jared. "Very well, I'll say it! I don't like the way you look at that little Goody Two-shoes. I may be what I am, but I've never been a liar. And last, but not least, I'm not dumb and I have *no* intention of continuing the role you want me to play. A secretary is one thing, but don't expect me to play the blithering idiot. Your little swamp girl is no fool. Remember when she came out to the yacht? Well, the first thing she asked was what you did for a living. I played my part to the hilt, and believe me when I tell you, she didn't buy it. Not one word of it."

Cathy, hiding in the shadows, saw Jared tense and his eyes narrow.

"What did you tell her?"

"I told her you sent out bills. Let her figure it out. If I'm supposed to be brainless," Erica complained, "it was the perfect answer." Her strident voice lowered and she moved a step closer to Jared. "Something's wrong, Jared. Something has come between us. Tell me not to worry, lie to me if you must," she pleaded. Seeing no response, she spat angrily. "It's Pollyanna, isn't it? You like that girl and all her homey talents. What do you suppose she'd be like in bed? She's shaped like a plank! Or haven't you gotten that far in your thinking? If you never believe anything else, believe this. That one is holding out for a ring and a marriage contract."

Cathy's face flamed and she was certain they could see it shining like a beacon from the dark alleyway. An anger which she'd never known she was capable of raced through her and stiffened her back. How dare they talk about her this way? A plank, indeed!

"That's enough, Erica. You know no more about the girl than I do, and if there's one thing I don't do, have never done, it's seducing sixteen-year-old girls."

"Sixteen!" Erica laughed shrilly. "Sixteen! Try adding eight or nine years onto that number and you'll have her age. She may look sixteen to you, but she isn't."

Cathy, from her hiding place, almost cried aloud in outrage. Sixteen! Even after this afternoon, when he had held her in his arms, kissed her, he thought she was sixteen! Her blue-green eyes ignited into fires. He had seen her naked, had watched her pull on her bathing suit. And still he thought she was sixteen! Cathy nearly moaned aloud with humiliation. She knew she was slender, but she had never thought of herself as being built like a plank nor of seeming underdeveloped. *Sixteen!*

Erica advanced a step toward Jared and wrapped her arms around his neck. "I'm bored, Jared. Can't you hurry Lucas so we can leave this place?" Her long nails trailed the soft hair at the nape of his neck. "Let's hurry back to the yacht," she whispered, and the hushed tone echoed through the alley. "I'm feeling lonely and I want you to do something about it…soon, very soon."

Cathy couldn't bear another moment of seeing them, hearing Erica's soft purr as she made her unabashed invitation to Jared. Couldn't bear to see the woman's long, painted nails trailing through Jared's hair, just as her own fingers had done hours earlier when he had swam out to her and held her in his arms and created an earth-shattering stir of her emotions. With a silent cry, Cathy buried her face in her hands and only knew that an eternity later, when she at last was able to lift her head, both Erica and Jared were gone.

BACK IN HER ROOM, Cathy tossed her beach bag and her purchases from the drugstore onto the bed. She removed the slim sheaf of Teak Helm's galleys and dropped them beside the sheets she had already read.

The house was quiet, disturbingly so. She didn't want to be alone with her thoughts; she didn't want to remember that scenario she had witnessed from the alleyway. She felt besmirched and foolish because of Jared Parsons, and stupidly chagrined to be betrayed by her own dog. "You," she accused Bismarc as he nosed hungrily at the zipper on her beach bag, "would sell your soul to the devil for an Oreo cookie." The setter whined pitifully at her stern words. "You actually sat there stuffing yourself while I made a fool of myself, naked as the day I was born. I actually came out and said I was saving myself, and I admitted I was a virgin to that…that man! Now I'm going to have to face him on the trawler in the morning when we leave to go shrimping. How can I look at him knowing he thinks I'm…I'm…sixteen! I hate him! And you can just get out of my sight, too, you…dog!" Cathy cried brokenly as she threw herself on the bed, crushing the galleys into a heap. At first she fought the tears but then gave in. She hiccoughed and sobbed, all the while beating the pillow with clenched fists. Cautiously, Bismarc poked his head around the door frame, then slinked his way to the bed. Cathy was asleep, the tears drying on her cheeks. He whined and tried to lick her hand, but gave up when she pulled away. Disheartened at this lack of attention, he left the room, but not before he managed to nose the package of cookies out of the beach bag.

# CHAPTER FOUR

THROUGH MOST OF THE NIGHT Cathy prayed for rain. The last thing in this world that she wanted to do was to spend the day on a small trawler with Jared Parsons and his "secretary."

But the heavens chose not to comply with her prayers and produced perfect shrimping weather. The sun was already making the promise of a beautiful day as it shed a red-gold haze on the horizon. A fine smoke mist was dissipating off the water, and there was just enough breeze to sway the highest tops of the tall pines. Drat!

As Cathy rose from her bed, Bismarc was already demanding to be let out. "Calm down, Bizzy, let a girl get her eyes open, will you?" Bismarc barked anxiously. "All right, all right, I'm hurrying!"

Hastily, she stripped off her light blue baby-doll pajamas and pulled on her two-piece bathing suit, covering it with jeans and a T-shirt. "Do you think I can have a chance to brush my teeth, if I hurry?"

Carrying her Top-Siders in her hand, she ran with Bizzy out the kitchen door and down to the dock. The early-morning dew was cool on her bare feet, and the sun was higher on the horizon, spreading its golds and coloring the landscape. Before she even reached the dock, she could hear the powerful motor of Jared's motor launch breaking the stillness. Her heart sank. Since she hadn't succeeded in her wish for bad weather, she had begun to hope that he and Erica had overslept and that she and Lucas could slip out on the trawler without them. Bizzy set up a rousing welcome, long before the runabout docked.

Jared threw the bowline with perfect aim, lassoing the piling and securing the boat. He spotted her and waved. "Coffee ready?" he called.

Cathy immediately bristled. Of all the insufferable... There sat Erica in the stern seat, looking as though she'd just stepped from the pages of *Women's Wear Daily,* and he was asking *her* if she had coffee ready! She knew his crew was still securing the new engine for the yacht, and so that left Jared and Erica alone on board; still, if Erica couldn't even make a pot of coffee what *did* she do? Cathy gulped, her face reddened. She didn't want to think about what Erica did for Jared.

"Hey, are you still sleeping? I asked you if you'd made coffee? Didn't you hear?"

"I heard," Cathy answered from between clenched teeth. "I knew Dad had invited you to come trawling with us. I didn't know he'd also invited you to breakfast."

"He didn't," Jared smiled an infuriating smile, "I only asked if you'd made coffee." He turned to help Erica onto the dock, warning Bizzy in a gentle command to stay away.

Cathy watched Bizzy, a russet-red form of eager impatience, sit down and control himself from rushing onto the pier and running to Jared. She eyed Erica's short shorts of yellow terry cloth and her skimpy white top which left little to the imagination. Cathy couldn't help but smile. Even Erica's "perfect skin" would show the effect of a long day on the trawler, with the burning sun reflecting off the water and with nowhere to take shelter but the cramped wheelhouse.

"Lucas up and about?" Jared asked conversationally.

"I suppose so. I haven't seen him yet this morning, but he's more than likely bringing the trawler around from the marina." Cathy turned on her heel, slapping her side in a silent call to Bismarc who was affectionately hugging Jared's thigh.

"Where're you going?"

"You seem to be dying for a cup of coffee. I'm going to the house to make it. Also, I've got to make the lunches for today. Hard work makes for big appetites, and there's no place on a trawler for anyone who doesn't intend to do his day's share of work." She looked pointedly at Erica who didn't seem to notice.

"Don't worry about the lunches," Jared said. "Erica whipped something up in the galley." He jumped back into the runabout and hefted out a wicker basket.

Cathy eyed the basket suspiciously and shrugged, saying nothing. Probably green molded bologna sandwiches and yogurt.

Jared and Erica sat at the kitchen table drinking coffee while Cathy busied herself. "What are you doing?" Jared asked between sips of hot coffee.

"Making lunch."

"I've already told you Erica whipped something up in the galley...."

"Then let me put it this way. I'm making *my* lunch. When I work, I get hungry. It's as simple as that." Cathy felt his eyes on her every move, making her self-conscious. The butter knife, thick with peanut butter, slipped from her fingers and clattered to the floor. She couldn't seem to control her shaking hands and the hot coffee which she was pouring into a thermos slopped over the sides, making a brown puddle on the shiny counter top. The hard-boiled eggs she had prepared the day before crunched to the floor, and even the apple she packed into the brown paper bag rolled out of her reach.

"That's quite an act you've got there, Miss Bissette. What do you do for an encore?" There was humor in his eyes, but his tone was deadpan.

Choking back a snarl, Cathy wrestled the peanut butter knife away from Bismarc. "I think I hear the trawler," she remarked as a low *putt-putt* of a marine engine came to her ears. "If you're ready, let's go."

Erica, who had been silent since arriving, stood and brought her coffee mug to the sink. Jared brought his, too, but at least he rinsed it under the running tap and turned it upside down in the dish drainer. Cathy sniffed. If Erica's lack of housekeeping instincts was any indication of the lunch, Cathy was glad to have the cracked hard-boiled eggs and gooey peanut butter and jelly sandwich. "Come on, Bizzy. Dad's here and rarin' to go."

"You're not bringing that…that dog, are you?" Erica asked, her expression clearly indicating her concern.

"Of course we are," Cathy snapped. "Bizzy always comes with us, don't you, boy?" She patted Bismarc's head. "He'd be heartbroken if we left him home.

C'mon, boy, Dad's waiting." She pointedly stood by the back door, holding it open for Bizzy and Jared and Erica.

Lucas waved from the bow of the trawler then went back to stringing line through the winches, which would haul the heavy nets out of the water.

Jared ran ahead carrying the wicker basket, Bizzy barking at his heels. "Can I give you a hand there, Luke?" he called.

Cathy watched Jared's easy movements, admiring, in spite of herself, his athlete's grace. Erica was having a difficult time making her way across the expansive lawn in her spike heeled sandals. "Dad's not going to let you on board wearing those things," she said, motioning toward Erica's shoes. "They're not safe, and they're murder on the decks."

"Oh, I won't wear them on board. I'll take them off."

"Erica, I suppose I should warn you. The decks of the trawler aren't plushly carpeted like they are on the yacht. And bare feet are treacherous on wet decks. Don't you have a pair of Top-Siders like these?"

"You mean those sneakers?" Erica curled her lip in distaste.

"They're not sneakers. They're deck shoes." She stopped and showed her the bottom of the shoe. "See, the grooves on the rubber sole act like little squeegies, even on a wet deck."

"Oh. Is that what they do?" Erica sneered, obviously disinterested, indicating that she wouldn't be caught dead wearing sneakers unless she was on a tennis court.

"Suit yourself," Cathy called, running ahead and leaving Erica to hobble down the grassy slope to the pier.

WHILE THE PULLEYS and lines did most of the hard labor of lifting the heavy nets out of the water, it was still a tedious and backbreaking job to empty the funnel-shaped nets and sort through, separating the assortment of fish, crabs' debris and the prized shrimp. Over and over again, when the lines became taut and dragged to the bottom, the winches were manned and creakily hoisted the nets to the decks of the trawler.

Erica issued shrill little shrieks whenever a fish bounced out of the net and flopped around the deck, and she turned up her nose at the sight of the shrimp, with their ugly little heads and threadlike little legs. But it was the crabs that were her undoing. Fierce and warlike, they battled with each other in the tall plastic cans, and Cathy couldn't resist pretending to accidentally drop a few of them onto the slick, water-puddled deck. Claws raised in self-defense, skittering in their peculiar sideways motions, their dark olive bodies raised up over their pale blue legs, they sought the shadowy recesses of the boat. Unable to control herself, Erica screamed, demanding that something be done before those monsters chewed off the tips of her little pink toes.

In her panic, Erica sought safety next to Jared, but before she could reach him, her bare feet slipped on the wet deck, and she went tumbling down.

Lucas turned to help her stand on her feet. "Watch out there, little lady," he said softly. "Bare feet and a wet deck are dangerous. You could go overboard." Erica smiled beguilingly up at Lucas, fully aware of her power over the weaker sex. Lucas cleared his throat. "Cat, why don't you lend your Topsiders to Erica? You're a lot more familiar with this boat than she is. What do you say?"

Cathy was beyond words. Her own father! For her answer, she glared at him. Sure, give over her own shoes to Erica, and she could take her chances barefoot. Grudgingly, seeing the plea in Lucas's eyes, she kicked off her shoes and tossed them at Erica.

She went back to work at the stern of the boat, her tasks taking her close to Jared. "That was very nice of you, Cathy. Erica's never been on a work boat before. I guess she didn't know what to expect or how to dress. Part of the blame is mine, I didn't even notice what she was wearing."

Biting remarks died in Cathy's throat. He hadn't noticed what the beautiful Erica was wearing! She supposed it just went to prove that any man could become impervious to a woman's charms when they were so blatantly offered. Besides, after praising her on her generosity, how could she tell him how deeply she resented giving over her Top-Siders? She didn't like Erica and she didn't like sharing her possessions with her.

Some of Cathy's bitterness at having to spend the day working the trawler with Jared Parsons melted away. She began to take notice of him as he worked the lines. He was skillful at everything he did, Cathy thought; but, somehow, in the back of her mind, she suspected that Jared was no stranger to hard work. Something about the way he used his hands when working the lines, and the way his muscles bunched in his bronzed back when he made the hoist, let her know that Jared hadn't always lived the easy life of a playboy.

As she worked beside him, they set about an easy pace, matching one another's rhythm in a harmonious determination to get the job done. From time to time she caught Jared looking at her and she knew it was with wonderment and appreciation that she could put in a hard day's work.

"We work well together. Have you noticed?" His voice was warm, friendly. And was she wrong? Had she detected a note of admiration? So Jared Parsons's interests didn't only lie in long-limbed, beautiful women who whiled away their days soaking up the sun and watching their fingernails grow. With renewed vigor, Cathy put her back into her work, liking the nearness of this tall, sun-bronzed man whose eyes could flash with something that could make her heart pound and her pulses race.

Lucas stepped out of the wheelhouse, his expression complimenting his crew on a good morning's work. "I was thinking of making a heading for Indian Island. We could have lunch and then head into Belhaven and see what we get for our catch."

UNDER THE TALL TREES on the isolated island, the shade was cool and the breeze refreshing. Jared waded ashore with the wicker basket Erica had packed, and Cathy followed, careful to keep her little brown paper bag out of the water. Bizzy leaped over the side and followed them.

Erica, now fully aware of crabs in their active state, refused to follow. With an indulgent smile Jared went back and carried Erica ashore.

"What have you got there, Cat?" Lucas asked, questioning the brown paper bag.

"My lunch."

"But that's a pretty heavy basket Erica packed…."

"No thanks, green bologna sandwiches and yogurt aren't my thing. Bizzy and I will share what I've got here."

Dropping down onto the sand, Cathy opened her lunch and pulled out her sandwich. She opened her thermos and poured herself coffee and was about to offer some to Lucas just as Erica opened the lunch basket. Jared spread a bright, checkered cloth and proceeded to help Erica empty the basket. Wine, cheeses, Beluga Caviar, assorted crackers, potted meats…a feast for kings!

"Sure you won't join us, Cat? This here is some spread Erica packed for us." The twinkle in Lucas's eyes challenged her, daring her to toss her meager peanut butter sandwich aside and join them in devouring all the goodies Erica had thought to bring.

"No thanks, that's a little too rich for my blood. Bizzy and I will…Bizzy! You come back here!" Too late. Cathy watched as her dog nosed around Lucas and Jared, begging for pieces of cheese and even lapping up a cracker spread with caviar. He was gobbling it down like he was born to gourmet goodies instead of dog food.

Cathy had never been so glad to get back on board as she was when they finished their lunch. It had been a long day, and it was going to be even longer before they got home late that evening. They had made surprisingly good time from Swan Quarter all the way up river to Belhaven, but it was still a long way home. She had humiliated herself at lunch. She had tried to make a fool of Erica, expecting the worst, and she had made a fool of herself. It was obvious to everyone, even to Bizzy, that her little sandwich couldn't compare with what Erica had brought. Why couldn't she have been gracious and accepted the lunch? Why was she so stubborn?

They trawled the nets eastward to the mouth of the Pungo River where they would swing into Belhaven. It was nearly four in the afternoon, and they would just make it to the fish wholesaler where they would sell their day's catch.

Lucas was excited by the size of their catch, praising Jared and promising to work extra duty in getting the yacht seaworthy.

The decks were slick with fish oil and water, and Cathy was finding it more and more difficult to keep her footing. She cast a murderous glance in Erica's direction and saw that she was sitting in the shade of the wheelhouse, her feet propped up on the bulkhead. And on her idle feet were the Top-Siders.

Her anger worked its way down to her fingers, and Cathy found it increasingly difficult to work the lines. She had been leaning over the rail when Erica came up behind her, startling her. Her bare foot slipped, her arms reached out, her fingers clutching at the lines. Quicker than the blink of an eye, Cathy went over the side and was underwater, sputtering and choking with shock. By the time she pushed herself to the surface, the trawler was more than fifty feet away. She could see her father's anxiety in the set of his shoulders and the way he was pointing. Jared was poised on the starboard rail, jumping feetfirst into the river.

"Oh, no," Cathy wailed. She was perfectly capable of swimming to the boat. Why did Jared think he had to save her? The last thing in this world Cathy wanted was to have Jared Parsons take credit for rescuing her.

Her arms stroked through the water, her legs stretched out and kicking, propelling her forward. But Jared had already left the boat and was swimming in long powerful strokes toward her. Twice in one week! It was too much! She was aware that Lucas had cut the motor on the trawler, and he and Erica were leaning over the side watching. She could have made it to the side of the boat within minutes. Even Bizzy seemed to know she was in no danger. She heard him barking and saw the russet streak as he plunged in over the side. He thought she was playing, and he had made up his canine mind to join her.

Jared swam toward her, meeting her halfway. "Go back. I'm all right, I don't need your help."

"This is the second time you've cried 'wolf,' Miss Bissette, and I think it's time you had a spanking. And I'm just the man to do it!"

She saw that he was suddenly angry, all concern for her leaving his face. He thought she purposely fell overboard to get him into the water to save her. She remembered the last time he jumped into the river, when she had pretended to be in trouble so she could get ashore and into her clothes. Cathy's face burned with embarrassment. There was no use in trying to explain to this insufferable, arrogant man. She swam away from him, her efforts taking her in the direction of the trawler.

"Did you hear what I said? I said you deserve a spanking."

"I heard. And what makes you think you're man enough," she sputtered.

Instead of an answer, he swam, overtaking her. "This makes me think I'm man enough." He reached for her, his fingers gripping her shoulders. She felt him pushing her down, down, under the water's surface. He dove, holding her against him, overpowering her struggles. His embrace was intimate, molding her body against his. Beneath the waters of the Pamlico, his mouth found hers, crushing her lips with his own, quelling her protests.

In spite of herself, Cathy wrapped her arms around his neck; her lips answered his kiss. She felt herself floating into a world of sensuality she had never known existed, until Jared Parsons led her through the portholes to a place where passions lay just beneath the surface and desire was a food for the soul.

Breaking surface, Cathy gasped, swallowing air. His hands were on her tiny waist, holding her firmly, refusing to release her. The sunlight sparkled off the droplets of water that tipped his dark lashes. He smiled at her and there was no hint of mockery to be found there.

"Everything okay?" they heard the call from the trawler. Jared waved and made the three ring sign, but his eyes never left her face, and they seemed to linger on her mouth. Cathy felt herself flush.

"We'd better get back," she said softly.

"Yes, we'd better," he answered, but regret was there in his eyes and in the husky sound of his voice.

Cathy felt herself thrill to the emotions Jared could arouse in her. She wanted him to drag her beneath the surface again, and to feel the pressure of his mouth against hers, to feel herself a prisoner of his arms and mistress of his desires.

Bizzy's arrival broke her out of her thoughts. And they swam back to the trawler, Bismarc following closely behind.

The sun was setting low in the west, and darkness was falling over the river. Lucas snapped on the trawler's running lights and left Jared at the helm in the wheelhouse. The night was soft and warm; the breezes from the motion of the boat were gentle and the sounds of the engines were monotonous yet somehow soothing. The door to the wheelhouse was left open so Jared could join in the conversation out on the stern deck. Lucas was triumphant over the price the day's catch had brought; and, as always, when in a particularly jovial mood, he became loquacious, this time bending Erica's ear.

"Yes, sir, lived my whole life on this river. I still love it. It's God's country. It's not the boondocks, either. Some pretty important people have pulled into these parts. Take Lefty Rudder, for instance."

Cathy sat on the cooler, sipping coffee. She smiled when she heard Lucas mention Lefty Rudder. She knew he would go on and on about the famous author until they pulled into Swan Quarter, a good two hours away.

Erica looked questioningly at Lucas. "You know Lefty Rudder?"

"Do I know him? Why he was just about the best friend a man could have. 'Course we were both young men when I knew him. He'd just started his writing career. But he was a good man, the salt of the earth."

Cathy noticed that Jared, in the wheelhouse, was paying rapt attention to this conversation. He visibly cocked an ear while his gaze was focused ahead as he took the boat down the river.

Erica spoke again, her voice denoting her incredulity. "If you were such a good friend of Lefty Rudder's, then you must know that Jared…"

Jared Parsons swung around, his eyes dark and warning. His abrupt movement caught Erica's notice, and her words were cut off. Cathy watched with curiosity. What had Erica been about to say about Jared and the venerated Lefty Rudder that he hadn't wanted her to reveal?

Lucas turned to look at Jared, and there was a devilish glint in his eye. Whatever the secret was, Cathy knew her father was aware of it. It seemed everybody knew—everyone except Cathy, but she was determined not to ask any of them what was going on.

# CHAPTER FIVE

CATHY SEETHED inwardly as she banged the copper pots in her kitchen. Her pretty features were tight and grim, knowing her father was grinning behind her back. "Why don't you say it? I know exactly what you're thinking and you're wrong. I did not, I repeat, I did *not* stumble and fall off the boat on purpose so Jared Parsons could save me. I've never fallen off a boat in my life and you know it!" Hands on her hips, she glared menacingly at her father. "Erica startled me and I lost my footing."

"Simmer down and get on with your cooking. You have to be at the judging booth by three o'clock and that doesn't give you much time," Lucas drawled. "Tell me, are you going to enter any of the other contests?" Lucas asked, hoping to sidetrack his daughter onto a more pleasant subject.

Cathy tossed the crab meat into the large copper pot, wishing it were Jared Parsons she was adding to the boiling water. She couldn't dwell on the handsome man any longer, nor his beautiful companion; she had to concentrate on what she was doing or she would never win first prize or any other prize for that matter. "I'm entering the disco contest with Dermott McIntyre."

"You *what?*" Lucas exploded. "Dermott has two

left feet and a mind to match." His tone turned fatherly as he patted Cathy on the shoulder. "Look, why don't we sit down here and have a little father-daughter chat. You're going about this all wrong," he said, not bothering to wait for her reply. "In my day, when a young woman wanted to snare a man, she did it...subtly. You've been acting like a goat in a field of orchids. You take your mother now. She caught me with the oldest trick in the book. She let me think I was doing the pursuing while she was actually manipulating me like a puppet. She never moved off that swing on her front porch. A wink and a little show of leg and I was hooked. She didn't go falling off any boat or get caught skinny-dipping. You young people!" he said disgustedly.

"That does it!" Cathy stormed, banging her spoon on the side of the stove. "I'm going back to New York!"

"Quitter. Only cowards quit when the going gets tough. Cut and run. What are you afraid of?" Lucas demanded as he stuffed his pipe with fragrant tobacco. His pipe drawing to his satisfaction, Lucas continued, "If you leave now, you'll be playing right into Miss Erica's hands."

"You still don't understand, do you? I don't *want* Jared Parsons. I don't *need* Jared Parsons! Also, I would appreciate it, Dad, if you would refrain from mentioning his name to me again. I'll handle this in my own way without any help from you." Tears burned Cathy's eyes, and she felt her hand tremble as she stirred the bubbling contents in the copper pot. Jared Parsons had made a fool of her. How was she going to look at him and not remember what he had said about looking like sixteen? She was going to handle it all right. Lucas was right, going back to New York wouldn't solve anything. She *was* what she *was*. There was no way she could even begin to compare herself to the ravishing Erica. At that moment, she would have given her back teeth if she could make Jared Parsons's eyes light up. She was attracted to him, but that was her secret. And if she responded to his kisses, that was her secret, too. If her body ached, no one would know but herself. Jared Parsons would never know that. Life does go on, she thought bitterly. Grandpa Bissette had always said when there was nowhere else to turn and nowhere to go, you simply pulled up your socks and started all over in another direction. Cathy looked down at her feet and giggled. She bent over and gave her tennis socks a tug and winked at her father. He nodded through a cloud of fragrant smoke from his pipe.

The She-Crab stew bubbling to her satisfaction, Cathy withdrew to her bedroom and began to straighten it up. Carefully, she folded the Teak Helm galleys into a neat pile and stood staring down at the fine print. Did she dare call her boss back in New York and tell him how disappointing the manuscript was? The Teak Helm fans would know immediately that this novel wasn't up to par. He could be ruined. How had it gotten as far as galley form? Why hadn't someone asked for a rewrite? A first year journalism major could see what needed to be done. Her cardinal rule had always been—never dupe a reader who has spent his hard-earned money to buy a book—and Teak Helm was very close to duping his fans. Cathy sighed. There was nothing she could do. She wasn't Teak Helm's editor and had little to say in the matter. Too many characters, too many inconsistencies to make the novel work. She slid the long strips of paper into her dresser drawer. She felt betrayed, angry, that a writer she didn't know but loved had disappointed her. The reviews would be horrendous. Well, it wasn't her problem, and she had to get on with the day.

The apricot-scented bubble bath was so inviting Cathy slid down into the slippery water and leaned back, relaxing her muscles slowly. She hadn't realized how tense she was. Come to think of it, she had been over-wrought ever since she first set eyes on Jared Parsons. How could a man, a man she knew nothing about, have this effect on her? Why did she tremble and her heart beat so fast when he was near or when she thought of him as she was doing now? No one had ever kissed her the way Jared Parsons kissed her. She flushed when she remembered how she felt with her naked breasts pressed against him. The alien ache and emptiness was back. She squirmed in the steamy wetness and forced her mind to think of Dermott and the coming disco contest. Just once she would like to win something besides a homemaker award. She was a good dancer. If she was lucky, Dermott's left feet would sprout wings at the eleventh hour and they would win the contest. It would be a fun night, regardless if she won the contest or not. The Fourth of July Fair was the biggest event of the year in Swan Quarter. She had always looked forward to the event and in years past enjoyed each and every contest. Jared Parsons would be there, thanks to her father's gracious invitation. She was going early, ahead of her father, so she would be spared sitting next to Jared and Erica. With her luck, she would spill her stew under Jared's gaze, and Erica would cluck her tongue, and she would be reduced to tears and make a fool of herself once more.

Cathy stepped from the tub and slipped into her robe. Bismarc whined and scratched at the door, forcing her thoughts back to the present. "Just a minute, boy." She bent over the tub and wiped up the excess water and then hung the towel neatly on the rack. She looked around the small bathroom and was satisfied that she was leaving it the way she found it—neat and clean. Besides being a country girl, she was clean and neat. Qualities that would certainly endear any man to her. "Ha!" she snorted, opening the door and fending off Bismarc. "Let's face it, Bizzy, I am plain and neat. Tidy, if you like that word better. And I'm dull. I blush when a man looks at me, and I get nervous if a man kisses me. No, that's not quite true, I get nervous and weak in the knees when Jared Parsons looks at me and kisses me, there's a difference." Bismarc cocked his head to the side and growled deep in his throat. It was evident to Cathy that the Irish Setter didn't care for her self-pitying tone. She tweaked his ears and chased him from the room. Bismarc took it as a sign that she wanted to play and leaped on the bed. Cathy dived for him and they tussled on the bed, Bizzy with his teeth pulling at her terry robe. Laughing and tugging at the belt, Cathy fell backward. Bismarc relaxed his grip on her robe and growled, his ears straight, his tail still.

"I do seem to find you in the oddest situations, Miss Bissette. I apologize for intruding on your frolicking, but your father said I would find you up here reading.

He needs the boat key, and he thought you might have it." He grinned down at her, enjoying the swell of her creamy breasts, which were spilling from the loose robe and the long expanse of thigh that was visible. Cathy blinked and then clenched her teeth. "There should be a law that prohibits men like you from…from entering women's bedrooms. I don't have the key, and if I did, I wouldn't give it to you." Now, why had she said that? She scrambled off the bed and tied the belt so tight she had to catch her breath.

"Your father seemed quite positive that you had the boat key. He said he saw you drop it in your carryall." Before she had a chance to reply, Jared had the yellow bag in his hand and was extracting the second half of Teak Helm's galleys from the depths. For someone who was interested in a key, he certainly was scrutinizing the printed pages in his hand. He said nothing, laying the rolled pages on the pine dresser. He fumbled in the depths of the bag and withdrew a shiny silver key. "Somehow, Miss Bissette, I didn't think you capable of a lie," he said coolly, his eyes narrowed as he stared at her.

"I'm not," Cathy said shortly. "Dad must have put the key in there himself. Now, if you'll kindly get out of my room, I'd like to dress."

Jared Parsons's tone was cool and mocking when he spoke. "For some strange reason I get the impression you don't like me very much." His eyes darkened as they narrowed to mere slits, making Cathy draw in her breath. "I find that strange, especially since I took my life in my hands to save you on two separate occasions.

One would think that you would be...grateful to say the least."

He was doing it to her again, and she was allowing it. How many times was she going to make a fool of herself in front of him? She should be saying something, anything, to make herself look less like a ninny. The words stuck in her throat as she stared at him. Let him think whatever he wanted, she thought rebelliously. He was staring at her differently. Her breath caught in her throat and her pulse hammered. She took a step backward and then another. Panic coursed through her when she remembered she wore nothing beneath the terry robe. Her eyes raked the room, coming to rest on Bismarc who was busy licking Jared's tennis shoe. She swallowed hard and backed still farther away from the man in front of her who was making no move to do anything beside scratch Bismarc's ears. He laughed. "Relax, Cathy. I'm not after your virtue. When I decide to make love to a woman, it's usually a mutual decision. And," he said, laughing again, "this is hardly the time or the place." His voice sobered as his stare locked with hers. "I've never attacked a woman yet. You're safe." His voice was cold now, the words clipped like chips of ice. "Thank you for the key, and I apologize for disturbing you."

Cathy all but fell on the bed, a sob catching in her throat. Did she hear his muttered words right as he walked through the door? Had he really said, "There will be another time and another place," or was that what she wanted to hear? "I can't handle this," she cried over and over. "Come here, Bizzy," she said, longing for the comfort of the dog's warm body. She needed something to wrap her arms around. "Bizzy!" Cathy sat up on the bed and sniffed as she dabbed at her eyes. The unmitigated gall of the man. He stole her dog. "Dognapper," she shouted angrily.

# CHAPTER SIX

CATHY GRACIOUSLY accepted the blue ribbon for her She-Crab stew and smiled winningly at the judges and then at her father who was beaming proudly. Jared Parsons's face held a decided smirk, and Erica looked like a sleek feline, her eyes narrowed in amusement. Cathy felt awkward under their gaze and stumbled as she was walking away from the judging booth. She jammed the prize ribbon into her slacks' pocket. It was Jared Parsons's smirk that made her wish she had never won. Just who was he anyway, this man who had come to Swan Quarter and upset her like this? What did he do and why was everything so secret? The only thing she did know was that Erica was involved in the secret, too. Cathy felt that if she knew what he did she could do a little sniping of her own, and at least she would feel better. It had often crossed her mind that Jared was involved in something illegal. That would explain his apparent wealth, at any rate.

Somehow, Cathy couldn't resolve herself to accepting the thought that Jared Parsons was linked with the underworld. There was an almost tangible aura of respectability about him; his clear gray eyes, his open smile. No, it was not to be considered, something in her rebelled, something she did not choose to put a name to. Perhaps Jared had inherited the wealth that supported his playboy lifestyle. She just wished she knew the answer. It would help erect her defenses against him.

But for now she had to get Bizzy from the kennel. He had proved his worth and came in second in the bird-dog class, it was time to take him home. The shaggy dog leaped for joy when Cathy came into view, his tail wagging furiously. "You're as fickle as that fiend out there. If he was here to open this door, you wouldn't pay any attention to me," Cathy said shortly, remembering Bizzy's unqualified loyalty to Jared. The moment the door of the cage was opened, Bismarc was off and running. No doubt to find his fickle friend, Cathy thought nastily. Now she would have to stomp the dusty festival grounds in search of the friendly dog.

Annoyed with herself and the world, Cathy settled down on a rustic bench and peeled the wrapper off a candy bar. Munching the crunchy sweet, she let her eyes rove the grounds for some sign of Bismarc. He was coming toward her at a dead run. She waited till he was near enough for her to reach out and grasp his collar. The dog backed off and barked, his front paws stamping the ground. He barked again and advanced a step and then withdrew. He barked louder and shook his head. He started off in the direction from which he had come and then turned to see if Cathy was following him. Again, he ran to her and backed off, barking wildly. "You want me to come with you, is that it?" Bismarc *woofed* loudly and this time ran off, Cathy on his heels.

Cathy's eyes took in the situation at the isolated river's edge behind the crab packaging building. Pieces of a homemade raft lay splintered on the shoreline and some distance out she could just make out flailing arms and almost hear a weak shout. She didn't hesitate. Quickly, she shed her wooden clogs and stripped off her slacks and hit the water at the same time Bismarc did. Her strokes were sure and powerful as she made her way to the swimmer in distress. Once she raised her head and saw the figure slide beneath the water. Frenzy drove her on as she prayed she wouldn't be too late. It must be a child, an inexperienced child, who had entered the contest with the homemade rafts. Probably a summer guest who wasn't too familiar with the river. The cry, when she heard it, was feeble and weak. It spurred her on. Her arms were getting tired, and there was a sharp pain in her shoulder. Bismarc barked behind her to show he was following her, his big paws daintily plunging into the water. "Hold on," Cathy called, "I'm coming. Tread water," she gasped as she herself began to tread and then struck out for the child who was almost within her grasp. "Chunky Williams!" she choked in dismay. Lord, she sighed, there was no way she was going to be able to tow him to shore. She was too tired and the boy was just too heavy, the complement of too many sweets and rich food. The most she could do was hold him upright and hope he hadn't taken in too much water. "Bizzy," she commanded, "go back and get Dad. Get somebody and *hurry!*" The Irish setter remained in the water, his paws lapping at the wetness. He appeared uncertain, should he leave his mistress and the boy or should he disobey the weak command? "Go!" Cathy ordered.

Cathy watched as Bismarc paddled through the water. "Go faster," she prayed, knowing full well the setter was doing his best.

"Th-thanks, Mi-Miss Bissette," Chunky said hoarsely. "I-I'm…so…cold."

"What happened?" Cathy asked, trying to keep the chubby boy's head above water as well as her own.

Chunky tried to grin and failed. "I… di-didn't use… rawhide when I bound the raft. I used mom's old clothes-line, and it stretched when it got wet…everything just…fell apart… My dad is going to…sk-skin me alive."

"No, he won't," Cathy shivered. "He'll be so glad to see that you're okay, he'll just take you out to the woodshed for a little father-son talk."

"Gee…do…you…really think…so?"

"You have my word. Parents are like that. It was a dumb thing for you to do, coming out here alone on the river after the race," she gasped, struggling with his weight, treading water, trying to keep them both afloat. It would be useless to tell Chunky to float, he was too frightened, too tense.

"I hate coming in last," the boy grumbled. "Mom told me I didn't have a chance because all the other kids were skinnier and littler, but I wouldn't listen. Are we going to die, Miss Bissette?" he asked fearfully.

"Not if I can help it," Cathy replied through clenched teeth. "Look, Bizzy just got to shore. Any minute now Dad will be here with the boat and you can look forward to that talk in the woodshed. Don't give up now, Chunky," Cathy said, trying to shift the boy's weight to her left side. Her arms were numb and there didn't seem to be much feeling. Cathy recognized their peril, yet it was incomprehensible to her that she could die here in the river that had been her friend since she was a little girl. The sun was bright and hot and glistened on the calm water like spilled diamonds. People drowned in the dark, with wind-churned waters greedily reaching out for them, not in the glorious brightness of the Fourth of July. "Do you think you could float on your back, Chunky?"

"No. I ate too much pizza and ice cream before I came out here. I have terrible pains in my stomach." Cathy groaned as she searched the shoreline for some sign of help. Even from this distance she knew it was Jared Parsons who made the clean dive into the glistening river water. Bismarc stayed behind, barking wildly. Other people gathered, cheering the swimmer on with enthusiasm. "Hang on, Chunky, your savior is about to arrive," Cathy said in disgust. "Just you wait till I get my hands on that dog."

"What did you say, Miss Bissette? I can't hold up any longer," Chunky said, sliding through her weak hold on him as he clutched his midsection.

Cathy slipped beneath the water and frantically searched for the boy. She had her arms beneath his armpits when she felt herself being shouldered out of the way. Gratefully, she surfaced and shook the water from her eyes.

Jared held the boy effortlessly as he stared deeply into Cathy's eyes. "While commendable, it was a foolish thing for you to do. Why didn't you get help before setting out here alone? How did you think one little slip of a girl was going to save this kid?" Not bothering to wait for a reply, he continued to scold. "Both of you could have drowned and that fool dog of yours is just about useless. Can you make it back to shore or should I call for someone to come and get you?"

"I can make it," Cathy said bitterly. "And you're wrong, Jared Parsons, my dog is not useless. If it wasn't for Bismarc, Chunky would be dead now. I did the best I could at the time. If it doesn't meet with your approval, it's just too…damn bad. And from now on, stay away from my dog!" Cathy shot as she used every ounce of reserve she had to stroke out and head for shore.

Even towing in the heavy Chunky, Jared Parsons reached the riverbank before she did. Men were clapping him on the back and women were oohing and aahing over him as he carefully laid Chunky on the ground. Some kind soul wrapped a blanket around Jared's shoulders as Bizzy licked at his toes in approval of his lifesaving venture. Tears streamed down Cathy's cheeks as she watched in amazement. They were ignoring her. The child she had kept aloft in the water, her dumb dog and her father were all crowded around the muscular Jared Parsons. No one offered her a blanket; no one asked if she was all right. "That does it!" she groaned. "That's it," she repeated to herself. "I'm going back to New York."

Cathy sniffed and hiccoughed all the way to the parking

lot where she searched for the pickup truck. Climbing behind the wheel, she drove home in a storm of tears.

FRESH FROM HER second bath of the day, Cathy dressed again and dried her hair. Should she go back to the celebration or stay home? Dermott would be waiting for her, and the least she could do was tell him she was no longer interested in anything concerning the Fourth of July festival. Lord, she was tired. Surely, Dermott wouldn't expect her to enter the dance contest now. Who cares anyway? She poured herself a cup of strong, black coffee and immediately drank it as tears began to well in her eyes. The scalding coffee had the desired effect, and she squelched the tears. She was mad. She wanted to scream and kick, to lash out, hurt like she'd been hurt, the way she used to do when she was a child. She was grown-up now and was expected to act like an adult. Ha! As far as she could tell, she had been the only one acting like a grown-up. Stupid, mysterious Jared Parsons, flighty, little girl in a woman's body, Erica, and Lucas in his second childhood. Who cares what they do; who cares what they think? Not me, she thought childishly. "I'm going back to New York as soon as I can get plane reservations." By now Jared would be the next thing to a national hero. Man of mystery saves little boy. Endears himself to all the residents of Swan Quarter. Mystery man steals dog's affection. Cathy grimaced. She admitted to herself that that was what hurt the most. Bizzy used to love her; they were inseparable, and for him to give his affection to that…that playboy was more than she could bear. This time the tears welled up and trickled down her cheeks. She sniffed and wiped at them with the back of her hand only to find more.

A shadow fell across the table and startled her. Cathy gulped and turned. "I looked for you but you were gone. I'm sorry if I seemed abrupt with you back there in the river, but I knew you needed something to make you angry. Angry enough to make you swim back on your own. You looked as done-in as the boy," Jared said softly. "For some strange reason, the mere sight of me seems to make you angry, and I thought… what I mean is…"

He was looking at her so strangely that she felt weak. She should be telling him off, giving him a piece of her mind, but she was just standing here, staring at him. She nodded, accepting his apology. She was certain it was an apology, the closest thing he would ever come to in taking the blame for anything. She accepted the snowy handkerchief and blew her nose. It smelled like Jared, and she held the linen cloth a second longer than necessary to her nose, savoring the manly scent of the man standing so close to her. When she did manage to get her wits together and speak, the calmness in her voice surprised her. "Where is my dog, Mr. Parsons?"

Jared Parsons smiled. "Believe it or not, he's sitting on the riverbank, guarding your belongings." The old mocking ring was back in his voice. "You can hardly blame me if your dog likes me. Short of kicking him or hitting him, what would you have me do? I happen to like animals, dogs in particular, and I guess Bismarc senses that." His eyes wore an amused look as he waited for her to speak. Cathy nodded and turned away.

"I'm going back to the celebration, can I give you a lift?"

"No thank you," Cathy answered politely.

"Then I suppose I'll see you later at the dance contest. Erica and I are entering. She's a superb dancer. I understand you and one of the local boys are entering, at least that's what Lucas said."

"And did my father tell you the local boy also has two left feet?" Cathy asked quietly.

Jared Parsons gazed at Cathy, his head tilted slightly to the side. "No, he didn't. You don't seem to have a very high opinion of your own worth, Miss Bissette. If you don't, how do you expect other people to measure you?"

"It's not the measuring that I mind," Cathy snapped, "it's the comparisons I object to." Jared Parsons understood perfectly, just as she had intended. He closed the door behind him, and to Cathy it was the most terminal sound she had ever heard.

CATHY WAITED SILENTLY next to Dermott McIntyre in the makeshift ballroom that was to be used for the disco contest. She knew Erica was nearby by the heady scent which wafted about her. Dermott's myopic gaze was all the proof she needed. She felt tacky next to the svelte, long-limbed woman who was smiling at her. "I never won a cup in my life. Jared says he's confident we'll win. We've danced at all 'the' clubs in New York City on more than one occasion. Have you, Miss Bissette?"

"No," Cathy replied shortly. "I…I wish you luck."

"Luck has nothing to do with it. Jared and I have perfected our routine over the past months. We dance very well, and from what I've seen of the entrants," she said, looking around disdainfully, "I see no competition. You aren't entering, are you?" It wasn't so much a question but a statement of fact.

"I wouldn't think of it," Cathy said quietly, nudging Dermott to remain quiet. If his life depended on it, he wouldn't have been able to speak, he was so busy eyeing the mid-thigh slit on the satin skirt and the matching spike heels that Erica wore to perfection. "Well, here comes Jared," Erica bubbled. Cathy couldn't bear the thought of dancing now.

"But I thought you wanted to enter this contest," Dermott complained. "I polished my shoes for nothing. Why, just tell me why?"

"Because we aren't good enough, and I have no desire to see you make a fool of yourself. We wouldn't have a chance against them," Cathy said, nodding in Jared Parsons's direction. Her eyes took in the white silk shirt, open almost to his waist, with his bronze chest showing, and the made-for-his-hips black pants. He was the focal point of every woman's eye and the envy of every man. It was evident in the way the young men hugged their young ladies to their sides. Dermott was not immune to Jared's threatening charms. Protectively, he put his arm around her waist. "That guy's a rover," he said curtly, never taking his eyes off Erica.

Cathy bristled. "If he's a rover, what does that make Erica?"

Dermott blushed.

"Oh, really?" Cathy asked happily, taking Dermott's flush of color for an answer.

"You bet, guys like that smoothie love 'em and leave 'em, I know their type. I'm a man," he said proudly.

Cathy wanted to tell Dermott next to a man like Jared Parsons he was a mere boy, but she held her tongue. Dermott was nice, perhaps he was too nice for her. He might have two left feet, but he had other sterling qualities which would endear him to some other young woman.

Suddenly, Dermott didn't seem to mind that they weren't going to enter the contest. He was affable, his eyes glued to the voluptuous figure of Erica who was holding out her hand for her card number. Jared, as always, looked loose, ready for anything, and Cathy knew the striking pair would win the contest hands down.

"Who decorated the hall, and where did that band come from?" Dermott asked.

Cathy looked around the makeshift ballroom and had to admire the artistic decor. The multicolored flashing lights and the earsplitting warm-up music made for a gala night with all the proceeds going to the local orphanage. "Pat Laird and John Cuomo are responsible, at least that's what Dad told me. Al Anderson rigged up the lights. Billy Jensen's band has played all over the South, so I expect we're going to have a sellout. They're good, aren't they?" Cathy shouted to be heard over the din.

"Yeah, great," Dermott replied, his eye on Erica's long leg, flashing through the slit in her skintight skirt.

If I'm lucky, she'll get a cramp, Cathy thought nastily

and immediately was sorry for wishing ill on the beautiful girl. I'm just jealous, she admitted to herself.

"What number are you and Dermott?" Lucas Bissette asked, coming up behind Cathy and laying his hand on her shoulder.

"We're not entering," Cathy said quietly. Lucas stepped in front of Cathy and stared down into her eyes.

"Can't handle it, eh, Cat?"

A sharp retort rose to Cathy's lips. Good heaven, what was happening to her when she couldn't handle her father's jibes? Cathy swallowed hard and said very softly, "That's exactly right, Dad, I can't handle it. And this is as good a time as any to tell you I'll be leaving the middle of the week. Make whatever you want out of that."

Lucas Bissette again patted Cathy fondly on the shoulder, then hugged her. "Whatever you do is okay with me, Cat, you know that." Cathy's eyes widened at his paternal tone. Then Lucas put the sting back in. "You're the one who has to live with yourself," he muttered as he walked away.

"What did your dad say?" Dermott asked as he shifted from one foot to the other.

"He said I was a Polish princess and I deserved a Polish prince, and since there isn't a prince available, he understood why I wasn't entering the contest," Cathy grimaced.

"Izat right?" Dermott grinned, watching the first contestants take to the floor.

Cathy watched the first four contestants with clinical objectivity. They were good, but they lacked the skills she knew she was going to see when Erica and Jared took to the floor. She felt defenseless, vulnerable as she watched the fifth couple make their way to the middle of the floor. Her eyes traveled the circle of people who were breathlessly watching the dancers. At this point she needed some paternal protection. Dermott was oblivious to her departure as she worked her way through the milling circle of people to stand next to her father. He looked at her and smiled. Cathy sighed, he understood.

"Cat, I'm taking Erica into town after the contest. I just happened to mention to her that the Lobster Pit was owned by a friend and…"

"Dad, you don't have to explain to me what you do. In turn I expect the same courtesy from you."

"I just wanted you to know where I would be in…"

"In case I needed you. And that also means Mr. Parsons is free and available." The two twirling contestants ended their number with their arms outstretched to applause. Cathy joined in, her mind whirling with excitement. Dad was taking Erica to the Lobster Pit. Jared Parsons would drive her home if her father had anything to say about it. Surely, Lucas wouldn't have the nerve to take the ravishing Erica to the Pit in the pickup, which meant he would take the Mark IV. Girls like Erica didn't ride in trucks. Girls like Cathy Bissette who won cooking contests rode in pickups.

Cathy clenched her fists tightly to her side as Erica led Jared to the middle of the dance floor. It was quiet, more quiet than when the other contestants had made their way to the center of the floor, possibly because most of the people in the room knew the dancers. Erica and Jared were strangers, New York strangers, sophisticated people with money. Cathy looked around and was stunned at the looks on the faces of the crowd. The women, old and young alike, wore admiring looks, and the men were openly leering at Erica who was smiling widely. No one had that many teeth, Cathy grimaced. Then her eyes widened when she glanced at Jared who wore a mocking smile and was staring directly at her. Darn it, he had seen the grimace and probably thought she was jealous, which she was, she admitted honestly to herself. She startled herself when she mouthed silently, good luck. Jared lost the mocking smile and stared at her as if she had said something obscene. Then she further amazed herself by waving and smiling at the couple.

"Good girl, Cat, I knew you could handle it," Lucas grinned.

"You know something, Dad, you might just be right. The music is starting. Here's your chance to see what they do back in the Big Apple."

They were fluid, their movements perfectly tuned to one another as they twirled and moved to the wild beat of the music. There was no envy in Cathy now, only appreciation of the dancers and their movements. The dance over, Cathy clapped wildly with the crowd. It was obvious that they won and the master of ceremonies was making his way to the middle of the floor to present the gold cup to Erica, who accepted it graciously. Jared was smiling and accepting the congratulations of the young crowd. He smiled down at a little gray-haired lady and then unexpectedly kissed her on the cheek. The woman brought a dry, wrinkled hand to her cheek in awe and then smiled happily.

Unreasonable rage coursed through Cathy. Steals dogs, kisses me whenever he feels like it, bamboozles my father, and endears himself to old ladies. "He'd make an excellent politician. I bet he even kisses babies," she said tartly to her father.

"There's nothing wrong with kissing babies. I've kissed a few in my day," Lucas grinned.

"I'm hungry, Dad, I think I'll get myself a hot dog or something. I don't see Dermott around anywhere, so if you see him, tell him where I am."

"Will do. Time to claim my prize. Do you want me to bring you some lobster back from the Pit?"

"No thanks, a hot dog will be fine. I guess I won't see you till morning. Have a good time, Dad," Cathy said, walking into the crowd.

Her hot dog finished, there was no sign of Dermott. Hopefully, he found something to occupy himself and he had forgotten her. She picked at her French fries and let her eyes rove the crowd. There was no sign of Jared Parsons. She felt annoyed. She would give him another few minutes, and if he didn't show up, she would go on home and let him find his way back to his boat on his own. If she went home now, she would miss the fireworks. She smiled secretly and then laughed. If Jared did show up, he was quite capable of making his own fireworks, only it would be Cathy Bissette who exploded, not the suave, debonair Jared Parsons. If, and it looked right now like a mighty big if, he showed up and drove her home, she was going to make up her mind not to act like a child. Behaving like a child was what made her lose Marc back in New York. She would act like the enlightened New Yorker her father kept telling her she was.

Fifteen minutes went by and then another fifteen and still no Jared. The couple working in the hot-dog stand were beginning to stare at her. Time to move on. Time to go home. Alone. What had she expected really? That Jared was going to fall all over her and declare undying love.

Yep, Cathy thought. And right now I'd even settle for a lie. Tears gathered in her eyes, and she was glad it was dark as she made her way to the pickup truck and found Bizzy sitting in the back of the payloader. She slid behind the wheel and the tears brimmed over and slid down her cheeks. Childishly, she wiped at them with the back of her hand. A sob caught in her throat. She stifled it and sniffed, needing to blow her nose. The offer of the snowy piece of linen, when it was offered, made her gasp.

"Your father asked me to drive you home, and I've been combing this infernal fairground for the past hour. The least you could do is stay put in one spot," Jared said coolly as he motioned for her to slide over so he could take the wheel.

Cathy stared at him. Duty. He was only taking her home because her father asked him to, and he needed a ride to get back to his boat. Thank heaven he couldn't read her expression. "Don't do me any favors," she said through clenched teeth just as the first Roman candle exploded into a kaleidoscope of color and sound.

Jared Parsons ignored the fireworks and stuck his head out the window to back up the pickup truck. When he faced the road again, the same wry smile played around the corners of his mouth. "Fireworks always remind me of a woman's emotions. Up and down, explosive and then...fizzle."

"You're insufferable. Still, if anyone should know about women, I suppose a man like you is the one to be an expert," Cathy said huffily, aware of the effect his nearness was having on her.

Jared's voice was harsh and somehow tender when he spoke. "What's that supposed to mean?"

"It means whatever you want it to mean," Cathy retorted, glad that she had gotten a rise out of the man. Quietly, she drew in her breath, marvelling at the sensuous expertise with which he was handling the old pickup. She felt like she was in the Mark IV and they were both in evening clothes.

"I get the impression you don't like me very much. Why is that, Miss Bissette?"

Cathy felt confused. Deny it or ignore the question. She opted for truth. "I don't know if I like or dislike you. All I know is I feel very uncomfortable around you. I don't like the feeling. If that means I don't like you, then I'm sorry."

Jared laughed and pulled the truck over to the side of the road.

The night song of the birds was music to Cathy's ears, and the dark night was a velvet cocoon where she rested in anticipation of her own Roman candle showering the two of them with emotion. Trembling, she inched away from his outstretched arms. How could a man, any man, have this effect on her? She wanted the feel of his arms around her as much as she wanted to draw another breath. What she didn't want was for Jared Parsons to know how she felt. Trembling women were something he was no doubt used to, and she didn't want to be just another one of his entourage of shaking, quaking, giddy women who fell all over themselves and then fell apart when he left them for someone new. But before she realized it she was giving herself up to the moment.

# CHAPTER SEVEN

CATHY HEARD the low sound deep in his chest as he reached across the seat for her. His fingers tightened on her shoulders, drawing her to him. She felt his warm breath in her hair, felt his lips against her ear and in the soft hollow beneath it. The crush of his mouth against her lips evoked a taunting fire that flared and raced through her veins. She was helpless, powerless against him. She fleetingly thought of all the vows she had made to repel him, to be safe from his lure, and consumed by the fire within, they went up in billows of smoke. All she knew, all she was aware of, was that this was Jared and she, Cathy, was in his arms, tasting his lips upon her own and reveling in the delights of awakened passion that he stirred within her.

Her arms wound around his neck, holding him, pressing her own mouth against his in an answering kiss. Her lips parted, her fingers wound in the dark, silky hair at the nape of his neck. She could feel the strength of him in his embrace, feel his breath against her cheek, feel her power as a woman who was wanted and desirable.

His hands caressed her throat, his fingers trailed down the length of the graceful column, and she could feel her pulses beating against his touch.

The tailored, blue checked blouse she wore was opened to the cleavage between her breasts, and when his hand slid inside and grazed her skin, it sent off little charges of electricity, which sparked and caused her to gasp for breath. Masterfully, he slowly undid her top button. His hand caressed her skin, molding itself to the curves of her body, ardently searching for its fullness in the cup of his palm.

Cathy's breath quickened with yearning as his touch ignited a flame on her already heated skin. She was losing herself, aware only of him, the scent of him, the strength of him, wanting only to know him. His effect on her was more heady than French wine and her senses reeled and whirled, making it impossible for her to think, to make any protest. She was a woman and she wanted, needed.

Jared released her mouth at last, his lips leaving hers slowly, reluctantly. He began a searching, tender exploration of the curve of her throat, his lips finding her pulse and resting there, seeming to draw the vitality from her. Her mouth pouted with passion and a longing climbed the length of her spine as his gentle caresses became deeper, more sensuous. He seemed to know instinctively where her vulnerabilities slept—in the hollow of her throat, in the valley between her breasts.

She found herself straining toward him, offering herself to him, welcoming him with her embrace. She heard a soft sound of pleasure and suddenly realized it was the sound of her own voice, coming from somewhere deep within her, from a hidden part of her that she had never explored.

There was an ache deep within her, and it was echoed in her response. Her lips sought his, finding and searching. Her fingers grazed his chest, sliding over the muscular expanse of it and stopping to wander through the soft furring she found there.

She heard her name on his lips, and the husky sound of it made her weak with longing. The moment became her eternity as she lost herself in her need for Jared.

His hands took possession of her, feathering against her soft skin. His kiss was a drug, his arms a prison, the sound of her name on his lips was food for her passion. There was only the here and now, only herself and Jared lived in the world, and he was a man and she a woman. Nothing, no one, mattered except that she was here in his arms and he was making love to her, loving her.

Her voice, when she heard it, was husky and passion filled. It was the only sound that broke the quiet of the night. "Jared," she spoke his name like a cry, a sound born of her soul and birthed on her lips. She offered herself to him, pressing against the touch of his hand, moving against him, lost in her need for him.

Imperceptibly, she was aware that his lips gave no answering response. That his hands had become still and that he was drawing away from her. What had she done? What had she said? Why had he released her from his embrace and was now looking through the windshield out into the darkness.

"Jared?"

"Button your blouse, Cathy." His voice was hard, stern, void of the emotions she could have sworn he had been feeling only a moment ago.

Ignoring his orders, only aware that right now, this moment, she needed to hear from his own lips the reason for his sudden coldness. She asked, "Why?" Even she could hear the choked sob behind her question; she could feel her eyes burning with tears.

He turned to look at her, his eyes burning her flesh as they glanced over her, taking in her open blouse that revealed much of her breasts. His eyes were cold and flinty, and even in the darkness she could see the flash of his white teeth as he smiled wryly. "Someone told me, Miss Bissette, quite confidentially, of course, that you were saving yourself for marriage."

He was laughing at her, mocking her and all her newly found tender emotions. He had made a fool of her. No, that was wrong. She had made a fool of herself, throwing herself at him, offering herself to him, wanting him as a woman wanted a man. She had been ready to satisfy their passions and now he was laughing at her. And to further her own humiliation, she had asked him why. The question itself had been tantamount to begging, pleading, imploring him to take her for his own.

With shaking fingers she redid the buttons on her blouse. "Forget I asked that question. I really don't care to hear the answer. I think you should know that you're the most insufferable man I've ever met. You are selfish and self-serving and you hurt people, Jared Parsons," Cathy hissed. "And you've got the hungriest eyes of any man I've ever met. Get out of my truck!" With a force that was surprising, she tried to shove him over to the side of the seat and push him out the door.

"Wait a minute," Jared laughed. "It's the girl who's supposed to walk home. You don't understand. I wasn't making fun of you. Not at all. I was only trying to respect you…" He was at a loss for words.

"Go ahead! Say it!" Cathy spit angrily. "Say what you're thinking. Go ahead, say 'your virginity.'" Doubling her hand into a fist, she lashed out, hitting him squarely in the eye. "That's for making fun of me, and this," she added, socking him again on the chin, "is for stealing my dog's affections. I hate you, Jared Parsons! I hate you! And if you ever come near me again… I…I'll…"

Her emotions were choking off all thought. Gathering the shreds of her dignity, Cathy swung open the truck door and jumped out and ran away down the road. She ran, away from Jared Parsons, as fast as her legs could carry her. Bizzy jumped down from the back and raced after her, his bark breaking the stillness of the night.

CATHY MOPED around the kitchen, the Irish setter on her heels. It had been three days since she last saw Jared Parsons. Angrily, she kicked out at the stove with her sandaled foot and immediately let out a howl of pain. He was out there, sequestered with the delectable Erica, doing only God knows what. It was her own fault; she had said she never wanted to see him again. The morning after their last encounter the pickup truck had been parked in the driveway, the only reminder that she had been in it with Jared Parsons. She felt her father knew something, but there was no way she was going to ask him even one word about Mr. Parsons.

The telephoned shrilled, and Cathy debated a moment before picking it up. It might be Jared. "Hello," she said cautiously. "Mr. Denuvue, what's wrong, why are you calling me here?" she asked fearfully. She listened a moment. "Of course I do. Why me? Tomorrow! Yes, yes, I can be there. Thank you, Mr. Denuvue, for giving me the opportunity. I'll do my best." Cathy stared at the phone a minute before replacing the receiver back in its cradle. "Bizzy, did you hear that?" she cried excitedly. "That was Mr. Denuvue, the president of the publishing house I work for, and he just told me I'm going to be Teak Helm's new editor. Mrs. English decided to go to California to live with her daughter who is expecting her first child. She gave up Teak Helm for a baby. I have to be in New York in the morning, which means I have to leave tonight. But, if I leave now, I'll never see Jared again. I was so excited when Mr. Denuvue called, I almost forgot about Jared. What am I going to do?" She reached for the telephone only to withdraw her hand. Three days and three nights on the boat with Erica. Why should he care if she went back to New York? She said she never wanted to see him again. How could he believe such a blatant lie? She was the one who said it, and she knew it was a lie. He was supposed to be an expert where women were concerned. Didn't he know a lie when he heard one? Of course not, she said disgustedly to the setter. He was the one who told the lies. All men lie.

It was a once in a lifetime offer; she couldn't turn it down, not even for a man like Jared Parsons. She would be a fool if she didn't go back to New York and take the job offer. In just a few days Jared's boat would be repaired, and he would sail off and never give her a second thought. So, why was she standing here even thinking of not accepting the offer? "And," she said to the sleeping dog, "I'll be making a lot more money, and I won't have to scrimp and save. Maybe I could get a bigger apartment that will take dogs and then you can come and live with me. Wouldn't that be great?" Bismarc ignored her as she rambled on, her voice breaking each time she mentioned Jared's name. "I'm going to accept the offer," she said firmly to the dog. "First, I'll pack and then we'll take the skiff out for one last ride, after that it's goodbye Swan Quarter till Christmas."

Inside of an hour she had her bags packed and her room straightened up. Quickly, she called the airline and made a plane reservation. It was now definite. She was accepting the offer and returning to New York.

Cathy packed a meager lunch for herself along with a fresh double bag of Oreo cookies for Bismarc. At the last minute she wrote her father a note and left it on the table. She didn't want him to think she was leaving in anger or in a pique over something or other: namely, Jared Parsons. He would understand about the job offer and be the first one to tell her to accept. Plus she knew Lucas would want to drive her to the airport.

THE WEATHER was typical for July in North Carolina. The sun beat down mercilessly and the humidity was high. Bizzy sat in the bow of the outboard and allowed the breeze to stroke his russet coat. Out on the river, alone with only Bizzy, Cathy regretted her decision to leave Swan Quarter for the sultry New York summer. This was home, where she belonged, with the sky and sun and the river, not in the concrete jungle with the smog created by the taxis and buses and the hectic coming and going of the subways. Here was God's country and she loved it.

The motor created a wide wake behind her, and once or twice she heard the engine cough in protest. Dad had been promising to give it an overhaul, but apparently he had never gotten around to it. And now, at the height of the shrimping and crabbing season, he had committed himself to repair Jared Parsons's yacht. "That leaves you and me out in the cold," she said, as she patted the motor housing, "just don't give up on me now." As though hearing her words, the engine returned to full power, and she made a heading for the beach on the point.

When she approached shore, she cut off the engine, drifting into the sandy beach until the keel scraped bottom. Quickly, from long years of practice, she climbed over the side into knee-high water and carried the Danforth Anchor ashore, burying it securely into the sand. "C'mon, Bizzy," she encouraged, as she lifted her lunch and an old blanket to take ashore. "This is our last day here till winter, let's enjoy it."

The afternoon was an idyll spent in the sun, playing with her dog and enjoying the cool, refreshing waters of the Pamlico River. Drying off from her last swim, she glanced at her watch. Plenty of time to get home and bathe and do her hair before leaving for the airport. She hoped Lucas was home and that she wouldn't have to scout him down. She knew her father would be disappointed that she was leaving so suddenly, but he would understand. Lucas was a businessman, and he knew you had to get while the getting was good. This was too great an opportunity to pass by.

Bizzy took his place in the bow while she set the engine to start and whipped the cord, expecting to hear it roar to life. Nothing. Dead. Again she tried, again nothing.

Exasperated, she lifted back the motor housing and fiddled with the spark plug. Again she tried. Nothing. She did all the things she thought she was supposed to do, even going so far as checking the gas tank, knowing full well that Lucas never left a boat on empty. Still nothing.

She was stranded, marooned. Not on an island, but on a slim strip of beach that was backed by thick woods and stubborn undergrowth. She looked back in the direction of the tall trees and moaned. This was a place that was only accessible by boat. If she had to make it to the road, she would find herself faced with three or four miles of forest primeval.

Bizzy whined as though sensing her dilemma. "Might as well come ashore, Biz. It doesn't look as though we're going anywhere. Not for a while, at least."

The sun had swung into the western sky and was beginning to dip to the horizon. She kept a careful eye peeled for a passing boat and even had her beach towel ready to flag it down. But boat traffic at this end of the Pamlico was a sparse and almost nonexistent thing on a weekday. With a groan, Cathy lowered herself to the sand and waited.

She looked at her watch for what she thought was the hundredth time and winced. If she wasn't found soon, she would miss the plane. Where was her father? Didn't he get her note? Surely, he would have read it by now and realized the time. Fathers were supposed to worry about their children. He knew where she always went with the skiff to picnic and read and swim. Maybe he didn't want her going back to New York, and he was deliberately making himself unavailable. He could have come in and read the note and decided to pretend he hadn't come home in time to take her to the airport.

No, that was silly. That wasn't like Dad at all. Closer to the truth was that he was still working on Jared's yacht and hadn't even bothered to come home at all.

Out in the distance was a small object, and she immediately recognized that it was a boat long before she could hear the engine. Jumping to her feet, she stood on the point's headland and began to wave her beach towel furiously. "Bark, Bizzy! Maybe they'll hear you!" She knew it was improbable, but Bismarc's shiny red coat might catch their attention as he raced up and down the beach.

It seemed to take an eternity for the craft to come within distance, and when it did, Cathy's heart sank. Jared's runabout!

Shifting her thoughts into neutral, she went back to the skiff and readied its lines for towing.

The minute she heard his voice she felt sick to her stomach. She had thought she could push down her emotions at him finding her and the memory of the night of the July Fourth celebration. Of all the people in the world, why did it have to be Jared Parsons who found her? She would have rather taken her chances with a barracuda.

Jared's face was cold and aloof as he stared at her and smiled. "Your father is working on my engine and, rather than have him stop, I told him I would look for you. Don't you ever think before you jump on your impulses? Lucas said you knew the skiff wasn't ready for water, so why did you take it out? Did you want me to come looking for you?"

Cathy's own voice matched his coolness. She was glad his presence hadn't started her limbs shaking as they usually did. Her blue eyes were steady and her mouth was a grim, tight line. "The reason my skiff isn't ready is because my dad has spent all his time working on your yacht. And, no, I didn't expect or want you to come rescue me. In another few hours you won't have to worry about me. I'm taking the evening plane to New York. In short, Mr. Parsons, you'll have no need to wet nurse me ever again." Cathy could see her words and tone surprised him by the way his eyes narrowed. As if she cared what he thought.

The ride back to Lucas Bissette's pier was uneventful. Jared kept his back to her, his hands clenched on the wheel. As soon as the boat slid next to the pier, Cathy was up and off with no help from the man at the wheel. Bismarc leaped to the pier and stood barking loudly at both man and girl. "Thank you for bringing me home," Cathy said formally. "I'm sorry for any inconvenience I may have caused you. I know what a busy man you must be," she said in a syrupy sweet voice. Jared stared at her, a frown on his face. He made no comment. He was making her uncomfortable again. After today, she wouldn't have to worry about feeling like that again.

Even to her ears her formal, quiet goodbye sounded final. Turning on her heel, she walked the length of the pier, Bismarc trotting alongside. Tears blurred her vision, but the dog at her side guided her expertly to the shore.

By midnight she would be back in her little studio apartment about to embark on a new phase of life and this brief interlude would be nothing but a memory. "Why," she said heartbreakingly to the dog, "couldn't it be more than a memory?" Because it wasn't meant to be, she thought, squaring her shoulders.

# CHAPTER EIGHT

SWAN QUARTER and Jared Parsons behind her, Cathy rolled the Teak Helm galleys into a tight bundle and with a deep breath walked into Walter Denuvue's office. If she was going to be Helm's new editor, then Walter had to be told now that she wouldn't be responsible for the sorry mess she held in her hands.

The social amenities and the congratulations over with, Cathy held the tightly rolled bundle in front of her, offering them to Walter Denuvue. "It's a mess, I can't take the responsibility for the manuscript. Have you read it?" she asked bluntly.

"I'm sorry to say, no. However, before Margaret English left she brought me up to date on it. I did glance over it," Mr. Denuvue said defensively. "You see, Cathy, Margaret had no desire to anger Mr. Helm. She tried to get him to do revisions and he refused. As a matter of fact, he claimed it was one of his best novels and went so far as to tell us if we changed one word he would change publishers. As long as we're going to be honest, we might as well be brutally honest. This house stays in business because of Teak's two novels a year. Without him we'd never get out of the red. If he threatens to pull out, then we have to go along with what he wants. We're a small publishing house and we need him."

"If he's so independent and so arrogant, why does he need an editor? What can I do except correct his grammar—and if what you say is true, I can't even do that. I thought you brought me back here to be his editor in every sense of the word, not just someone at whom he can take potshots."

Walter Denuvue shook his shaggy white head. "We can't risk alienating him—his new novel is due the first of next month. Teak Helm wants an editor and you're it. You're right about one thing, he takes pot shots from time to time, and I'm not proud of the fact that I've allowed Margaret to go home in tears on more than one occasion. I hate it, but my hands are tied. There are people I have to answer to, stockholders among them."

"When is Mr. Helm due to come to the office?" Cathy asked quietly.

Walter Denuvue sighed. "Teak doesn't come to the office. He sends his manuscripts by messenger. I've personally never met him nor has anyone on my staff. You know, he doesn't have an agent. Actually, when it comes right down to it, he's a man of mystery, and none of us has ever been able to figure out why he's so keen on privacy and secrecy."

"Where do you mail his money?" Cathy demanded, not believing what she was hearing.

"We mail it directly to his bank."

"And there's nothing we can do except accept his demands and publish whatever he sends in, in the condition it arrives?"

"That's about the size of it, Cathy. I know I didn't do you any favors by giving you this job. You'll be working on other things, so the best I can tell you is not to let it get you down."

Cathy wasn't finished. "Walter, if you want to get in touch with him, how do you go about it?"

"We don't. That was one of the conditions. Actually, it's weird in a way. He always seems to know when we need to talk to him and he calls. That, you see, is one of the conditions of his contracts. He always delivers right on schedule, never been a day late in the eleven years we've done business. Look, Cathy, I don't want you trying to stir anything up by trying to get in touch with the bank. Margaret English tried that one time and within three hours Teak Helm was on the phone blasting us and threatening to go to another publisher. He's a regular demon when it comes to privacy."

Cathy felt deflated. "I understand everything you've just told me. However, I want to ask you something. Will you give me your permission to do a revision letter with suggestions and mail it out to the bank? I'll do it on my own time, and I'll be most careful how I word it. If we lose just this one manuscript, hopefully, Mr. Helm will get the message and not make the same mistakes on the forthcoming novel. It's worth a chance, Walter. How long do you think the readers will continue to buy his books if they aren't up to the standards of his others? Two books, tops, and we both know it."

Walter Denuvue thought a moment. He nodded. "It's worth a try. Cathy, be very careful how you make the suggestions." The old man looked winsome for a second. "Just how bad is it?"

"Bad," Cathy said succinctly. "I can't believe that as publisher of this house you haven't read it."

Walter Denuvue shrugged. "I'm into motorcycles and fast cars. If you want the truth," he said sheepishly, "I was never able to get past the first page of any of his books. That's not for publication," he said sternly.

Cathy grinned, her mind already composing her cover letter to one Teak Helm, author of seafaring adventures.

ONE DAY RACED into another as Cathy pored industriously over the Teak Helm galleys. She worked in the office and then she went home to cook herself a sketchy dinner and then worked again until the wee hours of the morning. By the end of the third week back in New York she had her letter finished and, along with her suggested revisions, ready for mailing. How was the illustrious Teak Helm going to treat the contents of the manila envelope? She wrote the word *urgent* in capital letters on the envelope and then added stamps.

She was tired, exhausted really, from all the hard work she had been doing. She missed her father, Bismarc and Swan Quarter. Christmas seemed forever away. And Jared Parsons, where was he and what was he doing? As always, when she thought of Jared Parsons, she felt a hollow well grow in her stomach and her breathing would quicken. She had been grateful for the hard work she was doing on the galleys and was even more grateful when she climbed into bed, her eyes closing with just the thought of sleep. She felt she had

weathered the emotional storm of parting from her
memory of Jared Parsons by diving full force into work.
If that was true, she asked herself, why was she sitting
here thinking of him now?

When thoughts of Jared Parsons invaded her mind,
as they had in the past weeks, Cathy forced herself to
think of other things or to do something physical. She
reached for a sweater and picked up the envelope. She
would walk the six blocks to the nearest mailbox and
drop the envelope in the bright blue box. She would jog
home and accomplish two things at once.

The moment the envelope slid into the mailbox Cathy
felt as if a weight had been lifted from her slim shoulders. How was the secretive Teak Helm going to respond
to her letter and suggested revisions? Probably demand
that Walter Denuvue fire her, that's how, she told herself.

As she jogged along, Cathy wished Bismarc was with
her and then changed her mind. The big dog, used to
roaming the river edge, would not like all the concrete
and steel of New York. Maybe I should get a cat or something, she mused, as she skidded to a stop in front of her
apartment building. Someday, she muttered, as she fit the
key in the lock. Now, she was going to take a nice hot
bath and make herself a cup of black rum tea and then
go to sleep. She deserved a good eight hours of rest.

Cathy did sleep, fitfully, her dreams invaded by a tall,
muscular man with gray eyes and a wry smile playing
around his mouth as he chased her along the riverbank
in Swan Quarter. She woke, exhausted and hostile to her
new day. A hot shower and a quick cup of strong black
coffee made her, if not fit, willing to start the day.

Each time the phone rang she flinched. By the end of the day her tired sighs were the speculation of everyone in the office. She almost collapsed when the workday ended and there had been no word. When Margaret English had the audacity to get in touch with the bank officer, she had heard within three hours. Was it good or bad that she hadn't heard?

The days crawled by on tortoise legs. It had been almost a month to the day since she had mailed the manila envelope. In just two days Teak Helm's new manuscript was due. Would it arrive on time? What would it be like?

Cathy sat at her desk, her pencil poised over a manuscript she was supposed to be editing. She squinted at the printed words that held no meaning, wondering why in the world she was sitting there doing nothing; why she couldn't concentrate. She should be able to put it all behind her and concentrate on the day's work. She was too tired, too angry with her circumstances to realize what she was doing, she told herself. She had a job; she hadn't been fired by Walter Denuvue and that should count for something. Let Teak Helm and Jared Parsons do whatever they wanted. She had to pick up her life if it wasn't too late.

She had turned down all her friends' friendly invitations, been short with them on the phone, pleading one excuse after another until, finally, they stopped calling. She was alone and she didn't like the feeling. She needed a friend, a confidant. But, there was no one. Not even Bismarc was around to hear her sorry laments. She would spend another lonely night at home in the tiny apartment after a quick dinner of soup and a few crackers. One of these days, she told herself, she was going to cook herself a real dinner and put some of the flesh back on her bones. And what, she questioned, could be done about the dark circles around her eyes and her hollow cheeks? Makeup was wonderful, but it could camouflage just so much.

Cathy looked at the circlet of gold on her wrist and then at the big clock with the Roman numerals on the wall. Fifteen more minutes and she could go home. She looked around the office and noticed that no one appeared to be doing any work. She reached for her purse in her desk drawer and made her way to the ladies' room to repair the ravages of the day. She thought she heard her phone ring but decided she was mistaken. No one ever called her at this time of day so there was no reason for concern.

Deftly, she applied fresh eye shadow and then applied a beige cream to the circles beneath her eyes. A quick brush with the rouge pot and a dap of lipstick completed the job. Perfume? Why not? Even bus drivers need a little diversion after smelling exhaust fumes all day. She patted a few drops of VanCleef and Arpell's *First* behind her ears and at the hollow of her throat. She washed her hands, dried them and took another look in the bright mirror, wishing they would use less wattage. She would mention that to Walter tomorrow. A rosy forty watt bulb would be just perfect.

Cathy looked around the office and wasn't surprised to see that aside from one of the mail boys the office was empty. A bright pink message slip caught her eye on her desk. She peered at the scrawl and almost fainted. "Teak Helm called. He will call tomorrow morning. He sounded angry."

"Billy, who took this message, do you know?" Cathy shouted to the mail boy.

"I did, Miss Bissette. Why, did I do something wrong?" the boy asked anxiously.

"No, no, of course not. How do you know that Mr. Helm was angry?" she asked past the lump in her throat.

"Because he sounded just like my dad when my mother bangs up the car or when I let the car run out of gas," Billy said shortly. "He said he would call you back in the morning. I told him you were in the ladies' room and that you would be right out, but he said he couldn't hold on the wire."

"It's okay, Billy. Go on home. I'll see you tomorrow, and thanks for taking my message."

That night sleep was out of the question. Cathy paced the tiny apartment, her emotions in a turmoil. She hadn't felt this way since she left Jared Parsons in Swan Quarter. Was she falling apart? What was Teak Helm going to say to her? Would it end up being his way? Was she supposed to act like Margaret English when he called and yes the man to death? Did she dare defend her suggestions for revisions?

Cathy rubbed at her throbbing temples, willing the ache to leave her. Everything seemed to be going wrong with her. She knew she was run-down and not sleeping right. Vitamins just went so far. She hadn't had a good night's sleep since leaving Swan Quarter. And now there wasn't going to be any sleep at all.

Curling up on the chocolate sofa, she longed for Bismarc and her father. Someone to talk to, to confide in. Someone with objectivity. Her eyes went to the sunburst clock over the bookcase—11:20. Seven more hours before she could shower and leave for work. She felt marked, like the eye of the devil was upon her. The worst thing that could happen would be that Teak Helm would ask for a new editor and have her fired. The best thing that could happen would be that Teak Helm would say he agreed with her suggestions and rewrite his book. Or, she thought morosely, he would have second thoughts and not call her at all and just let things lie.

Cathy reached for a notepad and pencil that lay next to the phone. She swiftly calculated her finances and decided that she could stay on in the small apartment for approximately six months if she was fired. With her small savings account and her unemployment compensation, she might be able to stretch it to eight months. But would the unemployment office pay her if she was fired? If they didn't, she would only last in the apartment three months and that was stretching it a bit. If she sold her furniture piece by piece, she might be able to extend it a bit longer. Why was she torturing herself like this?

The phone shrilled, startling her. Who would be calling her at 11:45? All her friends had deserted her. Who could it be? In her befuddled state it didn't occur to her to pick up the phone. She sat staring at the squat black instrument in something akin to horror. She just knew that somehow Teak Helm had found out where she lived and gotten her number from the information operator. From everything she heard about the man he wouldn't think anything of calling someone at midnight to go through a tirade. Just like that insufferable Jared Parsons. No consideration for anyone else's feelings. "Well, I'm not going to answer it. I have an office and I do business in it, not at home, at midnight," she said loudly and clearly.

The shrilling phone followed her into the kitchen and lasted all the while she made herself a cup of tea. It continued to shriek at her as she cut herself a chunk of Monterey Jack cheese, and it was still shrieking as she carried the plate full of crackers into the living room. Her head started to pound so fiercely she bent over the sofa with the intention of ripping the telephone cord from the wall. Just as she was about to give the black cord a good yank, the phone stopped ringing. The silence was deafening in the small room.

"Now, he'll probably make some remark tomorrow that I was out partying all night and what kind of editor am I?" she thought nastily. She would agree if the subject came up. It was none of his business what she did or where she went. Why was she getting so hyper? She didn't even know if it was Teak Helm. But it had to be him. People, as a rule, were considerate of others and didn't call after ten o'clock unless it was an emergency. She knew it wasn't her father because he had the manager's number downstairs, and he would have had her come up and tell her any bad news. No, it had to be Teak Helm.

Cathy munched her way through the wedge of cheese and attacked the tiny wheat thin crackers. Just as she picked up the teacup the phone shrilled again.

The tea splashed over the rim and soaked into her robe. Everyone knew it was almost impossible to get tea stains out of something white. She was angry now, angry at her own clumsiness and angry at the noisy phone.

Her movements were savage when she scooped up the ebony receiver and placed it next to her ear. Her voice was cold, defying anything, save a civil hello on the other end. "Catherine Bissette please," said a nasally voice. Two rapid sneezes in succession followed.

"This is Catherine Bissette."

"Teak Helm here. I realize the hour is late, but I've been trying to reach you all evening and there's been no answer. One second please." Cathy waited, drawing in her breath, and listened to more sneezing and a hacking cough that sounded like gravel being pushed through a grinder. Liar, she wanted to shout, I've been here all night, but she remained quiet, remembering Mr. Denuvue's words of caution. "I received your…suggestions some time ago, but as you can hear, I've been laid up with pneumonia. I was discharged from the hospital today, and this is the first chance I've had to call you."

Cathy waited, hardly daring to breathe. What was he going to say about the revisions? Aside from the heavy cold he didn't sound like such an ogre.

"I'm willing to make several concessions," Teak Helm said. "I have a busy day tomorrow, so why don't we just go over them now?"

"Do you realize what time it is, Mr. Helm?"

"Only too well. If you had been home earlier, we

could have resolved this matter by seven-thirty. Now, write this down because I won't go over it again."

"Very well, Mr. Helm. I'm waiting," Cathy said tartly.

"I know what time it is and you've no doubt been partying all evening and have no desire to do this, but I don't much care at the moment. I, myself, don't feel all that well. Now on page sixty-six I agree to the change. On page one hundred forty-three the situation has been changed, and as you'll see, the outcome is the way you want. That's it."

Cathy gasped. "But that's only two changes. What about the rest of my suggestions? Mr. Helm, I'm only trying to help you make a decent book great. All the ingredients are there, but the spirit is lacking. In short, Mr. Helm, your lead character is peripheral at best. He has no depth. Your readers are going to be disappointed," Cathy begged, seeing her dream of a revised manuscript going down the drain.

Teak Helm sneezed again, this time not bothering to hold the receiver away from his mouth. "Why don't you let me worry about my readers and just stick to your job?"

"You are my job. And you're right about one thing, you had better worry about your readers, because once they read this book they're going to know it's far from your best. Let me say that I've read each and every one of your books and this one doesn't compare to your first one in any way, shape or form. Did you hear me, Mr. Helm, there's no spirit of sea adventure in this manuscript at all. Since you're writing sea adventures, it might behoove you to at least give me the courtesy of listening to me. I was looking forward to a long and lasting working relationship."

"If that's your intent, then I suggest you do what I tell you. I corrected the galleys and followed the two suggestions of yours that I agreed with. I have no desire to withhold my manuscript that is due the day after tomorrow. In short, Miss Bissette, if you persist in trying to sway me to your way of thinking I may not deliver the manuscript at all. Do we understand each other?"

"Perfectly, Mr. Helm. I just have one question. If I was a man and made the same suggestions, would you have considered them?"

"Thinking of burning your bra, Miss Bissette?"

Cathy sputtered trying to find the proper words. She looked at the receiver in her hand and then replaced it with a loud bang, but not before she heard a loud and lusty sneeze.

"I hope you choke to death," Cathy snarled to the phone. Why in all the world did she have to come across two obnoxious men as Teak Helm and Jared Parsons? They must have been whipped up from the same mold. She wouldn't cry; she was beyond tears. She had done her best and it wasn't good enough. Tomorrow she would tell Mr. Denuvue that she would finish out the week and then leave. She'd go back to Swan Quarter where she belonged. New York and all its polished apples could function without her. Who needs it?

Two changes and he acted as if he was doing her a favor. And to top it off, threaten not to deliver the new manuscript. And what business was it of his if she partied all night long? And to lie on top of that and say he had been trying to call her all night long. That business about the hospital. She just bet he was in the hospital. Hospitals didn't discharge patients that sounded like he did. Who did he think he was fooling; she knew a death rattle when she heard it.

Dejectedly, she climbed into bed and lay in the dark, her eyes dry. She should cry; maybe she would feel better. No, she was all grown-up now, and she had shed all her tears back in Swan Quarter. She had botched it up and tomorrow she was going to march in to Walter Denuvue's office, confess and then hand in her resignation. But the tears she held in check trickled down her cheeks while she slept.

# CHAPTER NINE

WHEN CATHY WOKE in the morning, no one was more surprised than herself to see her back stiff and her shoulders squared. She wasn't going to resign; she had never been a quitter and she wasn't quitting now. They would have to tie her and bundle her up and then ship her out in the late-afternoon mail before she would depart Harbor House Publishing. She would dig in and fight to the last ditch. The only thing she would be guilty of was trying to help a good author become a great author. Somehow or other he slid off the track on this last book, and if there was a way to get him back on, she would do it. Please God, she prayed silently, don't let Mr. Denuvue fire me. Not yet anyway.

The moment Cathy walked into the office she knew something was different. The other editors were looking at her with a mixture of awe and something that looked like naked embarrassment. Billy was staring at her with blank eyes, waiting for her to walk to her desk. Walter Denuvue himself was exiting his office, both arms outstretched. "How nice of you to get here early, Cathy, we've all been waiting to see what's in there," he said, motioning to her desk.

Cathy wet her dry lips and gaped at the area where

Mr. Denuvue was pointing. A meadow of wildflowers blanketed her desk and chair. Propped in the middle of the garden of color was a manila envelope bearing Teak Helm's stamp.

Overwhelmed with what met her eyes, Cathy found it hard to open the yellow envelope. Her eyes scanned the printed words on the slip of paper. A wicked smile played around the corners of her mouth. She handed the slip of paper to Walter Denuvue who grinned. "You did it, Cathy. You brought Teak Helm around. Good girl," he said, patting her on the shoulder. "What else is in the envelope?"

"The two revisions he originally agreed to do. Do you believe it, Mr. Denuvue, Teak Helm has actually agreed to all, not just a few, but all of my suggestions. Walter," she said, reverting to his first name, "this is going to be such a grand book when we're finished, his best to date. I'm so excited. You're not going to believe this, but last night when I went to bed I made up my mind that I was going to resign this morning. I was so sure after my conversation with Mr. Helm last evening that he would never, under any circumstances, come around to my way of thinking. I wonder what made him change his mind."

"Your charm, of course," Walter said magnanimously. "Right now, I think the most pressing problem of the day is what to do with this botanical garden."

"Walter, can't I keep them?" Cathy asked in a little girl voice. "I never saw so many wildflowers in my life. In fact, this is the first time a man ever sent me flowers."

"Of course, you can keep them," Walter answered gruffly. "Billy! Help Cathy move these wonders of nature so she can find her desk, but be careful, the petals bruise easily."

Cathy hardly noticed the day pass until her phone rang shortly before four o'clock. A cool, aloof voice informed her that her name was Megan White and she was Mr. Helm's secretary. "Mr. Helm wishes me to advise you that we are working around the clock to follow your suggestions. Someone from the office will check in with you every day to advise you of our progress."

Cathy was too stunned to utter more than a cursory, "Fine," and hang up the receiver.

The balance of the week passed, to Cathy's surprise, with a manila envelope arriving each morning, bearing the current revisions. Walter, if he noticed that the new manuscript was overdue, made no mention of it to Cathy, who was only too aware of the fact. Was all of this a blind of some sort? Was Teak Helm doing as she asked and was he then going to jam down Walter's throat that the house was in breach of contract or some such nonsense? He had never been late before on delivery. Was he going to go somewhere else with his book? Would she be blamed? She couldn't think of that now. For now she had to concentrate on the manuscript in her hand. Another three days, if Teak kept working at his present speed, and the manuscript could go. And go it would. It was the best, surely he could see that. And if Walter could light a fire under his promotion staff and have the book billed as his best yet and give it the proper promotion, then it would take off like a rocket. Personally, she loved it, from the first page to the last, and Teak was sticking strictly to her suggestions, neither adding nor deleting, doing exactly what she had outlined. She wondered vaguely how his cold was. She wondered other things, too—like why did a different secretary call her every day? Did men like Teak Helm surround themselves with gorgeous girls who posed as secretaries like Jared Parsons had with Erica? The last secretary hadn't sounded too bright when she said, "Mr. Helm doesn't mind a whit if y'all take a few liberties with his words."

"I wouldn't think of it," Cathy had replied.

"Well, feel free, sugar. Mr. Helm don't mind at all."

Friday afternoon arrived and so did another delivery of flowers from the florist. This time it was a colossal arrangement of multicolored daisies, Cathy's favorite flower. Gathering together her belongings, she made her way past Walter's office, the flowers held aloft like a beacon. Cathy grinned and rang for the elevator. The first thing she was going to do when she got home was call her father and tell him of her weeks' trials and of the flowers. Then she was going to wash her hair and clean her apartment. Her world was right side up and she loved it. Perhaps it still tilted slightly but good enough for now. Lucas was certainly going to be surprised about Helm's revisions on the galleys. Her heart fluttered like a trapped bird when she imagined that Lucas's first words would be news of Jared Parsons. First, she would start off by asking about Bizzy, that was always good for fifteen minutes. Another five to catch up on Lucas's health, which was always fine, and then the nonchalant question about Jared. But only if her father didn't volunteer news.

CATHY WAITED IMPATIENTLY as the phone rang in Swan Quarter. Four, five, six. "Hello," came the harried greeting.

"Dad. How are you?"

"Fine, and you?"

"Just fine. How's Bizzy?"

"Fine. He's out on the strip pretending that he's going to catch a fish any minute now. How's your new job progressing?" Lucas asked casually.

"Dad, you won't believe what I'm going to tell you, but I'm going to tell you anyway. Teak Helm came around to my way of thinking and has agreed to all of my suggested revisions. Dad, he sent me a whole carload of wild flowers a few days after I took over as his editor, and just today, a florist delivered a gigantic bouquet of daisies. It's the first time a man ever sent me flowers," she babbled, "and we've never even met. Actually, I just spoke to him on the phone once, and at that time he said it was going to be his way or not at all. I was going to resign in the morning, but sometime during the night he must have had a change of heart and decided I knew what I was talking about. There is one other little problem, however. His new manuscript hasn't arrived and I'm beginning to worry. Though Mr. Denuvue isn't concerned. I think! But we're all very careful not to mention it, hoping it will arrive in the next mail."

"It sounds like you're back in the swing of things. By the way, I mailed you a package the other day; it should be waiting for you in the mailbox."

"What did you send?" Cathy asked curiously, thinking she had left something behind.

Lucas laughed. "I sent you a very old book." He

laughed again. "My prize possession. Lefty Rudder's novel, *The Sea Gypsy.*"

"Dad, you didn't! Why?"

"I just thought you might like to have it since you're so involved with your Teak Helm sea adventures. Read it over and see how they compare."

Cathy's tone was puzzled. "But, Dad, I've read that book. A long time ago, as a matter of fact."

"That's why I want you to read it again. Now that you're grown-up," Lucas said dryly.

"Do you want a book report?" Cathy asked just as dryly.

"A phone call will do if it isn't too much trouble."

Cathy ignored his tone this time and wished there was some way she could tactfully ask about Jared Parsons. She decided to throw caution to the wind and bluntly ask outright. "Did you finish the repairs on Mr. Parsons's boat?"

"Sure did and he's gone."

"Oh," Cathy said, trying to hide her disappointment. Wasn't he going to say anything else? No, he was going to make her ask. "Have you seen Erica what's-her-name again?"

"As a matter of fact, I did see her. I drove her to the airport the day after the Fourth of July picnic. She went back to New York, a big modeling assignment was what she said. Something about her perfect skin being just right for this new cosmetic that's being advertised."

Cathy's heart pounded and then settled down to a dull throbbing. Then she hadn't been in seclusion on the yacht with Jared for three days as she had originally thought. Her voice was light when she spoke again. "Really?"

"Yes, really. Now don't you feel ashamed for all those nasty suspicions?"

"Not really," Cathy laughed.

"Cat, I hope you don't mind, but I gave Jared your address and phone number. He said he was going to be in New York for a while. And he said he would like to take you out to dinner. I thought you would enjoy it."

"Dad, don't lie to me. Did he ask or did you volunteer?" Cathy asked, holding her breath, waiting for his answer.

"I'm not even going to bother answering that question. I thought children were supposed to get smarter the older they got. I guess that means he hasn't called you. Probably changed his mind. He should have called by now."

Lucas's tone was almost petulant, making Cathy grin. Serves you right; fathers shouldn't meddle in their grown daughters' affairs. "Guess so," Cathy said airily. "If you say Erica is here modeling then we can both understand why he hasn't called, can't we, Dad?"

It was evident to Cathy from the lack of response that Lucas had not considered that particular possibility. "All I can tell you is he said he was going to look you up. Parsons is a man of his word and I, for one, believe him. He probably hasn't caught up on his business."

"Don't worry, Dad, I can handle it, and if I run into any trouble, I'll give you a call."

"Are you eating right and getting enough sleep?" Lucas asked, making it sound like an afterthought, not knowing how to end the conversation.

Cathy giggled. "Tonight I'm having Chicken Kiev

with green salad. I picked up some fresh corn-on-the-cob yesterday at the market, and for dessert I'm whipping up a peach cobbler. After I gorge myself I'm going to retire, which should be around eight o'clock," she fibbed, allaying his concern.

"I'm having leftover lamb stew," Lucas said wistfully. "Goodbye, Cat."

Cathy shrugged. She wished she had some of the stew he was talking about.

Her hair rolled into a thick turkish towel, Cathy placed her frozen dinner into a pot of boiling water and watched the plastic bag settle to the top. She shrugged. Chinese food had long been a favorite of hers, and she even had a fortune cookie tucked away in the kitchen cabinet to make the dinner complete.

While the Chinese dinner bubbled merrily in the pot, Cathy took a quick bracing shower and then wrapped herself in a faded flannel robe that had seen too many washings.

The table was set with her solitary plate and silverware, the luxurious vase of daisies making the table look festive. Carefully, she scooped out the contents of the boil bag onto her plate and placed the fortune cookie at the top of her plate. A bottle of beer and a glass were added as she sat down. The first forkful was poised in midair when her doorbell rang. Must be the landlady with her mail. Chewing enthusiastically, she opened the door and gulped the food she was chewing. Her eyes widened and then her face drained of all color. "He-hello, Jared," she managed squeakily. Of all the tacky luck.

"Are you coming or going?" Jared grinned.

"Well...I was...actually...come in," Cathy said, holding the door wide for him to enter. Her mouth was dry, making it difficult to swallow as she watched Jared's eyes rake the room and come to rest on her solitary dinner. Certainly, this could only compare to a hovel in his eyes, she thought defensively.

"Do you like my daisies?" she asked pertly. Why should she care if he did or didn't like her apartment, she was the one who paid the rent.

"A bit much, I think," Jared said coolly.

"Well, I happen to love them, and I don't think they're a bit much. I think the bouquet is just right. Teak Helm sent them to me," she said smugly.

"I think I understand," Jared answered. "The simple things in life please you, like this small apartment and the field daisies. I really didn't mean to interrupt your dinner, I just stopped by to ask if you would care to go to dinner with me on Tuesday."

Cathy's face flamed, knowing full well where he had been spending his days. Erica. Erica must be busy, why else would he be looking her up? "Fine," she said happily. Erica's loss would be her gain. "Where?"

"Where what?" Jared asked, puzzled.

"Where will we go for dinner? It would help if I knew, so I can dress accordingly."

"Forgive me, yes, I see what you mean. I was thinking of something else. I'm sorry."

"You said that twice, that you're sorry." Cathy frowned. This certainly wasn't the Jared she knew back in Swan Quarter.

Jared ignored the comment. "Are daisies really your

favorite flower?" he asked, then continued. "We'll go to the restaurant by Central Park. I'm sorry that your dinner is cold. I'll make it up to you on Tuesday."

Before she knew what was happening, Jared had the door opened and was gone. He hadn't said goodbye and he had made no move to kiss her, and, most important of all, he hadn't made fun of her. Strange, she thought, I think I liked him better the old way. Maybe it was a trick of some sort and he was going to spring some dastardly trick on her at the eleventh hour—like having her get all dressed up and then stand her up. It sounded stupid and Cathy was glad she hadn't said it aloud even though there was no one to hear.

Gingerly, she sat down on the wrought-iron chair at the table and stared at the mass of white and yellow daisies. Idly, she picked a bloom and started to peel the petals. He loves me, he loves me not. He loves me not! Cathy dropped the last petal as though it was a scorching brand. Only children played that game. She picked another bloom—he loves me, he loves me not. He loves me not! Best out of three, she muttered, her dinner forgotten. He loves me, he loves me not. He loves me! Who? Teak Helm, the flower giver, or Jared Parsons? Jared Parsons, of course. She didn't even know Teak Helm.

Cathy glanced at her watch as she cleared the table. If she hurried she could keep her word and be in bed by eight o'clock. Since dinner was a fiasco, she would at least not be a complete liar. First, she would have to go downstairs to get her mail.

Don't think about Jared Parsons, she scolded herself;

if you do, you'll spend another sleepless night. Let it be enough that he came by and invited you personally rather than use a phone. As she scraped her cold dinner into the garbage disposal, she noticed that her hands were trembling, and she knew her cheeks were flushed.

After gathering her mail and slipping back into her apartment, Cathy slid the chain and the bolt on her apartment door. She turned off the two burning lamps and returned to her room.

It was ten minutes to four when Cathy laid down the book her father sent her and stared at the bedside clock. It wasn't possible. It just wasn't possible that her beloved Teak Helm would stop short of plagiarizing the famous Lefty Rudder. That's why Lucas had sent the book. He wanted her to see with her own eyes. There had to be an explanation. There just had to be.

Why did she feel so betrayed? So wounded? Oh, what was she to do now? Could she ignore it, give the man a warning via one of his secretaries, or should she go to Walter Denuvue and give him the book Lucas sent along with the galleys. Why were all these things happening to her? Did she wear some invisible sign that said, "Dump on Cathy Bissette!" I know there is some explanation that will clear up all of this. I know it! Tears smarted in her eyes as she slid beneath the covers. It seemed like the whole world was crumbling about her. Would Jared Parsons stay around long enough to pick up the pieces?

Cathy sat bolt upright, a stunned look on her face. Her eyes were wide as she stared about the room, a wild look in her eyes. "I love him, I love Jared Parsons!"

# CHAPTER TEN

THE WEEKEND PASSED in a blur for Cathy who alternated between bouts of depression and nonstop eating binges. Sleep was something to dream about, and every bone in her body was weary because of her endless pacing. Monday morning seemed an eternity away. When it did arrive, Cathy was thankful even though there was a steady downpour that greeted her when she exited her apartment building. It suited her, gray and damp. By the time she reached the office her shoes were sodden and her hair hung about her face in damp ringlets, making her look like a winsome child of twelve.

Finding a note on Walter Denuvue's door that said he was not going to be in till Wednesday set Cathy into a near frenzy. Now, what was she going to do? There was no one to talk to, no one to complain to, no one to tell her what to do. She always seemed to be alone when it mattered most.

Cathy sat at her desk for what seemed like an hour before she picked up the phone to dial the number Teak Helm's secretary had given her. Quickly and concisely, she stated her problem, ending with, "I must speak with Mr. Helm, it's imperative." She listened a moment to the cool voice on the other end of the phone. "Very well,

Miss White, if Mr. Helm is not available then please tell him I would like to speak with him about the word *plagiarism* and what it means. As soon as possible." The squeal on the other end of the phone made Cathy rear back as she pulled the receiver from her ear.

"Are you saying Mr. Helm plagiarized someone?" came the excited squeal.

Cathy was fed up, fed up with Teak Helm and his unavailability. Privacy was one thing, but his insulation, provided by his secretaries, was something else. In his own way, the famous writer was as bad as Jared Parsons, who was still an enigma to her. Cut from the same mold, she sniffed. Her voice was cool, almost verging on ice, when she spoke, "The word, Miss White, means whatever Mr. Helm wants it to mean. I'll be in the office till three and then I'm leaving. If Mr. Helm wants to talk to me, tell him to call me before then or at the office tomorrow. I do not conduct business from my home, be sure to explain that to him."

"Goodness gracious, honey, don't go getting yourself all stirred up. I'll pass along your message to Mr. Helm, but in the meantime why don't you just explain it all in writing and send it along?"

Cathy didn't bother to reply. What was the use? Her head was beginning to ache, and she had a long day to get through, but she meant it when she said she was leaving at three. She was going shopping to buy a new dress for her night on the town with Jared Parsons. Teak Helm could just go fly a kite for all she cared. She had done all she could under the circumstances.

The morning passed uneventfully. Dutifully, Cathy

picked at a tuna sandwich at her desk and drank cup after cup of strong, black coffee. It was three o'clock and still no word from Teak Helm. Plus she had gone through the mail and all the messenger deliveries and there was still no new manuscript bearing the Teak Helm stamp. Her movements were sure and very precise when she covered her typewriter. She dusted off her desk with a Kleenex and then sharpened her pencils. She picked up a stray paper clip and tossed it into a tattered box sitting on her desk. She didn't like the way the rubber bands were spilling out of another small box, so she straightened them and then sat down. It was 3:10. So much for Teak Helm caring about what she thought. If he dared to call her at home tonight, she would simply hang up on him. If he couldn't give her the courtesy of talking with her during office hours, she certainly owed him nothing. Who did he think he was anyway? She was leaving!

Nothing pleased her in the department stores; nothing pleased her in the small boutiques. She picked and rejected; this color wasn't right; this style made her look too young; this one made her look like a matron and always she looked for something like Erica would wear. When it dawned on her what she was doing, she settled down to serious shopping for herself, Cathy Bissette. A simple, pale lavender linen was her final choice. With a deeper shade of lavender at the throat by way of a scarf, along with a deep purple braided belt, she felt she could hold her own.

Cathy's eyes sparkled when the salesgirl rang up the amount. It was outrageous, sinful, to spend so much money on one dress. Yet she paid it happily.

To take a taxi or not was now the question. Definitely not, the cost of the dress would probably haunt her for days to come, and the thirteen block walk wouldn't hurt her. She barely noticed the pouring rain, and she sloshed her way home, the expensive dress clutched next to her breast in the plastic shopping bag.

As the long evening wore on, she found herself wishing the phone would ring just so she could tell Teak Helm what she thought of him. She suffered along with the heroine through a two hour movie and then switched off the television only to turn it back on and watch the news. She might as well wait till after midnight before going to bed. Teak Helm didn't seem to have much regard for time. The last time he had called her at midnight. She wasn't going to sleep anyway.

The newswoman reporting the day's events finally put her to sleep. When she woke, it was four-thirty in the morning, and her shoulders ached from sleeping in an awkward position. She yawned and made her way to her bed.

The note on her desk Tuesday morning did not lighten her mood. So, he didn't have the nerve to talk to her. "Hrumph," she snorted as she ripped open the envelope. The sentence was short, curt, almost obscene, in its shortness. "'This time you're wrong,'" she read aloud. The signature was nothing more than a scrawl.

Cathy's eyes raked the office. "I refuse to become angry. I will not scream and yell. I will not cry. I realize there are perfect people in the world, of which I am not one. I will remain sensible and calm and wait for Mr.

Denuvue to return and then dump this on him." Dramatically, she dusted her hands together to show she had enough. Already she felt better. "Out of sight, out of mind, Mr. Helm," she muttered to herself as she rolled a piece of paper into her typewriter. Quickly, she dashed off a short note to Lucas bringing him up to date and explaining that she would not be making any calls for a while till she made up for buying her expensive dress for her date tonight. Carefully, she avoided any mention that Jared Parsons was her date. Just as she ripped the paper from the machine, her phone rang. Megan White, Teak Helm's secretary, inquiring if Miss Bissette had received his letter.

Cathy sucked in her breath. "But, of course," she purred, "messengers are most prompt."

"And…?" Megan White asked curiously.

"And nothing." Chew on that for a while, Cathy thought nastily. "Tell me," she asked curiously, "how do you stand working for such a perfect person?"

A small chuckle warmed Cathy's ear. Gone was the dumb, demure Southern drawl. "It ain't easy. The pay is terrific and the fringe benefits are great. Do you have a message for Mr. Helm?"

Cathy thought for a minute and then grinned. "But, of course, tell Mr. Helm to sit on it!"

"Gotcha. Verbatim, right?"

"You got it."

The moment Cathy replaced the receiver her world was right side up. For the first time since returning from Swan Quarter she felt in control. She had solved her problem, and she had a date with a man she was in love with. What could be better? The sun was shining and she felt terrific. As a matter of fact, she felt great.

Cathy sailed through the rest of the day smiling at one and all. Her mood seemed to transfer itself to the other girls, and before she knew it they were all laughing and talking, but working at breakneck speed to finish so they, too, could leave early.

CATHY'S HEART THUMPED in her chest at the sound of the doorbell. Should she wait for it to ring a second time? Nonsense, she couldn't wait to feast her eyes on the handsome Jared Parsons. She wanted to throw her arms around him and crush him to her. Instead, she stepped aside and didn't fail to notice the approving look in his eye. It was worth every cent she paid for the dress. More, I'd have paid twice that amount, she said to herself.

"I see you're ready. I like that. I don't appreciate waiting around for a woman to powder her nose," Jared said with a twinkle in his eye.

Seated in the restaurant, Cathy felt strangely relaxed in Jared's company. Cathy sipped at her margarita while Jared drank his Scotch as though he were dying of thirst. He finished it and ordered another. "I had a rough day," he offered by way of explanation.

"Really. I had a wonderful day," Cathy confided happily. "I solved a problem and I no longer have the weight of the world on my shoulders. To put it more simply, I no longer care."

Jared placed his drink on the table with what Cathy considered deliberate movement. "Tell me about your day. Tell me what you do at that office of yours."

Cathy stared deeply into Jared's eyes and suddenly wanted him to know everything there was to know about Cathy Bissette. "I work as an editor for Harbor House Publishing. I was just made Mr. Helm's editor. Don't be impressed. It's nothing more than a glorified title. He's an insufferable man. He actually had the gall to call me at home one evening and expected me to believe he had just been released from the hospital and that's why he was calling so late. He doesn't appear to have any concern or consideration for anyone. He told me straight out that he was not going to make any changes in his manuscript. You see, I felt the novel was wrong, all the spirit was gone from his writing, and I didn't want him to cheat his readers. Somehow or other, he got off the track on this particular book. I was objective, at least I thought I was, when I made suggestions. The following morning Mr. Helm sent me a garden of wildflowers along with two of the revisions that I suggested, saying he would follow all of my suggestions. But," Cathy said, holding up a warning finger, "he had a manuscript that was due in two days and so far it still hasn't arrived. I'm afraid that he may not deliver. You see, Jared, if Mr. Helm goes to another publisher, Harbor House Publishing would go bankrupt. The Teak Helm novels are keeping the house going. A lot of people would be out of work, some of them elderly who aren't quite ready to retire yet. They could never get another job." She was breathless when she finished speaking. She gulped at her drink, wishing she hadn't said so much.

"You sound like you don't care for Mr. Helm very

much. Why did you take on the job? And what makes you doubt the fact that the man said he just got out of the hospital?"

"I don't know Mr. Helm. I only spoke to him that one time. All of our contact has been through the mail or through his secretaries. He is the most unavailable, insulated man I've ever had the misfortune not to meet. I doubt that he was in the hospital because no self-respecting doctor would release someone who was coughing and sputtering the way he was on the phone. He sounded terribly sick. I guess what I don't understand is why a man as famous as Teak Helm needs all this privacy. It's almost like he's hiding out. Maybe he's afraid of people. I don't know what his problem is, and right now I care less."

Jared's tone was soft, intimate, when he spoke. "And what problem did you eliminate today?"

"I eliminated Teak Helm," Cathy said, smoothly sipping at her second drink. She was going to have to watch it, she was beginning to feel giddy. "You see," she said, leaning over the table to stare at Jared, "my father sent me—" why were Jared's eyes so flinty? "—sent me an old book written a long time ago by Lefty Rudder. Did Dad tell you Lefty Rudder used to be one of his closest friends? Well, anyway, I read it over, and would you believe, could you believe, that Mr. Helm has plagiarized an adventure right out of the pages of Lefty Rudder's *Sea Gypsy?*" She waited expectantly for Jared's comment, and when it came, she was disappointed.

"That's a very serious accusation, Cathy. Who else

have you told?" Jared asked smoothly, yet there was an intensity behind his words.

"Mr. Denuvue is out of town, but I certainly will tell him tomorrow morning when he returns," Cathy said adamantly.

"Do you always treat a man's good name so carelessly, Miss Bissette?"

"Of course not. I sent him a letter as his secretary requested and I made a copy for the records. Mr. Helm replied that I was wrong and that was the end of it." Her heart plummeted at the formal sound of Miss Bissette. She shouldn't have told him. She bristled at his piercing look. "Look, Jared, my first obligation is to my publisher," Cathy said, waving her arm in the air and coming to rest on the table. She suddenly felt out of her depth with Jared's gaze on her and, as usual, she made a clumsy move, knocking over her drink. Aghast, she drew in her breath at the stain on the snowy tablecloth.

A wry smile played around the corners of Jared's mouth. "I trust you can handle the matter in your own graceful style," he said smoothly, looking pointedly at the tablecloth. She had done it again!

When they arrived at the restaurant, Cathy was amazed at how quickly Jared could put awkward conversation behind him and go on as though nothing had happened. Unfortunately, Cathy felt strained and she kept her eyes lowered while she ate, answering only when Jared asked her a pointed question. She knew she was being childish, and yet she couldn't look into his eyes, fearful that she would in some way give away her feelings.

She heard Jared sigh. He was fed up with her attitude, she could tell. "Cathy, look at me," Jared commanded. Obediently, she raised her head and stared at the man across the table from her. "What's wrong, why can't you enjoy yourself when you're in my company?"

Cathy swallowed hard. "I feel very uncomfortable around you. It's not a bad feeling. It's a feeling that somehow or other you're going to…what I mean is I am very aware of you and how you make me feel. I won't lie to you. I'm not quite as sophisticated as your secretary and the other women you must have known…know. These feelings are rather alien to me. Oh, I've gone out with other men and was almost engaged at the beginning of summer, but I changed my mind. He just wasn't a person I felt I wanted to spend the rest of my life with."

Jared smiled. "What kind of man would you like to spend the rest of your life with?"

Cathy smiled, too, at his words. "Someone like you, perhaps, but only after I got to know you better," she said honestly.

Jared pushed back his chair and came to stand next to her. "I think," he said softly, "that this is as good a time as any for you to get to know me better." He held the chair for her. His touch on her arm was like wild fire. "I'm going to take you for a hansom ride through the park. Would you like that?"

"Jared, I would love it. I've lived in New York for two years, and I've never had a hansom ride through the park," she cried delightedly. "How wonderful of you to think of something like that."

"I have a confession to make. I come to New York

at least four times a year and I've never done it either."
He was like a little boy, Cathy thought, caught up in
her excitement.

It was a summer night to remember. The air was
kissed with the promise of fall, and the sky was black
as velvet. There was almost an air of celebration, and
the sidewalk strollers seemed enveloped in a conspiracy
of the romantic night.

Jared hailed a cab and gave the driver instructions.
Then he settled back against the seat, sitting close to her.
She was sensitive to him, aware of him, liking the aroma
of his cologne and the pressure of his shoulder against
hers.

Like two children, they ran from the taxi and raced
to the hansom cab. Jared helped her into the old-
fashioned carriage, and when the driver flicked the reins
and the horse obliged to his command, Cathy and Jared
settled back into their seats and caught their breaths.

Central Park revealed its magic as they took the
winding paths at an easy pace, and when Jared slipped
his arm around her as though it was the most natural
gesture in the world, Cathy knew the gentle happiness
of being with the man she loved.

Down through the dark arches created by the over-
hanging trees, over quaint little bridges that were barred
to traffic, they rode. Jared inhaled deeply. "It's almost
like a different world, isn't it?"

Cathy nodded in agreement, not daring to say a word
that would break the magic spell. Jared's arm tightened
around her, bringing her head to nestle on his shoulder.

She could feel his lips against her hair and then trail along her temple.

"You're a very special girl, Cathy Bissette, and I like being with you." The sound of his voice sent tremors up her spine.

Gently, as though he were afraid she would break, he turned her in his arms. "I'm going to kiss you, Cathy, because a girl like you should be kissed on a romantic evening like this, riding through Central Park in a hansom. But most of all, I'm going to kiss you because at this moment it's what I want most in this world. I've been watching you all evening. The way your eyes sparkle and change from blue to green. The way your mouth smiles and a tiny dimple shows just at the corner, there," he touched her mouth with the tip of his finger. "But, it's you I'll be kissing, Cathy, the woman you are. Not because I think you're beautiful on the outside, but because I know how beautiful you are in here," his hand fell to her chest, just below her throat.

Gently, with a tenderness that made her heart ache, he lowered his head and pressed his mouth to hers. Sparks ignited inside her head and burst into a flame that danced through her veins. A voice within repeated his name, Jared, Jared.

This was all Cathy wanted, all she needed. Any and all questions that had plagued her concerning him vanished. There was nothing else to know beyond this; Jared Parsons was the man she loved and she wanted to spend the rest of her life with him. She didn't care who he was or what he was, knowing in her heart that he could only be all things good and wonderful. And when the day came that he wanted to answer her silent questions, she would listen, knowing she had been right about him all along.

CATHY WAS THE FIRST one in the office, or so she thought, until she noticed Walter Denuvue on the phone. She motioned through the glass that she wanted to speak to him, and he waved at her, motioning for her to sit and wait in the small reception area. Seething and fuming, the Lefty Rudder novel in one hand and the Teak Helm galleys in the other, she paced the confines of the waiting area. The longer she waited, the angrier she became. The moment she saw Walter hang up the phone, she was through the door. Her voice was almost incoherent as she rushed to explain what was going on. Midway through her explanation she became aware of Walter's still impassive features. He was too calm, too unruffled. He didn't care! He really didn't care! She stopped and stared at the publisher, waiting.

"Cathy, don't concern yourself."

"Mr. Denuvue," she said formally, "I can't believe you said what you just said to me. How can you sit there and tell me not to concern myself over a case of plagiarism. It's here, in black and white. Teak Helm lifted this adventure right out of Lefty Rudder's sea adventure. He didn't steal words, he was too clever for that. He stole a creative idea and didn't even have the decency to do a good job with it. I quit!" she cried dramatically. "I'm going back to Swan Quarter where people know what decency and integrity are all about. I'm ashamed of you, Mr. Denuvue, not that you care, but I am. I'm ashamed of people like Teak Helm, too.

I don't want to be a party to any of this. Consider this my notice."

Walter Denuvue lit his pipe, his eyes and voice unconcerned. "Cathy, you have two weeks vacation left. You won't have to give notice. You can leave today if you'd like." Cathy clenched her jaw to keep her mouth from dropping open. Walter was so cool, so confident; this was not at all what she had expected. And to be dismissed so easily, it was insulting!

"If that's the way you feel about it, Walter, then that's exactly what I'll do. I'd rather shrimp for a living and get callouses on my hands for an honest day's work and eat the fruits of my labor. At least I won't get indigestion and heartburn, not to mention heartsick. I feel sorry for you, Walter, I thought you were a man of principle and that you knew what the word *integrity* meant."

Walter shrugged. "And take that damn pasture of flowers with you. I'm certainly not going to water them."

Cathy stared at the publisher. "You keep them, Walter. Mr. Helm made a mistake when he sent them to me. You should have been the one to receive them. I can't be bought," she said bitterly.

It took Cathy exactly seventeen and one half minutes to clear her desk and leave the office. No one paid any attention to her, and she was in no mood to explain anything to anyone. The ride down in the elevator was slow and she felt nothing. Her brief career in publishing was at an end.

Cathy spent the remainder of the day packing her belongings into cartons to be taken with her back to Swan

Quarter. She would rent a car rather than ship her belongings. This way she could take her time on the long trip, staying over one night in a motel. It was funny, she thought, she would get home around the same time her letter reached her father. Wouldn't he be surprised that he was now going to have a permanent hand on the trawler? As far as she could tell, the only thing she was leaving behind was her Blue Cross insurance. Jared! Her heart lurched and then stilled. He didn't live in New York, and he said he only came to the city four times a year. Well, if he ever decided he wanted to see her, he would know where to find her.

Tonight he was taking her to a concert in the park. He certainly was big on outdoor dates. Or was he a romantic at heart? Would he kiss her tonight? What did he think of her now that she had been so brutally honest with him concerning her feelings? Probably nothing, she answered herself. He had time to kill while he was in New York and, no doubt, in his own way was taking her out because he figured he was doing Lucas a favor by doing so. Take out Lucas's daughter to show he was grateful for the fine work Lucas had done on his yacht. Whatever it was, she had made up her mind to enjoy it for what it was and ask no questions. When he went away, she would handle it, and in her mind was sure she would be the best person for having experienced it.

Cathy pulled a calendar from the desk drawer and made up her mind to leave on Saturday. This way she wouldn't have to rush. She made a list of things she had to do: leave a forwarding address; have all the utilities turned off; transfer her small savings back to the bank in Swan Quarter; call the car rental company and reserve a car. Tell the landlady and thank her for not requiring a lease. If she did things in an orderly manner, she would have some time for a little leisurely shopping, perhaps a matinee or two and a little time left over for feeling sorry for herself.

Now, to tell Jared or not. No, she wasn't running away from him; she wasn't running away from anything. She was running to something. Home, the only home she had ever known. Swan Quarter was where she belonged, with or without Jared Parsons. Since she wasn't running away, there was no reason to tell Jared Parsons anything more about her business. When Saturday came, she would pack her belongings into the rental car and go home. It was as simple as that.

IT WAS SEVEN-THIRTY when her doorbell rang, and Jared Parsons entered her apartment, fifteen minutes late. He offered no apologies but simply waited for her to get a sweater. They made small conversation in the elevator. The ride to Central Park was companionable and easy. Jared seemed to be enjoying her company. In a quiet voice he told her he loved music almost as much as he loved reading.

"That's right," Cathy said in some surprise. "You told me back in Swan Quarter that you were a fan of Teak Helm. And that you had read all of Lefty Rudder's novels also. You did say you preferred Teak Helm, didn't you?"

"Yes, I did. I find his novels very moving. I can

almost envision myself in some of his scenes. To me, his characters are very alive."

"I wonder if you would have said that if you read his new novel before I made the suggested revisions. I wonder if you would have picked up, as a reader and fan, of course, the same lack of spirit I did."

Jared took his eyes from the road and stared at Cathy for a brief moment before returning to the traffic on the road. "I think I would have. I find that of late I'm a very critical reader. I'm not sure if that's good or bad. What do you think?"

"I think it's good, Jared. When a reader does that, it means the author has succeeded. Emotion, good or bad, is good. No two people read or look at anything in the same light. Do you understand what I'm saying?"

"Yes, I do. Tell me, has Mr. Helm's new manuscript arrived in the mail yet? Yesterday you said he was late."

"I'm afraid not." Cathy curtailed further conversation on the matter by telling Jared to start watching for the entrance to the park. Diverted for the moment, Jared concentrated on the road. Cathy watched him out of the corner of her eye. The grim set of his strong jaw puzzled her. What was he thinking? Why did he have to be such an enigma? Did he feel anything about her? Surely, he must feel something, some small twinge of something.

It wasn't his tone that startled her but his words, almost as if he knew. "What kind of day did you have?"

"A difficult one," Cathy said shortly, remembering her decision not to tell Jared of her leaving Harbor House and her decision to go back to Swan Quarter. She didn't want to explain to anyone, not even Jared Parsons whom she loved. She knew in her heart he would have something wise, something smart to say. He would mock her with his eyes if not with words.

"That sounds rather terminal," Jared said coolly. Cathy's mind raced as did her heart. What did that statement mean? He couldn't know, could he? Of course not. How could he? A guilty conscience on her part. Why should she feel guilty about not telling him she resigned?

Jared parked the car with smooth expertise and cut the ignition. He turned to look at Cathy. "You didn't answer my question."

"I wasn't aware that you asked a question," Cathy said, flustered at his usual mocking tone. "All I remember you saying was it sounded terminal."

"Yes, that's what I said. Most people would make some sort of comment to a statement like that."

"I'm not like most people," Cathy said, climbing from the car.

"That's true," Jared grinned as he, too, climbed from the car and locked it. "I find you most refreshing, Cathy Bissette. I think I can truthfully say I've never met anyone quite like you."

Cathy couldn't help it. "And I've never met anyone quite like you. Some day, Jared Parsons, I would like to know what makes you tick."

His touch on her arm, as he walked next to her, was familiar, and Cathy savored the feel of it. She did love him. Couldn't he tell? Did he care? How could one person love another so much and not have that love returned? Would she ever know?

The concert was long and lovely and Cathy, relishing every minute of it, was sorry when it was over. Jared, too, seemed caught up in the music. He held her hand in companionable silence, and from time to time he squeezed it to show he was aware that she was next to him. He made no move to put his arms around her or to kiss her like the other couples were doing in the darkness. Cathy felt resentful of his aloofness, his calculated aloofness. She didn't know why she thought that but she did.

Jared double-parked outside her apartment building. She handed him her key, and he deftly opened the door with no fumbling or bumbling. Why did she always have to stand there for ten minutes till she made contact with the lock? He did everything without wasted motion. "Good night, Cathy," he said softly. "How would you like to go see a Broadway play with me tomorrow night? My broker gave me tickets and I thought you might enjoy it."

"I'd love to go," Cathy said simply and honestly. "Thank you for asking me."

"It's my pleasure, Cathy. I enjoy your company, and you're an easy person to be with. I'll pick you up around seven-thirty."

"I'll be ready. Good night, Jared," she said longingly, staring into his eyes, willing him to at least kiss her on the cheek. Instead, he smiled and waved nonchalantly and left, telling her to be sure to slide the bolt and slip the chain. She nodded mutely. Maybe tomorrow, she sighed, as she followed his instructions. In some ways he was just like her father.

Cathy spent a restless night, her fitful dreams invaded

again by a tall, muscular man chasing her down the riverbank. He resembled Jared Parsons in build, but his face was blank. In his hand he clutched a book. Cathy woke, her forehead beaded with perspiration. She was no dream analyst, but she knew the man chasing her was a mixture of Jared Parsons and Teak Helm, the two men responsible for turning her world topsy-turvy.

The bedroom drapes open to her satisfaction, Cathy lounged around the tiny room, picking up a knickknack here and putting it down. She made the bed with grim purpose, twisting and tugging at the rumpled sheets till she had them as tight as any boot camp recruit could make them. She fumbled in her purse for a quarter and watched it bounce off the tight covers. So what, she snarled to herself. It just goes to prove I know how to make a bed.

Why hadn't Jared kissed her last night? What was the point of all this formality? Was he trying to lull her into a false sense of security, and when she was unaware, he would spring. Men did that, they were always doing it in the movies. "Spring already," she shouted to the empty room. Tears gathered in her eyes and she made no move to hold them in check. Who was there to see or care for that matter if her eyes were red and swollen? Nobody.

Cathy fixed herself a sketchy breakfast, one Pop Tart and a cup of Chinese tea. She looked with revulsion at the blueberry tart that had burned in the toaster and then tossed it into the trash. The tea was weak and smelled terrible. So much for breakfast. Blowing her nose lustily in a paper towel, she sat down with a thump on the yellow kitchen chair. What was she going to do to while away her day? She wasn't fooling anyone, especially herself. Inside of an hour she could have all her belongings inside a cardboard carton and be on her way. Why was she dillydallying? Because of Jared Parsons, of course. And because she secretly hoped that somehow, someway, Teak Helm would get in touch with her. Once the telephone was turned off, it would put an end to such hope. She knew he wasn't going to call and admit to a thing. Walter Denuvue had made that very clear. So clear in fact, her ears were still ringing with his words.

What to do? Go to the Empire State Building. One last look at New York. Why not? She dressed and set out. She felt like she was going on a mission of sorts. The people she passed were a blur to her. She nodded to some and smiled at others. Cathy paid her admission and waited for the next elevator. It was a dramatic tribute to engineering, she thought. She should feel impressed but she wasn't. Carefully, she edged her way over to the long windows and looked out and then down. This was her last look at New York. Had she given anything? Was she leaving anything behind? What had New York given her? Was she taking anything back to Swan Quarter with her? She decided the answer was a draw. She had given nothing and she had taken nothing. She was free to go. Free to go home.

The elevator ride down seemed endless. Impatience now to get back to her apartment made her rush through the lobby and out to the street. Quickly, she hailed a cab, knowing she couldn't afford it but doing it anyway.

Her apartment looked the same; there were no messages on the foyer table and no mail. Her telephone was silent. She felt lost, forgotten.

For lunch she fixed herself a plate of crackers and cheese and a glass of apple juice. She forced herself to eat, the dry crackers sticking to the roof of her mouth. The cheese didn't appeal to her, and she left it sitting on the plate till it started to dry out along the edges.

Television might make her feel a little more alive. The actors and actresses on the "soaps" always had so many problems maybe she could identify with them for a little while. She watched several soap operas and sat through seven commercials till the four-thirty movie came on, then waited impatiently for five o'clock so she could switch the channel to the news. She liked this all-women news show and watched it greedily until six o'clock when the male newscasters came on and rehashed the same stories with a delivery that said, *"This is the real news!"* It was time to take a bath and get ready for her date with Jared. She giggled as she turned the switch to off, collapsing the man to a thin white line.

As in the past two days, Jared was prompt, and she was waiting, dressed in a burnt-orange silk suit. Jared smiled and complimented her warmly. She basked in his intimate look, convinced that tonight Jared would kiss her or make his intentions known. That's what she wanted, would like to happen, but she knew it wouldn't come to pass. Jared was acting just as polite and formal as he had acted on the other date. A small wave of panic washed over her as she saw him glance at the two cardboard cartons that were standing by the door, sealed with masking tape. She was thankful when he made no comment.

Jared brought her a glass of orange juice during the intermission of the play. She sipped at the tangy drink, wishing the night would never end. She loved it when Jared stood over her like this, staring down into her eyes. Her heart fluttered and then stilled. Nothing was going to happen, so it was unwise to even pretend it was. This was here and now and people like Jared Parsons didn't carry off people like Cathy Bissette. For a while he was enjoying her company or pretending to; it was good enough for now. "I'm leaving in the morning," he said quietly. Cathy's eyes widened at his words. She should say something. The words wouldn't come. Where was he going? Why was he going? She swallowed hard past the lump in her throat. Suddenly, the tart juice was sour, bitter to her tongue. With a trembling hand, she held out the glass to Jared. His expression was unreadable and Cathy suddenly felt terrified. After tonight she would never see him again. The lump in her throat was getting larger. How in the name of heaven was she going to get through the second half of the play? All she wanted to do was take off her shoes and run, run far and fast, and never look back.

"Ready?" Jared asked. Cathy nodded as Jared held her arm. It seemed to her that he was holding her much too tight then she realized she was quaking like an aspen leaf and he was merely steadying her.

Thankful for the darkness of the theater, Cathy felt her body go limp with relief that now she could sit quietly and think. The figures on the stage held no magic for her, and she was barely aware of them or the presence of the audience around her. Jared was leaving.

He had to shake her arm twice before she was aware that the play was coming to an end. "Did you enjoy it?" Jared asked softly.

"Very much," Cathy lied. She hoped no one ever asked her how the play ended.

Somehow, on the ride back to her apartment, Cathy managed to make small conversation. They discussed the smog in New York and compared the teeming metropolis to Swan Quarter. Jared again complimented her on her suit by saying it was rare to see that particular shade and was it a favorite of blondes. Cathy nodded. She hated stupid, inane conversation. Why couldn't he say something interesting like: I love you. Come away with me; be mine. Oh, no, he had to talk about smog and suits the color of ripe persimmons. Men!

Jared paid the driver and tipped him generously. Cathy could tell the tip had been generous by the smile on the driver's face. And, he hadn't told him to wait. What did that mean?

"Do you mind if I come in for a few moments?" Jared asked, fitting the key in the lock.

"Please, I'd like that, but the only thing I can offer you is a glass of white wine or a cup of Chinese tea."

"Wine will be fine."

Cathy opened the kitchen cabinet for the glasses and winced. Two glasses, two Flintstone jelly glasses. Cathy poured the wine and carried both glasses into the living room. Jared accepted this, openly admiring Fred Flint-stone who seemed to be dancing around the glass in purple garb. "Very original, Cathy," Jared said, pointing to the cartoon character on the glass.

Cathy's nerves were already on edge. She replied curtly, "All the other things are packed away."

"Packed away! Are you going somewhere?" Jared asked, his eyes going to the packed cartons by the door.

"I'm going back to Swan Quarter. I resigned the other day."

"Why didn't you tell me?" Jared asked quietly.

"I didn't think you would be interested in what I did. I'm sure it can't matter to you what I do or where I go." Please, she cried silently, say it matters.

"Is the big city too much for you to handle?"

"No. Not the city, the people. If you don't mind, I would rather not discuss it."

Jared drew her to him and cupped her chin in his hand. "Then we won't discuss it, it's as simple as that." He took possession of her mouth, his hands wound through her hair. His breath, feathered against her cheek, was wine-scented. She slid her hands inside his jacket, feeling the hard muscles of his chest and back, bringing him closer.

His lips traced the delicate line of her jaw and followed it to the softness behind her ear. She was losing herself in him, just like the night when they had been parked along the road in Swan Quarter. She heard the sudden intake of his breath and heard him murmur her name. The heavens descended around them; they were lost in the world of one another as his lips once again claimed hers.

She felt herself go weak as though she were dissolving into him.

He drew away from her and looked deeply into her eyes. His voice, when he spoke, was heavy with emotion and betrayed a passion that vibrated through her. There was open yearning in his voice and his eyes had become a flinty gray, burning deep into her being. "Heaven help me, Cathy, but I want you. And someday I mean to have you, but not like this."

Without further explanation, he rose and stalked to the door, opening it and shutting it behind him.

## CHAPTER ELEVEN

CATHY'S EMERGENCE back into Swan Quarter's busy life left much to be desired. She worked the trawler with Lucas until she was bone weary and exhausted. It was the only way she could sleep. Bizzy had taken to never letting her out of his sight. Where she went, Bizzy was right behind. He had even taken to sleeping at her bedside. He whined when she tossed and turned, sometimes stretching his long body to lick at her face.

All her dreams were of Jared, all her torments had him at their center. The last she had seen of him was his tall, straight back just before he had closed the door to her apartment behind him.

Why? Why had he left her that way? He had told her he wanted her and even now, after all this time, she still believed him. Still, a small voice tormented, wanting isn't loving.

The empty ache grew inside her. It was a familiar feeling now, almost like an old friend. Nothing had changed; she loved Jared Parsons.

There were so many unanswered questions, and she would probably never know the answers. But Jared was a man to be trusted, she knew this as well as she knew her own name. Nothing could ever take the memory of him away from her, and each time she felt her heart skip a beat when she thought of him, it somehow brought him closer. And if this longing and hunger was the price she must pay to keep him alive in her heart, pay it she would.

The days crawled into weeks and the weeks into months until it was nearing the Christmas season. Teak Helm's book was due. Was it out, was it in the local book store? Cathy pulled on her coat and headed for the pickup truck, Bizzy at her side, barking his head off. "You can come, so stop it, you're giving me a headache," Cathy complained.

Cathy parked the truck and literally raced to the Book Nook, and there it was on display in the window. The *Sea Gypsy III*. Cathy frowned. That was the name of Jared Parsons's boat. Well, she wasn't going to buy Helm's book. No way. She stared at it a minute longer with hungry eyes. It took every ounce of strength she possessed to walk away from the book store. Bismarc nudged her leg, hurrying her along. "Now, what is bothering you? Oh, I see, it's snowing. Okay, come on, we'll go home and hope it covers the ground and then we'll play."

The girl and the dog sat by the bow window far into the night, watching the miracle of fat flakes fall to the ground. "First thing in the morning we'll take a walk. Come on, Bizzy, time for bed."

It was a winter wonderland, the world, her part of the world anyway, was covered with a sparkling white blanket that dazzled her eyes. Quickly, she pulled on her boots and a heavy sheepskin jacket and opened the door for the setter, who leaped through it as though there was a bag of double Oreo cookies at the end of the walkway.

They ran, the girl and the dog, laughing and whooping in merriment. Bizzy tugged at her slacks, pulling her over into a heap. Cathy made one snowball after the other, tossing them to Bismarc who thought he was supposed to fetch. The moment he got the round ball in his mouth the snow fell apart and Cathy would throw another to the dog's delight.

"When are you going to make a snowman?" a quiet voice asked.

Startled, Cathy rolled over and then sat up. "Jared!" she cried in surprise. "What are you doing here? How did you get here? Are you staying?" Seeing him again this suddenly, without warning, sent a shock wave through her body. "Why are you looking at me like that? I'm a mess," she babbled as she brushed the snow from her clothes and then straightened her scarlet knitted cap. "Would you like to come back to the house for a cup of coffee?"

"Stop talking, Cathy," Jared said in a commanding voice. "Here, I brought you a present," he said, handing her a gift-wrapped package. "I want you to open it. Now!"

Puzzled, Cathy untied the gay ribbon and removed the gift wrapping. *"Sea Gypsy III!"* She felt all the color drain from her face as she stared at the title. Her lips trembled. "How could you be so cruel? How could you?" she cried heartbrokenly. She thrust the book at Jared and ran as if the hounds of hell were on her heels. Once she slipped and fell. Quickly, she righted herself but not before she saw Bismarc go after Jared, his teeth bared, snarls ripping from his throat. Jared was standing still, a helpless look on his face. "Let him go, Bizzy, he's not worth your time. Come on, boy." The setter let loose with a deep snarl and then ran after Cathy.

"Good boy, you gave him a good scare. I forgive all those other times," she cried, wrapping her arms around the wet setter. "I hate him, hate him, hate him!" she shrilled.

"No, you don't," Jared said, drawing her to her feet and holding her in his arms. "Look at me. I love you. I've loved you from the minute I saw you sitting on your dock with your legs tucked under you. I even love that ridiculous dog of yours. I want you to marry me."

"Let me go! Your days of torturing me are over. I could forgive you almost anything but not that…" she said, pointing to the book Jared was holding.

"Open the book, Cathy, and read the dedication. I think that says it all. I'm Teak Helm. Now, do you understand?"

If Jared hadn't been holding Cathy, she would have slipped to the ground. Her vision was blurred, making it impossible to read the words. Jared read them for her: "For Cathy—this book needed her and I need her."

"But…you acted like, that time in the truck… Chunky…Erica. No, I don't believe you. Pneumonia. It's impossible," Cathy said in a dazed voice.

Jared's voice was tender and patient. "Cathy, I want you to look at me and believe everything I say to you. That time in the truck, I couldn't. You were too special. I didn't know just how special until that moment. I couldn't take advantage of you. If I had, you would have come to hate me. And as for that time when you saved Chunky, I had to be harsh with you. I had to make you angry so you would have the will to make it back to shore. There was no way I could have saved you both. Erica was never anything to me except a substitute secretary. Her sister is my regular secretary, but she had an appendectomy and Erica filled in for her till she came back to work."

"But what about this novel and Lefty…"

"I did not plagiarize Lefty Rudder. Lefty Rudder was my father. I was part of that sea adventure. In my father's book, if you remember, there was mention of a boy. I was that boy. The experience, the creative idea that you thought I stole from Lefty Rudder's book was my experience, the way I remembered it. Is there anything else?"

"You lied and said you were in the hospital," Cathy said, praying he had an answer.

"I was. I very foolishly discharged myself thinking I knew more than the doctors. I was wrong and I suffered for it. Is that it?" he grinned.

"You said I looked like I was sixteen."

"Darling girl, no sixteen-year-old ever looked like you. I knew you weren't sixteen. I swear it," he said, his eyes twinkling.

"Where have you been all this time? What took you so long to come for me?" her voice was choked with self-doubt.

Jared laughed. "It's all your fault. How could I turn in a manuscript that had the same difficulties as the last one. It had to be completely rewritten. Walter Denuvue says you're back on as my editor. I told him you'd be working at home, from now on."

"Did my father know?"

"From the day he first came on my boat. He saw a sailing cup with Dad's name on it. He recognized it. I knew all about your father. Just the way your father told you stories of my father, mine told me stories of yours. They must have been some pair. Just like we're going to be. You will marry me, won't you?" Jared asked anxiously.

Cathy moved closer into his embrace and brought her face up to his. "Was there ever any doubt?" Bismarc took that moment to race across the snow and sink his teeth into Jared's boot. "Not now, Bizzy." The dog whined and then lay down as Jared bent his head to kiss Cathy.

* * * * *

# GOLDEN LASSO

# CHAPTER ONE

JANICE WARREN shook her shining chestnut curls with a mixture of sadness and relief as she scrutinized the legal paper before her. The stiff, crackling letter, if she was interpreting it correctly, held the answer to her and Benjie's future.

"What's wrong, Jan?" the little boy in the bulky wheelchair asked fearfully, not understanding his sister's sudden silence. "Did the doctors say something scary about me? Is that why you look so funny?"

"Of course not, silly," Janice soothed, wiping the tears from her eyes. "This letter is going to make everything right for you and me. Do you remember Dad's brother? Uncle Jake? He owned the ranch in Arizona." At Benjie's nod, she continued, "Well, he left the Rancho Arroyo to me, and I'm going to share it with you. That's the happy part. The sad part is that Uncle Jake died and no one notified us. The letter says that he wanted a simple funeral. Uncle Jake was like that—fiercely independent."

With nine-year-old logic, Benjie asked, "How come he left the ranch to you? Didn't he have any children of his own?"

"Uncle Jake's wife died when she was very young and they had no children. I guess we're the last blood relatives and Uncle Jake was big on family." Janice blurted over a sob, "Oh, Benjie, do you know what this means? We can go to Arizona and begin a whole new life. I remember your doctor telling me there was a marvelous clinic in Phoenix that specializes in problems like yours. We've never been able to afford it; but now, since we'll be living close by, we can! You can go there and they'll help you and pretty soon…"

"I'll be able to walk again!" Benjie shouted happily, tossing his dark tousled head, his blue eyes shining.

"With God's help, that's exactly what's going to happen. I can't wait to see you out there playing Little League ball with all of the kids again. And you will," Jan said with determination. "I'll see to it if I have to work twenty-four hours a day to make it come true."

"What about your job here and that boyfriend of yours, Neil Connors—the one who doesn't like me?" Benjie asked curiously.

"Benjie!" Jan cried in surprise. "What a terrible thing to say. What makes you think Neil doesn't like you? And as for my job—pooh, I didn't like it anyway."

"I heard Neil say you were going to be saddled with me for the rest of your life, and he didn't plan on taking on a kid brother. I heard him," the little boy said past a lump in his throat.

"Well, if you heard that then you must have heard my reply. You did, didn't you?" she asked anxiously, her green cat's eyes studying her brother.

"No, I didn't hear what you said. I sort of…I thought Neil might tell you to put me in an orphanage or something."

Jan was off the chair and kneeling in front of Benjie. "Hey, this is Jan, your big sister. I thought we had an agreement that if something was bothering one of us we could talk it out. How could you think such a thing? I told Neil that you and I were a team, and if he didn't want to be part of that team, then that was his problem. I told him when Mom and Dad died in that car crash and you managed to survive I swore that I would take care of you for the rest of our lives. I meant it, Benjie. All we have is one another, now that Mom and Dad are gone. And now that Uncle Jake is gone, too, we're all that's left of the Warren family. We have to stick together. You're such a good little kid putting up with me and never complaining when other kids are out there playing and having a good time. You're going to play, too—you have my word on it. When we get to Arizona, you'll get lots of fresh air. There'll be horses and treatments at the medical center, and at night you're going to be so tired you'll sleep better than ever. What do you say partner? Is it a deal?" Jan asked huskily as she hugged the little boy.

"You bet! When are we going to leave? What about my schoolwork?"

"We'll leave at the end of the week. Tomorrow is going to be a very busy day. There're only three weeks of school left before summer vacation, and I doubt if it will be a problem since you're a straight A student. I'll make the plane reservations this evening and start packing our gear. We'll just close up the house and decide later if we're going to keep it or sell it."

"Tell me about the ranch, Jan. Did you ever see it?"

"Once, when I was about your age, maybe a little older. It's great, Benjie," Jan said enthusiastically. "The main building is made from logs and there're all kinds of planters with bright flowers at the windowsills. There were separate cabins for the guests—a dozen or so, if I remember correctly—and each of them is on what Uncle Jake called a trail that branches off the main path. He wanted his guests to have privacy so they're sort of scattered. When it was in season, he would have big barbecues, where he roasted a whole steer, and then have a square dance. The guests would wear cowboy outfits, and there was an old Indian who played the guitar. At that time he had a lot of really good horses that he kept for his own pleasure and others that were for his guests to ride. All of the people who worked for Uncle Jake seemed to love him because he really cared about them. It was homey and cozy, and I guess that's what I liked about it. Mom and Dad went there on their honeymoon, and I guess that makes Rancho Arroyo special, too. I hope we can make a go of it—I don't know the first thing about running a dude ranch. This letter," Jan said, tapping the legal paper, "says the reservations for the guests have all been confirmed and we're starting off with a full guest list. The first party of guests arrives the day after we do. Our worries are over, little brother," Jan cried exuberantly. "I'm going to pack some of my things now. Do you want to come upstairs or would you rather watch television?"

"I'm going to work on my model and sort of listen to the TV if that's okay with you."

"Sure. If you want me, just holler," Jan said, running

lightly up the stairs. Once she was inside her room she unfolded the letter from Uncle Jake's attorney and reread it. It was the last paragraph of the letter that bothered her. The printed words sent a chill down her spine as she reread the ominous-sounding words.

At the moment I doubt there is much cause for alarm; however, I feel that I must alert you to the fact that a new dude ranch, owned by Derek Bannon, had just been opened in the same vicinity. It caters to the entertainment crowd and its specialty appears to be a Las Vegas atmosphere. Your Uncle Jake was concerned up until the end about the effect of such a place on his little enterprise. However, he believed that family atmosphere and good home cooking at Rancho Arroyo would win out. I want you to be aware, Miss Warren, that while all the reservations have been confirmed, there is nothing that says a guest can't change his mind once he sees the glittering Golden Lasso. I want you to be prepared for any and all emergencies.

I feel it is imperative that you visit my office as soon as possible upon your arrival, as there are many facets of the business that need discussing.

Jan folded the letter carefully and placed it in the zipper compartment of her handbag. The Golden Lasso. A man named Derek Bannon. Jan's stomach curled into a hard knot. Suddenly, she was afraid. Could she handle it? She had to, for Benjie's sake and for her own. She had wept so bitterly that day at her parents' grave site when she promised to take care of Benjie. She wouldn't let a man named Derek Bannon upset her plans—not now, not when Benjie's welfare was at stake.

From time to time, as Jan busily packed and sorted and then discarded, she caught a flash of her reflection in the long mirror in her room. Was that grim, tight jaw hers? Of course it was—she was being threatened by an unknown named Derek Bannon. She could feel it, almost taste it. Benjie's future was being threatened more than her own. But now it was time for her to call the airlines and make their reservations. And she did it with all the calm she could muster. The die was cast. She would make a go of the ranch; she had to. Now she had to call Neil and tell him what was happening.

After putting the receiver back in its cradle, Jan applied a light layer of makeup around her eyes and then deftly added a little color to her cheeks. She couldn't give way to her feelings now, especially not in front of Benjie and Neil, who, rocked by the news that she was leaving, was due to arrive any moment now.

But it was Benjie with whom Jan was concerned. The youngster was so attuned to her feelings he could sense immediately if something was wrong. She had to think positively and act confidently in front of the little boy.

With trembling hands, she ran a brush through her short-cropped chestnut curls. She frowned at the smattering of freckles that ran across her nose and then winced as she thought of the effect the Arizona sun would have on those hated freckles. Her mother's comforting words, "Jan, don't worry about your freckles.

---

With those gorgeous emerald eyes of yours, no one will ever notice them," didn't help now. Twenty-one-year-old women weren't supposed to have freckles. Neil always poked fun at her freckles, but in a nice way. She supposed she would miss Neil when she went away, but Benjie was more important to her than romance. Not that there was much romance—not with her obligations to be both mother and father to Benjie. But still, Neil had always been in the wings waiting for her to have time for him.

Jan scowled. Romanticizing already? Face the truth, she told herself. Neil is great; he's nice to me, and he's always ready to give me a hand when I need it. He has a good job and he'd good-looking—a great catch, as the other girls in the office had told her. But somehow Jan couldn't stir herself up over a great catch. And the fact that she was willing to drop everything and go out to Arizona was proof enough to her that Neil just wasn't that important in her life.

There were times when she had thought he was about to ask her to marry him. But something always held him back. There were times, also, when Jan was so tired and disgusted with trying to make ends meet and taking care of Benjie that she knew that if Neil had only said the word she would have married him in a minute. It would be nice to have someone to lean on, she thought. But then, at other times, when she seemed to have control of the situation and she was well rested, she knew that marrying Neil would be a mistake. There was something lacking in their relationship, something she sensed in Neil that didn't

appeal to her. Or was it because she knew Benjie
didn't like him?

Neil Connors wasn't the kind of man who could
make the earth move under her feet, Jan decided. At
best, Neil might be able to move a small hill.

Jan descended the stairs calmly. It was time for Benjie's
medicine and his snack before bed. She watched him toil
away with his model and marveled at the child's patience.
He held the tweezers and the tiny sticks that held pinpoints
of glue on the end and matched them perfectly. He looked
tired, poor little kid, and yet he never complained. He just
sat and waited till she had time for him. He looked just
like their father with his crisp, dark hair and bright blue
eyes. Even now, at the age of nine, he had their father's
chin, complete with a small cleft. He was bright and precocious with a delightful sense of humor. She loved him
dearly. He was all she had left, and there was nothing or
anyone who was ever going to change that. Not ever.

Benjie was at the kitchen table, his wheelchair pulled
up close against the edge, when the doorbell rang insistently. Neil. Jan opened the door and in he stormed.

"What do you mean you're going off to Arizona?"
he demanded, pushing his fingers through his thick
blond hair.

"Just that," Jan railed. "And if you'll give me a
minute, I'll explain it all to you. Come on into the
kitchen and say hello to Benjie. I was just going to put
him to bed. I'll pour you a cup of coffee."

Jan turned back to the kitchen, Neil hot on her heels.
"Explain!" he demanded again, not bothering to answer
Benjie's polite "Hi."

As Jan poured his coffee, she began to explain, feeling her patience fail. Was Benjie right about Neil not liking him? She shrugged and handed Neil his coffee. "C'mon, Benjie. Ready for bed? I'll be right back, Neil. Make yourself at home."

"Can't he get into bed on his own, for chrissakes?"

"Yes, he can," Jan bristled. "But when you were nine years old, didn't you like to have someone tuck you in?"

Jan returned from the downstairs den, which had been made over into a bedroom for Benjie. "Whatever you do, keep your voice down," she told Neil. "He's going to find it difficult enough to get to sleep."

"Yeah, yeah, okay. Now, what's this all about?"

Slowly, Jan explained, watching the look of disapproval deepen on Neil's face.

"You mean you're just going to go out there and take over and run that place?" He laughed harshly. "What do you know about running a dude ranch?"

"Nothing. No more than I knew what it was to run a house and take care of a little boy," she retorted sharply. "But I learned real fast. And I don't think the idea is so ridiculous. I'm not stupid, you know."

"I never said you were stupid, Jan. Just inexperienced. Naive. You're going to lose your shirt—you know that, don't you?"

"Thanks for the vote of confidence. No, I don't know that I'll lose my shirt. There are people out there, Neil—my uncle's staff—who know all about running the ranch. And am I or am I not one of the best darn bookkeepers you know? I'm halfway through my courses to become a certified public accountant, and that takes brains, whether you like to admit it or not."

"All right, so you're not stupid. But going off to Arizona this way is! What about your life here? This house? Your job?" He slammed his coffee mug down onto the table, sloshing coffee onto the checkered cloth.

"In that order? My life in Arizona would be a change from the humdrum life I live here. The house? I was hoping you'd keep an eye on it for me. My job? I've already told you I'm not stupid. I can always find a job. But what's most important to me is Benjie. There's a clinic out in Phoenix that was recommended to me months ago, but I couldn't afford it. Now Benjie will have the opportunity to go there and be helped."

"So that's who's behind all this. That kid." Neil put his cup in the sink.

"Benjie is my brother, Neil, not 'that kid.' And no, he's not behind this. I would have taken this opportunity anyway. Benjie only validates my reasons for moving on this so quickly. I'm sorry you feel this way, Neil. I was hoping you'd cheer me on."

Neil looked at Jan, an expression of exasperation on his face that clearly stated that this was the dumbest move she could make. "Write out a list of instructions about the house. I'll take care of it for you. When did you say you were leaving? Don't bother telling me—I don't want to know. Leave the list of instructions in your mailbox. Goodbye, Jan."

Without turning around or saying another word, Neil pushed open the kitchen door and stalked out. Jan sat down moodily. Whatever reaction she had expected from Neil, this definitely wasn't it.

JAN WAS THRILLED by the attention Benjie received on the plane from the stewardesses. On boarding, the pilot had handed the little boy a pair of plastic wings, and at the last moment he had fastened them to Benjie's polo shirt. Benjie had beamed his thanks, and from time to time Jan watched him touch the pin during the long trip.

Benjie was happy and amenable to this change in their lives, trusting Jan to take care of him. For a moment tears blinded her. She knew she was guilty of being too maternal, too protective of him. She was going to have to let go in degrees. In New York it had been hard, but now that they were going to the wide-open spaces, perhaps she could manage to bring herself to relinquish her hold and let others have a chance at getting to know the little boy. He needed friends—good friends—who would love him as she did. They were making the right move, Jan told herself determinedly—she was sure of it.

Besides, the house in Upstate New York would be there for them if things didn't work out. Her cushion, so to speak. Now, with the income from the ranch, she wouldn't have so much difficulty meeting the taxes and insurance payments. And the money for Benjie's treatments wouldn't be so difficult to come by. She admitted she had become bone tired from holding down two jobs: her regular one at the dairy, where she was a bookkeeper, and her evening job as a receptionist at a health spa. Benjie's care hadn't presented a problem because he was at school all day while she worked at the dairy, and then at night he had been allowed to come with her to the health spa. Still, he had gotten to bed late, and more times than she cared to remember, they had eaten cold suppers from her lunch bag. But he had thrived and hadn't lost weight, and that was important, according to his doctors. What Benjie needed was her love and the security only she could provide.

Other niggling little thoughts plagued Jan as she stared out at the fluffy clouds far below them. What about me? the contrary little voice demanded. When am I going to have a life of my own? A chance to go out on dates or just for a simple dinner? For the past two years she hadn't even been able to accept an invitation. It was no wonder Neil had been so grudging of Benjie. What kind of date was it to sit and watch television after Benjie went to bed? And she had always been firm about ushering Neil out at the stroke of eleven. She didn't have much going for her either way she looked at it.

Dreamily, Jan closed her eyes and let her mind wander. It must be wonderful to be in love and thrill to another's voice. To know that the person loves you as much as you love him. Would she ever have the time to find that elusive thing called love? Would she ever be free to accept that love? She was almost twenty-two and so far it hadn't found her. She admitted she wanted to be swept off her feet. She wanted, yearned, to feel someone's arms around her, and she wanted to be kissed till she was left breathless and wanting more.

A sound of light laughter, feminine and crystal-sounding, captured Jan's attention. Across the aisle sat a fashionably slim, stylishly dressed woman about Jan's age. Her long, slim legs were crossed, and when she turned her head Jan saw that she was very pretty. The man sitting beside the woman seemed very attentive and kept glancing at her appreciatively as he spoke to her. Whatever he had said to her seemed to strike her as amusing and she laughed again, a lighthearted, abandoned sound that wrenched at Jan's heart. How long had it been since she had been carefree and laughed that way?

"...but I'm going to be married before the month is out. Do you think it would be right if I met you for a drink?" The woman's voice was light and teasing as she flirted with the good-looking, massively built man beside her. "It was only coincidence we took the same flight to Phoenix.... And my fiancé is rather jealous..." The rest of her statement was lost in the sound of the jet engines.

Jan watched the girl across the aisle covertly, a frown of scorn drawing her finely arched brows together. She didn't think much of any girl who could so lightheartedly announce that she was engaged to be married and at the same time flirt so blatantly with the first stranger she met on a plane. A jealous, green monster nipped at Jan's sense of propriety. Some girls just seemed to have it all—money, looks, someone who loved them—and still it didn't seem to be enough. A sudden rush of pity for the girl's fiancé forced Jan's pretty mouth into a thin, straight line.

"As long as you promise to behave yourself," the girl in the aisle warned. "I don't suppose a little drink would hurt anyone. I'll be at the Golden Lasso…" Again her words were drowned out as she turned her head away.

At the mention of the Golden Lasso Jan jumped to attention. Over the top of Benjie's head she took another long look at the girl and sighed. Women as beautiful as that always had men dancing attention around them, she concluded. Jan stiffened her back and sat up straighter in her seat. This was definitely none of her business, and she should be thinking about the kind of reception she would find at Rancho Arroyo and in what condition she would find it.

"I think we're going down," Benjie said, his eyes wide as he stretched to peer out the window. "Look, Jan, the seat belt sign just went on. Is someone going to meet us?"

A knot formed in the pit of Jan's stomach. This was the beginning of a new life for the both of them. She was the new owner of Rancho Arroyo. Boss lady. She could handle it—she would have to. Taking a deep breath, she leaned back and readjusted her seat as the stewardess requested. Quickly, she pressed the button on Benjie's seat, raising it to a full sitting position, and smiled at how happy he was. She had originally thought he would be terrified of flying. But nothing could have been further from the truth. Benjie took to flying like a duck to water.

As the airport came into view and she felt the jar of the mechanism lowering the landing gear, Jan said a silent prayer that the Rancho Arroyo would be a happy place to make their new home and that the medical center in Phoenix would be successful in helping Benjie to walk again. She was tempted to utter a small plea to grant her wish for love and romance and then changed her mind. That would be almost too much to wish for.

Once on the ground, Jan peered around the airport baggage area searching for a person who looked like they might be looking for her. Surely, Uncle Jake's attorney had told someone at the Rancho that Benjie was in a wheelchair. If they didn't recognize her, Benjie was certainly visible with his hundred-watt smile.

## CHAPTER TWO

"MISS WARREN? It is Miss Warren, isn't it?" a drawling voice inquired.

"I'm Jan Warren. Are you from Rancho Arroyo?" she inquired of the tall, slim man in the tight Levi's who was towering over her.

"You've got it, and this little guy must be your brother. Andy Stone," he said, holding out his big, sun-bronzed hand to Benjie, who shook it manfully. "See that man over there?" he asked, motioning to a tall, dark-skinned man standing near the luggage carousel. "That's Gus and he's full-blooded Cheyenne Indian. He's the man who's going to take your baggage to the van and then we're all going to the ranch for a proper welcome."

"Wow! A real Indian!" Benjie cried excitedly.

Jan smiled, "Thank you for that, Andy Stone. I really appreciate it." She handed him the baggage tickets.

"He looks like a nice little kid and it must be rough being glued to a chair like that. I have a little brother in Montana who isn't much bigger and I...what I mean is... Heck, ma'am, I'm just rattlin' on. But your little brother is going to be around people who really care about young ones."

Jan smiled brightly and alleviated Andy's embarrassment. "Look, Andy, there's a man who seems to be trying to get your attention."

Andy tilted his head and looked in the direction Jan was indicating. His mouth tightened and his eyes narrowed. "That's Derek Bannon—he owns the Golden Lasso. There must be someone important on this plane if he's here to meet him personally. You might as well know now before someone else tells you—he's approached everyone who works at the ranch to come and work for him. Some of the people he asked directly and others he sent his business manager around to them. I was one of the ones he approached directly. I turned him down flat. It was hard because he offered me quite an increase in wages. But I liked your Uncle Jake. He took me in and gave me a job when I needed it, and I don't forget that quickly. Looks like Bannon's coming over here. Let me handle it. Later, when you're up on all the goings on, you can take a shot at him yourself."

Jan was bewildered. Fifteen minutes on the ground and already she had a problem. Instinctively, she trusted Andy Stone. Her own gaze narrowed as she watched the tall, muscular Derek Bannon make his way through the milling passengers who were waiting for their luggage. He was tall—taller than Andy Stone—and he wore his extra flesh well. There was nothing lanky about Derek Bannon. He maneuvered himself gracefully, like a cat, and his low Western boots had just the right amount of shine to them. His Levi's fit to perfection as though they were tailor-made, as did the shirt he wore, open to reveal a massive, sun-bronzed chest. There was a slight curl to his crisp, black hair and just a trace of gray at the temples. Steely blue eyes stared at her and through her, making her feel uncomfortable.

"Have you given my offer any more thought, Stone?" he asked Andy in a deep voice that seemed to come from somewhere in his chest. His eyes, however, were on Jan.

"Not today, I haven't. I've been a little busy. This is Janice Warren, the new owner of Rancho Arroyo, and her brother, Benjie."

"Miss Warren, a pleasure." Jan knew he noticed that she hadn't extended her hand, and after a moment he turned his attention to Benjie. He held out his hand and Benjie grasped it and shook it heartily. "Benjie, is it? How old are you?" Derek Bannon asked.

"Nine on my last birthday, sir."

"Isn't it time you were called Ben instead of Benjie?"

Benjie flushed and stared at Jan and then at Andy Stone.

"But that's my name. My mom and dad gave it to me. They're dead and I can't change it, can I, Jan?"

"If you want to. Your real name is Benjamin and Benjie is just a nickname, like Ben. You don't have to decide right now, Benjie, and it isn't important. Is it, Mr. Bannon?" she asked in a cold tone that told the man it was none of his business what her brother's name was.

Derek Bannon shrugged. "Perhaps we'll see one another again." With a curt nod, he weaved his way through the milling crowd.

"What a strange man," Jan said in a puzzled tone.

"He's more than strange, Miss Warren. He's a hard man to fight, and believe me when I tell you you have a fight in store for you. He wants your ranch and he's not going to stop until he gets it."

·"I like him," Benjie chirped. "I liked the way he didn't stoop over and pretend I was a little kid. And I liked it when he said I should be called Ben. I liked him," Benjie said emphatically.

"Well, will you look at that!" Andy said in surprise, pointing to a group of men. "That's the entire Bison football team, and I guess they're staying at the Golden Lasso." Benjie's eyes boggled at the sight, and Jan didn't miss Derek Bannon wave his hand in the little boy's direction.

Jan tugged at Andy's arm. "Why does Mr. Bannon want my ranch?"

"Beats me, Miss Warren. All I know is he wants it. He was forever palavering with your uncle, and as far as I know Jake turned him down each time."

"Is our ranch a threat to the Golden Lasso?" she asked fearfully, afraid now that all her wonderful dreams were going up in smoke.

"I can't see how. Our clientele is different. We cater to families with children. Good home-cooked food, fresh air, and family-type entertainment. Bannon, on the other hand, is all glitter and frills. He's got show girls at the Lasso that would put some of those Las Vegas girls to shame. I don't mind telling you the people around here were just a mite disturbed over the whole thing. But then they all settled down nice and quietlike when they saw the Golden Lasso held pretty strict standards."

"Why would Mr. Bannon want to open a resort way out here in the first place? Why not Las Vegas?"

"Derek Bannon inherited the land from his father.

Over two thousand acres. The only piece he doesn't own is the five hundred acre spread the Rancho Arroyo is on. Your uncle Jake won that piece in a poker game from Bannon's father. He wants it back. Unless you're one hell of a poker player, I don't hold out much hope for you. Money talks, and Derek Bannon talks big. But for what it's worth, I'm on your side, Miss Warren."

"If you're on my side, then I want you to call me Jan. Is it okay if I call you Andy?"

"It's a deal, Jan. Looks like Gus is getting restless. I'd better get these baggage claims over to him. Then what do you say we mosey on back to the ranch?" He swaggered, pretending to be a cowboy, much to Benjie's delight. "Gus, now—he doesn't talk much, but he listens. There isn't much that goes on around here that he doesn't know about. A body would be hard pressed to try to pull the wool over his eyes," Andy said softly to Jan before he left to help Gus with the bags.

"Andy," Jan stopped him in midstride. "Did Derek Bannon try to wean Gus away, too?" she asked anxiously.

"You used the right word. Try was what he did. Gus listened and didn't utter a word. Oh, he was polite about it. After Bannon had his say, Gus just spit tobacco juice in the road and moved on. It's just a guess on my part, but some of the other hands back at the ranch figure that Bannon wanted to exploit the fact that Gus is Cheyenne. You know—dress him up in feathers and paint or something."

While Andy took Benjie over to the luggage carousel, Jan scanned the airport. Her eyes immediately fell on the escalator, where she saw the girl who had sat across from her on the plane. Now that she was standing, Jan could get a good look at her. The first thing she noticed was that she was alone; apparently, she had said her goodbye to the man seated beside her on the plane. Second, Jan could see what a terrific figure she had. Tall, slim and willowy, wearing a clingy jersey dress that set off every curve to an advantage. And her shoes! Just how some women learned to walk in those sky-high creations was beyond her.

Suddenly, it seemed as though the girl spotted someone, and before the escalator touched bottom she lifted her arm and waved in excited greeting. As lightly as a dancer, she was off the escalator and skipping across the floor right into Derek Bannon's arms.

Jan was staggered. The girl had spoken about being engaged to be married. Could her fiancé be Derek Bannon? From the way he was hugging her—swinging her up off the floor and twirling her around—it must be. For an instant, Jan felt smug. Well, Mr. Bannon, it seems as though Rancho Arroyo isn't the only thing you can't put your brand on. Your little girlfriend was making a date with another man. But the thought had a bitter taste.

Benjie demanded her attention. "Hey, Jan! Come on! Andy's bringing the van around to the front. Let's not keep him waiting!"

During the ride to the Rancho, which was about forty miles outside of Phoenix, Jan was entranced with the countryside. She remembered the beauty of the desert from her last visit to Arizona, but it hadn't seemed so majestic through the eyes of a little girl. Now she could view the shifting sands and the arrow-straight road with amazement that so close to a burgeoning city there could be such wilderness. Low mountain ranges lifted the horizon, and in the late afternoon the sun painted myriad color schemes from dull reds to vibrant purples with each scheme punctuated by black shadows and low-growing scrub. There was peace here—Jan could feel it—and she knew it was a sight she could enjoy for the rest of her life. Instead of becoming tired, her eyes picked up every nuance of color and symmetry. Gus, too, seemed intent on the scenery. Since climbing into the van beside Andy, his gaze never strayed from the window except to glance at Benjie to see how he was faring during the ride.

From the interstate highway Andy pulled onto a secondary road following a beaten signpost that pointed the way to Rancho Arroyo. "It's about four miles after turning off the interstate. That's where your property begins. From there on our own road, which we maintain, it's another two miles. Think it's too far from civilization for you, Jan?"

"There were some days in the big city, Andy, that I thought the moon wasn't far enough away. Where's the Golden Lasso from here?"

"Well, you follow this secondary road for about eight or nine miles, and you can't miss it. It's only about two and a half miles as the crow flies, though. The roads are indirect to say the least."

Jan watched through the windshield and gained her bearings. They had headed west out of Phoenix and now were heading north. As Andy turned into the private road leading to the ranch, Jan's heart pounded with excitement. And when they at last pulled through the split-rail fence and she saw the low, flat buildings of her new home, she nearly shouted with joy. It hadn't changed. It was still the same. And she loved it.

"This is really beautiful." Jan drew in her breath. "I had remembered it being this way, but I was afraid to see that perhaps it had become run-down with use and age. You see," she offered Andy by way of explanation, "it's been a long time since I was here. Not since I was a child not much older than my brother. It's just perfect." She eyed the colorful window boxes. "I know we're going to be happy here, don't you, Benjie?" But Benjie was off, his chair skimming over the smooth flagstone patio, Gus close behind.

"Don't worry about the boy—he's found himself a guardian. Gus loves kids, although you'd never think it from his rough exterior. Come on inside and meet your staff." Andy held the screen door open.

The dimness inside startled Jan for a moment after the bright light of day. But she recovered quickly and took in everything around her. The heavy pine tables were polished to a high gleam and the long, low leather sofas and armchairs looked inviting. The plank wood floor was buffed to a patina and Indian print scatter rugs seemed to follow the traffic flow and make intimate little conversation areas, almost like rooms within the room. The ceiling was rough adobe sectioned off by rough-hewn beams, and the far walls of the lobby were covered with used brick on which were hung gleaming brass plaques that offset the huge round wagon wheel chandelier with its brass lanterns. And everything sparkled—not a hint of dust anywhere, not even on the various plants and ferns showcased against the walls and positioned around the vast room. Off to one side of the door was the desk, and behind it the numerous nooks and crannies for mail and keys. Behind the desk was a door, and through it she could see a small, cozy office with one window that looked out on the corral. Her office, Jan told herself—her very own office.

She didn't hear the woman until she was standing beside her; she was wearing leather moccasins. Jan was looking down at the oval braided rug and knew it was handmade.

"You like." It was a statement, not a question. "I make it many years ago for your uncle Jake."

"This is Delilah, Gus's wife. Don't ask me where she got the name." Andy grinned.

"Hello, Delilah." Jan smiled. "I understand you're our chef."

"I cook, I clean, and I do everything. You like my name, Delilah? I pick myself. Gus no Sampson, but I am Delilah," the woman chortled.

Jan liked her immediately. She was small and round as a ball with shiny black eyes and a wealth of braids arranged on her head in a coronet. Deep laugh lines etched Delilah's face, and Jan thought her one of the most beautiful women she had ever seen. "I like your name very much. It shows you have character," she told Delilah seriously.

"You see," Delilah said, poking Andy in the ribs.

"One smart lady, Jake's niece. But you skinny like stick," she turned back to Jan. "One week, two, and I make you like Delilah." Jan pretended mock horror as Andy swooped her out of the lobby.

"Bannon offered Delilah a fantastic sum to come and work for him," Andy said sourly.

"But you said Gus turned him down. Surely Delilah wouldn't go without her husband."

"I hate to be the one to tell you this, but we only have Delilah's word that she's married to Gus. Gus doesn't commit himself one way or the other. Every now and then Delilah gets it into her head to try to make Gus jealous. He yanks her hair and gets her back in line until the next time. But she loves bangles and beads, so keep it in mind. You can buy a lot of doodads with the kind of money Bannon is tossing around."

"I'll keep it in mind. Let's do the tour so I can go into the office and get familiar with the way things have been done around here."

"If those books are anything like the way your uncle Jake did everything else, you'll find them in top order. I thought maybe you'd wait until that lawyer from Phoenix came down to give you a hand with them."

"Don't worry about me, Andy. I've been a book-keeper since I graduated from business college. I think I can handle them. Then you do know where they're kept?"

"Sure, everybody knows. There's a safe behind the desk and the combination is the numerical value of the word *Jake* in the alphabet. You know, A is the number one and so on. So working left, right, left, it's 10-1-11-5."

Jan smiled up at Andy. "Is there anything you don't know about the Rancho Arroyo?" She laughed.

"Oh, I suppose there's a few things." He seemed embarrassed and pulled the brim of his Stetson low over his eyes.

"Seems like my uncle Jake trusted you, Andy Stone. And I'm giving you fair warning—I'm going to trust you, too." Seeing a flush of color creep up from his shirt collar, Jan changed the subject. "Are you sure Benjie is okay?"

"He's fine. By now he probably has every ranch hand on the place eating right out of his hand. Little kids are kind of hard to resist around here, and he's automatically special if Gus adopted him."

They followed the main path down to the first trail leading to the cabins, where she followed Andy across the planked verandas and stepped inside. Every modern convenience had been installed in the cabins: air-conditioning, tiled baths—even a little efficiency kitchen. Some of the cabins were one-bedroom, but most were two-bedroom affairs, capable of housing a family with children. And each was furnished in Western flavor with heavy oak pieces and bric-a-brac and were kept in A-1 condition.

"There's a lot of work that goes into housekeeping around here. Who does it all?" she inquired.

"There's four women who come in on call when they're needed," Andy explained. "They live on the outskirts of Phoenix and make the drive in every morning. As for repairing fences and the like—you know, roof repair and painting and taking care of the stables and horses—that's what the ranch hands do to keep themselves busy. They're a good bunch of guys, Jan, and I know you'll like them. Between myself and Gus, we handle things during the off-season. Right now, you've got a full crew working for you. Delilah has two girls to help her in the kitchen and she rides herd on them. Come one, I'll take you down to the corral where you can meet the hands. On the way we can stop at the swimming pool."

By sundown Jan had taken her tour and had a bath and a cup of coffee. She pored over the account books until her eyes ached. Everything was right side up. Now all she had to do was keep it that way. A small cash flow, an emergency fund, a filled reservation list, and a storeroom full of every supply known to man—she couldn't ask for more.

At first she had been surprised and then relieved to discover that liquor was not served on the ranch. Applejack and a liberal dose of that potent liquor called white lightning was kept in the locked storeroom, and each had a label that stated it was the property of Gus: "Keep Hands Off."

After dinner she took Benjie and settled him down in bed after his long, exciting day. With guests arriving in the morning, she wanted to be fresh and clearheaded when she handed over the first key to her first guest. She couldn't wait and she knew she would have trouble dropping off to sleep. She only hoped that thoughts of Derek Bannon and his faithless fiancée didn't keep popping into her head the way they had all during the day.

# CHAPTER THREE

JAN WATCHED THE SUN come up from her room in the lodge. The sight was breathtaking. Only once before had she seen anything its equal and that had been a sunrise in Key West, Florida. She toyed briefly with the idea of waking Benjie and quickly negated the thought. There would be other days, other sunrises, for the little boy to see.

Benjie occupied the room adjoining hers on the second floor of the lodge. He had been as thrilled with his room as Jan had been with hers. She loved the dark mahogany furniture and the tall, heavy-paneled chifforobe that stood sentry just outside her private bath. Even here there was a flavor of days gone by. The floor was covered with an Indian patterned rug, and the walls were covered with a small-scale print of cranberry on federal blue paper. The bedstead was huge, and she had found the night before that she had had to literally climb into it. But the mattress was firm and the sheets smelled sweet, and she had almost immediately dropped off to sleep.

As Jan made up the bed and smoothed the dull cranberry comforter, which doubled as a spread, she wondered how she could feel so comfortable in a room completely devoid of the frills and ruffles she had had back home in New York. This room was handsome, almost masculine, the only feminine items being the Victorian globe lamps on her night tables. But comfortable it was, and it seemed to fit her new way of life. There was an austerity about it that seemed to compliment her new position of authority.

Jan washed and dressed herself in a comfortable pair of jeans and a long-sleeved blouse. As she stepped into a pair of wedge-soled clogs, she vowed to buy herself a pair of Western boots, and almost giggled at the thought. She didn't want to seem like a weekend cowboy, but she knew that the boots would do double duty against the hard-packed roads and trails leading to the various cabins. She would be covering a lot of territory on foot each day and she needed serviceable shoes.

She raked a brush through her chestnut curls and blessed the fact that her hair was naturally curly and, worn short, didn't require much attention. She'd be too busy from now on to fuss with elaborate hairdos. A last look in the pier glass, and Jan appreciated the fact that her jeans were well-worn and didn't look new, as though she were contriving to look the part of a ranchowner. She liked the way they felt against her skin and admired the way they fit. They had been worth every saved penny she had paid for them.

A glance at her watch and she sighed. She would have to awaken Benjie and get him ready to come downstairs. It seemed a shame to wake him from his sound sleep, but there was no help for it. Benjie required a considerable amount of diligence to get him out of bed, washed, dressed and into the wheelchair. After she had him ready, Gus would come up and carry him down the stairs to his chair. It hadn't been so long ago since Benjie hadn't been able to do anything for himself, but since he had gained the strength to maneuver on crutches, things had improved. But he still needed help in pulling up his trousers and tucking in his shirt. Jan smiled. Soon, with heaven's help and a lot of work, Benjie would be totally self-sufficient; but, she reminded herself, he would probably still need help to get him to wash behind his ears.

Breakfast was a perfunctory affair, with Jan being too nervous to eat more than a few bites of toast and drink several scalding sips of the best coffee she had ever tasted. She itched to get behind the desk in the lobby and wait for the Marshall family, which was to arrive at 10:00 a.m. She had it all planned. First she would greet them and register them in the large book on the desk. Then she would personally escort them to Cabin Six on Wayward Trail. She hoped they would like the seclusion and the scent of scrub pines that surrounded the three-room cabin. And after that she would drive into the Phoenix Medical Center with Benjie for his first treatment. She knew that was going to work out right also. It had to—it just had to!

Before leaving New York and on the advice of Benjie's physicians, she had phoned the Phoenix Medical Center and spoken to Dr. Rossi, who would take over Benjie's case. In her suitcase up in her room was Benjie's medical file, which she would give to Dr. Rossi. There had been a lot of preparation involved in having her brother continue therapy in Phoenix, and it was important that he not miss his first appointment.

A cup of lukewarm coffee at her elbow, Jan waited at the desk, her patience barely under control. It was now after eleven and Andy still hadn't returned with the Marshalls from the airport. She looked around the inviting lobby and was suddenly apprehensive. Surely nothing was wrong, but if the Marshalls didn't arrive soon, she was going to have to leave with Benjie for Phoenix.

She saw the dust and then heard the van. Even to her inexperienced ears, it sounded as though something was wrong. It hadn't coughed and spit like that yesterday when Andy and Gus picked them up at the airport in the minibus they used to transport guests to and from the city.

Andy looked disgusted when he ushered the Marshalls into the lobby with their luggage in tow. While Mr. Marshall filled out the registration card, Mrs. Marshall oohed and aahed over the plants and copper and brass and kept rein on her two precocious little daughters. Andy took Jan aside and whispered. "There's something wrong with the van. I'm going to have to call a mechanic out from town to take a look. Usually Gus tinkers with the wheels, but this is something with the transmission. We might have to tow it into the garage. We can use the pickup truck around the ranch so we aren't entirely without transportation. Hopefully, the mechanic can repair the van before tomorrow, when the other guests arrive. If not, we'll have to hire a limousine. Sorry."

"But, Andy, I have to take Benjie into Phoenix for his first therapy session this afternoon. Can I use the pickup? What about a taxi?"

"I don't recommend the pickup. It's old and it's been patched up so often with spit and prayers, it's apt to conk out on you two miles down the road. A taxi is out unless there's a fare coming in from the city. I guess you're going to have to cancel the appointment. I'm sorry, Jan. Where do you want me to take the Marshalls?"

"Cabin Six on Wayward Trail. There must be something I can do," Jan almost wailed. She had forgotten that she wanted so desperately to take the first guests to their cabin but it was too late. Now all she wanted was to get Benjie into Phoenix.

"Perhaps I can be of some help. I couldn't help overhearing. I'm going into Phoenix and would be more than happy to take Ben with me," Derek Bannon said quietly.

Jan was stunned by his sudden appearance. Where had he come from and what did he want? He looked so physically fit, Jan felt weak and ineffectual beside him. His tan was just the right blend of bronze and gold, making his blue eyes brighter by contrast. Again, she was uncomfortable with his nearness. Should she accept his offer to take Benjie into Phoenix. Would he feel imposed upon? Would it make her indebted to him? Especially when he discovered that Benjie's therapy sessions took over an hour and he would be obliged to wait. She decided she would hold her answer until she discovered what he really wanted. "Is there something I can do for you, Mr. Bannon? I know you didn't come here just to offer us a ride into Phoenix."

Derek Bannon's blue-eyed gaze was openly amused

and faintly mocking. "As a matter of fact, I did come here on business. I never beat around the bush. I want to buy Rancho Arroyo from you."

"I never beat around the bush either, Mr. Bannon. Rancho Arroyo is not for sale. Today, tomorrow, or any other day."

"Name your price, Miss Warren, and I'll have a check drawn within the hour," Derek Bannon said arrogantly, ignoring her reply.

Anger shot through Jan. "From reports I hear about your establishment I know that Rancho Arroyo couldn't compare to that glittering palace, and why you would make an offer for this ranch is beyond me. I plan to run this ranch and make a go of it. It's my and Benjie's home now, and one doesn't sell one's home on a whim. It's not for sale, Mr. Bannon," Jan said coldly.

"Everything is for sale if the price is right," Derek answered without emotion. "It might interest you to know that I was negotiating with your uncle, and we had about come to terms before he passed away. As I understand it, he died within minutes of suffering the heart attack. It was his intention to turn the ranch over to me."

"That's not the way I heard it. My people tell me my uncle rejected all three of your offers, and this makes your fourth rejection. Rancho Arroyo is not for sale, and, contrary to your opinion, everything and everyone does not have a price. Including me."

Derek Bannon leaned over the desk, the masculine scent of his aftershave making Jan's senses reel. He was so close Jan could have counted his eyelashes. Gently, he cupped her face in his hand and drew her closer to him. She knew his lips were going to touch hers, and she made no move to withdraw. Instead, she stared deeply into his eyes, aware of the intensity she saw there. It was a light kiss, feathery and fragrant, and left her feeling awkward and wanting more. This time she did withdraw. "Kissing me, Mr. Bannon, is not going to get me to sell you this ranch. At the risk of re-peating myself, I can't be bought." To her own dismay, her voice sounded breathless and husky, betraying the fact that she was more affected by his kiss than she cared to admit.

Derek Bannon's eyebrows lifted and a wry smile touched the corners of his mouth. "Everyone and every-thing has a price. One just has to find it. Now, do you want me to take your brother to Phoenix or not? I'm leaving almost immediately."

"I can't be ready that soon," Jan said curtly. "I'll have to find another way to get into the city."

"You didn't understand me. I didn't ask you to go. I offered to take your brother. Dusty Baker, the running back on the Bison football team, has to have hydrotherapy on his knee. I thought your brother would enjoy riding along and meeting Dusty. I'll wait for him while he has his treatment and bring him home safe and sound."

Tears burned Jan's eyes, turning them into glittering shards of green glass. "Benjie isn't for sale either, and I think it's rotten of you to try and get to me through a little boy."

"It doesn't matter to me what you think, Miss Warren. I offered to do you a favor. Take it or leave it,"

Derek Bannon said coolly, his eyes shooting white sparks of anger.

Jan knew she had no other choice. Benjie's appointment was important and she couldn't just cancel it because everything hadn't gone according to plan. Benjie propelled his chair through the lobby, and she watched as his eyes lit up at the sight of Derek Bannon. "Benjie, Mr. Bannon has offered to take you to the medical center along with one of the football players. Do you think you can handle it?"

"Wow! Sure, Jan. Really, Mr. Bannon, just you and me and one of the Bisons?"

"Dusty Baker," Derek replied, watching Jan's face.

"Dusty Baker! Jan, did you hear that? Gosh, he's my favorite player! Is it all right, Jan? Huh?" Benjie literally glowed with excitement.

Jan couldn't find her voice, but she nodded her agreement. "Just remember, Mr. Bannon," she finally managed through clenched teeth, "Benjie is a little boy who has gone through traumas even an adult couldn't handle. You hurt him in any way and you'll answer to me."

"That sounds like a threat and unworthy of such a pretty lady." Derek smiled.

"That's not a threat, Mr. Bannon, that's a promise."

Derek laughed, a rich, booming sound that seemed to fill the room and bounce off the walls. "I make it a practice never to offer advice, but I'm going to make an exception this time. Don't ever threaten me, or you might get more than you bargained for. And stop smothering the boy with your frustrated maternal instincts. He's going to have to make the best of whatever life has in store for him. Find yourself a cat and take your frustrations out on it."

"You…you arrogant, insufferable…"

"You ready, Ben? My car is out front. I'll meet you there," Derek said, striding through the open doors.

Benjie sensed Jan's intention of helping him. "I can do it, Jan. If Mr. Bannon thought I needed help, he would have offered. I can do it," Benjie insisted manfully as he turned the chair and expertly propelled it through the doorway without touching the wooden frame. "What did I tell you?" he called over his shoulder.

"Yes, I see," Jan said weakly. "I'll be right down with your medical file. Don't leave without it." Quickly, before she could change her mind, Jan ran up the stairs and dug into her suitcase for his records, then raced down the stairs.

Outside, Benjie was already situated in the car, his wheelchair folded in the backseat. She handed Benjie the manila envelope and turned to Derek Bannon. "You don't know the name of Benjie's doctor or where he's supposed to go."

Walking toward her, he grasped her arm and almost dragged her back into the lobby. He stood facing her, hands on hips, a look of disgust on his face. His voice was laced with sarcasm when he spoke. "Miss Warren, don't ever take me for an idiot. There's only one doctor at the center who can give the therapy your brother needs. And he's the same doctor Dusty Baker must see. I happen to know Dr. Rossi personally, and he mentioned to me that your brother was coming in for treatments. He felt it would be convenient for him if Dusty came in at the same time."

Again the words stuck in Jan's throat. He was insufferable. It had been natural for her to offer instructions as to where and whom Benjie was to see. After all, Derek had just popped in out of nowhere and had taken matters into his own hands. He certainly seemed like a man who had all the answers—and then some.

It took Jan the better part of an hour to get her emotions under control. There was no point in denying that Derek Bannon had an effect on her. He made her aware of the fact that she was a woman, a woman with feelings that had been submerged too long and were now creeping to the surface. She felt suddenly alive and vibrant. She liked the feelings and wondered what it would be like to be held in his strong arms and to feel his heart beating against hers and to know a deeper kiss than the feathery touch he had pressed upon her.

Jan felt herself blush. What was wrong with her? Derek Bannon was engaged to be married to that beautiful woman she saw on the plane. And what kind of person was he to kiss her and stir these emotions in her when he had promised himself to another woman?

And what kind of woman was Derek's fiancée to have someone like Derek Bannon dancing on a string while she amused herself with other men? A fool, that's what she is, Jan thought hotly. Derek Bannon was the kind of man to answer most girls' prayers, and there was his fiancée playing him for the fool. Or was that the normal way of doing things in that kind of glittering, glamorous society that the Golden Lasso suggested?

Was that the kind of morals those rich and beautiful people had? Well, it wasn't *her* way—not in the least. If she ever pledged herself to someone, she'd never amuse herself with flirting with other men. And she'd never, never be attracted to a man like Derek Bannon, who probably collected women the way other men collected stamps.

Why did some men think they were so clever? Didn't Derek realize she saw through his little plan? He would try to make her brother his ally, his friend, and he would state his demands again, once he had the boy wrapped around his little finger. Well, he wasn't going to get away with it. This was one of Benjie's relationships that she was going to nip in the bud.

The remainder of the afternoon was spent in meeting the housemaids and inspecting the linens and supplies. When she visited the stables, she developed a particular affection for a mare named Soochie. She promised herself she would brush up on her riding techniques and take the gleaming palomino out for a canter at the first possible opportunity.

From time to time Jan heard the Marshall children squeal in delight over their father's antics in the swimming pool. When she glanced at her watch again, she was appalled to see that it was after four o'clock. Benjie should have been home by now. Each session was only an hour. A smidgeon of worry shot through Jan. What if Derek Bannon had forgotten the little boy and left him there at the medical center? What if they had had an accident? What if...what if...scurried through her brain until she gained control of herself. Her face flushed a brilliant scarlet. Derek Bannon was a responsible man, and he truly liked her brother. Whatever else he may be, he was reliable, and she knew she could trust him with Benjie's care and safety.

Jan was busily working her way down to her third fingernail when she heard the high-pitched whine of Derek Bannon's sports car. She waited a second and then walked out onto the front veranda. The sight of Benjie's weary face went straight to her heart. Poor little guy, he looked so beat, and she hadn't been with him to help, if not with physical support, at least to cheer him on. Quickly, she opened the car door, intending to scoop Benjie into her arms and croon over him as their mother would have done.

"Don't! Ben can manage." It was an iron command, an order not to interfere. Jan stepped back in alarm, fearful that something was wrong with Benjie. Her eyes pleaded and implored the man in front of her to say something to reassure her. He said nothing, did nothing. Instead, he waited for Benjie to look up.

"What do you say, Ben? We can do it two ways. I can help you or you can help yourself," Derek said quietly, but encouragingly.

Benjie grinned. "If you push the chair closer, I think I can handle it, Derek."

Bannon gave the chair a little nudge with his foot and waited. The little boy slowly maneuvered himself to the edge of the car seat, his lower lip caught between his teeth. He slipped and Jan made a move to reach out a supporting hand. Derek Bannon caught her arm in a viselike grip and held firm. Benjie righted himself and slipped into the chair. "I did it!" he cried jubilantly.

Jan was suddenly aware that the man hadn't released his hold on her arm, although his grip had loosened. She liked that touch and hated the man. He was sadistic. "That was a brutal thing you just did," she hissed. "He's such a little boy, and he's absolutely exhausted. Why couldn't you help him or, at the very least, let me help him?"

"He didn't need any help. Leave him alone before you destroy him." Without another word, Derek slid behind the wheel of his car. His powerful hand moved effortlessly over the gearshift as he expertly reversed the sports car. "By the way, Dr. Rossi suggests you give him a call the first of next week. Benjie has a pamphlet describing the exercises he's to work on before his next visit to the center. And I suggest you get him out into that swimming pool. It's the best thing for him."

Benjie called, "Thanks, Derek. Thanks for taking me to the hospital."

Derek Bannon waved without turning around to acknowledge the boy's goodbye. He was insufferable!

"I'll bet you're starved. How about a snack like we used to have at home. Tea, cheese and crackers?"

"I'm not hungry. Derek and Dusty took me for tacos and I had two with a malted. Isn't he great, Jan? And Dusty Baker is a super guy—just the way he looks on television. He didn't talk to me like I was a little kid. We talked about plays and signals and he said I knew a lot about football. Derek is going to take me to the field behind the Golden Lasso to watch the Bisons work out tomorrow. He said you could come along if you wanted.

I told him you hated football and wouldn't want to come. You don't, do you?" he asked anxiously.

Jan felt deflated and defeated by Derek Bannon. And yet Benjie, who was usually so reserved with strangers, liked him. Maybe she was missing something.

"Look what Derek gave me," Benjie said pridefully, rummaging in his jeans pocket. "Four tickets to the Bisons salute dinner. I'm not sure what a salute dinner is, but Derek said I should get you to bring me. Can we go, Jan? Huh?"

Jan inspected the white cards with the gold engraving. "Benjie, these tickets cost one hundred dollars each! I can't afford to buy them."

"They're free, Jan. Dusty gave me two and Derek gave me two. The other two are for Andy and Gus."

"We'll see," Jan said, not wanting to make a decision at the moment.

But Benjie was not to be put off. "Don't, Jan. Just say yes or no. I don't like it when you tell me maybe," he said quietly.

"My 'maybes' never bothered you before," she answered tartly, knowing who she had to thank for Benjie's sudden independent behavior. "I want to remind you that you're only nine years old, and I'm the one who is taking care of you. It has to be my way, not Derek Bannon's way. Do you understand?"

"I understand, all right. I understand that you don't like Derek. Well, that's okay, too, because I heard him say he didn't like you. He told Dusty Baker you were on the verge of being a frustrated old maid," Benjie said with all the force he could muster. Mouth pressed into a grim line, he turned the chair and headed down the driveway.

Tears trickled down Jan's cheeks as she watched Benjie's slow progress in search of Gus. Things were falling apart, and they had only been on the ranch for twenty-four hours. What had she done to deserve those biting comments from Benjie? All she wanted was to love him and see that he was well again. Hadn't she given up two years of her life for him since he had been injured? And Derek Bannon swoops into their lives and it's all for nothing. Now I'm not good enough for Benjie. Whatever I can do, Derek Bannon can do it better. "In a pig's eye!" Jan snarled as she stamped her foot on the blacktop. "No way, Mr. Bannon!"

Still smarting from Benjie's comment on being an old maid, Jan made her way to the tiny mail room and began to sort through the mail. She was just on the verge of taking it back to her office when Delilah intercepted her. The little Indian woman was carrying a large wicker basket. "This come for you on a special truck. Man wait for money. Says is five dollars and two cents."

"Are you sure it's for me? I didn't order anything. What is it?" Jan asked as she dug into petty cash for the money to give Delilah.

"How should I know? You open, we both see." Delilah waited patiently. "Will you open before I pay man or after I pay man?"

"I'll wait for you to pay him," Jan muttered. "I have no idea what it could be. I'm certain I didn't order anything."

It was Delilah who finally opened the wicker basket lid. She cocked her head to one side and peered into the basket, her shoe-button eyes merry and full of mischief. "This funny present. I think you get stung. Is not worth five dollars and two cents. Must be tax, too?" she said authoritatively.

Swallowing hard, Jan moved nearer the basket and looked inside. A cat! Of all the unmitigated gall! Arrogant, know-it-all playboy! And she had paid money for it! He was cheap in the bargain!

Delilah's eyes widened. "You want cat? We have many for free in barn. You think maybe this is special cat?" she asked inquisitively.

"Nope. This is your run-of-the-mill, everyday alley cat, and from the looks of things she's about to bestow a blessing on us. Here, Delilah, you can have it," Jan offered generously.

"You pay, you stuck with present. Even for free, I don't want it. Maybe in New York you pay for cat. Here is free. You make little mistake but all right. Next time you look inside before you pay," Delilah indulged.

"There isn't going to be a next time. I should take this cat to the Golden Lasso and demand that…that…"

"He good-looking man, no? He make me itch all over." Delilah giggled as she waddled from the room. In spite of herself, Jan laughed. She would send Derek a thank-you card that would set his teeth on edge. Better yet, she would send him the whole kit and kaboodle after the litter arrived.

BEFORE GETTING into bed that night, Jan penned off a letter to Neil telling him all about Rancho Arroyo. She carefully omitted the fact that the minibus was out of order and that she had had a confrontation with the owner of the Golden Lasso, who was a stiff competitor for business. She did describe the landscape and the wonderful condition of the lodge and the cabins and the beautiful Arizona sunshine. Silently, Jan crossed her fingers and hoped that the trouble with the minibus and the disarming situation with Derek Bannon weren't an omen of things to come.

Hastily, before she was tempted to confide in Neil, she licked the envelope and pressed it shut.

# CHAPTER FOUR

JAN SADDLED SOOCHIE and rode out past the ranch into the wild terrain. Paying careful attention to the direction she was taking, she watched for the blazed trail and fence posts that would lead her around the entire circumference of Rancho Arroyo.

It was a beautiful day and promised to be hot, with the sun scorching down on the parched land. Yet there was beauty to be found here, so different from the verdant appeal of the Catskill Mountains with which she was so familiar. Here the eye could stretch, following the low, uninterrupted land right out to the horizon, where, in the distance, purple mountains stood sentinel and lifted the eye to the vibrantly blue sky. It was still early—hours before the heat of the day—and Soochie seemed grateful for her escape from the corral.

Relaxing in the saddle and instinctively trusting Soochie's temperament, Jan gave the palomino free rein. There was time to enjoy her new home now that everything seemed to be running smoothly—on the surface at least.

Andy had taken the guests on a ride into the desert and wouldn't return until well after sunset. A campfire and a sing-along was planned for them before their return to the ranch. She made a mental note to be on hand for the nine-o'clock pool party, complete with Delilah's scrumptious buffet goodies.

However, Jan was aware of vague undercurrents that had recently reared their ugly heads. A mantle of worry settled over her slim shoulders as she dismounted and tied Soochie's bridle to scrub pine. She sat down on the hard-packed earth and munched on the cheese and crackers she had thought to bring along. Andy's grim words that the van could not be repaired without a major overhaul on the transmission had been the last thing she wanted to hear. But when the mechanic discovered a cracked engine block, the world seemed to come to an end. The ranch would have to buy a new minibus. Momentarily, she had panicked. To pay cash or take it on time payments was a difficult decision. She had finally opted for cash because the dealer was offering her a sizable discount if she took it that way. Her small cash reserve was now seriously depleted. And if Andy was right about the air-conditioning unit in the lodge going on the fritz, she was going to have another gigantic bill facing her very soon. She couldn't very well expect her guests to eat in a hot, stuffy dining room and her guests wouldn't expect it either.

Jan leaned back against an outcropping of rocks, her hands trembling. Was it the bills or was it the fact that two of the ranch's prospective guests had changed their minds about staying at the Rancho Arroyo once they saw the glittering Golden Lasso? There had also been three future reservations for large families that were also canceled. At the moment they weren't in any serious difficulty and could weather the storm, but if there were any further cancellations, the ranch could bury itself in the red side of the ledgers. A devastating thought, especially since Benjie would soon be ready for his third treatment.

And to make matters worse, while the guests professed to adore Delilah's cooking, Jan had noticed that most of them preferred dressing up and going to the Golden Lasso for dinner and entertainment, leaving their children behind for her and her staff to tend to. There wasn't a thing she could do about it. And all the food that Delilah prepared was wasted because there was no one to eat it. Jan groaned and her stomach churned at the thought of the colossal waste of food every day. From the looks of things, there wasn't going to be any profits for a long time to come.

And then there was Derek Bannon. Each time she saw him she felt more drawn to him and more confused than ever. Clucking mother hen indeed, she sniffed. A lot he knew and what business was it of his anyway? He'd just better not think he was going to make any decisions where Benjie was concerned. She was his own sister and she knew best.

Tears of self-pity burned her eyes and she brushed them away with the back of her hand the way Benjie did. It seemed she was doing an awful lot of crying lately. Maybe I am a frustrated old maid, she thought sadly. A man kisses me and I go all to pieces. As if that kiss meant anything to me. I've got other things to think about. Like earning a living for myself and Benjie. There's no time to become attracted to anyone—especially not a man like Derek Bannon.

Jan was about to gather up the crumpled cheese and cracker wrappers when she noticed her feet were in shadow. She had been so involved in her thoughts she hadn't heard him approach.

"Littering, Miss Warren? And trespassing," Derek Bannon said mockingly.

Jan was acutely aware of her position: sprawled on the ground, her legs wrapped in faded jeans and tucked beneath her like a yogi. She felt the trail of scarlet begin in her neck and work its way up to her cheeks. Her hateful freckles must be lighting up like neon lights, she thought inanely. She should say something—anything—to wipe that know-it-all smile off his face, but the words stuck in her throat. Scrambling to her feet and belatedly remembering the papers in question, she bent over like a child who had been severely reprimanded and stuffed the cellophane into the pocket of her jeans. She was humiliated and embarrassed and knew Derek was reveling in it. She hadn't seen the girl astride the cinnamon-colored horse waiting behind the scrub. Jan's eyes widened. It was the girl from the plane—Derek's fiancée.

The girl sat upon her horse looking like a model with her precision-cut clothes molding her slim body. She sat comfortably in the saddle as though she were born to it, and the soft, white Stetson was worn on the back of her head with just the right amount of ebony hair showing in front.

Jan had envied the girl on the plane, had been shocked to learn in the airport, that she was Derek's fiancée, and now she knew she could hate her—especially when she called to Derek in a low and husky voice.

"Andrea, I'd like you to meet our new neighbor. Miss Jan Warren," he said coolly, "who owns the Rancho Arroyo. This is Andrea, my…"

Before Derek could complete the introduction, the girl's eyes widened. "Really! So you're Jake Warren's niece. And is Ben your son?"

Jan stared first at Andrea and then at Derek. "Yes," she answered airily. "I really am. And as for Benjie, I'm more what some people would call his clucking mother hen," Jan snapped as she slid her foot into the stirrup.

At first Jan thought she had imagined it, but Derek was grinning at her. "Touché," he said softly.

"I'm sorry if I trespassed and I did clean up my litter, so I presume I'm free to leave." It was plain to see Derek was enjoying her discomfort.

"Don't move, either of you," he said suddenly in a strangely hoarse whisper.

Jan looked in the direction of Derek's gaze and then she saw it at the same time Andrea's horse bolted and raced off. A coiled rattler had crept out from beneath the rocks. She gulped and tried to swallow as she watched Derek rein in her horse and lead it carefully away.

"Aren't you going to kill it?" she asked hesitantly, fighting back her own urge to bolt and run.

"You may have noticed, I don't make it a practice to carry my six-shooter," he answered sarcastically. "Besides, the Western rattler is an endangered species, and for the most part they're more frightened of us than we are of them."

A shudder ran through Jan. "I'm afraid of snakes and bugs," she babbled. "Thank you. Andrea—is she all right?"

"Andrea was born to the saddle. By now she's back at the Golden Lasso with a Bloody Mary in her hand. Here, let me help you—you look a little shaky."

"I'm all right," she snapped as she threw her leg over the saddle horn to slide to the ground. If there was one thing she didn't need at the moment, it was Derek Bannon's help, for that would require that he touch her, and then she would fall into his arms, weeping with fright.

She fixed a deliberate haughty expression on her face and slid from the saddle. Soochie sensed the change of weight upon her back and daintily backed up, throwing Jan off balance. Derek reached out his long arms and drew her against him.

Suddenly, she felt safe, protected, and it was with great difficulty that she forced herself to pull away from his grasp. She couldn't allow this arrogant man to see what he did to her.

"Your palomino is still a little skittish; give her a few minutes before you try to ride her," Derek said softly as he lowered his gaze to meet hers.

His blue eyes, shaded by the brim of his Stetson, had a hypnotic effect on Jan. It seemed, when she looked up at him, that all she could see was the blue sky framing his powerful shoulders and his face. Soochie was forgotten and the world seemed to tilt, and, like a moth to flame, she was drawn into his arms. For a long moment he looked down into her upturned face, and Jan was tingling with expectancy. His hand cupped her face, his long fingers coming to rest on her neck beneath her ear. Finally, at last, and with determination, he brought his face closer, touching his lips to hers. With an urgency that left her breathless, his arms closed around her, holding her against his lean, hard strength, and his mouth becoming more demanding, crushing hers, insistently summoning a response.

Derek Bannon filled her world. The sheer strength of the man, the wide width of his shoulders, the flaming touch of his mouth on hers became her existence. There was no world, no anything, beyond the reach of his arms and the touch of his lips. He was gentle, he was insistent, he was demanding, he was tender.

A rush of emotions pummeled her senses and the earth seemed to move beneath her feet. Jan clung to him, lifting her face to his, answering his demands, filling her own. He brushed the hat from her head, and his hands were in her hair as his mouth sought hers.

Jan felt her sensibilities leave her, and in their place, from somewhere deep within, came an answering response. As though of their own volition, her arms sought the rippling muscles of his back, the narrowness of his waist. Her thighs pressed against his, feeling their strength through the fabric of her jeans. He was no longer kissing her, and she was aware that his breath came in sharp rasps that matched her own. A deep sound of pleasure escaped him as he began to trail his lips along her neck and then down to the cleft between her breasts. Jan clung to him, welcoming him, pressing herself closer.

Derek Bannon smiled down at her. "Tell me you didn't like that."

Jan bristled, and with a huge effort she managed to regain control of herself. "Oh, I liked it, all right," she managed to say tremulously, "but you kiss like you do everything else—to perfection. The next time—if there is a next time—try putting some emotion into it. We clucking mother hens not only want, we demand, warmth and feeling. And, Mr. Bannon, I'm still not for sale and neither is my ranch."

Derek's face was set into grim, hostile lines. "Perhaps there's something lacking in you, Miss Warren. I've kissed many women, and you're the first who has complained."

"I'll just bet you have—kissed lots of women, that is," she snapped, thinking of Andrea. "And that makes you one up on me because I haven't kissed many men. But I do know what I like and what I don't like. Perhaps the reason no one has ever complained is because they're like you. Peripheral, without depth, no emotions. In short, Mr. Bannon, I find you sadly lacking."

Quickly, she mounted Soochie and dug her heels into the animal's flanks, riding off and leaving a stunned and angry man looking after her.

Soochie seemed to be aware of the emotions that embroiled her young rider. Jan's trembling hands couldn't control the reins, making the palomino skittish and unruly. How in the world had she managed to let him kiss her? And where in the world had she mustered up the nerve to say the things she had said? The full weight of the situation descended on her, seeming to block out the sun and chill the air. Liar. Jan Warren is a liar, a small voice hissed. You loved it, you loved every minute of it and you know it. Liar. Liar! You just didn't want him to know that he shook the earth beneath your feet.

Jan's backbone stiffened and she railed against the small voice. "He deserved it!" she shouted to the sky. "He's going to marry Andrea, and he thought he could play his games with me! He deserved it!" Still, on the long ride home Jan couldn't seem to erase the memory of his lips on hers or the way his hands touched her hair. And the soft sound of pleasure that came from him when his mouth found the soft flesh between her breast came back to her.

At Rancho Arroyo Jan was greeted with a broken air-conditioning unit and a mean, angry Gus, who was stomping around the lobby as though he wanted to kill. Benjie was watching the man with wide eyes, uncertain if he should maneuver his chair out of Gus's way or not.

"What's wrong? Will someone tell me what's happened? If whatever it is is going to cost me money, please, tell me gently. Where's Delilah?"

"That's what the problem is," Benjie whispered. "She quit and went to work for Derek at the Golden Lasso. She just left a little while ago. You should have asked her to stay," the little boy accused the tall Indian.

Gus continued his parade around the lobby, stopping once to light a foul-smelling pipe. He puffed furiously as he stomped out his anger.

"If Delilah is gone, who's going to prepare the buffet table for the pool party?"

"There isn't gong to be any pool party tonight, so we don't have to worry about the buffet," Benjie volunteered. "One of the ranch hands drained the pool and forgot to turn the water back on."

Jan sat down and wished she smoked so she could light a cigarette. Instead, she jumped back up and headed for the storeroom and uncapped a jug of Gus's white lightning. She took one gulp and recapped the bottle. She waved away the fumes and thought that flames were going to shoot from her mouth any second. When nothing happened, she locked the storeroom and made her way back to the stiflingly hot lobby.

"Well, Gus, aren't you going to go to the Golden Lasso and fetch Delilah back where she belongs?" Jan asked irritably, her throat burning from the alcohol.

Gus favored her with a withering glance and continued his furious pacing.

"Why?" Jan asked, throwing her hands helplessly in the air. "How could you let her go like that? The ranch is without a cook and I can't even begin to cook for all these guests. Gus," she implored, "we need Delilah."

"Delilah said Gus doesn't make her itch and she's tired of not listening to him. She said he never says anything," Benjie offered sadly, knowing he was going to miss the little round woman who made apple tarts for him with globs of icing on top the way he liked them.

"Then I'll go myself and get her," Jan said huffily. "I appreciate her even if you don't, Gus."

"Mr. Bannon won't give her back to us. Delilah said he was going to lock her in his kitchen and never let her get away. That's what she said," Benjie said at Jan's look of disbelief. "Honest."

"Where's the pickup? I'm going to get her, and when

you see me again, Delilah will be with me. You can count on it or my name isn't Jan Warren. Will you come with me, Gus?" He just continued with his furious pacing, which was becoming wilder by the moment. "Well, if you won't come with me, do you have a message to her you want me to deliver?"

"Yes," Gus replied. Jan was dumbfounded. She had been at the ranch over a week, and it was the first time she had heard him actually speak. "Tell her I'm not itchy," he said in perfect English.

"That's just exactly what she's going to want to hear," Jan said stormily as she flounced out of the lobby and went in search of the battered pickup truck.

She seethed all the way to the Golden Lasso. More than one scathing look was shot her way in the parking lot of the Lasso. The truck was definitely not Lasso material among the Cadillacs and Continentals, not to mention the Mercedes that peppered the ample parking area. Jan looked around and made her way to the back of the club. No sense causing more of an uproar by going in the front door. She flinched when she remembered Andrea's perfect attire. The Lasso's hired help probably dressed better than she was at the moment.

Jan found the kitchen by the aroma. Delilah must be making her specialty—corn bread with raisins. She stood for a moment and watched the small woman wipe at her eyes from time to time. Quietly, Jan opened the door and stood a moment till Delilah recognized her. "Delilah, please, you have to come back to the ranch. I'll pay you whatever Mr. Bannon is paying you. You can't let me down now. There's no way I can possibly cook for all the Rancho's guests. If you stay here, I'll have to send them here and refund their money."

"I make promise to Mr. Bannon. I give my word," Delilah said defiantly.

"That's wrong, Delilah. You gave me your word when I came to the Rancho that you would stay and work for me. If it's Gus who's bothering you, you have something you better learn right now. He will not come over here to get you. He belongs at the Rancho, and if you stay here he's…he's going to get another…well, what he's going to do is find himself a…a girlfriend, and then where will you be?"

"You think Gus do that?"

"Pirating my help, Miss Warren?" a cold voice inquired.

"Actually, you could say I was pirating my help *back* again. That was a pretty shabby, shoddy thing for you to do, Mr. Bannon. Your tactics are definitely to the left of Attila the Hun," Jan said in a furious, choked voice.

"A simple business proposition. I offered Delilah money and she accepted. What's wrong with that?"

"There's nothing wrong with a simple cut-and-dried business arrangement, but it didn't happen like that and you know it. You're trying to put me out of business and it isn't going to work. I'm not selling and that's final!"

"My dear Miss Warren, think whatever you will," Derek Bannon quipped. "You're trespassing for the second time today."

"Yes, I know, but I came to talk to someone. So I consider it fair for me to be standing in your kitchen. Delilah, are you coming with me?"

Delilah looked uncertain, and from Jan's vantage point it looked like Derek Bannon was going to win. Jan felt desperate. "Delilah," she pleaded, "think of Benjie. What's he going to do, Delilah? He's such a little boy and he needs you. I need you."

"Okay, I come," Delilah said, taking off her apron. Without a backward glance, she followed Jan from the spacious kitchen.

Jan allowed herself a smirk as she sailed past the astonished Derek Bannon. "And that's what I call fair."

Jan backed the pickup from the parking slot and headed for the highway. She took her eyes from the road a minute to look at Delilah. "I'm glad you're coming back with me."

Delilah shrugged. "I thought Gus come for me. I not plan on staying there. At Rancho I big boss in kitchen. At Golden Lasso, many cooks. Chefs, they call themselves." Delilah sniffed her disapproval of their self-appointed titles.

Jan was silent on the drive back to Rancho Arroyo, grateful that she had succeeded in getting Delilah to come back to work. And then it hit her. It had been too easy. Men like Derek Bannon always won. If he had wanted to keep Delilah, he would have kept her, and no amount of pleading on her part would have changed things. Men like Derek Bannon did not get where they were in the business world by being nice to their competitors. Suddenly, she felt like a fool. She had been maneuvered by an expert, and she had fallen for it. He was giving in graciously now; later, when she was lulled into a false sense of security, he would strike another blow in his quest for her property. Her hand trembled on the steering wheel. She felt uncertain, betrayed somehow. The only certainty on the horizon was that Derek Bannon wanted her ranch, and if he had to ruin her in the process, he would. Jan shivered in the hot, dry air. If that was so, then she would go down fighting. Derek Bannon would at least know he had picked a formidable adversary. She had to wait and play the waiting game just as Bannon was doing. Who would win? A fine bead of perspiration dotted her brow as she drove. She knew in her heart who was going to win, and all she could do was mark time.

# CHAPTER FIVE

ALTHOUGH THE PICTURESQUE facade of Rancho Arroyo pleased the eye, it was the *inner* working of the small complex that threatened to be the undoing of Jan Warren. The new car dealership kept reneging on delivery of the promised van, offering instead vague excuses, and the bills for the rental limousine Jan was forced to use kept mounting. The air-conditioning unit in the main lodge had to be replaced, and, to add insult to injury, the main generator gave out, and though the backup unit functioned, it failed to do the job efficiently, to the guests' acute discomfort.

The swimming pool had been inactive for three days, and the guests were becoming hostile, threatening to leave at a moments' notice. Her pleas that the filtering system was being cleaned and water pressure was low fell on unforgiving ears. All the guests cared about was the 105-degree temperature and how were they to cool off with the air-conditioning working on a hit-or-miss basis. There was no longer any cash flow and the small savings account had dwindled alarmingly. Food was being bought sparingly and paid for just as sparingly. Benjie's hospital bills were mounting faster than she could count. She was being beaten before she started. There was no way she was going to run this ranch by herself.

Jan gathered the mail and retired to her office. Slumping down in the swivel chair, she swung her booted feet on top of the desk. Lord, she was tired— more tired than when she had been holding down two jobs with a house to clean and meals to cook. It must be the heat, she told herself, plus the fact that she wasn't sleeping well.

Wearily, she massaged her temples, willing the approaching headache to evaporate. She felt like crying. No, she wanted to throw a furious tantrum. She wanted to kick and yell and scream and break things, then to cry stormily and get it all out of her system. But she couldn't do that, now that she was an adult. A pity— she would have felt so much better.

Jan pulled a piece of stationery out of her desk drawer and began to scrawl off a note to Neil. As she wrote she wondered how she could so blithely lie about how things were here at the Rancho Arroyo. Lies, all lies, she told herself. Even if she hadn't come right out and said that things were marvelous and wonderful and that she was making money hand over fist and that she was certain to make a success of the business, she had lied by omission. Consciously, she had worded her letters so they skirted the issue. She hadn't told Neil that the minibus had broken down, she had instead led him to believe that she had ordered a new minibus because there was enough capital in the ranch's account and because of a whim.

While she told him of Delilah and Gus, she had done

it to describe their colorful characters. She hadn't told him that she was worried sick that her cook would stomp out and go over to the Golden Lasso and that nothing in this world—not even Gus—could bring her back again.

The taste of the glue on the back of the stamp was bitter. She applied it to the envelope and slammed her fist down on it. She'd prefer to die rather than tell Neil that she couldn't handle managing the ranch. That would be tantamount to admitting she was stupid, and she knew that Neil was not gentleman enough to refrain from saying "I told you so!"

Frowning, Jan told herself that she wasn't lying to Neil; she was merely dreaming aloud.

To Jan's weary mind and body it was inevitable that Derek Bannon should be entering her office. She didn't move but deliberately reached for a Coke bottle and took a long drink. Now what?

"I've come to make you another offer for this property," Bannon said, seating himself across the desk from Jan. His easy familiarity annoyed Jan. She took another gulp of the lukewarm soda and set the bottle down with a thump. "It's not for sale," she said curtly.

"Why?" The question sounded obscene to Jan's ears, and she momentarily saw red. How dare he come here and harass her like this? Who did he think he was?

"Because I said so. You look like a reasonably intelligent man, Mr. Bannon. Why do you refuse to accept my decision not to sell? Why are you harassing me like this? The ranch is not for sale, period."

"If you keep on like you've been going, you'll have

to file for bankruptcy soon. Is that what you want? I'm willing to pay you three times what this property is worth. You're being very foolish in rejecting my generous offer."

"Why? Why are you offering me three times what the ranch is worth?" Jan asked coolly. "Nobody throws away money like that—not even rich people. Tell me why you want this ranch so badly. Your club seems to be a thriving place and equal to Las Vegas, if one is to believe my guests. What could you possibly want with this little place?"

Derek Bannon ignored the pointed question. "Shortly before your uncle's death we were in serious negotiations concerning this ranch. He agreed to sell at my price. I feel that you should honor his decision," Derek said harshly.

"I have only your word for that, Mr. Bannon. No one around here seems to know anything about your negotiations other than that you were here trying to pressure a sick old man. If I knew in my heart that what you say is true, I would sell you this ranch, but since I don't know for sure, I can't do it. My uncle had a will drawn up leaving me this property. It seems to me if he had any intention of selling Rancho Arroyo to you, he would have changed his will."

"Your uncle was not a sick old man as you imply. He was a sharp, intelligent businessman, and, let me tell you, I met my match while we were discussing terms. He knew exactly what he was doing. Why he agreed to sell I don't know. The day before he died he called me at the club and made an appointment to see me the following afternoon to finalize the deal. As you know, he died shortly after awakening."

"It's a pig in a poke, Mr. Bannon. Proof. If you can give me proof, then I'll sell—not a minute before. Now if you'll excuse me, I'm rather busy."

"I can see that you're busy," Derek Bannon said mockingly, his white teeth gleaming against his bronzed tan. "I'm giving you until August first to take advantage of my offer and after that it's withdrawn. If you file for bankruptcy, you lose everything. Think about that before you make any rash decisions," Derek said, getting up from the chair. Before she knew what he was doing, he swept her feet off the desk and stood towering over her. "Ladies," he said coldly, "never sit with their feet on a desk."

"What you mean is Andrea would never sit with her feet on a desk," Jan said spitefully. Now why had she said that? Her cheeks flushed and she was very aware of Derek's mocking eyes as he strode from her office. "I'm taking Ben back to the club with me," he called over his shoulder.

She should stop him, say something to prevent the hold he had over the boy. But how could she deprive her brother of the one main pleasure he had—seeing the Bisons work out in the field belonging to the Golden Lasso? It rankled her that Benjie had taken to the muscular man and was now calling him Derek. What did they do over there for hours on end? She admitted that she was jealous of the man's attention to her little brother, wishing secretly that it was herself he was courting.

Benjie arrived home shortly after four in the afternoon in the company of Dusty Baker. From her position behind the desk in the lobby Jan watched as Dusty opened the car door and pushed the wheelchair as close as possible for Benjie to maneuver. He tousled Benjie's hair and then followed him into the lodge. Jan smiled as Benjie introduced the famous ball player.

"I've heard a lot about you," Dusty said, indicating Benjie, who was grinning from ear to ear. "This," he said, holding out a sealed envelope, "is your invitation to the Bisons' testimonial dinner. It's this evening at eight. Formal dress."

"I almost forgot," Jan apologized. "Thank you for reminding me."

"Don't thank me—thank Derek Bannon. He said he would have my scalp if I didn't deliver this when I brought Benjie home."

"Have you known Mr. Bannon long?" Jan asked pointedly.

"Sure have. He's a great guy. When his father died, he took over the club, and, let me tell you, he's one heck of an owner—just like his father. He never interferes with the managers, and when he does offer advice, he knows where he's coming from. This testimonial and vacation for the club is a treat for us. He picks up the tab once a year. I've gotta get back now. See you this evening. Hang tough, Benjie," he said, ruffling the little boy's hair a second time.

"I have to wear a shirt and tie—Andrea said so," Benjie said happily. "What are you going to wear?"

"Didn't Andrea tell you what I should wear?" Jan snapped irritably.

"No. Was she supposed to? She's wearing a dress that doesn't have straps and has a slit up the side. I saw her show it to Derek and he said it was…it was… sen-sensational. Do you have something that's sensational?"

"I'm afraid not, Benjie. There hasn't been much money lately to buy sensational clothes."

"That's what I told Derek," Benjie said offhandedly, maneuvering the chair through the lobby. "I'm going out to see how the work on the pool is coming."

Sensational, huh? Jan muttered as she ripped open the invitation. Hmm. According to the invitation, she and Benjie were to sit with Derek at his table. There was no mention of Gus or Andy, and yet Benjie was given four tickets. It made no difference, since neither Andy nor Gus expressed a desire to attend the festivities. She and Benjie would have to wing it on their own. At that moment she would have sold her soul to have a gorgeous dress to wear for the evening's entertainment. It was a night out—her first real one in over two years. It would be whatever she made it, good or bad. Clothes didn't necessarily make the person, but they sure helped.

How was she going to sit at a table with Derek Bannon and not show how uncomfortable he made her. She would blush like a schoolgirl every time she remembered how he held her, crushing his lips to hers. That heady, wonderful experience had made her aware that she was alive and that her adrenaline flowed like everyone else's. How? She just might be able to carry it off if Benjie chattered away all night long. A twenty-one-year-old woman depending on a nine-year-old to carry off an evening. It was a disgusting thing to want or even expect. "Well, Mr. Bannon, what you see is what you get," she muttered to the empty room. Hair! She had to do something about her hair, she thought wildly.

Jan checked the kitchen to be sure Delilah had everything under control. From there she checked out the work going on poolside and was reassured that by nightfall the filtering system would once again be operational and the pool ready for use by morning. She stood watching Gus give a group of youngsters a lesson in using a lasso. She whirled around in time to see a rather matronly looking woman slide off a horse into Andy's outstretched arms. For the moment everything was under control.

A long, luxurious bubble bath later, Jan stepped from the tub and wrapped herself in a bright lemon bath sheet. She squinted down at her feet and decided not only on a manicure but a pedicure as well. The creamy mulberry nail lacquer went on smoothly, pleasing the excited girl. She had to look her best in case she found herself next to the ravishing Andrea in her sensational dress. How could she ever hope to compare to someone as gorgeous as Andrea? "I can't," Jan said dejectedly, sitting down on the edge of the tub while she fanned her nails in the air.

Her nails dry, Jan went through her closet slowly and methodically, searching for something to wear. There wasn't a lot to choose from. When she had bought clothes in the past, she had bypassed all the frivolous evening wear in favor of tailored suits and dresses she could wear to work or, if the occasion warranted, dress up with a colorful scarf or belt. There were two long dresses that were on the serviceable if not outdated list. Thoughtfully, Jan pulled a black sheath with a high mandarin collar from the hanger. It was too plain and there was nothing to dress it up with. Certainly a belt would add nothing and the high collar couldn't take a scarf. She shrugged and slipped into the dress and stood staring at her reflection. Maybe when she had her makeup on it would look better. Before she could change her mind she reached down and ripped the side seam of the gown to above the knee. A little flash of leg never hurt anyone. She had good legs—why not show them? Quickly, she threaded a needle and stitched up the seams so the frayed edges wouldn't show. Again she walked to the mirror and moved this way and that. It still needed something. Whatever it was, she didn't have it, so she would have to be content with the dress the way it was.

Jan slid her feet into wispy black sandals with spiked heels and immediately felt dressed. She toiled painstakingly over her makeup, diligently trying to cover the freckles across the bridge of her nose. Her attempt was less than successful. Well, she had tried—what more could she do? Derek Bannon probably wouldn't even notice her—especially with Andrea around.

Jan transferred the contents of her shoulder bag into a slim black envelope of a purse and left the room to wait in the lobby for Benjie. She hoped Gus had made him clean his ears. How good it was to see Gus take over the personal care of the little boy. Derek Bannon was right again. Benjie seemed to be thriving with all the male attention he was getting—especially from Gus.

Jan whistled playfully when Gus pushed the chair into the lobby. Benjie grinned. "You look… sensational, doesn't she, Gus?" The old Indian grinned and nodded, showing strong white teeth. Delilah took that moment to pass through the lobby and inspect them.

"You need something," she said, tilting her head to the side like a bright, precocious squirrel. "You wait, I get." She was back moments later with a heavy silver and turquoise pendant. "White Antelope, Gus's great-grandfather give to him. Is made for woman of beauty." Before Jan could say a word, Delilah had the heavy silver chain around her neck. Gus nodded his approval while Delilah beamed her pleasure.

"It's gorgeous, Delilah, and just what the dress needed. Now I feel dressed."

Delilah laughed. "Is good—you make Mr. Bannon itch much. But," she said, wagging a plump finger in the air, "you no let him scratch. You understand what I say."

"I understand, Delilah." Jan laughed. "Gus, you are driving us in the rented limo, aren't you? If we show up in the pickup, I'm afraid we'll be shown the back door. Gus certainly isn't big on words, is he?" Jan whispered over her shoulder to Delilah.

"Not many words, no. He do other things good," Delilah said, closing the lobby doors behind them.

Aside from the day she had flown down the road and circled back around to the Golden Lasso's kitchens to retrieve Delilah, Jan had never really seen Derek's glittering establishment. She'd heard reports of its elegance from the guests staying at the Rancho who had gone for dinner at the Lasso, but nothing anyone said prepared her for what she found.

Even the tarmac in the parking lot glittered with iridescent chips of vermiculite and that twinkled under the old-fashioned lamps like stars. There was a flavor of the Old West that was defined in the lighting and split-rail fences that were painted white. It was almost like taking a step backward into the past, but instead of wagon wheels, old ox harnesses, and bleached bone steers' skulls that one expected to find, the Golden Lasso had such ornate and antique decorations that would have been quite at home even in the sophisticated society of a city like San Francisco. There was nothing of the Old Frontier here. Instead, it was a shrine to the Victorian era, complete with gaslights and overembellished furnishings of dark mahogany and trappings of rich turkey red. While the decor could have easily become overdone and gauche, it was a marvel of good taste.

The floor of the main dining hall, except for the dance area, was carpeted in thick, Oriental-style carpeting of reds and blacks and golds. The tables were covered with lace cloths and the chairs were upholstered in a dark red tapestry. Mirrors—hundreds of them, all framed in gilt—reflected the massive chandelier hung in the center of the room, and its crystal lights danced over the silver bowls filled with roses.

Benjie seemed oblivious to all this elegance, and Jan supposed it was because of his frequent visits. She noticed that the main dining hall opened onto several

small rooms, all decorated on the theme of the elegant
Pullman cars that had carried passengers from the East
into the world of the New Frontier. Each room was
narrow, and the tables nestled against the walls, which
were hung with rich brocades. Even the lights hung
along the walls were gimbaled, making one almost
think they could swing gently with the rocking of the
train. The ceilings were paneled in gleaming dark wood,
and at the far end of each "dining car" was a glass-and-
mirrored bar.

"This is really something, Benjie." Jan let out her
breath in a silent whistle.

"Yeah. Didn't I tell you?"

"No, as a matter of fact, you didn't." Jan frowned,
wondering what else Benjie had failed to mention.

"Well, if you think this is something, you should see
Derek's apartment. Wow!"

"I didn't know you'd been to Derek's apartment. I
thought you just came here to watch the Bisons practice
on the back field."

"Yeah, I do that, too. But the day Derek wanted me
to meet Andrea he took me into their apartment. I got
to really look around because Andrea was in the shower
and we had to wait for her," Benjie said with all the in-
nocence of a nine-year-old.

Jan looked at Benjie sharply. He had said "their
apartment" and that Andrea was taking a shower. The
statement seemed to throw her off balance. In spite of
the fact that Derek and Andrea were engaged to be
married, she hadn't thought of them as living together.
This new realization struck a nerve in Jan, and she felt

herself blushing. Derek and Andrea could do whatever they wanted and it didn't mean anything to her, but when she thought of his arms around her and his mouth on hers, she died a little inside. What a fool she was, and what a bounder Derek was. He had committed himself totally to Andrea, and yet he wanted to play his little games with Jan. Fool, fool, she cursed herself. And you let him do it, and, more to your stupidity, you loved it.

"Hey, Dusty!" Benjie called to the tall, well-built man across the room who was motioning for them to join him at his table. "Come on, Jan. There's Dusty. We're going to be sitting with him at Derek's table."

Jan's feet moved like lead weights across the floor. The last thing in this world she wanted was to be here, in the Golden Lasso, about to sit down to a night's celebration with Derek Bannon and Andrea. Benjie maneuvered his chair over to the table where Dusty Baker waited and pulled up to the space where a place had been set minus a chair.

"Hi, remember me? I'm Dusty Baker." He extended a beefy hand that swallowed Jan's. "As I said earlier, I've heard a lot about you, Miss Warren, and all of it's good. Ben knows how lucky he is to have you for a sister. Isn't that right, Ben?" He smiled affectionately at the boy.

"You bet, Dusty. Where's Derek?"

"Oh, he's seeing to some last-minute details. It's still early—he and Andrea will be here soon." Dusty held a chair and waited for Jan to seat herself. Then he walked around to the other side of the table and sat down.

"Is this your first visit to the Golden Lasso, Miss Warren?" Dusty asked as he stirred the ice in his glass.

"Please call me Jan. And yes—I've never been here before. It's really something."

"It sure is. Andrea had a lot to do with it. She's an interior decorator, and she's outdone herself with the Lasso. It's been covered in quite a number of magazines, but I don't suppose you're the kind of girl who reads those kinds of books."

Jan blushed. It was obvious that the kind of magazines he was referring to were the girlie magazines that depicted nude women. Also, there was something about the way he mentioned Andrea. With a kind of proprietorial pride that denoted something more than a casual friendship. Dusty turned to motion to the waiter and Jan suddenly recognized his broad shoulders and the set of his head and immediately knew that Dusty Baker was the man on the plane who had joked and quipped with Andrea and made a date for a drink. As much as Jan was inclined to like the football player, she wondered what kind of man would try to make a date with his friend's fiancée. What kind of people were these who had no respect for friendship and loyalty and faithfulness? Even Derek—about to be married to Andrea—had made advances in Jan's direction. And gullible little fool that she was, she had allowed it.

Dusty ordered a drink for Jan and turned his attention back to Benjie, who preened with delight. Jan decided that whatever else she thought about these people, they certainly were kind to Ben, and that should redeem them at least a little bit.

The dining room began to fill and every so often Benjie would wave across the room at another of the Bisons. As he did, Dusty told Jan their names. Many of the players were accompanied by their wives and children, and Jan saw that many of the boys around Benjie's age waved their greetings.

"Pretty soon Ben will be out there with the other kids, running and swimming, won't you, Ben?" Dusty asked.

"You betcha! Dr. Rossi says I'm coming along real fine. Isn't that right, Jan?"

"That's what the word is, Benjie. But there's still a lot of hard work ahead of you."

Dusty turned to greet someone, and Benjie pulled on Jan's hand, making her lean over to hear him whisper.

"Jan, just for tonight, couldn't you call me Ben? I don't want everybody to think I'm still a baby."

Jan was almost speechless. Derek Bannon's influence over her brother was becoming insufferable. But when she looked into Benjie's eyes, she saw that this was very important to him. "All right, Ben," she whispered in return, "but I'm warning you—every time I have you alone, I'll still call you Benjie."

"Aw, Jan, that's okay for when we're alone. But not when there's somebody around, okay?" he pleaded.

"Okay," she assured him, "but don't blame me if I forget once in a while. You've been my little brother Benjie for a lot of years."

Dusty Baker rose to his feet and turned toward the entrance to the dining room. Andrea walked across the room, and, just as Benjie had predicted, her dress was sensational. A long, sleek, shimmering red that was slit from the hem practically up to her waist. It outlined every curve and line of her body, and the strapless bodice accented the smooth, flawless skin on her shoulders. The only jewelry Andrea wore was long, dangling earrings, which Jan supposed were real diamonds. Everything else about Andrea appeared to be real—why not her jewelry? Jan sighed to herself.

"Ms. Warren, this is Andrea…"

"We've met," Jan interjected hastily. She couldn't bear to hear Dusty Baker say "Derek's fiancée."

Feeling awkward and out of date in her black sheath gown, Jan accepted Andrea's welcome through stiff lips. Although Andrea's attitude seemed friendly enough, Jan couldn't seem to bring herself past the green-eyed monster to accept Andrea as a friend.

"Can you sit down with us now, honey?" Jan heard Dusty say to Andrea, and immediately she bristled at the familiarity of his tone and the pet name he used.

"I think I've done everything that needed doing." Andrea sighed wearily. "These affairs take more out of me than you could know, Dusty. Derek is settling some disagreement in the kitchen. He'll join us shortly. That is, if the chef doesn't quit and he has to broil the steaks himself." Andrea laughed, Jan supposed, at the vision of Derek, complete in chef's hat, bustling about the kitchen. Jan saw the way the girl touched the sleeve of Dusty's jacket and the way her fingers lingered there just a little too long. There was definitely more to this relationship than met the eye.

Andrea began talking to Benjie and offered him the dish of celery sticks and olives that the waiter had deposited on their table. Jan was suddenly jealous of the easy repartee Andrea had with Benjie, and she even thought she saw Benjie blush under the lovely girl's attentions.

"You know, I've always wanted a little brother," Andrea told Benjie. "Big brothers can sometimes be a pain in the neck. They're always telling you what you can and can't do and when to do it."

Benjie laughed. "Jan's not like that—she's the best sister a guy could have. She lets me be my own man, don't you, Jan?"

Looking at Benjie with a wide-eyed amazement, Jan managed to force a smile. His own man indeed!

Jan reached for a large black olive and clumsily dropped it onto the table and watched as it rolled across the cloth onto her lap. "Lose something, Miss Warren?" Derek had come upon her so unexpectedly that Jan nearly toppled her drink.

Muttering some inane remark, Jan found the olive in the folds of her skirt and dropped it into the ashtray. She knew her face was red and that her hand trembled when she picked up her glass.

"I'm glad you brought Ben tonight," Derek said conversationally.

Jan nodded. He was glad she brought Ben—not he was glad *she* had come. As Derek moved to take the chair beside her, Jan concentrated on sipping her drink. At all costs she wanted to disguise the fact that every fiber of her being was totally conscious of his presence. She picked up the faint aroma of his aftershave and the sleeve of his tuxedo jacket brushed her shoulder as he sat down. She saw his hand, sun bronzed and masculine, against the white lace of the tablecloth. Her emotions rushed away with her, and once again she was alone with him on the desert and those capable-looking hands were in her hair and on her back, holding her close, pressing her against his magnificent length. The scent of his aftershave came to her on a wave of remembered desire as it filled her senses and she remembered the taste of his lips on hers. Stop it! her mind screamed. You can't do this to yourself! There he is, right now, this minute, joking with the girl he's going to marry. But if he really loved Andrea, her heart whispered, would he have kissed you that way?

Before she was faced with answering her own question, soft music began playing from the violin of the strolling musician and the waiters were carrying in the trays of shrimp cocktail, which signaled the beginning of the meal.

Dinner was excellent and the table conversation exceedingly pleasant. In spite of herself, Jan relaxed and found she was enjoying every minute of the evening. Benjie—or Ben, as he now preferred to be called in public—was on his best behavior, and Jan was proud that she had instilled in the boy a good amount of table manners. Derek, especially, was particularly attentive to Benjie and herself, and no mention was made of his offer to buy the Rancho, for which Jan was grateful. Even Andrea was gracious and didn't seem to mind the attention Derek was paying to Benjie and herself. But when Jan dropped her napkin and bent to retrieve it, she understood why. Beneath the cover of the lacy cloth, Dusty and Andrea were holding hands! Right there under Derek's eyes! Practically.

After her discovery of Andrea's fickleness, Jan found it increasingly difficult to be more than barely polite. After several tries, Andrea ignored Jan altogether, behaving as though she wasn't even there. It was to the men at the table that Andrea directed her attentions, and it wasn't long before all three of them, Benjie included, were eating right out of her hand.

After dinner the Bison players assembled at the long table at the head of the room, where a podium and microphones were already set up. The testimonials were gracious and even amusing, and Benjie listened and applauded and laughed at inside jokes that Jan couldn't begin to fathom. But Benjie was enjoying himself and that was all that mattered.

When Dusty Baker stepped up to the podium to receive his award, Andrea clapped long and hard. Stealing a glance at Derek, Jan noticed that he didn't seem to mind at all that his fiancée seemed to be the man's biggest fan. Finally, unable to bear another moment of the duplicity of Derek and Andrea, she asked to be excused for a breath of fresh air. Without waiting for an answer from either Derek or Andrea, Jan stood from the table and walked across the crowded room to the doors she knew led to the garden. As she left, she was aware of Derek's glance piercing her back.

Like the parking lot, the garden was lit by tall, romantic gaslights, illuminating the paths and shrubbery in a warm, yellow glow. Shadows were accentuated and the pathways shimmered with metallic chips. Everything about Derek's Lasso was indeed golden.

At a sound behind her, Jan turned on her heel and for some reason wasn't surprised to see that Derek had followed her.

"Must you always come creeping up on me?" she demanded.

"Must you always walk around in a daze, Jan?" he replied.

"Lately, it seems as though every time I turn around, there you are," she said hotly. "Why don't you go back inside and join Andrea? She must be wondering where you've gone."

"Andrea can take care of herself. Besides, she has Dusty for company, not to mention Ben." His tone was offhanded and his mouth twisted into a wry smile.

What kind of man was he? How could he speak so offhandedly about Andrea being with Dusty Baker, and what was he doing out here in the garden with her. If he cared so little about the girl he was engaged to marry, Jan knew that he would care even less for her. She straightened her back and squared her shoulders.

"I came out here to get away from the crowd and for a breath of fresh air. And you, Mr. Bannon, are creating a crowd out here in the garden, and whenever you're around I find that the air is anything but fresh." Her tone was haughty, her eyes cold and disapproving, but it seemed that nothing she could say would daunt Mr. Derek Bannon.

Derek's eyes narrowed, and in one step he was against her, holding her fast to his lean, hard body. His lips were hot and wine scented as they pressed against hers. She could feel her lips part beneath his as she struggled to free herself, as though fighting for her life. Derek held her closer, enveloping her within the strong fold of his arms.

Weakened by conflicting emotions, Jan ceased her struggles. Derek's answer was a renewed ardor as he held her and pressed long, passionate kisses to her mouth. She felt his hands on her hair, on her breasts, on the small of her back, and reaching lower.

Resistance lost, she felt herself melt into him as though becoming a part of him. Her arms reached around his neck, her mouth was pliant and yielding to his. A spectrum of newfound desires coursed through her body as she clung to him, offering herself to his caresses, submitting herself to his demands.

Suddenly, violently, she fought his advances. What was wrong with her, submitting to Derek Bannon this way? If *he* couldn't remember that he was engaged to Andrea, *she* could!

Jan lashed out blindly, her hands beating at his broad chest and reaching for his mocking face. Fury inflamed her cheeks and shame and humiliation at what she had allowed to happen brought hot tears to her eyes.

"You devil!" she shouted. "Keep your hands off me!" She lashed out again, aiming for the cold blue eyes that seemed to burn through her, turning her veins to ice.

Derek sidestepped her flailing arm, caught it by the wrist, and pulled her against him, holding her there in his iron grip.

All the weariness of the past weeks overcame her.

Dry, wracking sobs of frustration caught in her throat. She was the vanquished, he the victor. Let him do with her what he would, then just leave her alone to crawl somewhere to hide.

Closely pressed against her, he held her; Jan's lips were burning from his kisses and an involuntary trembling took hold of her. Through their light clothing, she could feel the massive muscular strength of him as he molded her body to his.

Feeling his lips part from her, Jan opened her eyes and could read the desire in his. His caresses became more intimate, and again Jan surrendered herself as though all her energy was anticipating a most unexpected pleasure.

Abruptly, he pushed her away from him with such a force her teeth rattled. His eyes avoided hers; the pain of rejection pricked her eyelids. In a gruff voice he commanded, "Go home, Jan." Silently, he turned and stalked away from her.

Humiliation swallowed her and a bitterness rose to her throat. He had used her, and she, heaven help her, had helped him—enjoyed it, loved it! And now he was through with her as though she were a cast-off shoe.

Oh, how I hate him! she cried silently. I hate him! But, realizing the truth for what it was, she sobbed, "Heaven help me, I love him. I love him!"

# CHAPTER SIX

JAN REFUSED to glance in the mirror the morning after the testimonial dinner for the Bisons. How could she have made such a fool of herself? How could she have allowed herself to be drawn into Derek Bannon's arms and enjoy it? Gus must have thought her a raving idiot when she had run across the parking lot to where he waited in the rented limo and tearfully choked out the order to get Benjie out of the dining room; they were going home!

Why did Derek Bannon have this invisible hold over her? What was there about the man that made her heart pound and her senses reel? She had been in the presence of other men who were almost as handsome as Derek. Good looks and fancy clothes didn't account for the way he made her feel. She thought to herself, I can't be in love with him! I don't want to be in love with him! "I can't handle this," she cried in a broken voice. I have to see to Benjie and the Rancho, and I don't need all this emotional turmoil in my life—especially not now.

She looked around the room wildly, as though hoping some answer was going to leap out from the four walls and make everything all right. It was a new day; she had to get on with everyday living and not think about Derek Bannon and how he made her feel. It was an impossible order, and she recognized it for what it was. She could no more stop thinking about Derek than she could stop breathing.

He had given her till August 1 to decide about selling Rancho Arroyo. He was right about one thing; it would be better to sell the ranch than to file for bankruptcy and lose everything. And that was where she was headed eventually. The bills would mount and the ranch would be sold to cover the bills. And one thing was certain— on the open market, with her back to the wall, she wouldn't get half what Derek was offering for the ranch.

If she sold the ranch now, she could bank the money for Benjie's education and go back to New York to the big old house. Big old house. Maybe the bank would give her a loan if she put up the house as collateral. Aha! Derek Bannon didn't know about the house back East. How long did it take to get a loan? If she went to the bank today, she could at least set the wheels in motion. All the papers from her parents' estate were in a manila envelope in the office safe. She would take everything with her and hope the bank would realize what a valuable property she held title to. If it took only two or three weeks, she felt confident that she could stall off the creditors for at least that long. However, she thought morbidly, perhaps that would be a mistake. If guests kept canceling their reservations and moving over to the Golden Lasso, she would be pouring money down the drain.

If there was only someone to talk to, to go to for advice, to confide in. There was no one. She had only herself to depend on. Perhaps the banker would help her. If she was lucky, the loan officer might be able to advise her.

Three hours later, Jan exited the bank feeling more morose than when she had entered. While friendly and helpful, the loan officer had not been overenthusiastic about making her a loan. He used words like sizeable and pointed out that she was a novice to this sort of business and that there was the competition of the Golden Lasso to consider. His voice had dropped a degree when he said that appraisal took several weeks and one simply did not hurry a bank. Everything in good time. He would call, he told Jan, when he saw tears trickle down her cheeks. "If he had just patted me on the head, I would have felt better," Jan mumbled as she hailed a cab to take her out to the medical center.

Dr. Rossi's youth and exuberance were evident when he told her of the progress Benjie was making in his physical therapy. "Dusty Baker and Derek Bannon have had a great deal to do with that progress. You have those men to thank for Ben's positive attitude, Miss Warren. And, of course, your own patience and work in helping Ben perform his daily exercises."

Jan bristled. If there was one thing she didn't need right now, it was another Derek Bannon fan.

"Ben thinks a great deal of Derek," Dr. Rossi went on to say. "With his encouragement, I predict that Ben will be walking very soon."

"Dr. Rossi, I'm so happy! That's fantastic news! I'm so grateful. I had no idea things would progress so quickly." Jan smiled. Benjie's happiness depended upon his walking again, and anything that made Benjie happy was good for her, too.

"A positive attitude and hope are something we here

at the medical center never discount. As a matter of fact, we depend on them. I just wish all our patients responded as well as Ben."

Outside his office, Dr. Rossi's receptionist told Jan that the billing office would like her to stop by and see them. Jan smiled nervously and stepped out into the corridor. She didn't know if she was happy or sad. Certainly happy that Benjie was doing so remarkably well, but sad that she had to see about paying the bill. Would they refuse to treat Benjie once they discovered that she couldn't meet the full responsibility of the bill? There was no decision to be made. If it came down to Benjie, she would sell the Rancho to Derek Bannon if the bank refused to give her a loan. She wouldn't lose sight of the fact that Benjie came first.

Surprisingly, the woman who was in charge of the billing office understood her problem and worked on it accordingly. "It's not the center's policy to deny help to those who can't afford to pay. We have a very wealthy patron here in Phoenix who donates often and handsomely. You can pay when you're able, Miss Warren. Just fill out this pledge form. Actually—" the woman smiled "—it's not even a pledge. Mr. Bannon said it was important for people to feel that they weren't charity cases. And do you know, he's right?" The woman beamed. "Even several years after treatment, many of our patients continue to pay on their bills. Even if it's small amounts at first. So everyone benefits from Derek Bannon's generosity—the clinic and the new patients."

Jan left the credit office in a daze. Derek Bannon certainly was an enigma. No two people saw him in the same light. How could a kind, wonderful, generous person as the woman in the credit office described set out to ruin a poor girl from New York who only wanted to set the Rancho on a paying basis to support her brother and herself? And how could such a philanthropic, humane man stand in the wings like a vulture waiting for her to go bankrupt so he could snatch up her property?

A quick glance at her watch told her it was almost noon and time for lunch. She looked around for a suitable restaurant, but the only thing in sight was a cocktail lounge that had a sign proclaiming they served businessmen lunches. Why not? The next bus back to the ranch wouldn't leave till two-fifteen, so she had plenty of time. Jan decided to treat herself.

"A vodka and tonic. And I think I'll have a Waldorf salad," she said bravely to the waitress. She hated eating alone, and when the occasion came up, she never ordered a drink, thinking all eyes were on a solitary woman eating and drinking by herself. For the moment she felt the need of the artificial stimulation to get her mind in gear again. Why did Derek Bannon always toss her a curve? Just when she thought she had him figured out, he did something to confuse her and make himself look like the proverbial knight in shining armor.

"Drinking alone, Miss Warren?" a cool voice demanded. Jan almost choked on the liquid in her mouth. Maybe if she ignored him he would go away. But men like Derek Bannon never went away. It was impossible to ignore such a masculine presence. Setting her glass down with expert precision, she stared at the man who was seating himself opposite her.

"Permit me to recommend the baked sole." Jan said nothing. "Have you given my offer any more thought?" Derek Bannon asked quietly.

"Yes." She deliberately avoided saying more.

"What's your decision?"

"I haven't decided. You said August first. I'll give you my decision then." Their eyes locked, and it was Jan who flushed and lowered her gaze, remembering how his eyes had softened as he stared into hers right before she melted into his arms. Was he remembering, too?

"I meant it when I said I would withdraw the offer at that time," Derek said coolly.

"I'm sure you did. Your offer was more than generous. Why can't you understand how important it is for me to keep the ranch? I have to try to make a go of it. You can't possibly need it. You appear to be very wealthy, and your club must be making you a handsome profit. My ranch isn't an eyesore that would offend your guests, so if you would level with me, I might be more amenable to your request. Wanting something just for the sake of wanting it is not reason enough. You might have been born with a silver spoon but I wasn't. I've worked since I was sixteen, and for the past two years I've held down two jobs, seven days a week, to be sure Benjie got the best I could give him. This, Mr. Bannon, is my best, and I can't let you take it from us. No, that's not right—I *won't* let you take it from us. If you'll excuse me, I have to get back to the bus station."

Derek Bannon stared at the tight-lipped girl who

was sliding out of the booth. "I'm going back to the Lasso. If you want a ride, you're welcome to come with me."

Jan ignored him as she laid some bills on the table and paid for her uneaten meal. There was no way she could handle the ride back to the ranch sitting next to Derek Bannon. Right now it was all she could do to hold the threatening tears in check. She was through the revolving door and hailing a cab before Derek could get out of the booth. "And I'll bet that's the first time one of your women ever refused you anything," she muttered to herself.

Jan's bus was already boarding when she climbed from the cab. Derek Bannon wheeled his sports car in front of the bus and came to a screeching halt. Jan didn't look in his direction but immediately took her place in line.

"This is ridiculous. I'm going right by the ranch. If you take this bus, you have to walk from the highway to Rancho Arroyo. Stop being so silly and come with me," Derek said, taking her possessively by the arm. Jan pulled away, his touch, like a firebrand, scalding her bare arm.

"I'm taking this bus. I came on the bus and I'm going home on the bus. It's not my fault that you don't understand the word no. No, Mr. Bannon, I do not want a ride home. And," she said tartly, "you can just come by the Rancho and pick up that cat you had the gall to send me."

"Is this man bothering you, miss?" the bus driver demanded gruffly.

"He certainly is. He tried to pick me up in a coc— restaurant."

"Beat it, buddy, and leave the young ladies alone or I'll have to call a policeman. You good-looking play-boys are all alike. You see a pretty face and you think all you have to do is move in. Take that fancy rig of yours out of here right now so I can get this bus mov-ing."

Jan was delighted at the look of acute discomfort on Derek's face. Two put-downs in the space of five min-utes. She smiled winningly and waved a jaunty salute. She shuddered at Derek's cold, unreadable face. He looked as though he wanted to murder someone. Serves him right, Jan thought as she leaned back in her seat.

When Jan left the bus on the highway, she almost expected to see Derek waiting for her, and she was dis-appointed that he wasn't. The heat was unbearable and before she was halfway home she wished she had ac-cepted his offer. Her sandal straps were rubbing, and she knew she would have king-size blisters the moment she removed her shoes. She could feel her makeup run, and she knew her hair was wet and tangled, hanging limply to her head. She didn't know when she had ever felt so miserable.

When Jan hobbled up the flagstone walkway leading to the kitchen, she thought she was going to faint. Delilah clucked over her like a mother hen, bathing her face in cool water and then wrapping her blistered feet in an herb-scented cloth. A frosty glass of lemonade was placed in her hand to be refilled twice. "Where's that weird cat that came in the mail?" Jan demanded petulantly.

"Not one cat anymore. Nine cats now," Delilah said, pointing to a spot near the open-hearth fireplace in the gigantic kitchen.

"Remarkable," Jan said through clenched teeth. "He's sadistic, Delilah. Do you have any idea how much it's going to cost to feed nine cats?" Delilah shook her head mournfully. "A lot, a fortune. I can't afford it. Tomorrow I'm mailing them back to him C.O.D."

"You much mad at Mr. Bannon?" Delilah inquired, a frown on her face. "You much mad because he kiss you or because he no kiss you? He kiss good, no?"

"He kiss good, yes," Jan giggled. "Too good."

Delilah waddled over to the stove. "Much good kiss, so you send back cats. Not good sense," she muttered as she stirred a bubbling pot on the stove.

## CHAPTER SEVEN

As ALWAYS, after being in Derek Bannon's company, Jan felt inadequate. This was the third time he had reduced her to a mass of Silly Putty. She must be doing something wrong. It wasn't her fault she didn't know how to act around people like Derek and the beautiful Andrea. She admitted that she hated the word *homespun,* but that's exactly what she was—a down-home country girl. And while she hadn't just dropped off the watermelon truck, she was incapable of playing in Derek Bannon's league.

And on top of that was the niggling suspicion of why Bannon wanted her property. What possible use could he make of it? Why wouldn't he say why he wanted it?

Somehow Jan managed to work her way through the day without any mishaps of any kind. Things were running smoothly for a change and she wanted to enjoy the calm atmosphere, if not to revel in it. Derek Bannon was the stuff dreams were made of and that's where she would relegate him in her mind. She would allow herself the luxury of thinking of him only when she drifted off to sleep. If she allowed him to get under her skin, she couldn't function. Delilah was right—he made her itch.

The day's work behind her, Jan watered the tubs of flowers around the pool and then sat down to relax with a cold glass of ginger ale. She felt good, knowing she had worked a full day and somehow managed to cope and make everyone happy. She deserved this brief respite before putting Benjie to bed.

Delilah seemed always to be the bearer of bad tidings, and this time was no different. Jan watched her approach the pool area, her bright eyes searching out Jan in the dim lantern light. "Bad news," she said matter of factly. "Andy break leg here, here and here. Three places," she said, holding up three plump fingers. "I call ambulance."

"What?" Jan exclaimed, jumping up from the chaise longue. "How… Never mind." If there was one thing she didn't need, it was one of Delilah's explanations. "Where is he?"

"On floor in bunkhouse. He dreaming and fall out. Simple."

Jan was sure Delilah was right. Anything more would have been too confusing. Now what was she going to do?

"Andy, are you all right?" she asked, bending over the lanky man.

"Yeah, I'm okay, but the leg is busted in three places—at least, that's what Delilah said. I'm embarrassed," he said, gritting his teeth in pain. "I don't know how it happened. One minute I was asleep dreaming about all those lovelies over at the Golden Lasso and *wham,* I was falling out of the bunk. I tried to grab the rail and that's all I remember."

"Delilah called for the ambulance. It's on the way. Here, let me put a pillow under your head. Do you want me to have Gus ride along with you to the hospital?"

"I'd appreciate that, Jan. Listen, do you think you

could do me a favor and not…what I mean is, people might think…"

Jan grinned. "I'll tell them you did it in the line of duty. Don't worry about it. Do you think some brandy might ease the pain? I'm afraid to give you anything else."

"I get," Delilah said, waddling off to fetch the brandy.

"Did Delilah check your leg?"

"Are you kidding? She just looked at it and then went, '*Tsk, tsk, tsk,* is broke, three places.' When she says something, you can count on it."

"Amazing," Jan said, shaking her head.

"That she is. Your uncle regarded her as a real treasure."

The brandy arrived at the same time the ambulance did. The attendants vetoed the brandy, to Delilah's annoyance. She fixed her shoe-button eyes on the youngest attendant and said, "You stupid—brandy make him sweat. Where you learn medicine, Sears Roebuck? *Tsk, tsk, tsk,*" she muttered as she downed the fiery liquid and waddled back to the kitchen.

The young attendant looked at Jan and shook his head. "His leg is broken in three places—please be careful," Jan pleaded.

"How do you know his leg is broken in three places?" the older man asked.

"I just know." Not for the world would she admit that she was taking Delilah's word for the three breaks in Andy's leg.

Andy winked at her; he wasn't about to tell them either. His look clearly stated, "Why shake up medical science?"

By the time she checked on Benjie and found him propped up in bed with a Hardy Boys book, she was bone tired. She felt a tug at her heart as she looked at the little boy. How game he was; he never complained and he always had a smile for her. He looked wan and tired, though.

"Benjie, how do you feel?"

"I feel tired, but it's a good tired. Dr. Rossi and Derek say so. Dr. Rossi said I was making… re-remarkable progress and Derek said he was proud of me. Dusty Baker said so, too. You shouldn't worry about me, Jan— the guys are taking good care of me. Aren't they the greatest?" he asked happily.

Jan nodded. "If they're making you happy, then, yes, they're the greatest," she said, bending over him to give him a good-night kiss. "Ten minutes and lights out. Tomorrow is another day."

"Jan, would you like to go on a picnic to Rattlesnake Canyon with me and Derek. He said it was okay if you came along as long as you brought the food."

A sharp retort rose to her lips but Jan squelched it. "I'll think about it. Remember, ten minutes. Good-night, Benjie."

"'Night, Jan," Benjie mumbled as he joined the adventuresome Hardy Boys in one of their wild escapades.

What kind of left-handed invitation was that? You can come along if you bring the food. She dutifully answered Neil's letter, the thought of the picnic continually on her mind. *Humph,* she sniffed as she got ready for bed. She was planning the menu as she drifted off to sleep.

The digital clock on the night table read 3:18 a.m. when she heard Benjie cry out. She lay quietly, waiting to see if the sound was repeated. It had been a long time since he had had nightmares. He wasn't crying; he was groaning when she reached his room and flicked on the light switch. "What's wrong?" she asked anxiously.

"My legs. They're all cramped up," Benjie cried. "They hurt, Jan. Make it go away!"

"I'll call Dr. Rossi. Do you want me to get Gus to come and stay with you while I make the call?"

"Gus went to the hospital with Andy and they aren't back yet." Benjie groaned. "Please, Jan, do something…" His words were stopped by the effort to grit his teeth and bear the pain.

Jan ran into her room and called the hospital only to find out that Dr. Rossi had left for Tucson late that afternoon and wouldn't be back in his office until late the next day. Since it was an emergency, they would try to reach him and have him call her back.

"Jan, get Derek. He'll know what to do," Benjie pleaded. "He stays in the therapy room while I have my treatments."

"But, Benjie, Derek isn't a doctor…"

"I want Derek," Benjie said, crying now, tears streaming down his cheeks. "Please, Jan, please get him."

"Okay, okay, honey, I'll call him. I'll be right back." Jan raced down to the first floor and pounded on Delilah's door, waking her and instructing her to go to Benjie while she made the call.

The main switchboard at the Golden Lasso answered

and rang Derek Bannon's apartment suite. The line was busy. Trying to control her panic, Jan asked them to please break into the line. It was an emergency with Ben Warren down at the Rancho Arroyo. The young man at the switchboard was sympathetic and came back on the line.

"I'm terribly sorry, but the phone must be off the hook. If I can reach someone, I'll have them go over to Mr. Bannon's apartment. You do understand that I can't leave the desk."

Jan slammed down the receiver. She would have to go to the Lasso and get Derek herself. She would have to use the pickup truck; the rented limo had been returned that afternoon. Taken back, actually—she forced herself to face reality.

Jan ground the gears in the old pickup as she raced up the road. She would bring Derek Bannon back to the Rancho if she had to drag him out of bed. Benjie had said something about his private apartment being somewhere near the tennis courts.

Halfway to the Golden Lasso, the pickup coughed and sputtered, and before she had gone another five hundred feet, it died altogether. Jan shifted into Neutral and turned the key. Nothing. Twice more she tried. Again nothing. Climbing out from the truck, she slammed the door shut with a vengeance. Darn old dilapidated, confounded machine! Nothing worked. Nothing!

Now what was she to do? She was already halfway to the Lasso—turning back now would be foolish. She had to go on ahead. The night was chilly, as always in the desert. Her Western boots rubbed against the unhealed blisters. She had hurriedly pulled them on but hadn't taken the time to search for socks. At that moment she would have cheerfully given her back teeth for a skateboard.

By the time she reached the cobblestoned driveway to the Golden Lasso, she was perspiring with the effort of the walk. Her hair hung in limp strands about her ashy face. Her silk pajamas, emblazoned with green turtles, was plastered to her body, and she was limping from a bruise on the bottom of her sore foot. The thin robe that matched her pajamas flapped about her like bat wings. Somewhere along the way she had lost the belt. She wanted to cry, but she couldn't afford the luxury. Instead, she sniffed, wiped at her mouth, and headed for the rear of the Golden Lasso. If she couldn't find Derek's apartment immediately, she would scream to raise the dead. Someone would come running. She hoped.

Jan found the tennis courts and looked about for what might look like private apartments. Someone was up—there was a light in the window to the left of the courts. She squared her shoulders and marched over to the door and rapped on it sharply. Andrea, clad in a wispy affair of black lace, stood framed in the doorway, her eyebrows arched in amusement. "Jan, what are you doing here at this hour?"

Licking her lips and swallowing hard, Jan replied, "I'm looking for Derek…Mr. Bannon. Is he here? I must see him—it's very important. It's about Benjie…Ben. It's important." No one should look that beautiful at four in the morning. Jan knew she was going to cry.

Sensing her desperation, Andrea opened the door

wider and ushered Jan into the living room. "I'll go get Derek. I'll be right back. Can I get you something, Jan? Water?"

Wordlessly, Jan nodded her head. Her mouth was so dry and parched, her tongue was thick and sticking to the roof of her mouth.

Andrea brought her a tall glass of iced water and said she would go get Derek. Impatiently, Jan paced the apartment, oblivious to its elegance and charm. All she knew was that Benjie was home and in pain and needed her and that she'd been gone too long already. Her pacing took her near a glass and chrome desk at the far end of the room. On the desk were blueprints, and the lettering at the bottom of the page stopped Jan in her tracks. "Rancho Arroyo—Redevelopment."

Upon closer examination, Jan discovered the prints were indeed of the ranch. There was the main lodge and along the trails the twelve cabins and swimming pool…Derek Bannon certainly lost no time. He was so confident that she would sell him the Rancho that he'd already consulted an architect about redeveloping the site. Reaching out to turn the page and try to discover exactly what Derek Bannon intended to do with the property *if* she should sell it to him, a voice startled her.

"Trick or treating, Miss Warren?" Derek Bannon said coolly. "To what do I owe the pleasure of this visit at—" he looked at the clock over the mantel "—four o'clock in the morning. Are those turtles?" he asked, touching the collar of the thin robe.

Jan was exasperated. "Yes, they're turtles and, no, I'm not trick or treating for Halloween. I need you to help Benjie. I don't know what to do for him and Dr. Rossi is in Tucson. Benjie has severe cramps in his legs. He's crying for you. Benjie never cries. Will you come?" she pleaded.

"Of course, I'll come. Where's your car? I'll follow you back."

"My pickup broke down when I was halfway here. I came the rest of the way on foot. I had no other choice. Your phone is off the hook!" she accused hotly, holding back the tears. "That's why I came in person—the switchboard couldn't get through."

Derek cast an angry glance at Andrea, who shrank from his silent accusation.

"Do you mind if I go back with you?" she said, the tears that had been held in check now running in rivulets down her cheeks. "But first I have to take these boots off—my feet are covered in blisters."

Derek stared at her for a moment before he scooped her up in his arms and carried her to his car. "You weigh about as much as a postage stamp. Do you eat?"

"Of course I eat," Jan muttered as she settled herself in the bucket seat. She tugged at the leather boots and could feel the skin leave the backs of her heels. She winced and then sighed with relief. She felt Derek's eyes on her, but she refused to look at him, knowing that if she did she would cry.

The ride was mercifully short, and Derek was hardly out of his car before he asked where he could find Ben.

"He's up in his room, second floor. Delilah is with him," Jan responded, climbing out of the low sports car, her feet aching.

Benjie was rolling around in his narrow bed, groaning with pain and biting his lip against crying out. When he saw Derek, his face lit up a bit and he tried to smile.

"It looks like you're having a problem," Derek said quietly, the low sound of his voice instilling confidence in both Benjie and Jan. "Jan, run a tub. Delilah, go to my car and get the bag out of the backseat and bring it here." Both women rushed off to do his bidding while Derek pushed up the little boys pajama legs. "You're going to feel this and it's going to hurt like the devil in the beginning. Can you handle it?" he asked as his strong hands massaged the boy's thin calf muscle.

Benjie dug his elbows into the mattress and gritted his teeth. "Boy, does that ever hurt."

"I know. Take a deep breath and let it out slowly. Count backwards from one hundred and make sure you don't miss any numbers. How's the water coming?" he called out to Jan.

"It's ready," Jan called, testing the water for just the right temperature.

"Good, I'll put him in the tub, and when your cook brings my bag in, take the jar of yellow ointment and warm it in a saucepan." Derek came to the bathroom door, his blue eyes serious and his tone very low and deep. "We have a tough night ahead of us, Jan. It's going to be rough for Ben. We can do it, can't we?"

Jan looked up into his eyes. Derek instilled such confidence, such a positive attitude, it was little wonder that Benjie adored him. And the way he had said "us" and "we've" got a tough night ahead of "us" warmed Jan and made her feel as though she wasn't alone.

Derek went back into the bedroom for Benjie and lifted him from the bed. "Hey, Jan," he called, just as she was about to head for the kitchen, "do you think you can change your clothes? When I was Ben's age, I wasn't allowed to have a pet, a real pet. So my parents compromised and let me have a turtle. I hated that turtle. I still hate turtles."

"What happened to it?" Benjie asked inquisitively as Derek lowered him into the tub.

"You won't believe this, but that turtle lived for twenty years," Derek replied before breaking into the misadventures of himself as a young boy and his detested turtle, who seemed to have no other purpose in life except to torment the young Derek. Jan could see him bent over the tub, rubbing Benjie's thin legs. A smile played about the corners of her mouth as she reached for her jeans and a pullover. She could change in the kitchen while the ointment was heating. She suspected she understood why Derek had wanted her to change out of the thin, silky, clinging pajamas.

All through the night Jan and Derek took turns massaging Benjie's legs. It was eight o'clock when Benjie was finally dressed in clean pajamas and sound asleep. Jan's arms ached as well as her head. She smiled wanly to Derek who put his arm around her shoulder.

"You did okay, Jan. Ben will be fine now. But the cramps will come again. It's part of the healing process. When they do, call me. I'll come over."

"You must be tired," Jan said. "Would you like some breakfast?"

"I thought you'd never ask. I'd like the biggest and best breakfast Delilah can dish up."

"Then that's exactly what you'll have. Let's let Delilah surprise us."

Jan enjoyed watching Derek make a path through the bacon and eggs and weave his way through a stack of blueberry pancakes. She picked at her food, exhausted by the trials of the night. And into her head popped a vision of Andrea in her wispy black nightie. "I'm sorry if I interrupted your…your morning. As I told you, your phone was off the hook."

Derek frowned. "Sometimes Andrea is very careless. It won't happen again."

Jan was silent and sipped her coffee. What had she expected him to say? Benjie had already informed her that Andrea was living with Derek.

"Has Ben asked you about the picnic in Rattlesnake Canyon?"

Jan laughed. "In a manner of speaking. He said I was invited if I brought the food."

"Well?"

Suddenly uncomfortable under his scrutiny, Jan nodded.

"Just don't make peanut butter sandwiches. I hate them. Almost as much as I hate turtles," Derek said as he strode through the lobby.

"I'll remember that," Jan said, making a mental note to burn those pajamas the first chance she got. The second thing she would do was throw out all the peanut butter and jelly in the kitchen. It was a good thing Derek Bannon hadn't told her to jump from a second story window. She must be out of her mind!

## CHAPTER EIGHT

BENJIE'S EXCITEMENT was contagious; he was excited over the promised picnic with Derek Bannon. In spite of herself and her own confusion concerning Derek, Jan found she had to smile and was actually anticipating the day just as Benjie was. There wasn't any need to fool herself about Derek any longer. The few kisses had meant nothing to him, and she had to take the cue and not allow these strange emotions he aroused in her to take such importance in her life. Derek was probably sowing the last of his wild oats before he married Andrea. If she were fool enough to let him kiss her and fool enough to suppose—no, hope—that it meant anything to him, then she deserved whatever came her way.

It had taken a great deal of reflection and hard thinking to come to terms with how she felt about Derek Bannon. Now, after pondering the logic of it all, she knew that she had to accept the fact that she meant nothing at all to him. All the emotions were on her part. It was difficult to come to grips with something like that, but Jan resolved that when Derek married Andrea she wouldn't be left with a broken heart. Whatever it took to defend herself against the wonderful and stirring things he did to her whenever he was near, she would do it.

Jan busied herself in Delilah's kitchen under the little woman's watchful eye. Carefully, she packed the picnic basket with a wide assortment of food that had taken quite a while for her to prepare. It was the usual kind of picnic food that she and Benjie always enjoyed. If it didn't meet with Derek's gourmet palate, then that was his problem. If she had to torment herself by going on this picnic, she was at least going to enjoy what she would eat.

A sudden disconcerting thought occurred to Jan. What if Derek had invited Andrea to go along with them? Jan groaned and snapped the lid of the picnic hamper closed. She could almost see the beautiful girl wrinkle her nose at the hard-boiled eggs and paper napkins. And fried chicken! In those perfectly mani- cured hands! Gracious.

What did Derek see in Andrea? It was true she was beautiful and glamorous and dressed like a fashion model, but she certainly didn't rain affection down upon Derek. And at the testimonial dinner she had actually had the gall to flirt and hold hands with Dusty Baker under the table. And what kind of friend was Dusty Baker to play around with Derek's fiancée? It was all too much. Jan decided she had heard of the jet set and that they played by a different set of rules, but she didn't have to like it and knew she could never be a part of it. Some small voice echoed: But you already are. You let Derek kiss you and stir up all those strange, yearning emotions. You're no better than Dusty Baker or Andrea or even Derek.

"Well, not any longer," Jan spoke aloud without re- alizing it. "Derek Bannon's kissing days are over," she said tartly, puzzling Delilah, who watched her as she marched out of the kitchen toting the heavily laden picnic basket.

"Here he comes, Jan," Benjie cried excitedly. "Right on time. Derek is right on time all the time. He says punctuality is the mark of a successful man. He's not like you, Jan. You're always late. Andrea is always late, too. Derek says she has to change her clothing six times before she makes a decision. I told Derek you don't do that, but you look in the mirror a lot, and he said, 'Same difference.'" Benjie babbled happily as Derek climbed from the car.

"Is everyone ready?" Jan strained her eyes into the bright sun to see if there were any other passengers in the high-axled four-wheel-drive station wagon. Maybe Derek got tired waiting for the sixth change and left without Andrea. Jan smiled. She would make an effort to be more punctual in the future. She lumped that thought into the same category as the turtles on her pajamas and throwing out the peanut butter and jelly. It was a stupid thought. It wouldn't make any difference what she did. Derek Bannon was getting married to someone else. And the thought was always with her that his deadline to sell the Rancho was bearing down on her with bared teeth. She felt a headache coming on and she knew that if she gave into it the day would be ruined for Benjie as well as herself. Why couldn't she just enjoy it for what it was and then forget about it? Because, she thought, as she watched Derek's broad back as he held the door for Benjie, I'm in love with him.

Derek moved to the side in time to see the flush creep up her cheeks. "You better bring a hat—this sun is brutal today." Jan walked back inside on trembling legs for the worn and battered Stetson she had confiscated from her uncle's belongings. She didn't like this feeling of being out of control and at some man's whim, and that's what it was. Why couldn't he look at her the way he looked at Andrea? Why couldn't he say nice things to her the way he said them to Benjie and Andrea? Why was he always so cool and mocking when he looked at her? Why should he be anything else? He was engaged to marry Andrea. He was definitely a male chauvinist like Neil. She squared her shoulders. Today she wouldn't let him get to her. She could be just as cool and just as mocking. The only difference was she would have to work at it, whereas with Derek Bannon it was a natural trait.

"Did you forget anything?" Derek asked casually, eyeing the picnic hamper.

"Gosh, no, Derek. Jan was up before the birds packing everything." Benjie grinned from his seat in the back of the car.

"Then I guess we're ready for a day in the desert. After you, Jan," he said, holding open the door. Jan nodded coolly and slid into the deep seat. Their eyes met as Derek moved to close the door. Jan felt the familiar flush and was the first to look away.

"Aren't we taking my chair, Derek?" Benjie asked anxiously.

Derek leaned over the back of the seat. "How would you manage it in the sand? If I thought you needed it, I would have put it in the trunk. I brought along a canvas chair and that spare set of crutches you leave at the Lasso. That should do it."

"If you say so," Benjie said happily, leaning back into the seat. "I'm ready if you are."

Jan, too, leaned back, determined to enjoy the drive into the desert. Somehow she managed to keep up her end of the conversation in a limited way, always aware of Derek's nearness. Each time his hand moved to the gearshift she thought he was going to touch her leg; instead, he shifted expertly, the muscles in his thighs tightening and relaxing as he let the clutch in and out. Her heart alternated between wild flutterings and heavy pounding. What was wrong with her? He had no right, she thought angrily, to have the power to make her feel this way, especially since he was soon to be married. Surely he knew she was attracted to him. Why did he insist on being with her and using Benjie as an excuse? Or was she the one who was using Benjie as an excuse?

"Penny for your thoughts," Derek said softly.

Startled, Jan turned from viewing the roadside and stared at Derek. She smiled sadly. "They were deep, dark and dire, and I don't think you really want to hear them. Besides, I'd never let them go for a mere penny." Derek's eyes narrowed. He reached for the polished sunglasses on the visor and slid them on with one hand.

Jan sensed, rather than saw, the tightening of his shoulders. She grimaced as she turned to view the Arizona landscape. Benjie was chattering away and Derek was answering him. She was safe for a while longer before she had to contribute to the conversation. She should be thinking about what she was going to do when Derek's deadline to sell or not to sell the ranch was up. If she didn't sell out to him, she could be left with a white elephant. If she did manage to hold on and try to make a go of Rancho Arroyo, how could she live down the road from Derek Bannon and his wife, Andrea? She couldn't. There was no decision to be made. She wouldn't spoil the day for Benjie. She would tell Derek later, or tomorrow. She and Benjie would live in Phoenix until he completed his treatments at the center and then they would head back for New York. With the money from the sale of the Rancho, she wouldn't have to work so many hours to make ends meet. Somehow things would work out. The decision made to sell out to Derek, she felt drained, emotionally and physically. She risked another glance at Derek. He turned, his expression behind the polished glasses unreadable. She hoped he couldn't see the tears in her eyes. Impossible dreams were just that. Impossible dreams. This was reality and she had better learn to live with it.

The four-wheel-drive station wagon bounced easily on its high axles, affording an overview of the land. Neither Benjie nor Jan had come so far into the desert before, and Derek obligingly pointed out the sights. Low hills stained a dusky purple because the sun hadn't risen sufficiently to illuminate them rose in the distance. Barrel cactus raised their thorny heads out of the hard-baked earth, and Derek made them laugh when he said he could imagine the plants with huge eyes staring out of their limbless bodies and watching the world go by.

Derek seemed to be looking for something as he slowed the vehicle and pulled over to the side of the road close to an outcropping of tall, spiky cactus. There among the thorns was the most beautiful pink flower Jan had ever seen. Derek explained it was a night-blooming cactus, and because the sun hadn't reached it yet, it was still open. The delicate pink petals moved slightly in the breeze, and Jan and Benjie watched, transfixed, as the sun slowly crept among the branches of the plant and the lovely flower closed upon itself.

Derek drove slowly, pointing out ferns and the different kinds of cacti and flowering bushes, explaining that when most people thought of the desert they thought of a barren waste. Nothing could have been further from the truth, Jan thought. Here was life and harmony. The hills dipped and gave way to the roads; mesquite and tumbleweed dusted the earth, and yuccas and boulders kept a companionable silence. And above it all was the sky, scrubbed and blue and relentless. In a few short weeks she had come to love the desert even more than she had loved the green mountains of Upstate New York. And when she must leave Arizona, as she knew she must, she would remember and mourn.

"We're here," Derek announced, swinging the wagon into a driveway paved with gravel and cutting the engine.

"But this…where…I thought you said we were going to have a picnic in the desert," Jan said, looking around at the small adobe house with its red tiled roof that sat back from the driveway and was surrounded by lush foliage. "Where is this place?" she demanded, sensing a trick on Derek's part.

He laughed. "This is the desert. Ben's doctor Bob Rossi's idea of the desert. He calls it his oasis. How do you like it? There's a pool in the back, complete with a Jacuzzi for Ben. That's why I wanted to come here."

"How does he keep all the plants and trees? And roses!" Jan gasped.

"He was lucky and he tapped into an underground spring. Fantastic, isn't it? I've got the keys, if you want to go inside and freshen up."

"It's breathtaking! It rivals any garden back home," Jan said, climbing from the car, forgetting about Benjie as she examined first one colorful plant and then another. "And there's moss—I don't believe it!" she laughed, bending down to feel the velvety softness at her feet. "It's almost like back home with the trees and the roses! I can't believe the roses!"

"The place is for sale," Derek said quietly. "Bob Rossi is moving back to Rhode Island in October to open a clinic." Jan was too busy poking beneath the shrubbery to hear his words and missed Derek's sly wink in Benjie's direction.

The place was perfect and incredibly beautiful. Here was the majesty of the desert and the nostalgia of home. Here was the perfect blending of two opposite worlds, and she knew, without fail, that here she could be happy for the rest of her life.

"Where are we going to have the picnic? Are you going to carry Benjie? We should have brought his chair," she accused. "He could get around here," Jan said, motioning to the paved walkways.

Derek grinned and whistled sharply. A young boy of perhaps seventeen came around the side of the house leading a pony and cart. "Now if you had a choice, which would you prefer? A wheelchair or one of these?" Derek said, pointing at the pony cart.

"Oh, wow!" Benjie exclaimed as he peered out the car window. "Do I really get to ride in that?"

"All day, if you want. There's lots for you to explore. Nick will ride along with you on horseback to keep an eye on you. He'll be perfectly safe," Derek said sharply to Jan, who was about to protest.

Jan snapped her mouth shut and fumed. She hadn't been about to protest over Benjie's safety, but because it appeared that she was about to be left alone with Derek.

Nick lifted Benjie from the car and settled him comfortably in the pony cart. He handed the excited boy the reins and grinned down from his perch atop a tall roan horse. "The pony's name is Sally, and she works at two speeds. Slow and stop. Just hold the reins loosely, and she'll do all the work. I'll be right beside you."

"Gee whiz, this is great, isn't it, Jan? Boy, I wish I could ride a horse like you do." He looked up at Nick.

"If Doctor Rossi is taking care of you, you will. Five years ago I was sitting in that cart being pulled by a pony named Feather. If I can do it, so can you. Say *giddy-up* and Sally will take you wherever you want to go."

"Giddy-up, Sally," Benjie cried excitedly, his thin little hands shaking with the reins. Sally obediently trotted off.

"Hey, Nick," Derek shouted after them, "come back around noon and we'll have that picnic. I'm going to take Jan up into the hills to Prospector's Gap."

Nick signaled that he had heard and cantered beside the pony cart.

Derek grasped Jan's hand and led her around the house to the corral and barn. Two horses were already saddled and waiting.

As they rode side by side into the hills, Jan was once again aware of the beauty surrounding her. Derek pointed out a dry riverbed and said they were going to follow it into the hills, where she was certain to be surprised.

Long before they reached it, Jan could hear the joyous splash of water. The air became sweeter, more fragrant with greens, and lighter with moisture. As they rounded an outcropping of huge boulders, the sound of rushing water became louder. Eagerly, she dug her heels into her mount's flanks. When she saw it, she was overcome. Sunlight dazzled her and reflected off the waterfall in a crown of jewels. The pool into which the waterfall emptied played in the sunlight and winked back at the sun like a million Christmas tree lights.

Derek held back, watching the delight dance across Jan's features. There was no need for words; it was all there to be seen in her face. "You love the desert, don't you, Jan?"

"Oh, yes, I do. I never imagined that I would, but it's worked its magic on me."

"I wanted to bring you up here. It's one of my favorite places. Geologists say this used to be a rushing river that filled the whole valley. Now there's only this waterfall, which is fed by the underground springs and empties into the pool. The pool feeds that little brook, and I've heard it said that the brook weaves its way across the desert and all the way south to the Rio Grande."

Jan was mesmerized, and it was with regret that she followed Derek back down the hills to Bob Rossi's house. Time had flown, and Nick and Benjie were returning for the picnic. Derek turned the mounts over to Nick, who took them back to the corral to water them. He lifted Benjie's crutches out of the trunk space and help the boy down from the pony cart, positioning the crutches under his arms.

"Think you can make it, buddy?"

"Yeah, sure, Derek," Benjie answered. "Just lead me to the food! I'm starving!"

Around the back of the house was the swimming pool and a patio complete with picnic table and benches. After lunch they rested in the shade of the awning over the patio in companionable silence.

When Benjie began getting fidgety, Derek suggested Nick take him into the house and help him get into bathing trunks so he could benefit from the Jacuzzi.

While Nick and Benjie played a limited game of water polo with a giant beach ball, Jan and Derek prowled through the house. If possible, the house was lovelier on the inside than outside. The ceilings were high, allowing the hot desert heat to rise, leaving the cooler air below. Rafters and heavy beams were left exposed, and between them was plaster, roughened and swirled. The floors were red tiles and accented by frequent use of area rugs in wonderful patterns.

The house itself was larger than Jan had expected. Four bedrooms, den, living room, kitchen, dining room—each decorated uniquely and lovingly. "If I had a lot of money and didn't know what to do with it, I'd buy this place and live here forever and ever. I could paint and cook and just plain love it."

Derek smiled. "You really like it? You don't think it's too remote?"

"It wasn't too remote for Dr. Rossi, and he had to go into Phoenix every day. But I'm only dreaming—where would I ever get that kind of money? And even if it were possible, where would Ben go to school?"

"It's not as remote as you think," Derek explained. "This is even closer to Phoenix than the Rancho or the Golden Lasso. I have to confess, on the drive out this morning I took the long way around, using secondary roads. I thought you and Ben would enjoy an early-morning ride. I could see you were nervous and tense when I picked you up. I thought the ride would relax you."

"That it did. I used the time to straighten a lot of things out in my head," Jan laughed merrily as Derek led her out onto the patio again.

"I'm glad, Jan." Derek looked off to the pool, where Nick and Benjie were having a rousing good time. "I'd better water and feed the pony, Sally. Nick has spent his whole day with Ben and probably hasn't done it yet. Want to give me a hand?"

Jan followed Derek around to the barn, where the cool shadows and fragrant straw beckoned them in from the bright sunshine.

Derek unhitched Sally and watered her. As she drank, he picked up a currycomb and smoothed the coat on Sally's flanks. Jan watched Derek's hands move over the animal in sure and gentle strokes. For a fleeting moment, she imagined the feel of Derek's hands on her own flesh and felt herself blush.

"I hope you have room for Sally and her little cart in your barn, Jan. I intend to make a gift of her to Ben."

Everything inside of Jan railed against Derek Bannon. This would be one more thing she would owe him. She could never have given Benjie a surprise like owning Sally—never in her whole life. And when she sold out the Rancho to Derek Bannon and eventually went back to New York, what then? He had made himself a part of Benjie's life, and she would have to cut him out. And he would have to leave Sally behind, too. She would be the bad guy in Benjie's eyes and he would never, ever forgive her.

Adrenaline shot through her and she became more angry than she had ever been in her entire life. She backed off a step and looked measuringly at Derek Bannon. "You are the cruelest man I've ever met, and I hate you for it!" she hissed. "I know what you're doing, and I'm the one who'll pay the price. I can never do the things you've done for Benjie. How could you do this? He's just a little boy and he loves you like a brother and he trusts you. When I take him back to New York, I'll be tearing his heart out. You're thoughtless and insidious and I hate you!"

"New York? You're taking Ben back to New York? Why? He's doing so well with his therapy…"

"Yes, back home," Jan snapped. "I've decided to sell you the Rancho at the end of your deadline. August first. And when I do, what do you think I'm going to do? Pitch a tent? Isn't this what you've intended from the very beginning? Well, you can have the ranch—for your original offer, not a penny more. I don't want anything from you, Derek Bannon. But," she said, pushing a finger into his chest, her eyes spewing fire, "you're the one who's going to tell Benjie, not me. I almost thought you were different there for a while, but you're not. You're a user, Derek, and you prey on women and little children. So buzz off, Derek Bannon, and leave me and my brother alone," Jan cried, the tears running down her cheeks.

"Jan…" She paid him no heed, turning on her heel to head out of the barn. He caught at her arm and pulled backward. "Wait…you don't understand…"

"I understand, all right. I understand more than you think. Get away from me you…you…Arizona gigolo," she shouted, pulling herself free.

She nearly escaped him, thought she had, and the door to the barn was within reach, when she felt her ankles being swept out from under her and fell backward into a stack of hay in one of the stalls.

"Gigolo!" Derek shouted in rage, wrestling her onto her back and staring down into her face. "Of all the stupid, stubborn women…"

"That's it. Call me stupid. Well, I'm not stupid. I saw right through you from the beginning. You're stupid for what you're trying to do to my little brother! I'm one thing, but don't mess with Benjie. He loves you, and when I have to take him away he's going to be heartbroken."

Derek held her firmly, pressing her back into the fragrant straw, a wry smile playing about his mouth. "And does his sister love me?" he asked quietly.

"Love you!" she spit out. "I hate you! I wish I had

never set eyes on you. You're disgusting. What kind of man are you anyway? I've seen the way you treat Andrea and here you are trying to…to…"

"Seduce you?" he asked, laughing, pressing his full weight on her to control her strugglings.

"Go away—leave me alone. But I'm warning you— I'm going to steal a page from your book and do as you suggested. You said I should let Benjie accept whatever life has in store for him. When he's devastated because of all this, I'll let him know exactly how you are. How dare you laugh at me?" Jan cried, gulping back the tears for a second time. "I'm warning you, get away from me," she said through clenched teeth as she was paralyzed into immobility as she watched Derek lean closer, holding her tighter, squeezing her between the haystack and himself.

"I mean it, get away from me. This is the last time I'm going to tell you…I'll scream." He lowered his head and covered her mouth with his.

There was no escaping him. He held her roughly, molding her body to his. Jan summoned all her determination to speak. "Leave me alone," she gasped as he lifted his mouth from hers. Her voice came out thin and weak—hardly the strong emotional statement that she had made to him a moment ago. But that was before he was looking at her as he was now. Before he had trapped her in his embrace and held her against him. So close, so very close.

Derek looked down at her and the world was in his eyes. Tenderly, he touched his finger to her chin, lifting her face to his. A tear slowly traced along her cheek, and he brushed it away. "You're trembling. Do I make you tremble, Jan?" His voice was soft and gentle, belying the strength in his arms. The sound of her name on his lips, the way he said it, sent a stirring through her veins. "Why do you think I'm such a dragon?" As if he hadn't expected her to answer, he pressed her head to his chest and held her, quieting her, soothing her, as though she were a wild colt.

Once again his finger tipped her face to his and he covered her mouth with his own, bringing her back in close contact with his lean, tall frame. Jan felt the hard, manly boldness of him, and she closed her eyes as his searing lips traced feathery patterns over her face and throat. His hands caressed her, leisurely arousing in her a varicolored array of emotions.

A warm, tingling tide of excitement and desire washed through her. Her mind whirled giddily and a soft sigh escaped her lips as she welcomed his kiss. Her trembling lips softened and parted as his mouth possessed hers. Her arms came around his back, aware of his strength and masculinity, and they held each other, offering to one another and blending together like forged steel. Their kisses became fierce and hungry, making them breathless.

Jan fought against the chaos in her mind. She should be fighting him, running away from him, raking her nails across his arrogant face. Instead, she lay back in his arms returning his kisses, bending her body against his, loving the touch of his mouth on hers, the touch of his hands on her neck, her throat, her breasts.

Clasping her tightly to him, as though he would draw

her into himself, Jan felt the thunderous beating of his heart while her own pounded a new and rapid rhythm.

Their moment became an eternity before Derek loosened his hold on her. His eyes held her softly, with tenderness, and when he spoke, his voice was thick with emotion and husky with desire. "I'm not such a dragon, Jan. And I don't breathe fire on little boys or on their beautiful sisters."

Jan turned away, not able to bear the hurt she saw in Derek's eyes. She had hurt him cruelly when she had accused him of using Benjie.

Suddenly, as though a curtain had dropped between them, Derek regained his composure and usual cool tone. "I didn't mean for this to happen. I didn't want anything to spoil Ben's day."

Jan nodded in agreement, not able to face Derek. Benjie had been looking forward to this picnic, and the day was almost at an end. She didn't want to spoil it for him now any more than Derek did. He helped her to her feet and began to brush the hay from her back.

"I won't mention the pony to Ben. Perhaps you're right—I was being thoughtless." He took her arm and led her back to the patio, and Jan noticed a new, almost imperceptible possessiveness in the touch of his hand. And when he spoke to her the brittle tone of his anger was gone. While not exactly lighthearted, she heard herself reply in kind and she began to relax. Derek was as good as his word. Benjie's day wouldn't be spoiled by hidden currents of bitterness between them.

For the remainder of the day, Jan remembered the taste of his mouth on hers and the strange and wonderful emotions she had experienced in his arms. She basked in Derek's attention and reveled in the sound of Benjie's laughter. And at the end of the day, when they loaded into the car for the drive home, she was saddened that it had come to an end.

As Derek drove them home in the deepening twilight, Jan rested her head back against the seat and relived the moments she had shared in Derek's arms, and she knew with certainty that she would remember this day always.

# CHAPTER NINE

JAN WOKE with a throbbing headache, knowing that the day was somehow going to bring disaster; she could feel it, sense it in every pore of her body. She felt drained as she swung her legs over the side of the bed. Drained and foolish. How could she have allowed Derek Bannon to do the thing he did—to kiss her like that, to touch her that way? She had behaved terribly, giving in to her emotions like some wanton hussy. "Oh, heaven," she cried, "how could I allow myself to…" It was over and done with. From this moment on she would make sure she was never within a mile of him. She would let an attorney handle the sale of Rancho Arroyo, and she would never have to come in contact with him again. At the end of the month she would be back in New York and all of this would be behind her. A brief interlude in her life—no more and no less. She could do it; she had no other choice. If she had to, she would work day and night, twenty-four hours a day to make up to Benjie the loss he was going to feel when Derek Bannon was no longer around to serve as a big brother to him. Surely the little boy would understand—or would he?

The cold, bracing shower helped a little in brightening her spirits and so did the bright tangerine pullover. However, Delilah's gloomy countenance in the kitchen dampened her fledgling spirits. "Don't spare me—just tell me what's wrong," Jan muttered as she sat down at the wide, butcher-block table with a cup of coffee.

Delilah stood with her hands on her ample hips, her dark eyes sad and gloomy. "Is bad. Freezer ruin all food—Gus throw out now."

"What?" Jan exploded, knocking her coffee cup onto the polished floor. "How could the freezer be broken? And what happened to the emergency generator? It can't be broken. The food can't be spoiled—it just can't be. Tonight is the going-away party for our guests. Are you sure, Delilah?"

"Yes, the fuses blew. No power all night. You have to cancel party. Or you go to town and buy more food. Guests expect big wingding. You promise on brochure. Everybody dress up and have good time. No good time," she said, shaking her black braids. "You have big problem."

The sound of Benjie's chair caught Jan's attention, and she immediately began to pour cereal into a bowl. Her hand trembled and she dropped the spoon as she set the dish in front of Benjie. He waited patiently for another moment and then gulped the sugary flakes as if he was in a hurry. "Why don't you call Derek and ask him if the guests can have dinner at the Golden Lasso? He told me he always keeps six tables in reserve for special guests. Do you want me to ask him?"

Jan stared at the little boy without seeing him. It was a solution. But where was she to get the money to pay for the night's entertainment? "No, don't ask him. I'll think about it. Is Dusty Baker taking you to the hospital or is Derek doing the driving?"

"I never know. Whoever shows up," Benjie said blithely as he put the chair in motion. "I'll see you this afternoon."

"Okay, Benjie. Have a good day." Jan sighed. It was the perfect solution, if Derek agreed. Maybe there would be some advance reservation checks in the mail, and she could make some kind of deal with him. And you weren't going to go within a mile of him, a niggling voice harassed. Sometimes we all have to do things we don't want to do, she answered herself.

By late morning the mail had arrived with a fifty-dollar check for a deposit for a family of three due to arrive in three weeks. She wouldn't be able to get inside the door of the Golden Lasso for fifty dollars. Could she lay her pride on the line and ask Derek Bannon for credit until the sale of the ranch went through? Oh, she could ask him, and he would look at her with those mocking eyes of his and be very gracious, not to mention condescending, and say, yes, of course, he would help her out. He'd probably take it one step further and pick up the tab himself, compliments of the Golden Lasso. She didn't need his charity and she didn't want it. But the guests—what was she to do?

Delilah was hovering, making Jan jittery to the point of exploding. "When you make phone call to Golden Lasso?" Delilah demanded. "Is late."

"Look, if I go to the guests and explain the situation, maybe they'll understand. I can offer them a refund at some future date," Jan said, grasping at straws.

"*Tsk, tsk, tsk.*" Delilah clucked her tongue. "You no understand. No food for any kind of dinner. They pay and want to eat. You want guests to go to bed hungry? *Tsk, tsk, tsk.*"

Jan was outraged. "Are you telling me there's no food at all? Nothing! What about the refrigerator?"

"Wienies," Delilah said curtly. "We have one string of wienies. The rest is what we serve for breakfast."

Jan stared at the cook and trudged dejectedly to the office. There were no options, no choices. She would have to call Derek Bannon and plead her case. Each time she reached for the phone she withdrew her hand, and then the sound of the children in the pool stiffened her spine, and she would again reach for the phone, only to draw away. Thank heaven the guests were leaving, and the new batch wasn't due to arrive till Sunday. Instead of sitting here like some ninny, she should be making calls, canceling the other reservations. She couldn't put it off any longer. She had just dialed the first three digits of the Golden Lasso when Delilah ran into the office. "You come see. Now. *Tsk, tsk, tsk,*" she said, turning and waddling back to the kitchen.

"Oh, please let there be water." What *else* could it be. Everything that could possibly go wrong had gone wrong. When she walked into the kitchen, there was food everywhere, packed in ice. "Where, who... how..." she said to a broad-shouldered man hefting a heavy carton.

"You Jan Warren?" At Jan's nod he handed her a slip of paper. Tears burned her eyes as she scanned the brief, curt note. "Ben explained. Call this Arizona hospitality or, if you prefer, one businessman helping another." It was signed simply: DEREK BANNON. Darn! He must want something in return. Her ranch. No, she had already told him she was going to sell it to him. Protecting his investment ahead of time, that's what he was doing. And humiliating her in the bargain. She would have felt better if she had asked and arranged the terms. This made it sound like a gift—charity, for want of a better word. She didn't need his charity or want it. Yet she had to accept it. And she had to call him and acknowledge his generous help. That was going to be harder to do than asking for his help the way she had originally intended. When it came to Derek Bannon, she was always on the receiving end of things.

Jan thanked the deliverymen and started to help Delilah stack the meats into the large kitchen refrigerator. There was enough for an army. Evidently the illustrious Derek Bannon didn't want her weak from hunger when it came to signing on the dotted line. She hated herself for such opinions but didn't seem able to control her thoughts when it came to the owner of the Golden Lasso.

As soon as the cartons were emptied, Jan left the kitchen, needing no further reminders of Derek Bannon and wanting no more confrontations with her emotions. Perhaps a ride would clear away her headache—if not clear it away, at least reduce it to a dull ache. Delilah had things under control; Benjie wouldn't return for another three hours. She was more or less on her own. Gus was seeing to the freezer, and all the guests were doing their thing. She shook her head as she saddled

Soochie and admitted to herself that she didn't like the feeling of not being needed. Everyone deserved to be needed. Why should she be any different?

Tugging on the reins lightly, she let Soochie have her head. The golden animal reared once and then headed for the open. Jan sat the horse with ease, reveling in the hot breeze the galloping animal created. She felt free, more free than she had felt since coming to Arizona. She rode for what seemed like hours before dismounting. She withdrew two apples from her saddle bags, gave one to the horse, and started to munch on the other.

She felt so tired and yet she had done nothing really physical since coming to this beautiful state. Mentally tired, she corrected herself. How terrible to be in love and not be able to do anything about it. It was such a devastating feeling. How could you love someone so much and not have the other person love you? Tears gathered and she wiped at them with the back of her hand. That was another thing—she had to stop this senseless weeping and wailing every time she thought of Derek Bannon. Crying never solved anything. All it did was give you the hiccups and red-rimmed eyes. She fixed her watery gaze on the quiet horse and muttered, "Emotionally, I can't afford you, Derek Bannon."

The hot Arizona sun, along with the horse's quiet grazing made Jan drowsy. The past day's tensions evaporated as she fell into a deep, restful sleep. She neither saw nor heard Soochie as she trotted off on her own to explore the terrain.

Jan woke, stiff and disoriented, from her sound sleep to see darkness falling. What happened? she wondered wildly as she struggled to her feet. She rubbed grit from her eyes, and gradually her eyes became accustomed to the indigo shadows around her. It took her seconds to realize Soochie was gone. She whistled and called the mare to no avail. How far had she come? She had ridden for over two hours and an hour of that had been fast, hard riding. To go it on foot, providing she didn't get lost in the darkness, would take her more hours than she could stand. The blisters on her feet were not healed sufficiently to make the long trek back even if she were wearing rubber-soled canvas sneakers. What time was it? How long had she slept? Surely by now somebody should be looking for her. When she didn't show up for the guests' farewell party, someone would start wondering about her whereabouts. Benjie. Benjie would worry and call Derek. But they didn't know which way she had come. All they would know was that Soochie was gone.

She couldn't sit here all night and do nothing. She had to move. She had to try to find her way back on her own. How could she have been such a fool as to let the animal graze and not tether it? Why did she always have to learn her lessons the hard way? She wasn't going to find any answers sitting here.

She started out, her head high and her shoulders straight. She trudged for hours under the full moon, wishing a tall, blue-eyed man named Derek Bannon would swoop down on her and carry her back to the ranch. She sighed wearily. At this point she would settle for Gus and a painted wagon. She was tired! She had to keep going and not think. One foot in front of the other, over and over. The blisters on the backs of her heels were sore and running. Disgustedly, she removed the offending boots and hurled them into the darkness. The moment she did she was sorry. Alone and lost in the desert was bad enough. Barefoot, it was intolerable.

Twice within minutes she stumbled and fell. She managed to get to her feet and start walking, only to fall into a crumpled heap. Bitter tears of frustration rolled down her cheeks. She couldn't give in, not now. The highway must be close. A while ago she thought she had heard the engine of a car, but it was too dark to see anything with the moon sliding behind a giant cloud cover.

It was the feel of the macadam road on her sore, bare feet that told her she had finally found a road. Where it was, she had no idea. She shivered violently as she tumbled down the road. She prayed silently that she was going in the right direction.

Jan raised her eyes and for the first time was aware that dawn was fast approaching. She had been stumbling along with her head down and her eyes closed. Now she would be able to see where she was. Hopefully, a car would come along and offer her a ride.

Jan heard a car and teetered on her feet in an effort to steady herself. She was so tired and numb from the night air that she fell, skinning her hands and knees. Angry beyond belief, she pummeled the road with her clenched, bleeding hands. Why wasn't someone helping her? She had to get up and walk. The car—it was stopping. "Please, don't let it be a mugger," she gasped.

The voice was angry and… What was that in the tone that reminded her of her father? Who cared? She was picked up in strong arms and carried like a baby. That was okay—she felt like a baby with the tears running down her face. She knew she was safe; she could feel it even if the voice was chastising her.

"You aren't safe to let loose, do you know that?" the voice was saying over and over. "Half the state is out looking for you. How could you be so thoughtless, so careless, and for heaven's sake, don't you care about that little boy back at the ranch who is crying his eyes out over you?" And then the arms tightened around her.

She burrowed her head in his chest and muttered. "I care, I really do. I knew you'd find me. I want to go home—my feet hurt." And then she was asleep.

Derek gently lowered the sleeping Jan into the depths of the bucket seat. A smile played around his mouth as he watched her curl into a ball and then sigh. He fastened her seat belt securely and climbed behind the wheel. Before he fastened his own seat belt he bent over and touched Jan's tousled hair. He kissed her lightly on the mouth and heard her murmur in her sleep, "I knew you'd find me." He whistled softly as he slid in the clutch and headed back toward Rancho Arroyo.

# CHAPTER TEN

LEANING BACK against a nest of pillows, Jan contemplated first the gray, overcast day through her window and then her bandaged feet, which were propped up with cushions at the foot of her bed. She had been guilty of some foolish moves in her life, but getting lost and trekking through the desert all night long was, without a doubt, the most stupid to date. What did Derek Bannon think of her now? She moaned. He had been so angry with her, so upset with her stupidity. And then her falling into his arms with such abandoned relief! Jan cringed and tried to make herself invisible by hiding under the bedcovers. She couldn't hide from what she had done any more than she could forget what a fool she was. It was over, done, and she was safe once again in her own bed with a cup of black rum tea at her elbow.

*"Tsk, tsk, tsk..."* Delilah muttered as she waddled into the room to check on her impatient patient. Deftly, she replaced Jan's bandaged feet on the cushion and ordered her to remain in bed. "You have a visitor in the lobby. I bring him to see you—you don't get out of bed," she ordered as she exited into the hallway.

"No! Wait! I don't want... Oh...I don't want to see Derek," Jan yelped. "Can't you see I'm a mess? Just look at me! Delilah, please, don't bring him up here. Look at this…this…thing I'm wearing," Jan wailed, pointing to her oversize football jersey with the number seventy-seven printed across the chest. "Delilahhhh!" she pleaded.

Delilah looked back and shrugged. "So, you number seventy-seven on list. Is funny nightgown but not my business," she shrugged again. "Your visitor not Mr. Bannon but lady in tight pants. I bring her tea and maybe cookies."

Jan's curiosity suddenly peaked. "What lady in tight pants? Are you sure it isn't Derek and you're only teasing me?"

"I sorry you disappointed, but I know lady when I see one. You want to see Mr. Bannon, I call Golden Lasso and tell him," Delilah clucked as she closed the door behind her.

Jan settled back against the pillows, her pretty features turned down into a frown. The visitor had to be Andrea— who else could it be? Beautiful, stunning Andrea. Jan slid beneath the covers and pulled them to her chin. She'd die before she allowed Andrea to see the football jersey that doubled for a nightgown, especially since she had seen the cloud of black lace that was part of Andrea's wardrobe. Darn! Why did these things always happen to her?

A cautious knock on the door alerted Jan to Andrea's approach. "Come in," she called weakly.

"I came as soon as Derek told me what happened. I'm so sorry about what happened to you last night. You must have been frightened to death. Do you have any idea how lucky you are that Derek found you? You could still be out there wandering. It was foolish, Jan, and it could have been a fatal accident. I hope you're more careful in the future."

Jan was puzzled. Andrea sounded so sincere, so concerned. Would she still sound that way if she knew that Jan, too, was in love with Derek? Not likely. "I realize what a fool I was, and you don't have to worry about me doing such a stupid thing again. I really did learn my lesson." In spite of herself, Jan found that she was warming to Andrea's sincere concern.

"We were all concerned about you. Especially your little brother. I can't tell you what the little guy went through when Derek had to tell him that they couldn't search for you during the night. You put Ben through a lot of anguish with your foolishness. Please." Andrea held up her hand to stifle Jan's protests. "I saw Ben and what he went through. He's told me about the accident that took your parents, and all he could think of was that something had happened to you, too! That was unfair, Jan, and Derek and I hope you'll take Ben's feelings into consideration in the future."

Jan bristled and she felt as though the hair at the nape of her neck was standing on end. How dare Andrea? How dare Derek? Who did they think they were? As if she had planned her bad luck the night before just to put Benjie through a bad time. If there was anyone in this world who could get Jan's back up, it was Derek Bannon and Andrea.

"This is hardly any of your business," Jan growled, her face stiffening into hard lines of anger.

"You're wrong, Jan. It is my business and Derek's,

too. We care about you and we love Ben." Exasperated, Andrea emitted a deep sigh. "Look, Jan, I didn't come here to stage an argument. I'd like us to be friends because we're neighbors, and we're so close in age a friendship would seem natural. But it's evident you aren't interested in my friendship, and I'm truly sorry for that. Derek's been pleading me to come over here and get to know you better. I tried to tell him you seemed less than receptive to the idea, and this will prove to him that I was right. However, just so my trip isn't wasted, I'd like to invite you and Ben to my wedding. It's the last Saturday in July. In the gardens at the Golden Lasso. I hope you'll put aside your hostility for me and bring Ben. I really want both of you to attend."

Jan couldn't believe what she was hearing. Derek had pleaded with Andrea to come over and try to be friends? After the times he had taken her in his arms, the way he had kissed her? He wanted her to be friends with his wife-to-be? Jan realized she was glaring at Andrea, who had turned her face away rather than subject herself to Jan's open hostility.

"Take care of yourself, Jan. Blisters can be a nasty problem. If there's anything I can do for you—"

Jan had turned her head away.

"I see. I don't know what I've done to make you feel this way about me, Jan. And I'm sorry." Not waiting for a reply, Andrea turned and left the room.

Jan sat and stewed until Delilah came back into her room. "Delilah. Do you know what she wanted?" Jan sputtered. "She had the gall to come here and rail me out for what happened last night. She told me what anguish I put Benjie through—as though I'd planned it! As though I wanted to scare the life out of him! And then, after telling me how stupid I was, she had the nerve to invite me to her wedding! Even after blaming me for the fact that she and I aren't friends!"

"Reason you're not friends is your fault," Delilah said calmly, puttering around the room with a tired old dust rag and flicking the cloth haphazardly over the surface of the furniture. "Sometime you have face like cigar-store Indian. Much frown, much anger. Me, I think sometimes you scared, so I still like you. Other people, they don't understand like Delilah."

"Is that what you think?" Jan challenged.

"How else to think? That you really one nasty person? No, I think you scared sometimes," Delilah answered matter-of-factly, seeming to concentrate on flicking the dust cloth between the bottles of hand cream and perfume that dotted Jan's dresser. "You tell her that you go to wedding?"

"I did not! Why should I want to go to *her* wedding? I don't care that Derek told her to come here and make friends with me! And I don't care to go to the wedding!"

"Oh, sure. You only care that they very nice to Benjie. You only care that Mr. Bannon take Benjie to hospital for treatments. You only care that he come here at night to take care of boy because you can't. I see," Delilah said offhandedly, still busying herself with straightening the room.

Desperate to justify her decision without revealing the true reason to Delilah, Jan persisted. "What kind of people are they anyway? I have every reason to believe that Andrea is living in sin with—with—her fiancé. Just because they're going to get married now, is that reason enough for me to condone what they're doing? And to bring Benjie to that wedding?"

"Is reason enough because Mr. Bannon is good to you. You think somebody live in sin? Big deal!" Delilah snorted, stuffing the dust cloth into her apron pocket and coming to stand at the bedside. Her hands were propped on her hips and her shoe-button eyes snapped with anger. "You look at me, I live 'in sin' with Gus for forty years. Is nothing wrong with me. Is nothing wrong with Gus. We get married, we have plenty wrong. He tell me what to do and I have to do it. Now we live in sin. When I tell him, 'Buzz off, you old Indian,' he listens. I marry him and he stick like fly to honey. Is good for some, is not good for others. You not judge other people, Miss Warren. I go get you something to eat. Later I give you advice."

Delilah left Jan alone in the room, and the hard sound of the closing door announced the woman's anger. Jan pummeled her pillows. Maybe she really was "one nasty person," as Delilah had said. But how could she go to the wedding and watch the man she loved marry someone else? What kind of people were they? What kind of man was Derek Bannon? There he was about to marry Andrea, and yet he seemed bent on seducing Jan. And Andrea—openly flirting with Dusty Baker at the testimonial dinner! And on the plane! What kind of marriage was Andrea going to have? Maybe they were planning on having one of those open marriages. Well, she wasn't going to get involved. Never! A fresh wave of tears drowned out her hiccups as she continued to pound her pillows with a vengeance.

Nearly an hour later, exhausted from her crying, Jan dried her eyes and sat up in bed to gulp some coffee from the breakfast tray Delilah had set on her nightstand. The coffee was less than steaming, but it made little difference—she couldn't taste it anyway.

Within the past hour Jan had reached a decision. There was an old saying that when you were down and out the only way to go was up. Perhaps some people were cut out to be martyrs, but she wasn't one of them. People got married every day of the week; some of them lived happily ever after and some didn't. When she got married, if she ever did, she would live happily ever after because she wouldn't marry anyone who didn't love her as much as she loved him. How could that—that weasel kiss her until her teeth rattled and then go off and marry someone else? She sniffed and blew her nose with gusto.

The next step was to get out of bed—gingerly, of course—and hobble around and see to her business. Life didn't stop just because you were laid up in bed and were moaning about fate and the way the cards were being dealt. She would spend the rest of the day on the veranda at the back of the lodge with a tall glass of lemonade and the ledgers from her office. And she would try to force her thoughts to remember the finer details of the blueprints she had seen in Derek Bannon's apartment the night she had gotten him to help her with the sudden, terrifying cramps that had plagued Benjie. She had a right to know what Derek Bannon was planning for the Rancho Arroyo.

Climbing out of bed was less painful than she had imagined. Delilah's poultices were working their magic. She dressed in Levi's and a colorful sleeveless blouse. Her feet were tender but not too painful, and she noticed the cane Delilah had brought for her so she wouldn't be putting her full weight on her blistered feet. Jan felt decrepit, old beyond her years, as she made her way down the stairs and through the lobby out to the veranda. Gratefully, she dropped into a wicker chair and winced with relief. She wasn't going to be doing much walking in the next few days, that was for sure.

By midafternoon Jan was certain of one thing. She was on the verge of bankruptcy. With the payment from the guests that were due within a few days, she would just be able to meet her expenses. That was providing nothing else went wrong.

Jan had just closed the last ledger when Delilah came to the door and motioned to the phone she was plugging into a jack on the veranda. "For you. They say they call from bank." Jan picked up the receiver, her heart leaping wildly.

"Janice Warren," she announced in her most businesslike tone.

"Miss Warren, this is Michael Davis at City Trust. The bank has approved your application for a loan using your house in New York as collateral. If you would care to stop by the bank sometime tomorrow, we can set the wheels in motion, and I can guarantee you'll have your money within ten days."

"Why, thank you, Mr. Davis," Jan said coolly,

fighting to keep her excitement from creeping into her voice. "I'll come by tomorrow afternoon."

She was solvent again, or would be in ten days. Now she didn't have to sell out to Derek Bannon, who seemed all too greedy for her land. She wouldn't have to go back to New York and lick her wounds. She could stay in Arizona and so could Benjie. And the first thing she was going to do was hire reliable help to get this business off the ground in the proper manner. She would take a few business courses at night in the off-season and learn whatever there was to learn about managing a resort. With just one phone call her world was right side up again. If Derek Bannon would call and say he decided not to marry Andrea, her life would be perfect. She stared at the black phone, willing it to ring, willing it to be Derek.

When the instrument shrilled, Jan's heart almost jumped from her chest. It couldn't…it couldn't…it must be! "Hello," she said cautiously, breathlessly.

"It's Neil, Jan."

"Neil! What a nice surprise," Jan stuttered, regaining her composure. What a fool she was to think that her prayers would be answered and that the voice she would hear would be Derek's. "How nice of you to call," she choked into the receiver. "How are you? How's the house? Nothing wrong, is there?" she asked anxiously. Just what she would need. She could imagine the old house in New York burning to the ground and then the bank refusing her the loan.

"I'm fine," Neil answered in brisk tones. "And your house was fine when I saw it this morning. I'm not in

New York, Jan. I'm here in Arizona. I decided I couldn't live without you and here I am. Tell me how to get to the ranch, and I'll soon be walking through your door."

Jan was stunned. Neil in Phoenix? He couldn't possibly have chosen a worse time to pay her a visit. "How…how nice," she said, trying for a light tone. "It's very simple. Take the interstate east and watch for the signs about thirty miles out. They point the way to Rancho Arroyo and the Golden Lasso."

"Gotcha," Neil assured her. "Tell me you missed me as much as I missed you. I'm going to sweep you right off your ever-lovin' feet. You got that?"

"Yes, I heard you. Neil, you should have told me you were coming so I could have prepared," Jan said tartly.

"And spoil the surprise? No way! I knew you'd be eager to see me right about now. I purposely planned it this way. From now on I'm not letting you out of my sight. And look, Jan, do us both a favor and keep the kid out of sight for a while. We have a lot of catching up to do. By the way, how is the kid?" Neil asked as an afterthought.

Jan's jaw tightened. "If you mean Benjie, he's fine. He's making remarkable progress with his therapy. I thought I told you that in my letters."

"Great, just great. Remember now, I want to spend my time with you, not the kid. By the way, I quit my job. I'm going to help you out there at the ranch. I've decided we're a team and teams work together. See you in a little while."

Jan looked at the phone and winced. Team. He quit his job. He wanted to spend all his time with her. She shrugged. At least she'd have an escort to Andrea's wedding and wouldn't look like an unwanted old maid. Jan shook her head. What was wrong with her? Was she crazy? What did it matter whether or not she had an escort? To save face? What face? Derek Bannon certainly wouldn't be impressed; he'd be too busy with Andrea on their wedding day.

AN HOUR LATER Jan watched from her chair on the veranda as Neil careened around the circular driveway on two wheels, finally bringing the rented Pinto automobile to a grinding halt. Jan shivered and frowned. What was wrong with Neil? Didn't he realize there may have been guests or children who could have been hurt by his reckless driving. Jan's frown deepened. She hadn't liked Neil's "surprise" visit, and the idea that he quit his job gave her cause for concern. What did he have on his mind? What was she going to do with him during his visit?

She watched with a kind of detached interest as Neil hopped from the car, resplendent in cowboy attire that some fast-talking salesman must have palmed off on him. No one dressed that way! Certainly no one here in Arizona. Perhaps on the backstage lot of a Hollywood studio Neil's outfit would have seemed natural, but certainly not here! Talk about Rhinestone Cowboys! Jan giggled as she likened Neil to a cross between Tom Mix and Gene Autry. If he said, "Howdy, pardner," she would laugh in his face.

Neil was up on the veranda, teetering on his high-heeled boots, before she could blink an eye, and he was sweeping her off her feet. "Howdy, pardner. What say we mosey out to the old corral and snatch a few quick kisses?"

"Neil, put me down! We don't have a corral, and we don't 'mosey' anywhere. We walk or we use the pickup. I'm not in the mood for kisses, quick or otherwise. You're behaving like Benjie. Now put me down!" she squealed.

"You haven't changed. I was just having a little fun," Neil said loudly. "I thought you'd be glad to see me."

"I am glad to see you, Neil. It's just that you're so exuberant. Sit down here—let's talk. What made you decide to come out here? Vacation?" she asked, mentally crossing her fingers. "What ever possessed you to quit your job? I thought you liked it! Who's looking after the house? You did make arrangements, didn't you?"

"Of course I did. My aunt Mary is going to stop by there several times a week to check on things. As for my job, it was boring me to death, and all the challenge was gone. It was time to start looking around, so here I am. Why do I have the feeling you aren't happy to see me? I haven't seen you smile yet?"

Jan managed a wan smile for his benefit. "I guess I'm just a little tired. I've been working pretty hard lately, and I haven't had too much time to sit around and relax. We're taking a breather before another wave of guests descends on us. It's not easy running a dude ranch."

Neil rolled his eyes. "I saw the sign at the turnoff for that Golden Lasso. You never mentioned it in your letters. I'll bet it gives you a run for your money. It looks like a swinging place to me. Who owns it?"

"I do," said a voice from the screen door leading onto the veranda. Derek held the screen door open for Benjie and then stepped into the porch himself. Jan swallowed hard as she watched Benjie maneuver himself along on his crutches. The boy was looking in stark amazement at Neil, and it was apparent he wasn't pleased with Neil's turning up on the doorstep.

"Neil Connors," Neil said, introducing himself, holding out a too starkly white hand. Derek looked at the hand a moment and then covered it with his.

"Derek Bannon," Derek said curtly.

"Derek owns the Golden Lasso and the Bison football team," Benjie offered proudly, "and he introduced me to all the players. Dusty Baker is a good friend of mine, too."

"How are you, kid?" Neil asked, stepping over to and putting his arm around Benjie. The boy shrugged off his arm and moved out of Neil's reach. It was apparent Benjie wanted nothing to do with this interloper.

"Neil is a friend of mine from New York. He'll be staying with us for a while," Jan said softly, mostly for Benjie's benefit.

"We're engaged to be engaged, if you know what I mean," Neil said brashly, winking at Derek Bannon.

"Neil!" gasped Jan in exasperation. "We're not engaged!"

"Not right this minute, maybe, but we will be. Why do you think I came out here? You aren't getting away from me again. Nice meeting you, Banyon," Neil said jovially, as he took Jan's arm to lead her into the lobby.

"His name is Bannon, not Banyon," Benjie cried with a catch in his voice.

"See you tomorrow, Ben." Derek nodded in Jan's and Neil's direction and left the veranda, his back stiff and straight.

"Listen, little fella, it was rude of you to do that. Don't you ever correct your elders. And don't ever embarrass me like that again. You mind your manners and we'll get along just fine." Neil scolded through tight lips.

Benjie stared at Jan a moment and then headed for the kitchen and some of Delilah's cookies and buttermilk.

Jan's shoulders ached with tension. She should have defended Benjie right then and there, but somehow the words didn't come. The little boy had given her every opportunity to come to his defense and put Neil in his place and she had failed. Jan knew she had trouble and his name was Neil Connors.

"Who was that guy, anyway? What's he doing with your brother? Looks like one of those aces to me."

"He introduced himself to you. His name is Derek Bannon and he does own the Golden Lasso and the Bison team, just as Benjie told you," Jan retorted curtly. "I don't have to explain anything to you, Neil. Derek Bannon happens to be a very nice person. He's gone out of his way to take Benjie to the Phoenix Medical Center every day. Benjie is crazy about him."

"Yeah, and why are you so defensive of him?" Neil demanded, watching Jan very closely.

Jan hedged. "Am I? I told you, I think he's a very nice person, and he's been great with Benjie."

"Well, if he's been going out of his way to take the kid into the city for his treatments, I can relieve him of that chore right now. I'll take the kid from now on. That way you won't feel obligated to him."

"I don't feel obligated. He takes Benjie because he wants to take him. He offered—I didn't ask."

"I've seen guys like him before and believe me, they never do anything without a reason. Especially lugging some lame kid around. I'm a guy. I should know. You've always been such a babe in the woods, Jan. From now on just leave everything to me."

Jan turned in a fury and lashed out. "Don't you ever call Benjie a lame kid again. And I don't need you to tell me about men like Derek Bannon. Let it drop, Neil, before we say things to one another that we'll regret later. If you don't like Derek, keep your thoughts to yourself. Benjie likes him and so do I."

It was immediately apparent to Neil that he had overstepped the bounds in Jan's private life, a life that somehow involved Derek Bannon. "Okay, sorry if I offended you. If you and your brother like him, then I'm certain he's a great guy. End of matter, subject dropped." Neil grinned as he put his arm around her shoulder to draw her closer. "Look, how about a tour of the ranch?" Noticing her cane for the first time, he asked, "What's wrong?"

"My feet are a little tender. I've acquired some nasty blisters. It's not serious, just uncomfortable. I'll have Gus show you around and assign you a cabin."

"You mean I don't get to stay here in the lodge? That's where you stay, isn't it?" Neil leered.

"That's exactly what it means. Paying guests stay in the cabins. You *are* a paying guest, aren't you?" Jan challenged.

The leer vanished, replaced by a look of stunned surprise. He recovered quickly and grinned. "You didn't think I was going to freeload, did you?"

Again Jan hedged. "Can you ride, Neil?"

"I'm not an expert, but I've ridden the trails in New York the same as you. I think I can manage. Bring on your old Indian guide," he joked.

Jan turned and Gus was waiting patiently, just as he did everything. Benjie must have told the Indian about their new guest.

"Well, I'm ready if you are," Neil said, perching a ten-gallon hat on his head, covering his golden hair. He seemed uncomfortable with the hat, just as he seemed unfamiliar with the studded Western-cut shirt and narrow slacks that were stuffed into handsome Western boots that were too obviously new. Jan fought back a giggle at the ridiculous sight he made and even Gus turned his head. But not before Jan saw the wicked grin that ripped across Gus's usually solemn visage.

Neil turned to follow Gus and then wheeled back toward Jan. "You didn't say how you like my Western togs. What do you think?"

"Neil, I can truthfully say those are the fanciest duds I've yet to see around here."

"Thought you'd like them. See you later."

Delilah stood framed in the doorway to the kitchen. *"Tsk, tsk, tsk.* Your friend smell like vanilla pudding," she chirped.

"What do you think of him, Delilah?"

"I tell you, that man very pretty. Maybe turn some girls' heads, but not mine. That man not make me itch, he give me rash!"

Jan's giggle turned into helpless laughter, doubling

her over. "He's not so bad when you get to know him," she gasped between bouts of hilarity.

"That why you laugh at friend?" Delilah said tartly as she shook her head, a perplexed expression on her face.

"Okay, okay, I shouldn't laugh, but he actually thinks that's the way cowboys dress. With bangles and beads. I can't help it. I think it's so funny!"

Delilah held her hands over her ample belly and joined in Jan's laughter. "I see but I not believe. First time I see Gus laugh in many years."

JAN DRESSED for dinner in a raspberry silk shirt and tan slacks. She added a belt of natural twine braid and stepped back to admire the effect. She wasn't going anywhere but to the dining room in the lodge so it didn't really matter how she looked. Neil never noticed other people's clothes, and right now he was overly impressed with his own flamboyant "togs," as he called them. Neil probably thought of himself as a dandy, but once the ranch hands got a look at him, they'd know him for what he was. A dude. A genuine, bona fide Eastern dude.

How had Derek looked when he saw Neil on the veranda with her? Angry, amused, startled? He looked, she decided, as though he was barely controlling his anger. Serves him right, she mused. Did Derek really think no other man in the world could find her attractive? And when Neil had made that brash statement about them being engaged to be engaged, what was the expression that crossed his face then? Jealousy? Jan sighed. The probability of Derek being jealous of Neil was so far-fetched as to be ridiculous. At this point in time it made little difference. Derek was getting married at the end of the month, and Neil was going to save the day by escorting her to that wedding. Afterward, she would tell Neil there was no hope of furthering their relationship as he had implied. If there was one thing she knew, it was that she would rather end up an old maid than settle down with Neil Connors. It would be like driving a wedge between herself and Benjie. There was little to say about the relationship between Neil and her brother. There was no relationship. Period.

If it was a spinster she was meant to be, then a spinster it would be. A vision of herself rocking sedately at the age of eighty-five with nothing to carry her through the days but the old memories of Derek Bannon kissing her and the feelings he evoked in her was such a vivid picture she winced. She clenched her small hands into tight fists and brought them crashing down onto her dressing table. The pain was welcome. If she wasn't careful, she could end up a basket case with Delilah spoon-feeding her.

With the aid of her cane Jan made her way onto the veranda to wait for Neil. Benjie was already there, watching a small portable TV that Gus had rigged for him. The small boy turned to his sister and with a break in his voice asked, "How long is he staying?"

Jan ruffled Benjie's hair and smiled. "Not long. I want you to be polite. I can't force you to like Neil, but I want you to be courteous. He is our guest. What are you watching?"

"It's an environmental program that Derek told me

to watch. He said he thought I might find it interesting. He's really smart, Jan. He knows what I like and what I don't like. I don't even have to tell him. He's a super guy. He never gets mad and he always explains things to me. He explains even when I don't ask him questions. He listens to me and he hears what I say."

"You really do like him, don't you?" Jan said softly.

"You bet I do. Derek is my friend. He said he'll always be my friend, no matter what happens. And I can always count on him. That makes him a good friend, doesn't it?"

"I'd say so," Jan replied quietly. No matter what happens—now what did Derek mean by that? Probably his marriage to Andrea.

"You don't like him as much as I do, I can tell," Benjie complained.

"I like him, Benjie. It's just that with me it's different than it is with you. You're a little boy, Derek is a man. He relates to you differently that he does to me. I'm a girl." She smiled.

"Derek says some women are wily and tricky, and they like to manipulate men. That means to wrap them around their fingers. I had to get Derek to explain that to me because I didn't understand. He said that some women—like you, Jan—aren't like that at all. He said it's something dumb women have to practice."

Jan flushed. So Derek thought she was dumb and she hadn't practiced enough. Of all the insufferable, egotistical men, he took the prize. "Is that what he said?" Jan muttered through clenched teeth.

"Yeah. But Derek likes ladies. He said they make the world go round."

Jan gulped. She had to put an end to this conversation and now, before Neil made his appearance. "What do you feel like having for dinner?" she asked lightly.

"A hamburger, French fries and a Coke," Benjie said, rattling off his favorite menu, knowing full well he wasn't going to get it. "But, I'll settle for roast beef and baked potatoes. Delilah said that's what she was making. And strawberry-rhubarb pie. She made an extra one for Derek. I'm going to give it to him tomorrow when he picks me up. It's his favorite."

"What's who's favorite, sport?" Neil inquired as he walked up to Benjie clad in another brand-new set of togs.

"Derek likes strawberry-rhubarb pie, and Delilah made an extra one for me to give him tomorrow," Benjie said curtly.

"Listen, sport, you won't have to do that. Now that I'm here I'm going to take you to the hospital for your treatments. It's the least I can do for your sister to show her my appreciation. Your friend Derek can have some time off. Sometimes squiring little kids around can be a real drag. Running that fancy hotel up the road must take a lot of time. I'm sure he'd appreciate the time off. It's settled then," Neil said, looking from Jan to Benjie. Both remained mute, stunned at his words. He did have a point, Jan thought. It was impossible to read Benjie's face as he stared at the small screen.

As far as Jan was concerned, dinner was a dismal affair. Benjie picked at his food and stirred it around his plate with the fork, making scraping noises on the plate. Jan ate little, watching Neil wolf down his food and go back for seconds. Somehow he managed to keep up a running conversation dealing with things he saw wrong and how they could be improved.

"The way I see it, you have a thriving little investment here, and with the proper management you could do a lot better, Jan. You could add at least another dozen cabins and make them closer together. Of course, you'll have to cut back on some of the nature trails and cut down some of the timber, but in the end your bank balance will win out."

"Environmentally, it's not a good idea," Benjie said hotly. "We have to keep the trees and the trails. If Uncle Jake wanted to build on, he would have. Even Derek said people are ruining this country just so rich men can get richer."

Neil's voice rose an octave. "And who is it that owns that glittering neon palace down the road? He must have cut down a good many trees to build that! What's good for him is only good for him and no one else."

"That's a lie!" Benjie said belligerently. Before Jan could gather her wits about her, Benjie had his wheelchair backed away from the table and was whizzing through the dining area and out the wide doors to the patio and pool area.

"Opinionated little bugger, isn't he?" Neil managed through bits of Delilah's pie.

"Why shouldn't he be? Derek Bannon is his friend and that means a lot to Benjie. You attacked Derek and he didn't like it, so he defended the man the only way he knew how. You're too blunt, Neil. And for the rest of your stay here I don't want you to antagonize him anymore. He has enough to contend with as it it."

"Okay, okay. If you want to coddle him that's your business. If you remember correctly that was our problem back in New York. You worry about the kid too much. I'm here now, and I want you to worry about me and show me some consideration. Listen, I have a great idea. Let's go to Bannon's place and make up for lost time. A few drinks and take in the floor show. If you're such a good friend of his, maybe the guy will pick up the tab and it won't cost us a cent. What do you say?"

"Not tonight, Neil. If you want, you can go. I wouldn't be able to dance with the blisters on my feet, and you know I'm a one-drink person."

"Would you mind if I go?" Neil asked hopefully.

"Of course I don't mind. I have a book I want to read, and Benjie and I try to spend some time in the evening together since he's at the hospital most of the day. You go ahead and have a good time. I'll see you in the morning."

"You're terrific. That's why I came here." He swallowed the last of his coffee and rose from the table. Bending over Jan, he gave her a slapdash kiss and was gone before she could speculate on his hasty behavior.

Delilah stood over the table with her hands on her hips, making it clear that she had something to say. It was also clear to Jan that the woman wasn't going to speak until invited. Whatever it was, it must be a shocker, Jan thought. "So say it already," she said wearily.

"Your friend is phony and a freeloader. Gus no like, Benjie no like, and I no like," she said forcefully. "He stay too long, I quit."

"He's just visiting for a while," Jan said hotly, hating

herself for defending Neil. She didn't like him either; he didn't belong here, and if it came right down to the matter, she would rather go to the wedding alone than go with him. How had this happened? Why hadn't Neil called her first before making the trip? She couldn't dwell on the matter now. "We're just going to have to wing it for a while. You can't quit and you know it. Gus wouldn't let you. I'll keep Neil in line and see that he doesn't bother you. What makes you think he's a freeloader?" she asked curiously. "He's going to pay like any other guest."

"No see deposit in book for money. I check out his room," Delilah said slyly. "Much credit cards. No bank book. No cash money. Everything new, still tickets hooked on clothes."

"Shame on you, Delilah. You were spying on Neil. Don't do it anymore," she said sternly, trying hard not to smile at Delilah's indignation.

Delilah sniffed. "You see—he go to Golden Lasso and pick up...how you say...chick."

This time Jan did laugh and so did Delilah. "If he does it might be the best thing that happens around here. And I didn't have a chance to get a deposit from him. He just got here. We do take American Express, you know."

"For you, big problem," Delilah muttered as she started to clear away the dinner table. "Your friend a gigolo."

THE FROWN ON Benjie's sleeping face tore at Jan's heart. He didn't like Neil and he saw him as a threat to his and

Jan's security. Somehow, tomorrow, she was going to have to try to make him understand that Neil was just visiting and nothing was going to come of his visit in the way of a romantic entanglement for herself.

Jan adjusted the thermostat on the air conditioner and straightened the covers. Benjie stirred slightly, muttering something indistinguishable in his sleep. She waited to see if he would wake, and when he didn't, she released a sigh of relief. Turning off the lamp, she closed the door softly behind her.

A quick glance at her watch told her Neil would be just about ready to leave for the Golden Lasso. If she stayed in her room, she could avoid a meeting with him and at the same time she could make the call to Derek she was dreading. There was no reason to put it off, no reason for her to dread telling the club owner that the bank had agreed to her loan application. As one business person to another, he should be happy that she wasn't going to go under and had another chance at making the Rancho Arroyo a paying proposition.

Was it the phone call she was dreading or was it the sound of Derek's voice that was making her stomach churn and her heart pound like a trip-hammer? Twice she picked up the receiver and twice she replace it. Her throat felt dry, so dry she could barely swallow. Maybe, if she cleared her throat and took a sip of water from the bathroom it would help. Nothing would help. Do it and get it over with and go on from there. How would he take the news, she wondered fretfully. Just how badly did he want Rancho Arroyo and for what? A vision of the blueprints on Derek's desk floated before her. The worst he could think was that she was wishy-washy and unable to make up her mind. So what if her credibility came under his close scrutiny. She shouldn't care, but she did, even knowing he was marrying Andrea. She cared; it was as simple as that.

Dial the number, a niggling voice urged. Dial it and say what you have to say and hang up. Do it! Jan dialed the number Derek had given her and waited. Six, seven rings—he must not be home. Eight. "Hello."

"Derek, this is Jan Warren. I hope I didn't take you away from anything. I was just about to hang up."

"Is something wrong? Is Ben all right?" Derek asked in concern.

"Benjie is fine. That's not why I called. I called to tell you that I won't be selling the ranch after all. I applied to the bank for a loan, and they called today to say my application was approved. I'm sure that you understand and you won't hold it against me if I have to go back on my word to you. I have to do what's best for Benjie, and staying here and trying to make a go of the ranch is what I have to do. Your offer was more than generous, but I want you to know that I would have sold it to you for the original offer. I wasn't trying to hold you up or gouge a higher price out of you. Your original offer was more than fair." Jan's hand was clutched so tight on the receiver her knuckles were white as she waited intently for his reply. The creak of the floorboard outside her room didn't register. Neil's shadow in the dim light also went unnoticed as Jan waited.

"I understand, Jan. In a way it was my own fault. I apologize for placing a deadline on the transaction. If you decide to sell at some later time, I hope you'll give me first consideration. And I do hope that you can successfully make a go of the ranch for your own sake as well as your brother's. Good luck."

Jan blinked and looked at the receiver, a foolish look on her face. He certainly had accepted the matter better than she could have hoped for. He was even gracious and he had apologized. And she had worked herself into a frenzy over the matter. Men! He was probably in some kind of tizzy with his fast-approaching wedding and had other things on his mind. Which, she thought tartly, just went to prove that he probably didn't want the ranch so much after all. It would have been just another investment to him. What did he care about her or the people who worked here? Investments, tax dollars, write-offs—that was all people like Derek Bannon thought of. Lust—she had to add lust to the list. And as long as she was making a list, she could add cheating on Andrea and heaven only knew what else. A philanderer, that's what he was. Well, she wasn't going to cry over Derek Bannon. Her days of crying were over. She was going to go on about her life without him.

Darn! She forgot to tell him not to pick Benjie up in the morning. She picked up the phone and then replaced it. She couldn't, she wouldn't, make the second call. She couldn't bear to hear his voice a second time in one night, and this time she would be the one who had to apologize. She would explain in the morning when he arrived for Benjie. It would be harder to do face-to-face, but she would do it. She wasn't a coward. Derek would be annoyed and justifiably so, but he would have to live with his annoyance. She had been forced to live with things over the past weeks that she didn't like and he could do the same.

While she prepared for bed and brushed her teeth, she wondered how long Neil was going to stay. She made a mental note to ask him point-blank on the morrow. She hoped she wouldn't be forced to ask him for an advance payment. Surely he would offer it on his own. He couldn't think he was a nonpaying guest. She would explain, and if he didn't like it, he, too, would have to live with his annoyance at her blunt business manner. She was in business to make money, not give it away. Neil was going to be a problem in more ways than one—she could sense it, feel it in every pore of her body. She would be diplomatic, of course, but she wouldn't beat around the bush with him. How had she ever seriously considered him a possible suitor? She shook her head wearily and slipped into her football jersey.

If she had anything to be thankful for this day, it was that she hadn't paid much attention to her feet. What with the news from the bank and Neil's appearance and Benjie's apprehensions, her feet had stopped hurting. Delilah's herbal bandages had worked their magic, she thought to herself as she slipped beneath the covers.

Jan tossed and turned in her sleep. On the brink of wakefulness, she thought she heard a sound outside her window. Groggily, she crawled from the bed and slipped open her window. She wiped her eyes, trying to clear them and to see into the inky darkness outside. Leaning over the sill, she was stunned at the sight that greeted her. Neil and a girl—obviously a showgirl from the Golden Lasso from the looks of her costume—were chasing around the perimeters of the swimming pool. From where Jan stood, she could make out the bare flash of long, silky leg as the girl scampered away from Neil. Eventually, she allowed Neil to catch her, and Jan flushed at the ardent kiss he was bestowing on the willing girl. His arms around her, he led her toward the trail that led to his cabin. His first night in Arizona and he had made a conquest. Suddenly, Jan hated him. She hated all men.

Slamming the window shut, she paced around the room. What she should do was march right over to Neil's cabin and tell him that she didn't run that kind of place and that if he wanted that kind of extracurricular activity he would have to go somewhere else. This was a family place! That was what she should do, but she wouldn't. But she was going to let him know what she had seen. She wouldn't put up with it—especially not around Benjie. If necessary, she would move Neil into the bunkhouse with the other hands for the remainder of his stay. Gus would keep him on the straight and narrow.

Jan tumbled back into bed. Move him out! By rights, she should throw him out! Out! Right off the Rancho! It didn't seem as though Neil was going to pay for his stay at the Rancho anyway. What did she have to lose?

Escorting her to the wedding so she wouldn't look like an undesirable old maid was no reason… "Oh, *no!*" Jan cried aloud. Here she was thinking she could hide herself from Derek and Andrea behind a seemingly interested suitor, and all the while that suitor was up at the Golden Lasso flirting with the showgirls. She would look more than ever like a fool! Jan's face became heated and red and she felt as though it could light up the dark corners of her lonely room.

# CHAPTER ELEVEN

THE FOLLOWING MORNING brought a fresh set of problems in the way of Delilah and Gus. When Jan entered the dining room for breakfast, Benjie was already seated at the table, his tight little face an indication of what the day was going to be like.

"Where's breakfast, Benjie? It doesn't smell as though anything is cooking," Jan said, a note of apprehension in her voice.

"That's because there isn't any breakfast cooking. We're having cold cereal and Gus is fixing it."

"Is Delilah sick? What's wrong?" Jan demanded, heading for the kitchen.

"I quit is what's the matter," Delilah announced as she pulled a heavy suitcase through the doorway.

"Why? What's wrong? What's happened this time?" Delilah sniffed disdainfully and pranced for the lobby.

"Delilah, I demand an answer!"

The rotund woman turned and her dark eyes snapped at Jan. "You say living in sin is not good for young boy. You say it is wrong. Right? So I tell that old Indian that I want to marry, don't want to live in sin anymore."

Jan turned to Gus, who was pouring milk over

Benjie's cereal. "And what did you say, Gus?" she asked, feeling more like a monkey in the middle by the moment.

"Darn fool woman," Gus growled. "She said she wanted to get married so I said okay. Now she's changed her mind. I won't ask her again."

"Not what he said at all," Delilah said angrily. "He say we have big Indian wedding. Humph! Me not stupid Indian woman. I know the law. Indian wedding not count for that!" She snapped her fingers. "Indian wedding is nothing. Must have license…everything! So I tell the old man Delilah only get married in Presbyterian church or nothing."

"You're throwing away a chance for Gus to marry you because of that?" Jan said incredulously. "I thought you said you didn't want to get married. Something about a fly sticking to honey. Which is it?" she asked wearily.

"So, I change my mind. Church wedding, marriage license, or nothing. Gus has one foot in happy hunting grounds. When he go, I want Social Security."

"I don't believe this," Jan said, rubbing her temples wearily. "Why can't you two get married because you love each other? Why do you have to put each other through all this torment?"

"I tell you if we marry we have problems," Delilah groaned.

"What's wrong with the Presbyterian Church, Gus?" Jan asked.

"Indian wedding or nothing," Gus answered flatly.

"No, you wrong. Presbyterian church or nothing," Delilah shot back hotly.

"Then it's nothing," Gus muttered, stalking from the room.

"Why don't you have them compromise and get married by the justice of the peace and have an Indian reception afterward?" Derek asked as he walked into the dining room. Jan groaned in echo to Delilah's groan. Why did he always show up when she was in a spot? This time she was grateful for his advice. She didn't need a rebellious cook and a surly handyman.

"What do you say, Delilah? A justice of the peace sounds good to me. You give a little, Gus gives a little."

"No problem with Social Security later on?" Delilah demanded of Derek.

Derek grinned. "No problem. I guarantee it."

"Then it's settled," Jan said gratefully. "All you have to do is decide on a date and that's it."

"Is good thinking," Delilah said, waddling back to the kitchen pushing her heavy suitcase in front of her.

"Is Ben ready?" Derek asked. "I've got the car running."

"I could eat a horse! Where's breakfast?" Neil interrupted as he entered the room, rubbing his hands together briskly as though he were expecting to sit down to a long-awaited meal. "Oh, Bannon, are you here to take Benjie? No need, old buddy. I'll be doing it from now on. Jan wanted to stop by the hospital and see one of her employees, and I offered to drive. Right, Jan? Get you off the hook, Bannon," he said loudly, slapping Derek soundly on the back.

Derek's eyes narrowed as he stared first at Neil and then at Jan.

Jan felt her heart race up to her throat, and she felt powerless to tear her gaze away from Derek's. She had to say something. Derek didn't wait. He turned on his heel and stalked out the door.

Feeling as though she'd been kicked in the stomach, Jan watched him leave. She had never seen Derek look at her like that, as though he hated her. And Benjie was avoiding her glance, his own mouth grim and tight. She might have one problem solved, but she had another now, a worse one.

"When do we eat? Who's cooking?"

"Whenever you want to eat, as long as you cook it, Neil. Delilah is taking the morning off. And from now on, Neil, you either get here on time for breakfast or you'll cook it yourself. Even when we're full with guests, breakfast is served between certain times. Anything else would be less than fair to Delilah. By the way, Neil, I'd like to have your American Express card so I can properly bill you for your stay here. Give it to me now so I can take care of the paperwork while you prepare your breakfast."

"My American Express card!" Neil said in surprise. "Do you mean you're really going to charge me for my stay here? And I still have to make my own breakfast? I came here, Jan, to see you, and I intend to help out in order to earn my keep." He laughed as he made his statements.

"I'm sorry, Neil. I don't operate a give-away establishment, and after today you'll have to move into the bunkhouse with the other hands. If it was a job you wanted, you could have said so from the beginning.

Also, all hands eat in the kitchen. Ask the men what time. You'll be sitting at their table from now on."

"Move me to the bunkhouse? But I like that cabin—it affords me privacy, and I won't be in your hair," Neil said, a note of panic in his voice.

"I'll just bet you like your privacy," Jan said tartly, remembering the scene below her bedroom window in the wee hours of the morning. "I'm sorry, but hands stay in the bunkhouse. Also, there are guests arriving in the morning. The cabins have been reserved. I can't let them down now. In case you don't understand, I'm in business to make money, not to give it away. That cabin has to be free to accommodate a guest."

"Is it reserved?" Neil demanded.

"No, not yet. But if I have an opportunity to take a reservation for it, I will."

"If that's the way you feel about it, here," Neil said, whipping out the plastic credit card. Jan accepted it and walked to the office, praying that the card was good. Neil was angry and behaving like a spoiled child. Her original instincts about him had been correct. He had thought he was going to be her guest in every sense of the word. What would he do and say when he realized that she had seen him bring the showgirl to his cabin? Somehow she knew he would try to weasel out of that, too.

NEIL STAYED IN attendance while Benjie had his physical therapy as soon as he realized that was what Derek Bannon had always done. Benjie had protested, saying that it wasn't necessary, that he could make out just fine on his own. But Neil had insisted.

Jan took the opportunity to visit Andy Stone.

"Don't say it." The cowboy grinned as he watched Jan eye the apparatus that held his leg in its sling. "You aren't going to believe this, but I'm having the time of my life. There's this great little nurse on the three-to-eleven shift and she adores me. All she wants to do is give me sponge baths and back rubs. She says I'm her most willing patient."

"Just what I need, another wedding. Well, they say it always goes in threes," Jan grimaced.

"Who's getting married?"

"Delilah and Derek Bannon."

Andy laughed raucously. "Somehow I didn't think Delilah was his type!"

Jan laughed in spite of herself. "No, silly, not Delilah and Derek. Delilah and Gus and, of course, Derek Bannon."

Andy Stone whistled softly. "Derek Bannon is getting married? I didn't think there was a woman good enough for him. Surprises me that he's finally going to tie the knot. He's the sort of guy you always expect to end up a bachelor."

"Same difference. Marriage won't change anything for him."

"Aha, so that's the way the wind blows. You fell for the guy, right? Look, Jan, this is none of my business but you're real people. Down-home. Bannon is in a different league. I'm real sorry you got hurt."

"Andy, I've known what you think of Derek right from the first time I met you at the airport. But, believe it or not, he does have his saving graces. Did you know he's been bringing Benjie in for his therapy almost every day. Not only that, but he saw Benjie through some pretty bad times. I walked into that whole thing with my eyes wide open. I've been hurt before and lived through it. What do you think about Delilah and Gus?" she asked, hoping to change the subject.

"I never thought he'd get married either. What did she do? Club Gus over the head? He's pretty set in his ways, Jan. Do you think he can handle a piece of paper that says he belongs to Delilah?"

"It was touch and go there for a while, but I think he's going to come around. Gus wanted an Indian wedding and Delilah was holding out for a Presbyterian church. I think they're going with the justice of the peace and then an Indian reception."

"When is the wedding? I hope I'm out of here. I want to give the bride away." Andy grinned. "Delilah's been good to me. Almost like a mother. You should have been there the day I tried to explain the Social Security system to her."

"Let me be the first to tell you that you got through to her loud and clear." Laughing and giggling, Jan explained about the meeting in the kitchen that morning. She felt happy sitting here with Andy, and it was with regret when an hour later she had to leave when the nurse said that visiting hours were over.

THE RIDE BACK to the ranch was made in silence except for Neil's comments from time to time. Jan hated the sour look on Benjie's face and wondered if her own countenance was similar. This was best, she kept telling herself. Benjie had to be weaned from Derek's company sooner or later because when he got married he would forget the little boy. And, she thought bitterly, let's not forget the honeymoon. Benjie had said just a few days ago that Andrea said the honeymoon was thirty days in Europe. Wearily she closed her eyes. This was the best solution, the only solution, for both of them.

Her plan to hire summer college students to help at the ranch could now be put into effect. One of the stipulations for the job would be that Benjie be kept occupied. Hopefully, Benjie would be able to relate to the young people. If not, then she would have to come up with some other plan, but she would cross that bridge when she came to it. She was going to do the best she could by her brother and what more could anyone ask or expect of her?

"We're home, Benjie. I'll get Gus to help you into the Jacuzzi for your thirty minutes."

"Help me out of the car, I'm tired," Benjie complained.

Jan frowned. He did look tired—as a matter of fact, he looked utterly exhausted. "Okay, I'll help you today, but after this you have to do it yourself. Is that understood?" Benjie ignored her as she and Neil struggled with his limp form. He made no effort at all to maneuver himself into his wheelchair.

The minute he was out of sight Neil reached for Jan's arm. "I thought you said he was doing well and would be walking soon. He looks the same to me and that therapy session was a waste of three hours. Are you sure you aren't pouring your money down the drain?"

"The doctor says he's coming along nicely, and I'm

not concerned about spending the money for Benjie's treatments, so don't worry about it. Benjie's just tired—those therapy sessions are hard on him—and he still has the Jacuzzi to get through. He's doing remarkably well, and I have every confidence in the doctor's prognosis."

"Exactly what is the doctor's prognosis?" Neil asked intently.

"That with proper treatment over an extended period of time Benjie will walk again," Jan said curtly. "Why?"

"I'm concerned over the little tyke. After all, we may one day soon decide to take that fateful step, and I want what's best for the kid just as much as you do. I'm not callous, you know."

"What fateful step are you talking about?" Jan asked, remembering the girl from the Lasso in the pool area.

Neil appeared flustered. "You know—we're engaged to be engaged, that sort of thing. I'm certainly willing to marry you if you decide that it's what you want. I wanted to give you enough time to get Benjie squared away before I asked you for a commitment. We'll work something out. Later," he added hastily.

Jan pretended puzzlement. "Work something out. Oh, I see, you mean you'll try to fit me in between visits to the Golden Lasso and all those luscious beauties scampering around. Thanks, but no thanks. I really think it's my destiny to be an old maid. A rich old maid," she added viciously as she stormed into the lobby. Of all the gall. Did she wear some invisible sign that she was good enough for certain men when they didn't have anything better to do. Bitter tears of frustration burned her eyes at the thought.

Nonchalantly, she looked around. Neil hadn't even bothered to follow her inside to say something trite, as was his manner when she got the upper hand.

She felt angry and humiliated as she plopped down on the swivel chair behind the desk.

Delilah marched into the room, a broom in one hand and the mail in the other. She laid the mail on the desk and turned to leave.

"Delilah, I've been thinking. I don't think you should get married after all. Men are terrible and they take advantage of women. We don't do that to them. I want you to think about it some more before you decide for sure."

Delilah's eyes widened. "First, you say live in sin no good. Then you say marry and live happy life. Now you say sin okay. I want Social Security and real wedding. Gus agree to all my demands. If I chicken out now, I make fool of myself."

"Don't you see? That's the whole point. All we women ever seem to do is make fools of ourselves over men. Do you really want to get married or not? If you don't want to get married, then don't do it."

"How else I get Social Security?"

"Didn't Andy explain to you that my uncle, and now I, pay your Social Security? You can collect on your own without marrying Gus. Look," Jan said patiently, "all I'm trying to tell you is don't get married for the wrong reasons. If you love Gus and want to get married, that's fine. If you're marrying him for his Social Security, that's the wrong reason."

"Gus have many...how you say...defects," Delilah

said, comimg up with the right word. "He sometime drink too much and no good for much."

"That's another thing. If he's drunk all the time, how do you handle it?" Jan asked.

Delilah shrugged and grinned toothily. "For me no problem. I put him to bed and play with him later."

In spite of herself, Jan laughed. "Do what you want, Delilah, but make sure it's what you really want. And don't worry about your Social Security—it's all taken care of. Where are you going with that broom?"

"I chase Gus to help Benjie."

"Why didn't you just tell him instead of going after him with the broom?" Jan asked, knowing she wasn't going to like the answer.

"And have Gus think I not love him? Shame," she said, wagging her finger under Jan's nose. "Gus expect me to go after him. He like it when I chase him. Is love game we play. Like when you get lost in desert and Mr. Bannon come for you. Was big trick you play, no?"

"No, it wasn't a trick. I really was lost."

"I hear that story before. All young guests that come to ranch do that so Andy go after them." Delilah sniffed as she marched from the room, the broom held straight in front of her.

# CHAPTER TWELVE

THE DAYS continued to pass, each of them bringing Jan closer to having to attend Andrea's wedding. There were, however, several distractions that proved to be welcome. Another wave of guests arrived at Rancho Arroyo. With the help of two part-time workers things were working out nicely. Andy would be home from the hospital in another week, complete with a walking cast. Although he would be unable to resume his strenuous activities, his advice and know-how would be invaluable.

Delilah had postponed her wedding plans, much to Gus's relief, and was spending whatever time she could steal away from the kitchen with Benjie. The youngster had become withdrawn and had regressed alarmingly, according to Dr. Rossi's latest reports. Jan had relinquished her care of Benjie to Delilah because the boy seemed to become even more sullen and uncooperative whenever she was around. As much as she wanted to believe that this was a temporary state of affairs between her brother and herself, Jan was plagued with concern.

As she took care of the paperwork at the desk in the lobby, Jan's eyes fell on the calender near her elbow. Her heart thumped painfully when the red circled date denoting the wedding date leaped out at her. She had neither seen nor heard from Derek since that morning in the kitchen when Neil told him he would be taking Benjie for his regular visits to the medical center. Out of sight, out of mind, she thought wistfully.

Even before she saw him, Jan picked up the heavy scent of Neil's cologne. He approached the desk and said encouragingly, "It's two o'clock. You are ready to go riding, aren't you?"

If there was one thing she didn't feel like doing, it was going riding with Neil, but she had promised and she would have to honor that promise. Besides, it was time she had a long talk with Neil and found out exactly what his plans were. The past few days everything concerning the tall blond man annoyed her, and she found herself hoping that each day would be his last on her Rancho. The thought made her feel guilty, and she smiled to let him know she was ready to leave with him. "I'm ready whenever you are. Benjie is in the Jacuzzi so I have a little free time."

"I knew that, so I saddled the horses and have them out by the paddock waiting for us. Come on, slowpoke, get a move on," Neil joked.

"You go ahead. I want to change into riding boots and I'll meet you in a few minutes." Neil banged out the screen door and Jan added a column of figures before she closed her ledger and headed toward the stairs and her room.

Looking neither to the right nor the left, Jan crossed the lobby and walked smack into Derek Bannon. It took only one glance for her to see that he was furious to the point of rage.

"You little fool, do you have any idea what you've

done?" he demanded coldly. "Do you have any idea at all?"

"Let go of me!" Jan said, frightened by the viselike grip he had on her arm. "What are you talking about?"

"What am I talking about? Don't you know? Are you so blind and wrapped up in your Rhinestone Cowboy that you've lost sight of what's happening to Ben? Open your eyes! Look at your brother and tell me what you see!"

Frightened by his fury, Jan could only stare at Derek. She could feel her knees tremble and the pain in her arm from his grip was tooth rattling. "What are you talking about?" she repeated.

"I'm talking about Ben and the phone call I received from Dr. Rossi. He tells me Ben has regressed almost to the point he was at when he first began attending the clinic. He chewed me out for neglecting the boy. He also said that when I start something I should finish it and that I had no right to play around with a child's life. Are you listening to me, Jan Warren? Do you hear me? Dr. Rossi said Ben isn't responding to the therapy and he has no desire or will to walk again. He said Ben gave up. Now," Derek said angrily, shaking her arm so viciously that her head almost snapped, "I want you to tell me what's going on, and then I'm going to tell you what I'm going to do."

Jan was terrified both by his verbal and physical onslaught. "Dr. Rossi told me several days ago that Benjie had a setback. That he was regressing. He said he was optimistic and would continue with the treatments. Benjie is…Benjie isn't very happy. He missed you. I knew you would do this to him. You don't care about him. If you did, you would have come around to see how he was doing. Regardless of who takes Benjie for his therapy, you never should have deserted him the way you did. Also, I thought when you found out I wasn't going to sell the Rancho that you didn't want to be bothered with either Benjie or me. I thought…"

"Do me a favor, Miss Warren—don't think. I can't afford it when you think. From now on I'll be taking Ben for his treatments, and if that neon sign that poses as your engaged-to-be-engaged boyfriend interferes, his lights are going to be punched out! When I start something, I finish it. Now where the hell is Ben?"

"He's…he's out in the Jacuzzi. He still has five minutes to go and I think…"

"I've told you, don't think!" Derek snapped "Even Delilah has more sense than you do. Feebleminded…" The rest of his words were lost on Jan as Derek made his way to the pool.

Jan stood on the side and wanted to die at the look on Benjie's face when he saw Derek stoop down on his heels. "I knew you wouldn't forget me! What are you doing here? How come you came? How are all the guys at the Lasso? Gee, Derek, I missed you. How long can you stay?" Benjie babbled nonstop.

"Whoa. One question at a time. From now on I'm back to taking you for your therapy. What in the world made you think I could forget my good buddy? I had some business that needed my attention. I came to see you. The guys miss you, and Dusty said I was to bring you back for the barbecue tonight. I missed you, too,

Ben. So what do you say? Shake off the water—your time is up. Let's make tracks for the Lasso. There's a lot of your friends who are eager to see you."

"Just you and me, Derek?" Benjie asked hopefully as he waited for Derek's reply.

"You got it—just you and me. Andrea and the guys will be at the barbecue, but with a little luck we can shake them easily enough. Between the two of us, we should be able to handle it."

"Wow! I can't wait! Derek, I haven't been doing so good with Dr. Rossi. I didn't make any...progress since you left."

"I heard about it and I'm here to see that you get back on the track."

"I can't get out of the Jacuzzi by myself. I can't do anything by myself anymore," Benjie said quietly, his blue eyes solemn, the dancing lights that had been there when he first saw Derek extinguished.

"I guess I can help you this time around. Starting tomorrow, though, you're on your own."

Jan watched with a catch in her throat as Derek bent down and lifted Benjie from the Jacuzzi and wrapped the boy in a thirsty towel. Carefully, as though he were handling eggs, he settled the little boy in his wheelchair and bellowed for Delilah. "Dress him and bring him back here. Ten minutes," he thundered.

Derek Bannon made no move in Jan's direction but stood glaring at her in stony silence. His eyes clearly said all, and she knew the words. Hadn't she been saying them to herself over and over these past few days? She had neglected Benjie. She had refused to see what was happening to the little boy. She had been so wrapped up in the ranch and fending off Neil that she had neglected the most important person in her life. If it hadn't been for Derek, how long would she have allowed it to continue? She had no defense; there was no defense. Her shoulders drooped as she headed for Benjie's room.

As Jan turned and walked away, she had half expected Derek to call out to her, to rail her out, to yell and holler, but he hadn't. Why should he? There was no sign that he even knew she was visible.

Delilah was just wheeling Benjie through the door when Jan got to his room. Gus waited patiently for Delilah to help Benjie dress so he could carry him back down the stairs.

"I heard you were going to the Lasso for a barbecue. Have a good time, Benjie," Jan said, her eyes brimming with tears.

"Are you crying because I'm leaving?" Benjie asked in surprise.

"Heck, no. I think I have some kind of allergy."

"Yup," Delilah muttered from where she rummaged through Benjie's dresser for a shirt. "Me get allergy, too. Whenever the dude with the big hat come around. He make my eyes water, too," the woman sniffed.

"Derek says the desert is the best place for allergies. Derek is finished with his business and he's going to take me for my therapy again, starting tomorrow. It's okay, isn't it?" he said anxiously.

"You bet it is," Jan said, blowing her nose.

"Jan, if Derek asks me to sleep over, can I? He said

there's a guest room and it's got my name on the door. Can I, Jan? I never did before, because I didn't want you to be alone. Your friend is here, so, if he asks me this time, can I stay?"

Jan was aware of two things—one, that Benjie really did care for her and was concerned about her, and the other, that he still never called Neil by name but always referred to him as "her" friend.

"I think it's a great idea. I know you're going to have a good time. Give me a call, though, just so I know your plans. Okay? I'll be fine. You'd better get a move on. I heard Mr. Bannon give you ten minutes and you're on overtime right now." Quickly, she gave Benjie a peck on the cheek.

Later, Neil found Jan leaning against the wall outside the kitchen door. Tears were streaming down her cheek, but he didn't seem to notice. "Do you have any idea what time it is? I've been standing out there with two saddled horses for over half an hour and I feel like a fool! Are you going riding or not?" he demanded arrogantly.

"Shut up, Neil. Shut up and don't say another word," Jan cried as she ran into the lodge and slammed the door shut behind her. Up in her room, she threw herself on her bed and buried her face in her pillow.

THE SOFT, VELVETY NIGHT enveloped Jan as she strolled the grounds of the Rancho Arroyo. For the second time in days she made a decision to sell the ranch to Derek Bannon. She knew now she could never live in such close proximity to Derek and still survive emotionally.

Today had been proof of that fact. Instead of calling Derek, she would write him a formal business letter and spell out the terms for him. She would be asking his original offer, not the elevated, inflated price he had offered when he thought she was being plain stubborn.

If Derek didn't want the property or had changed his mind, then she would have to sell it to someone else. Surely there were other businessmen who would be interested in the Rancho for investment purposes.

She would have to work something out with the hospital and Dr. Rossi as far as Benjie's treatments were concerned. Jan's anger rose and her sense of justice was assaulted. It was fine for Derek to storm into the ranch and tell her he was taking over Benjie's treatments again because she had sloughed off on her job. But what and who was going to take care of Benjie while Derek was away on his thirty-day honeymoon in Europe? I'll just bet he never gave *that* a thought, Jan sniffed.

A deep feeling of loneliness swept over her. Why couldn't someone fall in love with her and cherish her the way the heroes did in books? She wasn't ugly; she'd been told she had a pleasing personality. Was she unaware of something about herself that was a definite turnoff as far as men were concerned? Men, she said to herself. Be honest; when you talk about men, you're thinking only of Derek Bannon.

A deep sob rose in her throat and she squelched it immediately. No more crying, she told herself firmly.

How bright the stars were. It was a beautiful night, a night made for lovers and close embraces. Someday she would have another night like this and someone special to share it with her.

"Jan, I've been looking all over for you," Neil's voice called from somewhere deep in the shadows. "I want to talk to you."

From where she stood Jan picked up the excitement in Neil's voice. What now? she groaned inwardly.

Neil emerged into the flickering lights that surrounded the pool and motioned for Jan to sit down on a yellow chaise. "I have something I want to tell you," he said exuberantly.

"That's good. Because I have something I want to tell you," Jan said quietly.

"Whatever it is, it can wait. This is important. Jan, I want you to marry me! I've just discovered something that will make us millionaires. Are you listening?"

"Of course I'm listening, and so is half the Rancho. Lower your voice, please," Jan admonished.

Neil's voice dropped a tone. "Jan, don't sell the ranch to Bannon. I found out why he wants it. We can beat him to the punch and do it ourselves and make a fortune."

Jan laughed. He hadn't even bothered to wait for a reply to his marriage proposal. She raised her eyes heavenward and grinned. "This isn't exactly what I had in mind when I prayed for someone to love and cherish me," she mumbled almost silently.

"What did you say?" Neil questioned. "Never mind. Listen. Don't sell Bannon the Rancho."

"What? How did you know? I never told you Derek wanted to buy the Rancho…"

"I know, I know. I overheard you talking to him on the phone…"

"You what?" Jan hissed, starting to rise from her chair. "You spied on me? That's despicable…"

Neil pushed her back down onto the chaise. "Look, there's no time for that now. I know about it and that's all that counts. But don't do it, Jan. We'll take over his plans and make ourselves a fortune. Today I took a run over to the shopping center for some shaving supplies, and there's an architect's office right next to the drugstore. And whose car do you think was parked right outside? Your friend Bannon's. There were some rolled-up blueprints on the front seat and I sort of took a look at them. Don't worry, he doesn't know anything about it. I saw him go into the drugstore with Benjie."

"You what?" Jan demanded, fury lighting her eyes to shards of green glass.

"Shut up. Let me finish. I saw those blueprints, and believe me when I tell you that Bannon is out to steal this place right out of your hands. You can't sell it to him."

"Don't you mean you spied on Derek Bannon, and you spied on me, too? You didn't just happen to see the blueprints—you spied. You should be ashamed of yourself!"

"Well, I'm not!" Neil answered loftily. "It's Bannon who should be ashamed for what he's trying to pull over on you. Well, I won't let him do it to you, to us. I'll pull the rug from under him and we'll roll in clover from now on."

"Neil, I don't love you. I don't want to marry you. Stop saying 'us.'"

Jan's words penetrated and made an impression.

"Okay, then I'll be your business manager. We'll clean up," he said, rubbing his hands together. "Say, you didn't even ask what the plans were. Don't you care? Oh, I see. You really don't care and you'll leave it up to me."

"You're right about one thing—I don't care. Listen, Neil, I'm selling the Rancho to Derek Bannon for his original offer. I have no intention of gouging him or keeping this place. I have to do what's best for Benjie and myself. I can't worry about you or Mr. Bannon. I really am tired, Neil, so, if you'll excuse me, I'll go up to bed and you can go back to the Golden Lasso and your nocturnal prowling. By the way, you're going to have to vacate the bunkhouse. Andy Stone will be discharged from the hospital over the weekend, and he'll need his bunk. All the cabins are either filled or reserved, so you'll have to vamoose. You should be able to get a room at the Lasso. Sorry," she said, getting up from the chaise.

Neil appeared stunned but recovered rapidly. "I don't believe what I'm hearing," he snapped. "This guy is out to rip you off and you tell me to move out, when all I have is your best interests at heart? He's going to build some kind of treatment center for cripples like Benjie. How do you like that? If you keep this place and do the same thing, you could make a fortune. Do you know how easy it is to apply for federal aid? Everybody's got a soft heart when it comes to crippled kids. We could make a fortune just skimming off the top. You're a fool, Jan. I can't believe you're selling out! You could have a gold mine here. Open your eyes!"

Jan's face froze into shocked lines. Could she believe

what she was hearing? One look at Neil's determined features told her. "You are the most despicable man I've ever known," she hissed. "You can't stand the sight of Benjie because he's disabled, and yet you'd make the Rancho into a treatment center for children just like Benjie and then steal from them! Get back under your rock, Neil. I want you to clear out of here before morning."

"Listen, Jan. I've put up with a lot from both Benjie and you, and I'm not going to let you go until you see things my way!"

"You don't know *my* way, Neil," she said savagely, lifting her hand and slapping him soundly across his hated face.

"Why, you little…!" Instantly, Neil was on his feet, dragging her up with him and holding her fast. "You love him, don't you? You think if you sell the Rancho to him that will make him come around. I've seen him at the Lasso. Women follow him as though he were the pied piper. He's the kind of man who takes everything and leaves nothing behind but tatters and frayed ends. You aren't his type." Neil's voice had become shrill.

Jan struggled for her release, her fingers curling into claws reaching for his face. "I know one thing, Neil— Derek Bannon doesn't steal. If his plan is to make a treatment center for handicapped children, it isn't with the intention of skimming off the top. Regardless of his romantic adventures, he's a man of honor and principle. But, then, you wouldn't know anything about that, would you?"

"You're not going to cheat me out of this, Jan. This

is the chance of a lifetime, and you're not going to stop me!" Unleashing his rage, Neil tossed her backward, knocking her off balance and throwing her down into the chaise. She saw him lift his arm, his hand bunched into a fist, ready to strike her.

Suddenly, a figure stepped out from the path and seized Neil's arm. Derek Bannon. Neil turned with fury upon Derek, now aiming his blow upon him. Derek blocked, stopping Neil's fist in midair, and directed a well-placed blow to Neil's midsection. As Neil doubled over to clutch his stomach, Derek pounded his fist into Neil's face, knocking him backward onto the grass.

"Now, get up and get out of here. You heard the lady! And don't ever show your face around these parts again!" Derek's voice was harsh, filled with menace and fury.

Neil touched his hand to his nose and mouth, and his fingers came away stained with his own blood.

Stunned by Derek's sudden violence, Jan stood abruptly and loomed over Neil's reclining figure. "I've told you once and I'll tell you again—this time for the last time. Go back under your rock, Neil—that's where you belong." Unable to stomach the sight of him for another instant, she turned on her heel, squared her shoulders, and headed for the lodge.

Derek caught up with her on the veranda and held the door open for her. "I just came by to tell you Benjie is staying the night with me. He's with Dusty and the guys right now. I tried calling you, but Delilah said you were outside somewhere. I came by hoping to find you."

Why was he looking at her that way? Had he heard her defense of him to Neil? Or had he just happened upon them just as Neil was about to strike her? Even if he had heard, what difference did it make? It couldn't matter to him; he was going to marry Andrea in just a few days. "Good night, Derek. Thank you for going to all this trouble to tell me about Benjie."

"Jan, wait. I want to talk to you." Derek gripped her wrist, stopping her hasty retreat.

"Regardless of what you want, Derek, I've had enough. *E-N-O-U-G-H!* Go back where you belong and I'll stay where I belong." He reached for her, his hand cupping her chin, forcing her gaze to meet his. Desperately, Jan tried to avoid his penetrating stare. In agonizing defeat she knew she was helpless against him. Slowly—ever so slowly—she raised her eyes to meet his. The past few minutes had been too emotionally charged. She had discovered so much, and yet there were so many mysterious shadows remaining. She admitted it hadn't been so great a shock to discover what a heel Neil Connors was. Hadn't she always suspected it, based on the way he treated Benjie? And it hadn't really come as a devastating revelation to learn that Derek intended to use the Rancho Arroyo as a camp for handicapped children. Hadn't she learned about his generosity at the medical center? But, still, it was all becoming too much to handle. It was the havoc her own emotions created within her that was bringing tears to her eyes. Derek touched his finger to the glistening tear as it raced along her smooth cheek.

"You're coming with me," he stated simply, pulling her across the porch and pushing her into his station wagon, which was parked out in front of the lodge.

All the fight had gone out of her. Somehow she knew that her protests would fall on deaf ears, and she was so tired. So very tired. Drained emotionally. Obedient to his demands, she allowed herself to be put into the car and sat quietly as he climbed in beside her and spurred the engine to life.

The night was black, the only light coming from the headlights as they drove along the road leading to the interstate highway. Jan cowered against the door, too numbed to wonder where he was taking her, too defeated to even ask.

Just before the turnoff for the interstate, Derek swung the long station wagon onto a side road and parked. The lights from the dashboard struck his features, turning his eyes dark and delineating his chiseled jaw. His dark hair was tousled and falling across his forehead, lending him a boyish look. But his mouth was grim, tight—little more than a thin line of anger.

"Now will you tell me what this is all about? What goes on in that silly head of yours? Jan," he said in exasperation, "sometimes I feel as though we're so close. Then suddenly, without warning, something comes between us and I don't understand it. I know you feel something for me. You proved that the day we were in Dr. Rossi's barn."

Jan was silent, refusing to answer. What did he want her to do? What did he want her to say? He had no right to bring her here, to corner her, to demand she confess she loved him when in a few days he would be marrying someone else. Or was that his little game? Did his male ego demand she throw herself at his feet and plead and beg with him not to marry Andrea? Never! She warned herself. Regardless of how close and tempting those words were to her lips. She would never beg. How could he not know that his relationship with Andrea was the only thing that kept her from throwing herself into his arms and declaring her love?

"Jan?" His voice was so close it startled her. Suddenly his arms were around her, pulling her closer. His lips found the soft skin below her ear and his breath was warm and stirred her senses as he whispered, "Don't pull away, Jan…" And then his mouth covered hers and blocked out the universe.

Jan was moved by his plea. How could she deny him anything? This was Derek, the man she loved. She relaxed against him, her head tipped upward and resting against his shoulder. She felt the featherlight caress of his lips on her hair. "You always smell so sweet," he murmured as he bent his head, searching once again for her lips.

Her arms slid around him, aware of his hard-muscled torso against her touch. Unconsciously, her hands wound around him, hugging him closer. Derek kissed her, a warm, searching, drugging kiss, teasing Jan's senses and licking the flames of passion that were banked within her. Slow to passion, deliciously slow, touching, tender, loving, adoring…his lips traced a pattern that evoked her response.

His hands took possession of her, roaming lazily over her body, molding her to him. And he breathed her name, so softly she thought she had only imagined hearing it.

Her parted lips followed the strong line of his jaw

and descended to the hollow of his neck. She gave herself up to the pressure of his touch on her body, feeling as though the world began and ended within the circle of his embrace.

The night was dark; the moment was rapture. Derek held her tenderly, quieting his passions, yet arousing her own. And when she felt his fingers fumbling with the buttons on her blouse, she made no protest. Being with him, loving him seemed the most natural thing in the world.

His touch against her skin ignited a spark that blossomed into a shower of flames. The sound of her name on his lips before he covered hers was as heady as imported brandy. And the air was sweet and the night was silent. Only the whisper of his name rode on the desert breeze.

And when he followed the curve of her chin along her throat and touched his lips to the hollow between her breasts, she arched her back, welcoming his touch. Within her burned the new sensation of an indescribable budding, a splintering emotion that swelled and bounded from deep within her.

When she heard it, she thought it was merely wishful thinking. But he said it again—this time louder, hesitantly, as though unsure of her response. "I love you, Jan."

The words that she longed to hear and should have made her the happiest woman alive instead broke the magic. Jan's spine stiffened and he sensed her immediate withdrawal.

Puzzled, he sat back, looking at her as she struggled

with shaking fingers to redo her buttons. Softly, so softly she had to strain to hear him, he said, "I thought you wanted me to love you, Jan."

Jan's eyes flashed with fury. "To repeat one of your own phrases, Mr. Bannon, you shouldn't think! Now, take me home!"

She was angry, angrier than she'd ever been in her life. Derek had no right to do these things to her! He had no right to tell her he loved her—not with Andrea waiting for him up at the Golden Lasso!

Without another word, Derek started the car and expertly maneuvered it around and onto the secondary road leading to the Rancho. Although he was silent, when Jan sneaked a peek at him she saw his features were stricken. He gripped the steering wheel with a fury that whitened his knuckles. She couldn't think! She wouldn't think! She wouldn't be Derek Bannon's new plaything until something better came his way. And what of his wife-to-be? Jan never imagined that she would find cause to pity the beautiful Andrea, but at this moment that was exactly what she did.

A few moments later Derek drove the station wagon up to the front of the lodge. An instant before Jan found the door handle Derek turned to face her. His features were stiff with rage and his voice, when he spoke, was rife with menace. "Get out of my car, Miss Warren. I'll do my best to forget what a fool I made of myself tonight, and I hope you'll have the decency to do the same. Get out."

Jan was paralyzed by the menace in his tone and the naked hatred in his face. "Decency!" she cried. He had

already turned his head away from her and his foot
pressed the accelerator and revved the engine impatiently. Exasperated beyond words, Jan sprung from
the car and slammed the door shut, hearing the window
rattle and wishing it would shatter into a million pieces.
It would be fitting. That's exactly what her heart felt
like—as though Derek Bannon had crushed it in his
hands and shattered it into a million pieces.

## CHAPTER THIRTEEN

JAN DESCENDED the stairs early the next morning and pasted a stiff smile on her face. There was no sense in parading around with her heart on her sleeve for all the hands to see. The night had been interminably long and lonely. Thoughts of Derek kept turning over and over in her head, denying her peace and stealing her sleep. And when she did fall asleep, finally, it was only to awaken with a start, expecting to find him there beside her, whispering her name and holding her close. She must put it all behind her now, push it out of her mind and out of her life. But all through the night she heard him whisper, "I love you, Jan," and yet the dreaded vision of the naked hatred on his face as he ordered her out of his car returned to confound her.

Quickly, she entered the kitchen where Delilah was busy at the stove while the ranch hands stood in line waiting for her to drop a stack of wheat cakes onto their plates.

After saying good morning, Jan poured herself a cup of coffee and looked inquiringly at Delilah. "When did you start humming to yourself in the morning?"

"When your friend make tracks in the night."

"Neil?"

"*Tsk, tsk, tsk*—you have only one friend. Yes, Rhinestone Cowboy leave early this morning. Not even leave one rhinestone behind. Is good, yes?" Delilah grinned, showing her strong white teeth.

"Is good, yes," Jan mimicked. "But I'm not surprised. He received his walking papers last night."

"Yes. And also he got something else," Delilah said as she served another ranch hand. "Your friend got himself one swollen lip, two loose teeth, and banged-up nose. Right, fellas?" She addressed the four men sitting at the long table, devouring her luscious wheat cakes.

"Right!" they called in unison.

Jan grimaced, Neil had lived with the hands and yet he had been unable to become friends with any of them. That had a lot to say about the man.

"Wonder who punched your friend out?" Delilah muttered. "Me? I not give him time of day."

"Hmm. I wonder." Jan pretended bafflement.

"Sometimes I think you maybe not so dumb as you look," Delilah said heartily. "You just take longer than most."

Jan gulped. "I'll take that as a compliment and leave the rest unsaid." She grimaced. "How's breakfast coming? Need any help?"

"No, you sit down and eat. You too skinny—like stick!"

Jan took her place at the table and picked at a breakfast plate that Delilah had put in front of her. Should she tell everyone that she was selling the ranch to Derek Bannon? Should she wait? No. It wouldn't be fair. It was important to everyone to know her plans so they wouldn't be left high and dry at the last minute. She was glad Benjie wasn't here to hear it like this. She would have to handle him very delicately when she broke the news.

When breakfast was over and some of the men broke out cigarettes, Jan called for their attention. "I have something to tell everyone and I hope you'll understand. You all know the unexpected expenses we've been faced with lately. It's been difficult keeping the ranch in the black. Matter of fact, there were several times I thought we would go under. Also, there's the competition from the Golden Lasso to contend with, and that's not easy. We just can't afford to offer the accommodations they offer there. So—" she took a deep breath "—I've decided to take Derek Bannon's offer and sell him the Rancho." There, she had said it, but she hadn't expected the crestfallen faces of her staff.

There was silence. Total and complete.

"Listen, everyone. It's not what you think. I haven't given up and I'm not selling out for a higher price. As a matter of fact, I'm accepting Mr. Bannon's first offer. I believe him when he said that Uncle Jake died before he could sign the necessary papers. But I do know this. He's going to need help. Mr. Bannon isn't just going to make this Rancho a part of the Golden Lasso and use it for his staff's living quarters. I've discovered he wants to open a treatment center for handicapped children. He'll be needing all the help he can get."

"Miss Warren, is there anything we can do to help you change your mind? We hate to see you leave and we'll miss Ben. We really care about that kid, and you, too." It was the first time Gus had said more than five or six words.

"Gus, no, I'm sorry. I just can't handle it financially. Sooner or later it would have to come to this and it would have been even more difficult. I've got to secure Benjie's future and I can't do that if I have to file for bankruptcy. Understand? And I would appreciate it if none of you mentioned this to Benjie. I'll find the right time to tell him."

There were mutters and finally agreements around the table. It was heartwarming to know that in a few short months she had come to be so well thought of at the Rancho. The atmosphere was dismal, subdued to the point of a funeral.

Groping for something to lighten the mood, Jan turned to Delilah. "When are you and Gus getting married?"

Delilah shrugged.

"What do you say we have the wedding here? You could invite all your friends, and it would really be something for our guests to attend. And the Rancho will empty out its food locker to feed everyone. What do you say, Delilah?"

"I say you too late. Gus and me get married yesterday afternoon in Presbyterian church."

Gus stood up from his place at the table and raised his coffee mug. "To Delilah." He offered the toast to his new bride. Then, in a most unexpected display of affection, he rounded the table, caught Delilah in his arms, and squeezed her tightly. With a resounding smack, he put a kiss on her chubby cheek. Everyone praised Gus for his choice in women and immediately the mood lightened.

Jan smiled brightly, but inside she was dreading the thought of telling Benjie of her decision to sell the Rancho. He had come to love these people just as she had. It was cruel, but, then, life was cruel. She, too, had come to love someone, and she knew the pain of not being able to be near him. She would weather it; she would have to. And so would Benjie.

JAN CLOSETED HERSELF in her office to accomplish two things. One was that she would manage to avoid Benjie's eyes when he returned from the Golden Lasso with Derek; and, two, it would give her an opportunity to discuss selling the Rancho with her uncle's lawyer.

As she was on the phone with the lawyer, she heard Derek's powerful sports car pull up the drive. Gus went out to help Benjie, who was looking marvelously improved. The boy was using his crutches again and he refused Gus's helping hand. Derek had remained in the car with the motor running. As Benjie waved good-bye, he shouted something that sounded like "See you at the wedding!"

For a moment Jan was so distracted that the lawyer had to repeat something twice before she heard him. "Just draw up the papers and I'll come into town next week to sign them. Anything, as long as it isn't necessary for me to come face-to-face with Derek Bannon."

If the lawyer thought this a strange request, he didn't say so, he just muttered something about wanting to play golf this weekend, and now he was going to have all this paperwork.

Jan buried herself in the ledgers and receipts and

bills. A few minutes later, Benjie knocked on the office door and entered. "Hey, Jan, Derek's gonna pick me up to take me to the medical center in about two minutes. I asked him to wait around for me when he dropped me off, but he said he had something to do up at the Lasso. Why don't you come out and say hello to him when he comes for me?"

Jan looked up at Benjie's bright blue eyes. Derek Bannon had worked his magic on the little boy once again. "I can't come out, Benjie—I've got so much work to do."

"Aw, come on out, Jan. It won't take but a minute. Please, Jan?"

Unable to deny Benjie this one small request in the face of the news about selling the Rancho, Jan smiled. "Okay, sport. I'll wait on the veranda for you."

The midmorning air was already heavy and hot, but it was a balm to Jan, who, ever since Derek had dropped her off the night before, felt as though she could never be warm again. Benjie prattled something about the preparations for the wedding, and Jan only half listened, insulating herself against the pain. From Benjie's report, the florists were already decorating a small dining room that would serve as the chapel, and the cooks were preparing the most scrumptious food Benjie had ever seen. The boy's eyes widened as he described the ice sculpture of turtle doves that would be used for the champagne fountain. "It's really something, Jan. I bet you've never seen anything like it! Andrea says that the man had to come all the way from California to do it!"

Smiling stiffly, Jan tried to show enthusiasm for the

news Benjie was reporting. The last thing she wanted to hear about was Andrea's wedding plans and the elaborate showing she and Derek were planning to make. *"I love you, Jan."* The words seemed to float on the desert wind. *"I love you, Jan."* The remembered tone of Derek's voice as he whispered those words sent Jan into a panic. Nervously, she turned to Benjie, asking him inane questions about the medical clinic, Dr. Rossi, the Bison football team—anything to blot out the wound of those words.

"What's the matter with you, sis? You're as jumpy as a cat on a griddle." Benjie questioned her, piercing her with his stare.

"Nothing," she snapped. "I thought you wanted me to come out here and keep you company. I'm keeping you company!" she insisted, hearing her own voice rise two octaves.

As though saved by the bell, Derek's car rounded the drive. He honked his horn and Benjie hurried out to the car on his crutches. "I won't be needing these before long," he called out to Jan. "Someday I'm just going to run off that porch and right over to Derek!"

The conviction in the boy's voice convinced Jan. If nothing else, she had to be grateful to Derek Bannon for her brother's bright prognosis.

The whole time Benjie was settling himself in the car, Derek kept his face turned away. It seemed as though Derek had spoken the truth about feeling like a fool the night before. Well, it served him right. But in her heart Jan knew there was no bigger fool than she. The sight of Derek's head turned away from her ate at her soul. She had to hurry the lawyer, do everything she could to facilitate the deal about selling the Rancho. She had to get away from here, away from the desert, away from Derek Bannon. Her heart beat thunderously in her breast, her breath caught in her throat, and tears stung her eyes. Heaven help her, whatever the man was, whatever he did, she loved him. *"I love you, Jan."*

The fickle desert wind had returned his words again. *"I love you, Jan."*

"COME ON, JAN! You're gonna make us late!" Benjie admonished through the closed bedroom door.

"I'm coming. Just a minute!" she answered, desperately trying to keep her voice light.

"You said that ten minutes ago! Come on!"

"All right, all right! Just give me a few more minutes without your badgering. Now get away from the door and wait for me in the lobby. I'm hurrying."

Jan sighed deeply as she stroked the brush through her hair. She felt as though she were marching to her own execution. Today was going to be the worst day of her life. First, she was being forced to attend Andrea's wedding; and second, she was going to have to tell Benjie of her decision to sell the Rancho.

There was no avoiding it. The boy had to know. And the longer she put it off, the harder it would be on him.

Jan surveyed herself in front of the pier glass, checking her hem and the back of the pale blue linen dress she had decided to wear. If she had to watch the man she loved marry someone else, at least it would be while looking her best. Her cinnamon-colored hair shone, and there was just the right amount of color in her cheeks. The linen sheath dress hugged her hips and emphasized her long, lean legs. Satisfied that everything was where it should be, she hurried out of her room and down the stairs into the lobby.

Benjie emitted a long, low whistle, which caused Jan to raise her brows. "Where did you learn a thing like that?" she demanded. "Riding through town with Derek, no doubt." Her tone was harsher than she intended and Benjie looked at her curiously. "Don't look at me like that," she scolded. "You were the one in a hurry. Now, let's get going."

Even as they drove through the gates of the Golden Lasso, it was evident there was a festive note in the air. Garlands of flowers lined the drive, and crepe-paper wedding bells were entwined around the lamp posts. A parking attendant, resplendent in livery, claimed Jan's pickup truck and drove it around to the back lot. Benjie was impatient and became insistent when he heard the organ music coming from the small back dining room. "I told you you would make us late! Now hurry up or I'm gonna leave you here!"

The last thing Jan wanted was to have to enter the makeshift chapel all by herself, so she hurried behind Benjie, who was making fast tracks for the chapel.

Inside the chapel soft organ music played the "Wedding March." The interior was decorated with hundreds of flowers and white satin ribbons. The center aisle had been overlayed with a white carpet that led to the makeshift altar where Andrea and Derek would pronounce their vows.

Jan's eyes became misty and her throat choked up. How could she sit here and watch Derek swear his love for Andrea when only a few days ago he had whispered those words to her. A great heaviness weighed on Jan's heart. Her impulse was to run—run away as fast and as far as she could. Instead, she sat there paralyzed, incapable of motion, knowing only that the one man she could ever love was standing there at the altar waiting for his bride.

"Derek looks great in his penguin suit, doesn't he?" Benjie whispered.

"What?"

"His tuxedo. Derek calls it a penguin. And, hey, doesn't Dusty look nervous?"

"Shh!"

The organist began the "Wedding March" again, and the outer doors swung open to reveal two pretty girls dressed in yellow and carrying baskets of flowers. Behind her bridesmaids, Andrea stood, awaiting her cue. Jan caught her breath when she saw the dark-haired girl, who was beautiful in her antique lace gown and fine Holland lace veil.

Suddenly, Derek was standing beside Andrea, murmuring something to her and giving her a slight chuck on the chin. Derek! What was he doing back there? He should have waited for Andrea at the altar!

Benjie was pulling on Jan's arm. "Jan, Jan. When you get married can I give you away like Derek's giving his sister away?"

The full import of Benjie's words didn't penetrate Jan's consciousness for a full minute. Giving his sister away? Andrea was Derek's sister? No! It couldn't be! Jan's thoughts raced backward, trying to remember who had told her that Derek was marrying Andrea. No one. No one had told her. Back, through the haze of the days…Andrea, sitting beside Dusty Baker on the plane, telling him that she was going to be married. That was a flirtation, a coyness. And that time at the Golden Lasso when Dusty Baker introduced Andrea and she had interrupted him, not wanting to hear the words "Derek's fiancée." Jan's eyes followed Andrea and Derek and jumped ahead of them to where Dusty Baker was waiting. Andrea was going to marry Dusty! That was why Derek hadn't been jealous at the tribute dinner. How could he be jealous of his sister?

Back again, to where she had seen Andrea hug Derek in the airport. What made her think it had been more than sisterly affection? Had hearing Andrea's words on the plane and her own instant jealousy of the girl colored everything she knew about the girl?

And of course Andrea lived with Derek. Where else should she live while waiting to be married? Andrea had had every right to answer the door in the middle of the night wearing her nightgown.

*Fool! Fool! Fool!* she cursed herself. Always jumping to conclusions. The agony she had caused herself thinking Derek was in love with Andrea. The pain she had inflicted on everyone because she had assumed that Andrea was going to marry Derek!

Derek! Jan's heart leaped in her breast. Derek had said he loved her. *"I love you, Jan."* Again she heard the words, listened for the warm timbre in his voice. Fool!

Fool! What had she done? Her pride had kept her from discovering the truth. All those times when doubt had ruined what it was that she and Derek had between them, all she had had to do was say it. Tell him. Even if she had openly accused him of being engaged to marry Andrea while toying with her emotions—Derek would have laughed and then taken her in his arms and told her that she was such a silly because Andrea was his sister. His sister!

And Andrea, coming to see her when she was laid up with blisters on her feet and offering her friendship again. How many times had she insulted the unwitting girl by rebuffing her offers of friendship? Even now, she couldn't remember Andrea saying or doing one nasty thing to encourage Jan's hostility. No, it had all been Jan.

She covered her face with her hands to stifle her sobs. Benjie was embarrassed and she heard him whisper to someone: "Girls. They always cry at weddings."

Again the music reached a crescendo and filled the chapel with brightness. Andrea raced down the aisle with Dusty, her face as bright as the Arizona sunshine, and Dusty looking as proud as a peacock.

The wedding guests emptied out after the bride and groom, and Jan knew the impulse to turn and run. Fool! Fool!

Leaving Benjie behind, she followed the crush of guests out into the elegantly appointed lobby of the Golden Lasso. Tears streaming down her face, Jan longed for escape. Suddenly, she heard someone call her name.

"Jan!"

She turned to see Andrea standing on the stairs, looking down at her. "Jan! Catch!" The bridal bouquet flew through the air, and with the accuracy of the Bisons' quarterback, Andrea's toss went directly into Jan's arms.

Fresh tears stung Jan's eyes and, clutching the bouquet to her, she ran out of the Lasso and across the wide expanse of lawn. Over and over the words, "Fool, fool!" shrieked through her head, blocking out all other sound.

The remembered sight of the hatred on Derek's face swam before her. She could never make it up to him, not if she lived to be a hundred. The most wonderful man in the world had told her he loved her, and she had destroyed that love, crushed it beyond repair. "Fool! Fool!"

"I love you, Jan."

The words seemed to come from a distance, and yet they were close enough to touch her heart. She turned and saw him walking toward her. Through the mist of her tears, she saw he was smiling. "I see you've caught the bridal bouquet. You know what that means, don't you?"

He was standing beside her, offering her his snowy handkerchief to dry her tears. "Weddings make me cry, too. Especially when it's not my wedding to you, Jan." His voice was gentle, quiet, almost somber.

"Derek, I've been such a fool…you don't know. I thought—I thought—"

She was in his arms, her heart beating fast against his. His eyes held the sky as he looked down at her and a smile played near the corner of his mouth. "Kiss me. Tell me that you love me. To coin a phrase, Jan—don't think."

And she didn't as he held her tighter and gently parted her lips with his own, robbing her mind of all thought except him.

* * * * *

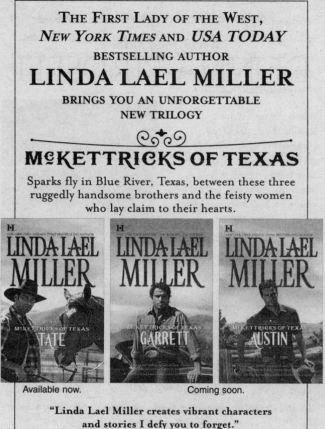

# REQUEST YOUR FREE BOOKS!

## 2 FREE NOVELS
## FROM THE ROMANCE COLLECTION
## PLUS 2 FREE GIFTS!

**YES!** Please send me 2 FREE novels from the Romance Collection and my 2 FREE gifts (gifts are worth about $10). After receiving them, if I don't wish to receive any more books, I can return the shipping statement marked "cancel." If I don't cancel, I will receive 4 brand-new novels every month and be billed just $5.74 per book in the U.S. or $6.24 per book in Canada. That's a saving of at least 28% off the cover price. It's quite a bargain! Shipping and handling is just 50¢ per book in the U.S. and 75¢ per book in Canada.* I understand that accepting the 2 free books and gifts places me under no obligation to buy anything. I can always return a shipment and cancel at any time. Even if I never buy another book, the two free books and gifts are mine to keep forever.

194 MDN E4LY    394 MDN E4MC

| | |
|---|---|
| Name | (PLEASE PRINT) |

| | |
|---|---|
| Address | Apt. # |

| | | |
|---|---|---|
| City | State/Prov. | Zip/Postal Code |

Signature (if under 18, a parent or guardian must sign)

### Mail to **The Reader Service:**
**IN U.S.A.:** P.O. Box 1867, Buffalo, NY 14240-1867
**IN CANADA:** P.O. Box 609, Fort Erie, Ontario L2A 5X3

Not valid for current subscribers to the Romance Collection
or the Romance/Suspense Collection.

**Want to try two free books from another line?**
**Call 1-800-873-8635 or visit www.morefreebooks.com.**

* Terms and prices subject to change without notice. Prices do not include applicable taxes. N.Y. residents add applicable sales tax. Canadian residents will be charged applicable provincial taxes and GST. Offer not valid in Quebec. This offer is limited to one order per household. All orders subject to approval. Credit or debit balances in a customer's account(s) may be offset by any other outstanding balance owed by or to the customer. Please allow 4 to 6 weeks for delivery. Offer available while quantities last.

**Your Privacy:** Harlequin Books is committed to protecting your privacy. Our Privacy Policy is available online at www.eHarlequin.com or upon request from the Reader Service. From time to time we make our lists of customers available to reputable third parties who may have a product or service of interest to you. ☐ If you would prefer we not share your name and address, please check here.

**Help us get it right**—We strive for accurate, respectful and relevant communications. To clarify or modify your communication preferences, visit us at www.ReaderService.com/consumerchoice.

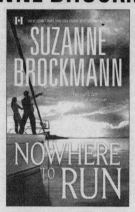

# FERN MICHAELS

| | | |
|---|---|---|
| 77424 DREAM OF ME | ___ $7.99 U.S. | ___ $9.99 CAN. |
| 77338 PROMISES | ___ $7.99 U.S. | ___ $7.99 CAN. |

*(limited quantities available)*

| | |
|---|---|
| TOTAL AMOUNT | $ _____ |
| POSTAGE & HANDLING | $ _____ |
| ($1.00 FOR 1 BOOK, 50¢ for each additional) | |
| APPLICABLE TAXES* | $ _____ |
| TOTAL PAYABLE | $ _____ |

*(check or money order—please do not send cash)*

To order, complete this form and send it, along with a check or money order for the total above, payable to HQN Books, to: **In the U.S.:** 3010 Walden Avenue, P.O. Box 9077, Buffalo, NY 14269-9077; **In Canada:** P.O. Box 636, Fort Erie, Ontario, L2A 5X3.

Name: _____

Address: _____ City: _____

State/Prov.: _____ Zip/Postal Code: _____

Account Number (if applicable): _____

075 CSAS

\*New York residents remit applicable sales taxes.
\*Canadian residents remit applicable GST and provincial taxes.

**HQN™**

We *are* romance™

**www.HQNBooks.com**

PHFM0210BL